FURTHER CONFESSIONS
OF ZENO

In the last years of his life Svevo was working on a sequel to *The Confessions of Zeno.*
It was never completed, but from the fragments he left it is possible to conjecture what kind of work it might have been. The five narratives included in this volume deal —like the astonishingly funny and accomplished three-act play with which it ends —with Svevo's obsession with old age, its miseries and consolations. In the humour, tenderness and gentle irony of these final works, and in the beauty and complexity of their prose, the voice of *The Confessions of Zeno* and *As a Man Grows Older* will be found to be as steady, the laughter as sharp, the insight undimmed.

Volume 5 in the Uniform Edition of Svevo's works

Volume 1: Confessions of Zeno
Volume 2: As a Man Grows Older
Volume 3: A Life
Volume 4: Short Sentimental Journey & Other Stories

Further Confessions
of Zeno

ITALO SVEVO

TRANSLATED FROM THE ITALIAN BY

BEN JOHNSON
AND P. N. FURBANK

LONDON
Secker & Warburg

First published in the Uniform Edition 1969 by
Martin Secker & Warburg Limited
14 Carlisle Street, London W 1

SBN: 436 50804 4

BRN 290370

Printed in Great Britain by
Northumberland Press Limited
Gateshead

Contents

Bibliographical Note	7
THE OLD OLD MAN	11
AN OLD MAN'S CONFESSIONS	27
UMBERTINO	71
A CONTRACT	113
THIS INDOLENCE OF MINE	141
REGENERATION: a Comedy in three Acts	167

Bibliographical Note

The present volume contains the various surviving fragments and drafts of the sequel to *The Confessions of Zeno* on which Svevo was working during the last year or two of his life. The first two fragments, "The Old Old Man" and "An Old Man's Confessions" appear to be alternative openings to the novel, and from the latter it appears that the new work—at least according to one projected version—was to have begun with Zeno, exasperated by the humiliations of old age, resorting to a rejuvenation operation. The three-act comedy, *Regeneration* which belongs to his last year, is evidently, though the protagonists are given different names, a dramatic treatment of the same incident.

None of these pieces were published in Svevo's lifetime, "The Old Old Man" ("Il vecchione") having first appeared in *La novella del buon vecchio e della bella fanciulla* (1929), the other novel-fragments in *Corto viaggio sentimentale e altri racconti*, ed. Umbro Apollonio (1949), and "Regeneration" (*La rigenerazione*) in *Commedie*, ed. Umbro Apollonio (1960).

THE OLD OLD MAN

Translated by Ben Johnson

IT WAS IN APRIL THIS YEAR THAT IT HAPPENED, A MONTH THAT brought us one dismal, rainy day after another, punctuated with brief, marvellous bursts of sunshine and even warmth.

I was returning home by car with Augusta after a short ride out to Capodistria. The sun had tired my eyes and I was drifting into a state of repose. Not sleep exactly, but inertia. My feeling was that of one who is far removed from the landscape round him, though, for lack of a substitute, I still permitted myself to register its presence: it fled past with no meaning whatever. After sunset, much of its colour went too, and all the more so because by that time the green fields had been replaced by the dingy houses and squalid roads I knew so well that I saw them in my mind's eye beforehand, and looking at them was hardly different from sleeping.

In Piazza Goldoni we were stopped by the policeman, and I pulled myself together. At that moment I caught sight of a very young girl coming towards us; trying to avoid the other cars, she passed so close as to brush up against our own. She was wearing a white dress with bright green stripes and green ribbons at the collar, and over it a light, green-striped mantelet that partially covered it. Everything about her was a vigorous affirmation of the season. What a good-looking girl! The evident danger in which she found herself was making her smile, and all the while her wide-open, big black eyes were darting about, gauging distances. Her smile allowed one a glimpse of the white glow of her teeth in the rose-colouring of her face; her hands were held high, at her breast, in an effort to make herself look smaller, and in one hand she was clutching a pair of limp gloves. I could see her hands perfectly: their creamy complexion, their shape—long fingers and tiny palms tapering into the curve of her wrists.

And then—I hardly know why—it occurred to me that it would be too cruel a thing if I were to let that moment escape without establishing some sort of relationship with her. Too cruel. But I had to hurry, and my haste threw me into confusion. Then I remembered! Such a relationship already existed. I knew her! Leaning towards the window to let her see me, I nodded with a smile intended to show my admiration for her youth and courage. But remembering my mouth was full of gold, I stopped smiling at once and confined myself simply to gazing at her, seriously and intently. The girl had just time enough to give me a curious look, and she responded with a hesitant nod that lent her a conscience-smitten expression— her smile vanished and her face changed, as if a prism had been put between my eyes and her.

Fearing that she might witness the death of the girl under the wheels of one of the motor-cars, Augusta had hastily raised her lorgnette. And imitating me, she nodded too. Then she asked: "Who's that girl?"

Her name had completely escaped me. But really wanting to remember, I sent my mind backwards through time to find out, going one by one through long-distant years of the past, finally coming upon her at the side of a friend of my father's.

"The daughter of old Dondi," I muttered, none too sure.

Once having spoken, however, I seemed to remember more clearly. The girl's image also recalled to mind a small villa surrounded by a little green garden. Something the girl had said, which had made everyone present laugh, returned along with the memory—"Why is it that tomcats never come down from a roof alone, but always with a pussy cat?" That was precisely the way then, as just now in Piazza Goldoni, that she had shown her unabashed innocence. Back in those days I was very innocent myself, for, beautiful and desirable as she was, I had laughed along with the others instead of sweeping her into my arms. Thinking of her made me momentarily younger; I remembered having had the capacity to seize, to hold, to struggle.

With an outburst of laughter, Augusta cut short this disquieting reverie of mine: "By this time Dondi's daughter is as old as you are! So who was it really that you nodded to? The Dondi girl was six years older than myself. Think again! You know if you had seen her out there just now, instead of grinning in the face of danger like that girl, she would have been hobbling along—she would have been close to meeting her Maker under the wheels of our car."

Once again, as though coming to me through a prism, the light suddenly changed. I didn't feel like joining in Augusta's laughter. But I had to! Otherwise she might learn the importance of this adventure of mine, and it would be the first time I had made a confession to her.

"You're right. It hadn't occurred to me. Day by day everything changes a little, so that in a year the change is considerable, and in seventy years very considerable." Then I spoke from the heart. Rubbing my eyes as though I had been asleep, I added: "I forgot that I was old myself and that everyone of my generation can't help being old too. Even those whom I haven't seen grow old, even the ones who have gone into hiding and whom you never hear anything about, who are not watched by anybody—they're getting old too, every day." In my attempt to conceal the flash of youth I had been granted, I was becoming childish. A change of tone was indicated, and with the most nonchalant look imaginable, I asked: "Where's the daughter of old Dondi living now?" Augusta didn't know. After marrying some foreigner, she had never returned to Trieste.

And then I visualised the poor Dondi girl, still in ankle-length skirts, pottering about in some corner of the world, unknown—that is, living among people who had never known her when she was little. I was touched by this vision of her, because it had been my own fate, though I had never gone anywhere.

Augusta is the only person who claims she can remember

me exactly as I was, with all my youthful virtues, and some failings, the most outstanding of which was my fear of growing old; this was something for which she still has not forgiven me, though she should be able to see by now how well-founded my fear was. But I doubt whether she really remembers. Apart from what I actually see, I myself don't remember much about her. What is more, she knew only a part of my youth; I mean, she knew it only very superficially. I, on the other hand, remember the adventures of my own youth better than I remember what I looked like or felt. On certain unexpected occasions my youth seems to return to me, and whenever it does I have to hurry to the looking-glass to find out where I really belong in time. Then, so as to return to my proper place, I look at the wrinkles in the loose skin under my chin.

I once spoke to my nephew Carlo about these illusions of youth that occasionally possess me. Carlo is a doctor, and young besides, so he knows something about old age. With a malicious smile, he told me that unquestionably they were symptoms of old age, if I had so completely forgotten how it feels to be young and had to look at the skin on my neck in order to recognise myself. Then, with a loud laugh, he added: "It's like old Cralli next door; he honestly believes he's the father of the baby that young wife of his is about to have."

No, hardly as bad as that! I am still young enough not to make mistakes like that. Time is an element in which I am not able to move with absolute sureness. But I am convinced it cannot be my fault entirely, though I dare not say so to Carlo, who, not understanding what I mean, would only make fun of me. Time wreaks its havoc with a firm and ruthless hand, and then marches off in an orderly procession of days, months, and years, but when it is far away and out of sight, it breaks ranks. The hours start looking for their place in the wrong day and the days in the wrong year. All of which accounts for the fact that, when we recall them, some years strike one as being nothing but summer and sun and others seem one long shivering. And chill and cheerless indeed is the

year in which one can't remember the rightful place of anything: three hundred and sixty-five twenty-four-hour days,
each one dead and vanished. A hecatomb!

Upon those dead years, sometimes, a sudden light is cast
that illuminates a particular episode, and then one discovers
a rare and intensely fragrant flower in one's life. Thus, never
before had I felt Signorina Dondi so close to me as that day in
Piazza Goldini. Before, in that little garden (how many years
ago could it have been?) I had paid hardly any attention to
her, and being myself young, I had passed her by without even
noticing her grace, her innocence. Now, no sooner had I re-
joined her, than the others, seeing us together, began to laugh.
Why had I not seen her or noticed her, before? In the present,
perhaps, all events are obscured by our own preoccupations,
by the dangers hanging over us. We don't see them, we
don't feel them except when we are far away from them, in
security.

Here in my little room, however, I am able to arrive at
such security; by concentrating with these sheets of paper in
front of me. I can examine and analyse the present in its own
inimitable light; I am able to reach that part of the past which
has not gone for ever.

Thus, I will describe the present and that part of the past
which has not yet vanished; and not to preserve my memory
of it, but to collect myself. If I had always done this, I would
have been less surprised, less upset by the encounter in Piazza
Goldoni. I would not simply have looked at the girl, like a man
whose sight has been restored by the good Lord, from head to
toe.

I do not feel old, but I have a feeling of being rusty. I have to
think and write in order to feel alive; for the life I lead—with
all the virtues I possess or people attribute to me, and all the
affections and duties, to bind and paralyse me—deprives me of
all freedom. I am living with the same inertia one dies with.
And I want to pull myself together, to rehabilitate myself. Perhaps I may become even more virtuous and affectionate—
passionately virtuous—but it will be a virtue all my own and

not one that is imposed on me by others and cramps me when I wear it. I shall stop wearing such borrowed outfits, or else tailor them to fit me.

Writing, therefore, which I look forward to doing every evening just before taking my physic, will serve a hygienic purpose. And it is my hope that these pages of mine may contain the things I don't normally say aloud, because only in that way can the treatment be successful.

Once before, I wrote with this same idea in mind—of being sincere, that is; and hygiene figured in it then, too, because my writing was intended to prepare me for psycho-analysis. The treatment failed, but the pages remain. How precious they are! I re-read them yesterday. Unfortunately I did not find any mention of Signorina Dondi (Emma?—yes, Emma), but I came across all sorts of other things. Including an important happening which had not been entered but is suggested by an empty space in which it clearly belongs. I would insert it at once, if I hadn't forgotten it. But it isn't lost, because by reading those pages again I shall certainly find it. They are here, those sheets, always at hand, protected from all confusion. Time is crystallised in them and can always be located if one knows how to open at the right page. Like a railway timetable.

Naturally, everything I set down I really did, but re-reading it all, it appears more important than my life itself, which I seem to remember as having been long and uneventful. Of course, when one writes about life, one makes it out a more serious thing than it actually is. Life in practice is diluted, and therefore obfuscated, by many things which, when one is describing it, never get mentioned. One does not mention breathing until it becomes panting, neither does one mention one's many holidays, meals, sleep, until some tragedy deprives one of such things. In actual fact, however, they occur with pendulum-like regularity side by side with a variety of other such activities, arrogantly presiding over so large a portion of our day that there is not room for too much shedding of tears or laughter. For this reason the descriptions of lives—of which a considerable part is omitted : the things everyone experiences but no one ever mentions—become more intense than the lives themselves.

In other words, when recounted, life is idealised; and now, trembling as though entering the presence of the sacred, I address myself to the task for a second time. Who knows but that, closely examining the present, I shall recover some aspect of my youth which my weary legs won't allow me to pursue and which, by evoking it, I can make come back to me instead. Already in the few lines I have written, I dimly made it out; it took hold of me enough to lessen the weariness of old age in my veins.

There is, however, a vast difference between my state of mind now and the last time I described my life. As I have remarked, my situation has simplified itself. I continue to struggle between the present and past; but at least hope—anxious hope for the future—does not come crowding in between. So I continue to live in a mixed tense : this is the fate of man, though his grammar also contains pure tenses—they seem designed for the lower animals, who live joyously, when not frightened, in a crystal-clear present. But for an old man (yes, I am an old man : I admit it now for the first time, and it is the first conquest I owe to my new effort of concentration), the amputation, whereby life is deprived of what it never had—the future—makes life simpler, but also so senseless, one might as well employ one's brief present tearing out the scattered strands of hair still remaining on one's deformed scalp.

But I, on the contrary, am determined to do something else during the present; and if, as is my hope, there should prove to be room for activity in it, I shall have shown that it is longer than it seems. Measuring the present is difficult, and the mathematician who tries would be making a gross mistake and proving the whole thing is not within his province. I at least think I know how one should approach measuring it. When our memory has been able to eliminate from a given occurrence everything that might produce surprise, fright, and

confusion, one may say that the occurrence has been translated into the past.

I have pondered this problem for so long that even my own
inactive life has given rise to an experiment that might settle
the matter, if others would repeat it with more precise instruments; that is, by replacing me by a man better trained in
scientific observation.

One day last spring Augusta and I plucked up courage to go
for a drive out to Udine, where we lunched at a well-known
inn which still practised the slow, unerring art of the spit.
Afterwards we went a little farther, in the direction of Carnia,
to have a closer look at the great mountains. In a short while
we were overcome by the weariness of old people, which comes
from sitting still too long in a comfortable position. We got
out of the car and, feeling a strong wish to stretch our legs,
climbed the low wooded hill that rose alongside the main road.
At the top we were rewarded by a surprise. We were unable
to see the highway now or the fields at the foot of the hill
we had climbed: only innumerable, gentle green foothills,
cutting off our view of all but the enormous mountains near
by, and their peaks of blue rock, regarding us with great
solemnity. We had managed to bring about a change of scene
more quickly on foot than by motor-car, and I breathed a deep
sigh of relief; it was a joy I have never forgotten. Was my joy
due to surprise or to the balmy air, free of the roadside dust,
or to our sense of being utterly alone? Joy made me feel
adventurous, and I went on to explore the far side of the hill.
It was easy: there was a footpath through the tall grass. And
from there I could see, at the bottom of the hill, a cottage,
with in front of it a man bending a piece of iron on an anvil,
giving vigorous strokes to it with his hammer. Like a child,
I marvelled at the way the metallic sound of the anvil reached
my ear long after the hammer had been raised to strike again.
I am a real child, but Mother Nature is very childish too, creating such contrasts between light and sound.

I remembered my joy at the colours and the solitude, and the
clash between eye and ear, for a long time. Then the serious

side of memory intruded, and my mind's logic brought order
to the confusion of nature; so that now, whenever I think of
that hammer, I hear its sound immediately it strikes the anvil.
At the same time, the rest of the scene falsified itself somewhat, too. The disorder of the present gave way to the disorder[1]
of the past. The cluster of hills became even more numerous
and more wooded. The peaks of the mountains grew darker,
too, and more serious, perhaps even closer than they actually
were; but everything became well-ordered and harmonious.
Unfortunately, I did not take note of how many days that
particular present required for such a transformation. But
even if I had noted it, I would not have been able to say more
than this: "In the mind of the septuagenarian Zeno Cosini
things mature in a certain number of hours and minutes." How
many other experiments would have to be performed on all
sorts of different individuals, with all their differing ages,
before one could formulate the general law establishing the
frontier between the present and the past?

And so I shall end my life, like my dead father, with a notebook in my hand. How I used to laugh at that book of his! And
in fact, I still smile when I think about it, remembering that he
intended it for the future. He jotted down things he had to
attend to, the dates of periodic visits, and so on. I still have
one of his notebooks. Many of his notes start with a reminder :
Don't forget such and such a thing on such and such a day.
He had confidence in the efficacy of the reminders buried in
that notebook. But I have proof that his confidence was ill-
placed. I found one note that read: "I absolutely" (and this
word he underlined) "must not forget to tell Olivi, when the
occasion arises, that, upon my death, my son must seem to be
the actual director in everybody's eyes, although he'll never
be so really."

One can only suppose that the occasion to speak to Olivi
never arose. Anyway, all effort to project oneself from one time
to another is futile, and it takes a naïveté like my father's to
believe one can direct one's own future. Perhaps, as the philo-

---

[1] *Sic*, in Svevo's MS. A slip for "order"?

sophers assert, time does not exist; but certainly the containers that hold it do, and they are virtually watertight. Only a few drops seep from one to the other.

I want to look round me a little more, so as to end this memorable day by preserving for tomorrow the hour I have spent writing. About my study—a cosy and attractive room, which to my great perturbation has been refurbished several times by Augusta over the years, though without making much real change—I have little to say. It is pretty much as it was shortly after our marriage, and I have already described it elsewhere. For a short while now there has been a thoroughly distressing innovation. In the last few days my violin, and even the music stand, have disappeared from their places. True, the gramophone thereby gained the extra room it needed to deploy its vigorous voice. I bought it a year ago. It cost a good deal, as do the records which I am constantly buying. I do not regret the expense, but I should have liked my violin left in its place, though I have not touched it in years. In my hands it had not only become arhythmic, not to say wobbly, I also seemed to be losing my power to produce tone. All the same, I liked seeing it there, in its place, waiting for better times; whereas Augusta could not understand why I left it there to clutter up my room. Driven by her mania for order, she removed it one day, assuring me that if I asked for it I could have it back at once. I shall certainly never ask her for it, but it is not so certain that, if she had left it where it was, I might not have picked it up again. The decision now required is of an entirely different nature. I would have to start by begging Augusta to bring it back, and playing it as soon as I had it. I cannot assume such long-term engagements. And so, here I am, permanently severed from another part of my youth. Augusta has not yet learned how much consideration is needed in dealing with an old man.

And there would be no other changes in the room, if it weren't that, at this very moment, it is filled with sounds that have nothing to do with my gramophone. Twice a week (never on Sundays, but on Mondays and Saturdays) a drunken

music-lover wends his way up the sloping path that runs beside our villa. He annoyed me at the beginning; later I laughed
at him, and finally I came to love him. Small, lean but not
stooping, his mouth turned heavenwards, I often used to
watch him from my window after I had switched off all the
lights in the room; I could make him out on the white, moon-
lit path. He walks slowly, not because the climb is difficult,
but so as to reserve all his breath for his notes, dragging them
out lovingly. And sometimes when he comes to notes that
make him hesitate, because they strike him as especially difficult, he even stops dead in his tracks. I recognise the utter
innocence of that singer even in the fact that his song is always
the same. Far be it from him to consider improvising! He has
a few appoggiaturas, by which he creeps towards the proper
notes, but these he needs; they make the notes easier to reach.
Perhaps, not realising he has altered the music, he now loves
it the way he has to sing it. He is devoid of all ambition and,
therefore, of malice. So, if I were to meet him one night on
the path, aware of his lofty, selfless humanity, I should not be
frightened; instead I would go up to him and ask if I might
sing along with him. He always sings from *Un ballo in
maschera*. He would be greatly taken aback if a policeman
told him to keep quiet. Singing *Alzati! la tua figlia a te concedo
rivedere. Nell'ombra e nel silenzio là . . .*[1] he is addressing
Amelia in person.

Behind that singing of his, of course, there is a great deal
of wine, but wine has never performed a nobler office. My
minstrel inhabits that ancient story. Re-born for him twice
weekly, it surprises and moves him like something fresh and
new. How is it that on all other evenings he can abstain
from wine, which provokes such bliss in him? What an
example of moderation!

Fortunato, my chauffeur, knows him. He says he's a carpenter who lives above us in a humble little cottage. He is
married. He is not yet forty but has a son of twenty. Which

---

[1] Arise! I permit you to see your daughter once more. There in the
shadow and silence. . . .

is why he thinks himself old and harks back to a past even
more remote than the one I am in search of. What morality
there is there! It has taken me seventy years to break away
from the present. And still I am not happy and am trying to
recapture it in these pages at this very moment.

I shall never try to make his acquaintance. That hoarse
voice of his seems to come from bygone times. It brings me the
feeling of them; being a lament, it has in it all the disorder
of a real-life story. Yet that lonely voice out there, and I here
at my table analysing its pauses and its moments of fervour
—it makes a perfect order! Future hours will not be able to
alter that voice for me. The next time I hear it I shall look at
these notes of mine to see if the new present finds things to
correct in my account, proving me wrong.

I am tired of writing this evening. Augusta, who called to
me a short time ago from the passage will be asleep by now,
in her neatly-made bed, with her head in a net, knotted under
her chin. She puts up with this to keep her close-cropped
white hair in order, a constraint and a burden that would stop
me from sleeping.

Her sleep is still light, but noisier than in the past. Especially
her first breaths, in the initial moments of abandon. It is as
though other organs, all unprepared, have been called on to
take charge of her breathing, and, woken up unexpectedly,
are grumbling. Ours is an awful machine when it is old!
Whenever I witness Augusta's efforts, I dread what I shall have
to go through myself and can never get to sleep without taking a double dose of sleeping pills. So it is a good thing I do
not go to bed until Augusta is already asleep. True, I disturb
her a little; but then she sleeps less noisily afterwards.

And here, emulating my father, I shall jot down a reminder:
Remember not to complain too much about old age in these
notes. You'll only aggravate your situation.

But it's going to be difficult, not mentioning it. Less naïve
than my father was, I know at once it is a useless reminder.
Old all day long, without a moment's respite! And ageing
by the second! I struggled to get used to being as I am today,

and tomorrow I shall have to struggle again to re-seat myself in this chair, become still more uncomfortable than before. Who dares deprive me of my right to speak, to shout, to protest? All the more since protest is the shortest route to resignation.

AN OLD MAN'S CONFESSIONS

Translated by Ben Johnson

Introduction

4th April, 1928

WITH THIS DATE A NEW ERA BEGINS FOR ME. NOT LONG AGO
I found something of great importance in my life—indeed the
only important thing that has ever happened to me: a description made by myself of a certain phase of my life—a bundle
of notes I had stacked up and laid aside for my doctor who
had prescribed them. I read and re-read them now and find
them easy to complete; I find it simple to make everything
fit into place, as my inexperience would not let me do before.
How alive that part of my life is! And how completely dead
the rest, the part I did not record! Sometimes I go in search
of it, anxiously, feeling myself maimed without it; but it is
beyond recovery. And what is more, I now know that the
things I put down were not the most important: they became
so, simply because I put them down. And now what am I?
Not the one who lived, but the one whom I described.

Oh! the only part of life that matters is contemplation.
When everybody understands that as clearly as I do, they will
all start writing. Life will become literature. Half of humankind will devote itself to reading and studying what the other
half has written. And contemplation will be the main business
of the day, preserving it from the wretchedness of actual living. And if one part of human kind rebels and refuses to read
the other half's effusions, so much the better. Everyone will
read himself instead; and people's lives will have a chance
to repeat, to correct, to crystallise themselves, whether or no
they become clearer in the process. For good and evil, they
won't go on being as they are now, flat and insignificant,
buried as soon as born, with all their days melting into each

other, piling up indistinguishably into years and decades.

I mean to take up writing again. I intend to record my whole self in these pages, my every vicissitude. Here in the house I have a reputation as a grumbler. I'm going to surprise them. I won't open my mouth again: I shall complain in these pages instead. I wasn't cut out for fighting, and when they tell me I don't understand things any more, instead of arguing with them—trying to prove that I'm still able to manage my own affairs, as well as my family's—I shall hurry back here to restore my serenity.

I may find to my surprise that the man I am now describing is different from the one I described years ago. Life, even when it's not put down on paper, still leaves its mark. With the passage of time, my life has, I should say, become calmer. I no longer have those absurd remorses, those awful fears for the future. What could I be frightened of? It is the future I am living now! And it glides away without preparing the way for any other. So it is not even a *bona-fide* present. It is outside time. Grammar does not possess a *final* tense. It is true, the business of my rejuvenation operation made a great stir in my life. But having decided upon it in a moment of pique, I underwent it very much in two minds, in a state of confusion, ready to back out at any moment, with my ear cocked all the time in case my wife or daughter or son would make an eleventh-hour outcry to stop me. None of them did so; they were probably keen to watch this unique experience, offered to them gratis. And I managed to reconcile myself to this and conceal my chagrin. I had compromised myself with my wife and daughter at the very outset, when, in an effort to frighten and punish them I shouted my decision aloud, and again afterwards, on the 'phone to the doctor, so as to frighten and punish them all the more. And so, completely against my wishes, I ended up on the operating table. Then there were the boils, which have kept me in my room for a month.

But be that as it may, old age is the serene period in one's life. So serene that it is hard to record it. How can I seize hold of it, to describe what led up to the operation? From that point on, it is easy. The very expectation of youth, which was to result from the operation, was itself a sort of youth, enough to create a distinct period in my life; so much so that I can describe it, with its great sorrows and great hopes.

And now I see my life, commencing with childhood, passing on into turbid adolescence, which one fine day settled down into young manhood (something in the nature of a disillusionment), then hurtling on into marriage (a state of resignation interrupted by occasional rebellions) and then entering upon old age, the main characteristic of which was to push me into the shadows and rob me of the rôle of leading actor. For everyone, including myself, my *raison d'être* from now on was to provide a background to others—to my wife, my daughter, my son and my grandson.

Then came the operation, and they all looked at me with wonderment. I was active and stirring again, and was given a new lease of life—almost like a real one, I mean the kind of life that doesn't call for operations, the natural kind, the kind everyone has; and the agitation ended by driving me back to this paper, which perhaps I never should have abandoned. This scolding I am giving myself seems to me fully justified; fundamentally, however, it is no more reasonable than that which that other old man gave himself, the man who thought he must be decrepit, because he had given up women. I am writing now because I must, whereas in the past merely holding a pen in my hand would have made me yawn. So I think, after all, the operation has had a salutary effect.

I · Alfio

AND I OUGHT TO BEGIN MY STORY WHERE I LEFT OFF.

With the war ended, in the way everyone knows it did, I was looking forward both to the general triumph and to a private one of my own: I was waiting to see old Olivi to show him how successfully I had managed affairs without him. But old Olivi, who had always snubbed me, avoided having to pay homage to me by dying of the *grippe* in Pisa. This happened after he had already told me when he planned to arrive and I had written to him to explain what his new duties were to be: he was to have charge of the office, whilst I would take over as business manager. I was waiting for him rather impatiently. And in fact, if he'd arrived in time I might perhaps have been spared a ruinous loss. This was that purchase of mine of all those truckloads of soap in Milan, where, as soon as the frontier was opened, there was an enormous profit to be made. All I had to guide me in this *coup* was my war-time business experience, and Olivi, after all, had another kind of training which, once the armistice was signed might prove valuable too. I had bought up what seemed to me a vast proportion of the consignment, and, following war-time practice, I saw no urgency to sell it. After all everybody has to wash—! One had only to ride on a tramcar in Trieste to notice the appalling stench—it was perfume to my nostrils, and reassured me of my success. When I learned of Olivi's death I was annoyed; he had evaded his defeat. Later, I was glad of it—for nobody in Trieste seemed to be interested in my soap. Had they all stopped washing? It would have been a bad business to have had Olivi arrive and find that most of our war-time profits had been wasted in a deal contracted during the armistice. I was left to liquidate the affair on my own. I could not reproach myself at all. The world had changed so rapidly, I had lost my bearings completely; I was entirely at sea. The soap I had bought didn't contain the fat content prescribed in Trieste under Austrian law, to which the town still clung despite the presence of the Italian troops. I later sold the soap on three months credit to an Austrian, who took it back with him to Vienna. There—I do not know whether because they were in desperate need of it or because it was sub-standard—the soap was immediately confiscated. It was turned over to some bureau and, in the end, paid for in full. But the money arrived here when *kronen* could no longer be exchanged; and so, redeemed for a few lire, the money returned to Austria.

That was my last business deal, and I still talk of it occasionally. One forgets neither one's first transaction, which fails from too much innocence, nor the last, the fatal result of too much cunning. And I have a further reason for remembering it; for there was something that made it rankle. Just before I had liquidated the affair, young Olivi came home from the war. A bespectacled youth, he returned a lieutenant with a chest full of medals. He agreed at once to take back his old job in my office, as my immediate subordinate. And before long I had settled down in a comfortable position of a king who doesn't rule. Soon I did not know what was happening in my affairs at all. Every day new laws and decrees showered down in Italy, written in impossible jargon: the only thing in the least clear about them was the numeral after the King's name. I saw to it that the tax stamps (it was then that the nation started licking such quantities of stamps) and all official documents were handled by Olivi. Then I began to find him rather obnoxious, and I started avoiding the office. He did a good deal of talking about his service and hardships during the war and never let an opportunity go by of reproaching me for not contributing to the victory.

Constantly talking about the soap as I was, and the *kronen* that had arrived too late, one day I said, "But isn't there something we can do about those Viennese? After all, we won the war, didn't we?"

He burst out laughing, in my face. And I am convinced that just to prove to me that I had not won the war, he wouldn't take a single step to make the Austrians indemnify me for the soap.

On the other hand, he goes on attending to my affairs with his usual integrity. What is more, he is fond of my son Alfio who, having left school, used sometimes to come to the office to get experience. Later on, when he took up painting, he stopped; but it was clear Olivi didn't mind having his work supervised.

Nor did he mind being supervised by my son-in-law Valentino either. There was a worker for you! He devoted the whole day to business, after which, every evening, he would put in an hour or more checking Olivi's books. Then, unfortunately, he fell ill and died; but as it is, as a result of his work, I cannot help having the same confidence in Olivi's son as I and my father before me had in his father. Indeed, greater confidence, one might say, because Olivi *père* was never closely supervised at any time in his career. My father, I suspect, knew nothing about book-keeping; and as for me—I used to go to the office now and again, but more to attend to my own affairs than to supervise other people. Besides, as is apparent, I have never been a book-keeper myself. I can initiate transactions, can think of them for myself that is to say—and I can carry them through as well, but once they have been transacted they dissolve into a fog in my mind, and I can keep no written record of them. I think this must be true of all real business-men; otherwise, having closed one deal, they would be unable to conceive of any other. Anyway, I stopped going to the office. I am ready here, if required. I'll go back to work if another war breaks out.

And since I have mentioned him, I will say something about Alfio. It will do me good to collect my thoughts on paper; because, really, I don't know how to handle him.

He arrived home after the war, a youngster of fifteen and

not at all like the child, thin, pale, lanky and carelessly-dressed, who had left. I noticed at once a streak of absent-mindedness in him, an inability to pursue today what he began yesterday—in short, qualities I was very well acquainted with, but which I had been irrevocably cured of by the great whirlwind. I had imagined that I would avoid making my father's mistakes and should manage to handle my own son differently. But my God, what if my father had had a son like mine! With all my knowledge and experience, I was so much better prepared to meet new situations, yet for all that, I didn't know what to make of Alfio—indeed, I didn't know how to put up with him. I let him do completely as he pleased. He left the *Ginnasio* directly after the Gentile Reform, which was not to his liking, and I didn't say a word. I simply told him with a touch of sadness in my voice that he was losing the chance to make his mark in the academic world; it meant the end of a private hope of mine. He took this as an intolerable interference and told me there was not merely a difference in age between us, but something much more. The war had divided us. We were now in a new world in which I, born long before the war, had really no part. As I thought myself perfectly able to understand the world around me, being told I was an idiot enraged me considerably.

But if the truth be told, our disputes were fomented by others. One of these disputes arose on a Sunday after lunch. We were all gathered together: my wife, my daughter Antonia, Valentino, and Carlo (the son of Ada and Guido) who was studying medicine at Bologna and was spending the holidays with us. Carlo started it by trying to talk to Alfio out of leaving the *Liceo*, arguing very simply that the *Ginnasio* and the *Liceo* might be a little dreary, but that made going to the university all the more enjoyable.

"You study there," Carlo said, "and you hardly notice you're doing it."

I was in a slightly irritable mood. The vegetarian diet prescribed by Dr Raulli hits me especially hard on Sundays, when I see choice platefuls of chicken being wolfed all round me.

But I'm sure I didn't bring a tone of martyrdom into the discussion. I was the mildest of all. Only I felt I couldn't rebuff such useful allies, all trying to keep Alfio on the right track, when I couldn't keep him there by my own efforts.

Suddenly Valentino, a true bureaucrat who thought that everything under the sun could be proved, and that when you had drawn up a balance sheet you had solved everything, began to lay down the law. He said that everybody had to be ready to make sacrifices for the sake of his own future, his dignity and his family. This was the truth; there was no question about it. Anybody who refused to obey it, would regret it later. He knew it to be true, having often witnessed it. He was not speaking out of his own experience, because he himself had always understood these things from the very outset and from early youth had always done what was best for his future.

Carlo now pulled Valentino's leg a little: "Somewhere in the world, I suppose, there must be people who, instead of always thinking of the future, prefer the present. Grammatically speaking, the two tenses are as good as each other. People are free to choose the one or the other."

It was meant as a joke, but I think it helped to poison the discussion. Alfio did not side with Carlo, being such a very different person; it made him want to assert his independence all the more, with the result that he jumped on Valentino even more fiercely. "Everybody can't know everything. For instance, a clerk can't be expected to understand an artist; nor a doctor either."

As for Carlo, who had inherited a great many of his father Guido's weaknesses, but not the lack of humour which ruined him (Guido could draw up the most ridiculous balance-sheets without a smile), Carlo extricated himself perfectly coolly, saying, with his glass at his lips: "To be sure, all we doctors can know about artists is the acts of God which strike them down from time to time. And then, I admit, they're no longer artists and are in no position to bother people any more."

Valentino did not answer. He was a timid soul. Having been occupied with my accounts for some time, he had come to imagine it was his duty to look after the welfare of the whole family. He discovered his mistake, and was inclined to retreat, after one luke-warm protest to Alfio: "I can only give you the advice suggested by my own experience."

But Antonia was terrible. As a rule she was rather motherly towards Alfio, but now she had seen him attack her husband. She felt that even Carlo's levity, about a matter which Valentino had taken so seriously, was an act of contempt towards her husband. She became violent, rebuking me for letting my son behave like a fool (I raised my arms, imploring God for help), and rebuking Alfio for thinking himself superior to everyone—it was a presumption he would repent of. Why wouldn't he at least complete his intermediate studies? He would be an inferior for the rest of his life! Moreover, when someone was kind enough to give him good advice, it was intolerable of him to reply like an oaf.

And the upshot of all this, with which I had about as much to do as cabbage at tea-time, was that Alfio bore a grudge against me. It is quite true that I failed to back him up, indeed that I couldn't avoid siding with the others. But, after all, it's a serious business when one sees one's own son renouncing, at the very outset, the sort of chances that others would give their ears for! Moreover, I daren't risk making things worse for Valentino, when Antonia was so upset on his behalf. I had been determined for so many years to prevent any repetition between me and my son of my own relations with my father, and now everything seemed to be leading exactly to that. I had behaved so that there would be no excessive manifestations of affection between us—not like that morbid anxiety about my future which my father showed on his deathbed, for instance—at that moment, with him already in such agony, it had been almost like a passionate kiss, and it was certainly the cause of that long and painful illness I suffered later—an illness which, even after it was cured, made the sun shine less bright for me and the air hang heavy.

So I had resolved to avoid great effusions of affection between my son and me—and, on my own part, any patriarchal presumptions. I avoided the effusions without the least difficulty while he was in swaddling clothes, as I could never stand squalling babies. As for the patriarchal presumptions, I could not refrain from them altogether. Whenever things got too much for Augusta, she called for my help and I would intervene with a great bellow which solved everything. But it was a brief affair, directed at him and his sister indiscriminately, as a general might dress down a battalion, and I cancelled it at once with a joke, so as to show there was no ill feeling. And I always abstained religiously from demanding acts of contrition. With Antonia, my system, I am sure, was successful: she will be able to watch me die with perfect serenity and carry on her life with her husband and child as though I had never existed. And once a year she will placidly come with flowers for my grave, convinced she is giving me all the pleasure I have any right to.

With Alfio, though, I am less sure. I know he doesn't think much of me. For him—the artist—a respectable businessman is a poor brute no one can take seriously, and convictions of this sort are just the kind that death sometimes reverses. And, moreover, whereas it should have been so easy for my father and me to have come to an understanding, seeing that we lived alone with each other, and any complications that there were had to start with one or other of us, in the case of myself and Alfio there were a whole crowd of people coming between us and confusing things. To take a single instance, let's go back to that Sunday discussion. At one point I raised my arms in a gesture which, par excellence, is that of the patriarch; and I did it to calm down Antonia. And then again, instead of leaving my son to look after his own affairs, I had to interfere with an admonishment, which I may have pretended was out of fatherly concern, and was actually done for Valentino's sake.

Alfio, in short, is a much more difficult young man for me to cope with than I ever was for my father. My father used to scold me for laughing at everything, and my son scolds me for the same thing. Apart from my bitterness at this like-

mindedness on their part, Alfio's attitude is much harder to
bear than my father's; my father's used really to make me
laugh, but my son's is no laughing matter. I put on a serious
face, and whenever a piece of nonsense crosses my mind I do
my best to repress it. It vanishes and afterwards I look back
upon it with regret. Nonsense, when not put into words,
loses all its efficacy, and life slips away more monotonous and
sadder than ever.

I honestly believe that my son is angry with me, and with
his mother too. At every little difference between us, an edge
of resentment comes into that slightly feeble voice of his. Just
after the war he was angry with us in the name of Commun-
ism. He was, in fact, not a Communist in the least, but he
really felt we were wicked for taking up so much room in the
world—so many rooms in our house—and for keeping to
ourselves so much of what would be useful to others. Augusta
was in dread that he would turn up at the house one day
with new lodgers. But in all the world he didn't know a single
worker. He walked the streets alone—concerned, just then,
about social justice, and later, still just as alone, with art, and
personality.

And it was then that I made fun of him, mildly, which
was a mistake. We only discussed theories, since he had not
yet started to paint. This business of being a personality seemed
to me carrying things too far: it was presumptuous of him.
One could aim at having a lovable personality or an attractive one. But personality in itself—!! Sometimes "real"
personalities ended up with life sentences. "What a personality!" I used to say, speaking of our Giacomo, a night watch-
man we hired to guard the villa during the recent troubles.
All in all, Giacomo was a real personality. When he was full
of drink he was as brutish as a drunkard, but he could not
act the drunken part: he looked a brute but not drunk. He
never staggered, and his walk was just the same, a bit stiff,
but perfectly steady. I resolutely refused to sack him. He
did his duty; he never went to sleep. Though for that matter
he never had anything to do and let us sleep in peace, since

nothing out of the ordinary ever happened. A real personality, our Giacomo!

But Alfio got angry and, as usual, by way of explaining himself more clearly, he insulted me. I became a bit fierce too, and threatened to disinherit him. The quarrel went on for days, and Augusta kept running from one to the other to explain, to soothe, and to reconcile us. My anger had already passed when, to please his mother, he finally asked me to forgive him, which meant he never really forgave *me*. To tell the truth, always being fairly busy, I wouldn't have worried all that much, except that I didn't like seeing how upset he became every time we met. Death was hanging over me more and more, and I felt pity for Alfio, who was in such danger of the same disaster as overcast my own youth. I felt sorry for myself too, at the thought that when I died my only son would breathe a sigh of relief, would say to himself "Ouf!" And Alfio had the kind of sincerity which must say what it feels, just that and nothing else. Whereas I should have liked to die mourned, though of course in proper moderation.

Augusta told me one day that Alfio, in his solitude, had become addicted to painting. He would leave the house in the morning with his portfolio and paints under his arm. He took his lunch with him. He would not have anyone give him lessons for fear a teacher might somehow cripple his personality. Dead tired, he would return home after sunset, but would go out again to talk shop with his friends at the café. From me he had inherited only this part of his day. The rest was not mine, nor did it belong to the grandfather I had given him, or the grandmother. Where did he manage to get his itch for painting and for solitude? From his "personality"? I, who had striven in vain to be like other men, had never given it a thought. From his rebelliousness? Whenever I felt like rebellion I repented of it at once. And his grandfather did not even know what it was, sitting comfortably as he did, so massive and corpulent, on other people's necks. Innate rebelliousness in a person, as with Alfio, is a sure sign of weakness.

But even the shape of his body is his own idea; none of his

forebears had one like it. Long and lanky, with a peculiar warp in the trunk, which bends back at one point but then thinks better of it, and in righting itself forms a curve (though not a hump), forcing his head forward so that it is never perfectly erect, which means that to look anyone his own height in the face, he has to roll his eyes upwards. He is not good-looking. I know, because others have told me so. But Augusta and I admire his pale, gentle face. There is all the difference between knowing someone intimately and seeing him once in the street, with all his imperfections on display. We knew Alfio's strong points and his weak ones. His long legs carried more than a mere shape. Indeed, Augusta and I often used to talk about the marvellous expression in Alfio's intensely blue eyes, one of which squints a little (but not as much as his mother's)—those blue eyes pleading for succour and support and desperately struggling to focus, even when his mouth was repeating harsh words out of Marx, whom he had not read and in whom he did not believe.

I felt myself called upon to make peace with him. There came a day when I was feeling worse than usual: I felt myself threatened by a stroke—one of those visitations that takes away one's speech, one's hearing and one's sight, even when it doesn't carry away life itself. The stroke announced its approach by certain noises in the ears. And considering I had once had a blood pressure of 230! I was deeply moved as I pictured Alfio before my dead body, sobbing as I had done at his age, "Now . . . from now on . . . life is finished for me."

That evening, as soon as I knew he was at home and dressing to go out to the café, I went to his room. He had a little study on the other side of the house; it was ill-lit, but Augusta had furnished it attractively.

"May I?" I asked, hesitating after I had half-opened the door. I saw Alfio in front of the mirror, gazing upwards at himself as he knotted his tie. It is a great sign of sincerity, to look at oneself the way one looks at other people.

He turned to me, his tie dangling from his grubby shirt. He

seemed taken aback and concerned: "What made you bother, Papa? You could have called me, you know."

Relieved, I started to laugh: "This is a business matter; it's better we talk on our own. . . . Your mother tells me that you finish a picture a day. Do you think I might have one?"

He looked at me dubiously, shy, with his ever-supplicating eyes: "But Father! My art isn't for everybody. It's something new. It's got to be understood first. And being new, it's bound to be rough; it's a collection of uncensored brush-strokes in response to an impression."

"What difference does that make to me?" I laughed. "Art can be bought, whether it's old or new. That's what it's produced for. Sell me one of your canvases. I'll be your first customer."

He seemed about to protest, but instead, thinking it over for a moment, agreed. Then, shyly, he muttered something which must have been the price.

"How much?" I asked, raising my voice a bit.

He looked at me hesitantly, red to the ears. I realised he thought I wanted to bargain with him. This really frightened me. What if he were to reduce his price now just to please me and I were to come in for the resentment felt by anyone who is forced to reduce his price? Where would be our reconciliation then?

I adopted a cajoling tone: "I'm an old man and I don't hear very well. Tell me how much you want. I'll pay whatever you ask so as to bring myself closer to you, closer to your art. I'll hang the picture on the wall in my study and I'll look at it every day. And in the end I'll understand it, too. I'm less of a cretin than you take me for. I'm an old man, it's true. But that means that at least I've had some experience. It's true I've never been concerned with painting. But music now. Recently I've even reached the point of putting up with Debussy. Not liking him, you understand; because his music sounds to me like things that have just been blown up by a bomb. The fragments are all smoking still, but that's all they have in common."

His deciding to gratify me was due, I think, to my rigmarole about Debussy.

Making up his mind he named his price: eight hundred lire.

I took a thousand-lire note out of my pocket and, with the air of a punctilious business man, said, "You owe me two hundred." Then, pretending to be impatient: "And the painting. . . ?"

He gave me the two hundred lire. Where money is concerned, I notice, he has a scrupulousness that does not tally with his unseemly notions about wealth. In this respect he is by far my superior, and this superiority of his, so much admired by his mother, delights me too. He does not spend in a way that brings him closer to his poorer fellow-humans; on the contrary, he keeps his wallet well lined—which, clearly, broadens the gulf between him and them.

As for the painting itself, he couldn't bring himself to give it to me there and then. I would have it in ten minutes, he said. He wanted to give me the best he had. Evidently he was ashamed to let me see some of his clumsier efforts.

I stopped in the doorway, presently coming back in again.

"Look," I began, "you and I are alone in the world." I stopped, terrified at having said the very same thing which, with considerably more truth, had been said by my father; and I corrected myself. "I mean we're the only men of the same blood in this house. Why shouldn't we understand each other? I'm going to do everything I can to come closer to you. Will you follow my example? I can't teach you anything any more, and I don't want to act like a tutor. I'm too old to teach and you're too old to learn. You've got your own personality, and it's up to you to assert it."

I kissed him on the cheek and, flustered, he kissed the air.

"Yes, Papa," he said, touched.

I started for the door, cheerfully: "You'll have to bring some nails so your painting can be put on the wall straight away. I'm not so good at things like that, you know."

"But a painting has to have a frame," he said. "I'll buy

one myself tomorrow . . . A modest little frame for a modest little painting."

"All right," I said; "but in the meantime, right now, I want to begin studying your work. You'll know how to put it up without damaging it."

In the ten minutes I spent waiting for Alfio I was very nervous. It struck me that I had succeeded in bringing off something tremendous—something important for me, for him, and for the family. And it also occurred to me that my father would not have been able to do it. And yet between him and me there had not been the Great War. The War? Well really! It was merely a question of intelligence, knowing how to make contact with another generation.

But the War came back to my mind when I got a look at the painting—a small square sheet of paper. I first saw it over Alfio's shoulder as he busied himself nailing it to the wall.

"Thank you, thank you, so much," I said.

He stood and gazed at it admiringly. I aped his pose. Then he left in that slouching way of his.

Returning to the painting, I thought, "He's swindled me! He's given me the worst!" It is not at all unpleasant discovering a shrewd business man in one's own son. I was not complaining.

At first, having that daub of his in front of me made me uneasy. Before seeing it, I had asked Alfio to hang it so that I could look at it when I was sitting at my writing-table. In this he succeeded beyond expectation: not only could I see it sitting down, but also when I sat reading, with the lamp at my back, and even when I was stretched out on the couch to rest, if I did not lie on my left side—something I couldn't stand, any more than my father could—with my nose up against the wall, and even then I could sense the presence of that monstrosity in the room.

The more I looked at the painting, the more I became convinced that with my stability and good sense I was quite an exception in my family (meaning me, my father and son).

The picture could not be removed without the risk of offending Alfio all over again. The frame arrived, and the picture stayed where it was, despite my timid proposal to move it— so that it might be put in a better light. With an air of authority, Alfio pronounced that it was right just where it was. He gazed at it once again, affectionately, admiring it in the isolation the frame had given it, and then left.

The frame, certainly, served as a kind of commentary. I believe that whenever a thing is framed it acquires a new value. A thing only has to be isolated to become something in its own right—without its frame it is overshadowed by whatever there is around it. Even Alfio's painting became something when framed. I looked at it at first with anger; then, as I began to see what he had tried to do, with pleasure; and finally with admiration, when I suddenly discovered that he had actually done something.

All along, it had been apparent that Alfio had wanted to paint a hill. There was no doubt about that. The colours had not been varied to indicate either distance or height, but when I came to understand and like the painting I arrived at conclusions that changed all my pre-conceived ideas about atmosphere. On top of the hill there had been constructed (or at least it had been his intention to construct) three parallel rows of houses. And studying it, I had the pleasant feeling of actively collaborating with Alfio. I was painting, myself! At the bottom some purple strokes marked a roadway. It was not the usual colour for earth. All the same, it was easy enough to make out that it must be earth. Above it stood the first row of buildings—a long low wall painted yellow, with a lone house on one side; the upper part of the house painted yellow as well; the bottom left bare, in white, the colour of the paper. But this house was the most habitable of them all. Its walls were absolutely perpendicular, perfectly squared, the only defect being that they hadn't enough windows—two on the second floor and one on the first; but they had been fitted out with matching grey shutters which I really came to like, later. This was undoubtedly the manor house.

On the far side of the first row there were some more purplish brush-strokes which, as one gathered from the key provided by the picture, again indicated a road. And then there were two more rows of houses separated by the same purplish colour which, owing to the distance—that is, so that it could be seen better—had been made darker. But my God, what houses! They had been painted with all the compassion of a poet for poor, ramshackle dwellings—an unspoken lament. Nearly all the walls were upright, but the houses had no windows; that is, wherever they had them they were noticeably black and shapeless, indicating that these poor windows had neither shutters nor panes. Instead of reflecting the daylight outside they gave off a pitchy gloom from within.

It's extraordinary how one can accustom oneself to anything under the sun. I quite took to that picture, and whenever I glanced up from my book (I had resumed my philosophical education and was reading Nietzsche) I felt genuine pleasure at finding myself vis-à-vis with the synthesis of life as Alfio felt it. I peopled his houses for him. In the manor house I installed landlords who, being as rough as their dwelling, were exploiting the tenants of the black-windowed houses. Only, in the background, quite some distance away, at the top, there was another solid, well constructed house, which, though it had black windows, might have been another manor house. It led me to think that with two such houses, the lot of the others would suffer all the more. Poor, long-suffering little houses, ramshackle abodes of sorrow! And there were even signs that the houses of the poor might become still more numerous: there were little towers scattered about which in time might come to be used as dwellings.

My relations with Alfio during this period were very pleasant. My admiration for him was sincere. See how, by simply painting shutters on a house, he had led me to visualize an entire landscape! It was certainly an art, what he was doing. It was modern art. And by understanding it I grew younger myself.

I talked to him about it with deep satisfaction. And he listened to me. But, full of youthful energy, he interrupted my praises, which were therefore wasted: earth seen from a certain point at a certain hour actually was that colour, and it did not take daring, but merely the analytical eye of a painter, to recognise it.

"Use your eyes, learn to use your eyes," he said.

I wanted to continue with my own analysis and mentioned those buildings of his which, though not yet houses, were on the way to becoming ones.

He protested, laughing, "But those *are* houses—real houses! You only have to look at them to tell. You simply have to know *how* to look. You've got to remember that light not only reveals but sometimes conceals and obscures things. Look at that house you claim isn't one yet; note the faint brown mark indicating a window . . ."

For me, his picture was easier to bear than his commentary. I continued to enjoy looking at it; but when we talked about it, not caring to state exactly what was in my mind, I fell back upon Alfio's own expressions. Be that as it may, I eventually reached the point of being able to roam that landscape of his with such assurance that I never had to worry about getting lost. And this pleasant period in my relations with Alfio lasted for some time. Though I was a bit disturbed, one day, when Alfio wanted to present me with another of his pictures—one I did not at all want to hang on the wall in my room. I put it in a drawer, assuring him that I looked at it every day. It was a lie, but I couldn't spend my whole time peopling my son's rickety houses. Then, again, any great effort on my part was pointless, as I had forbidden myself to speak my mind and had made up my mind to repeat what Alfio said. So it was easier simply not to look at his paintings.

The blissful interlude ended abruptly. At a very happy moment: precisely when I would least have expected it. I had invited an old friend of mine named Cima to lunch. It had been roughly a half-century since I had last seen him. Such meetings in one's old age are like the words printed in italics in a book: they stand out in a very special way. For a variety of reasons I had never forgotten Cima. He was a wealthy landowner from southern Italy who had come to Trieste in his youth to study German. (In those days they made such mistakes in southern Italy.) Cima learned Triestine with ease and subsequently spent his days wenching, hunting and fishing. He was richer then than he was ever to be again in his life.

I could not possibly have forgotten him because he had symbolised for me a number of failures, but a success as well. And I, judging my life and trying to be scrupulously objective, forgot neither.

My success was one of observation.

At the time, I was studying political economy. Or rather, it was a period when I was studying law, but my enthusiasm had led me to study too much political economy, which should have remained a marginal study.

This country gentleman was obviously an absentee landlord, an excellent description of whom is given in all the textbooks. And one day I was there when Orazio received a letter from his steward.

"From my overseer," he mumbled. (Even now, as an old man, he mumbles his thought aloud, no doubt to help to set his clear but slow-moving brain into motion.) Then, having read the letter, he murmured, "No."

And I said to him, "I'll bet your steward is suggesting some improvements you refuse to make."

His surprise confirmed it. "How did you know?"

I was able to show him the exact passage in the textbook which had told me.

My failures are so numerous that I can scarcely be expected to remember them all. Once I got him to join me in swearing off tobacco. Naturally, I promptly went back on it. He, on the contrary, in the course of a week, underwent every conceivable hunting adventure both good and bad, without weakening. One day he tramped the Carso for ten hours with no luck at all, and the next day he bagged so much that he had to return to town so as not to overburden himself; and his anti-smoking vow remained firm. This was astonishing to me, who, as I kept saying, could never manage to give up smoking, because my good resolutions weakened in the face of good news, bad news, or no news at all.

He possessed a will power like the force of gravity; it was a state of being, like the determination of water to run down-hill. When you confronted him with a desire on your own part, if it did not coincide with what he wanted, he became completely deaf to it. Once—I remember this as though it were yesterday, for moments of towering anger are never forgotten—I was expected at six o'clock by a woman who could only manage to give me an hour of her time. At three o'clock I made the mistake of getting into a gig, with him at the reins, and letting him drive me to Lipizza. I happen to know that it was a magnificent, clear autumn day, but I remember it as dark and wrathful.

At a certain point we could still comfortably have got back to Trieste in time; but in spite of all my protests, he took me on a drive through the Carso, which I was so ignorant of that I thought we were returning towards Trieste. At last we arrived back in town, and I found myself standing in the middle of the piazza, where he had left me, torn with craving and remorse. And there was Orazio, saying in perfect innocence to me: "You should have told me when we left."

I *had* told him! But it was one of those things he was deaf to. It had all happened, as I later found out, because his vet had told him his horse should put in a certain number of kilometres a day.

And now that he had returned to Trieste, he was glumly asserting that after living so long and experiencing so much sorrow, he was utterly without will. For my part I declared I was no longer the spineless man he had once known. I didn't really believe what he told me, because that very day I had the feeling I was returning to Lipizza with him—only this time with me trotting rather than being carried by his horse. He wanted me to accompany him everywhere he went.

"Afterwards I'll walk home with you," he said.

As it turned out, we went to an insurance company, where he had to fill up a declaration stating that he had changed his address; thence to a shipping agent who still had some of his furniture in storage; and lastly he inflicted an old fellow called Ducci on me.

Like myself, old Ducci had remained in Trieste, but from the day we left school at the age of eighteen we had not exchanged a single word. I recalled that the last time I had spoken to him he told me he was toying with the idea of seeking his fortune in Japan. Afterwards, small as our town is, we saw each other at least once a week and waved, without ever saying a word to each other. With the passage of years our waves gradually became more cordial. The fact that we were the only persons in the city who had known each other for so long created a kind of intimacy between us. And since he had found his fortune in Trieste, I regarded it as only natural that he had given up the idea of going to Japan. Now here we were, the three of us together, pounding the pavement with our accumulation of nearly two centuries' living. We looked at one another sympathetically, with our slightly bleared eyes, and for a moment I forgot my impatience. But it returned when I learned that Ducci could not recollect having ever having thought of going to Japan. Good God!—my whole world was becoming topsy-turvy. For years, whenever I saw him, I used to think, "There's a man who almost went to Japan!" Could I have made a mistake? Could it have been someone else who had told me, fifty years ago, that he wanted to emigrate? But later, seeing Ducci on other occasions while Cima was in town, I discovered he was planning various grand tours. For instance, he had a hankering to go to Norway. Certainly, with so many trips running through his mind, it was altogether possible that he might, in fifty years, also forget wanting to go to Norway; whereas I, who avoid making plans because they worry me, might, living from day to day as I do, remember this astonishing plan of his.

Anyway, the first time Cima came to lunch at our house he told me an old story, one dating back to our youth, and which he couldn't remember the whole of, but which I was able to finish for him; and it sent us into such paroxysms of laughter that, in the heat of my enjoyment, it led me to hurt poor Alfio's feelings irretrievably.

It must be remembered that when young Cima arrived in Trieste I was looking round for models of strong will and resolution to help me overcome the spinelessness I had begun so much to suffer from. Where could I find a better example than Cima? Cima always imposed himself as the master wherever he went and, though less intelligent than myself, never knew embarrassment or doubt: he was a man I could learn from. Even physically, he suggested youth and strength, with his little imperial, his black eyes and his great head of curly hair. I couldn't imitate his good looks and strength, but I didn't think his power of domination, which gave him such calm and self-confidence and happiness, depended on these things. He was the master because he felt himself to be.

It struck me that the habit of slaughtering animals must have contributed to Cima's strength. It was really a weakness of mine—in fact the greatest of my weaknesses—this business of not being able to kill animals. My squeamishness reached the point—it comes back to me clearly, because I still, very faintly, feel something of the same kind—that once, one evening before going to bed, I happened to give a light swat to a fly that was pestering me. Crippled, the poor thing managed to get away from me and, wanting to put it out of its misery, I looked for it in vain. I couldn't find it; and time and again throughout the night I thought of it, doubtless in agony, in some out-of-the-way corner of the room, consumed with rancour and pain. So, under Cima's tutelage, I resolved to harden myself against such pangs of remorse. I paid large sums for a hunting licence and bought one of those splendid outfits, with a feather in the hat, that sportsmen used to wear then. Cima lent me a double-barrelled shotgun.

It began with a hunting trip in the marshes. We went out to the marshland around Cervignana. On the way out I tried to fill my heart with hatred for animals. After all, the birds I was going out to kill were predatory too. They lived on animals smaller than themselves. Not only that, it was said that when they encountered a dangerous animal they were capable of carrying it up into the air and dropping it to its death. Moreover, I discovered that if I killed any game I had an advantage over Cima who, like a true sporting dog, did not eat game. I could at least stifle my remorse with a delicious meal. All the same, I was very much on edge, and my first act of violence against animals struck me as such an important occasion that I smoked a good many cigarettes, telling myself that once I possessed a powerful will, a murderer's will, I would stop smoking.

(I meant to give an account of happenings a few weeks old, but I find myself deep in the past. What a vast importance distant things take on when compared with those of a few weeks ago—like the bouquet of a vintage wine, all its elements blended and returning as soon as you lift it to your nose. And yet, my wife claims I don't remember anything. Of course, if I were to be asked where I left my gold pen or my glasses, I should be surprised at being expected to make such an effort; but bygone things come crowding back of their own accord, in great quantity, embellished with all their details.

So there we were in the marshes, each in a barrel stuck in the mud, at a certain distance from one another. Orazio had urged me to keep quiet and not to move, our aim in spending so many hours of misery in waterlogged barrels being to outwit the birds—suspicious creatures that, long before taking to flight, examine their route with their tiny, sharp, eyes. Another reason to hate them: all that prudence. Up over the distant mountains it looked as if the sky was beginning to grow light. Dawn? I was becoming restless. Slow processes like this wear out my patience. But how could I speed things up, crouching in such an uncomfortable place? Confound Cima! He might at least have got me a larger barrel and put a chair in it for me. I tried to look at my watch. It was a way to make the time pass more quickly. But the accumulated glow of the motionless stars above—an enormous example of patience!—was not sufficient to light the tiny dial. And a thought occurred to me: I might stop smoking at that unknown hour.

This was a unique resolution; it would be harder to break too; there would be no more calculations, no more time limits. I would be starting out from an unknown point, to travel towards another unknown point, far remote from me.

I studied the direction of the wind and, leaning against the side of the cask, faced into it. I carefully struck a match.

Whereupon an extraordinary thing happened. Cima fired at me. I heard the whistle of buckshot past my ears. I was filled with a towering indignation. In those days my indignation fell on anybody who tried to stop me from smoking my last cigarette. You will imagine how I felt an interference like this! I didn't think twice. Instead of replying to the abuse Cima was hurling at me, I yelled "I'll kill you!"

I aimed the gun at him and fired.

"You idiot!" Cima shouted. "What do you think you're doing?"

"What do you think *you're* doing?" I retorted.

"But I know how to shoot."

"And if I hadn't ducked in time I'd have got an earful of buckshot."

"Look, I've got a hole in my hat."

He jumped out of his hide and brought the hat over to let me see. I was sorry. I could have said that I had aimed at his hat and not his head, but he wouldn't have believed me.

"I'm sorry," I said, "but you made me angry."

His eye fell regretfully across the broad marshland, and he walked away.

"You can stay," I said, sulking, smoking furiously. "*I'll* go."

"Go where?" he said, lighting a cigarette himself. "By now all the birds for miles know we've got guns. And besides, you don't know how to get out of the marsh. Just look at yourself, up to your knees in mud."

He turned around and started off.

It was his way of making me follow him. I tried not to obey. But I was in real danger of drowning. I struggled up out of the mud to the path he had taken. I had no alternative but to resign myself, for the last time, to submission. But I made a vow: in future, whenever he went to the Boschetto[1] I was going to Servola.[2] There was solid ground there.

We walked on for ten minutes. Then, suddenly, he stopped and burst out laughing: "You're really quite a character!" He began to laugh so much he could hardly stand. He just managed to stammer out "I fire . . . so you fire . . . as if it were the same thing . . ." And, after lighting a wax vesta: "And now you're angry with *me*."

He took hold of my arm and stroked it. I finally burst out laughing too. It would have been stupid to give up smoking at an unspecified hour.

A good laugh, now—there's something that's never wasted; all the more so that we now re-discovered it intact, in fact better than before. In this meagre little old fellow, with his body still erect, not out of vigour but because, weak and wispy as he was, it was no effort to him to keep it erect (so long as nobody happened to push him over), with his head still partly covered with white hair, far thicker than mine, but by no means enough to hide the reddish scalp beneath, I found my old friend again, but gentler and less dangerous. He didn't command the respect that, as model and mentor, he had enjoyed in our youth; he was a teacher with nothing more to teach and content to be treated as an equal. We laughed over my idiocy in having wanted to go hunting, and his, in having taken me. Then we laughed simply at my idiocy, Augusta having brought up the subject of my endless anti-smoking campaigns. They came to the conclusion that, to my great credit, my disease must be cured, seeing that I never mentioned it, though I went on smoking. That was what *they* thought! Still it was true I had had to teach my disease not to reveal itself, except in soliloquies, immediately forgotten, and in resolutions neither written down nor spoken, nor indicated in any

[1] A wooded area on the outskirts of Trieste, a favourite resort of the Triestines.

[2] Village (now a suburb) at the other end of Trieste. Svevo himself lived at Servola.

way on the calendar or the face of my watch—all of which left me in a rather pleasant state of freedom. There's no doubt, living so long cures all diseases!

During that lunch now, I had not drunk a thing; I had even abstained from the delectable meat everyone else was eating. Nothing had been introduced into my impoverished bloodstream to heat it. It was boiling simply from laughter. I made fun of myself: I had gone out to kill beasts, and had proved such a marksman I had not managed to hit Cima with a single buckshot. Then, to needle Cima, I corrected myself: I had set out to shoot beasts and a beast had ended by firing at me. For his part, Cima thought up something I can't recall, which everyone else laughed at but not me, it being such a poor little thing I would have had to tickle myself to get a laugh out. But there was no resentment between us. Only, as was natural, the laughing stopped, whereas I should have liked it to continue. It was healthy exercise, the only violent form of exercise old men are permitted.

And to prolong it, I began to talk about Alfio's painting— something I had laughed bitterly over in the past, and over which I now smiled, thinking of my effort to supply all the things that were missing in that picture of his, and of how I had come to be fond of it without ever ceasing to laugh at it. At that time there was a great deal of talk about earthquakes, and exploding into a whoop of laughter, I told him how I had gone running to the painting to see if the little houses had all collapsed: "No, they hadn't. You might think they had collapsed, but they were just as they had always been."

Not even the way Alfio's face, which was always pale, went even paler, could restrain me. My attack had come so without warning that he had only glanced up from his plate a little, staring me in the face with those gentle eyes of his, scrutinising me to see if under the surface derision there might be a quite different meaning. I realised nothing. I felt perfectly innocent. I felt like laughing, and so any subject would do.

Alfio then broke out: "Listen, if you like, I'll give you back the money you gave me and take my picture back."

But I objected: "And who's going to pay me for all the work I put into it?"

And as Cima, with his slow brain, did not understand what I meant, I explained that with great effort and perseverance I had completed and populated my son's houses, and that now I had put them in such good order I wasn't inclined to give them back. As it was—as completed by me—I liked the picture. And as soon as I found myself in good health again (for a month now I had been taking a tonic with this in view), I was going to take on another of his pictures—one I kept hidden away for the moment so that I shouldn't overtax my strength.

Alfio tried attacking me: "D'you know, what you manage to do with all this effort, others with more training in art do without trying, simply by looking, the way one looks at nature itself."

I lost my temper and refused to admit that the effort it had taken me sprang from any weakness of mine. I got so angry, in fact, that I forgot my good resolutions and called Alfio an idiot. I am sorry for it and ashamed of it. How strange relations between fathers and sons are! No amount of effort makes them any better. I, who had always claimed to know nothing about painting, got furious because my son was shouting the same opinion.

But the others behaved even worse. With his grave official sententiousness Valentino said, "It's clear that an artist isn't on the right track if he doesn't please a large public."

Alfio thought so little of Valentino's judgement as not even to trouble himself to answer. But Antonia, distressed at her husband's interference on this second occasion, after he had left the first encounter limping, tugged at his sleeve to warn him of the danger. Valentino, never very alert, straightened his jacket, examining it with curiosity to see what was stretching it. And after a brief pause Alfio said to his sister, "Let him talk. What's the difference?"

A new offence, with another and more serious one following close behind: after lunch Orazio wanted to see the painting, whereupon Alfio declared that he had no intention of assisting at such an examination; and he went to his room. Later, though, the torture proved irresistible, and as Orazio, standing in front of the paintings, started guffawing, holding his non-existent paunch, Alfio appeared in the doorway of my study, leaned against the jamb, and looked on intently, very far from joining in the laughter, but mastering himself enough not to show any signs of suffering.

"Houses for horses!" Orazio said, and actually discovered something that looked like the muzzle of a horse under one of the houses.

But I think it was from that day on that my relations with Alfio began to deteriorate. I did all I could to improve them. Only, I couldn't tell him that I liked his painting. He had told me I was an ignorant boor, if only where painting was concerned. I could scarcely agree: "Yes, I'm a boor, though only where painting is concerned." I courted him, I gave him money, I put my arm around him, I kissed him on the cheek any number of times, while he kissed the air. It was all no good, because I never again dared to speak to him about painting.

One day I met him as he was returning home with his little box and portfolio. "Has your painting gone well?" I asked.

"I do what I can," he said. And he hurried off. He was truly frightened I might ask him to let me see some of his work.

Enduring his behaviour was a tough business for me. All the theories I had drawn from my dealings with my father could be of no service because I had behaved quite differently with my father. Still, I continued to be kind and considerate towards him. At table whenever there was a discussion I always sided with Alfio. When he asked me for money I gave it to him without batting an eyelid. I employed nothing but kind words when I talked to him. My behaviour, of course, must have looked strange and not really affectionate. And meanwhile, as I had my arm around him, a voice cried within me, "How good I am, how good!" The feeling of being so good has a tendency to make us less good.

What's more, I think our good relations did not revive

because he did not really care very much how he got on with me. Time and again I begged him to keep me company. He escaped at the first opportunity.

He was developing passionate friendships first for one, then another, of his colleagues. For a while he concentrated all his affection on a painter who turned out really beautiful portraits. And I said to him, unpleasantly: "Ah, so things can also be painted the way they are?"

Alfio turned pale, as only he can, and answered, "Everyone has his own personality."

To him—that is, to us—had been allotted that crooked personality, with its disorganised colours. There was nothing to do but grin and bear it. He always got his revenge.

So I was forced to the conclusion that if death and death-bed agonies turned out to be a terrible punishment for Alfio, it was his own fault. I could set out towards death now with a clear conscience. Death was a visitation we could all expect, and I had to get used to mine. By now I had good reasons for believing that its consequences would not be too serious: Augusta would weep over me, very sensibly; Antonia would not weep at all; and Alfio could react in the way I had done, or not, as the case might be—it was all the same to me.

II · Antonia

MY DAUGHTER IS ESTIMABLE AS HER MOTHER WAS; EVEN more so; in fact she is too admirable. Physically, she resembles Ada, with her stately bearing, and the elegance of her fine little head and figure. I gather from Augusta that men find her attractive, but when still a girl she made an iron resolve in favour of virtue, and she has remained faithful to it not only in everything she has done, but in her every word as well— every glance, even. And that is taking virtue too far. It may be accounted for by the fact that part of her education was received from nuns; but her organism itself, I suspect, in- herited cells with a tendency to exaggeration. I like to think that she inherited virtue from her mother, and exaggeration from me. I am here alone before this sheet of paper, which perhaps will never be seen by anyone: so what I am saying need not be thought ridiculous nor presumptuous. Although my own virtue has not been great, my desire for it has been excessive. It occurs to me I have just made an important dis- covery in the law of heredity, the accuracy of which may be verified by research. Antonia provides concrete evidence: from her mother she inherited a certain quality, and from her father the particular degree to which it manifested itself. In my heart I am excessively modest. It was a misfortune that Augusta's good qualities, as manifested in Antonia, should have had to be measured out by a scale provided by me.

As far back as her girlhood, life for her had developed into a series of duties. Study, it is true, was not her *forte*: she never learned a single foreign language or science. But she was an angel. The sisters loved her and made life for her as comfortable as possible. There was a period when Antonia talked about dedicating herself to the monastic life. We—Augusta and I—spent some anxious hours, as we suspected that this was just what the nuns themselves wanted and that they would get their way. Everyone warns you about monks and nuns and their passion for recruiting for their own order. In fact, however, the good sisters wouldn't hear of it and successfully helped us in dissuading her from such a step. I suspect, now that I am writing about it, that they had studied Antonia and foreseen she would have been the same nuisance in the convent as she is about the house just at present.

Fundamentally, though, as a girl she was a joy to us, a joy magnified by admiration for her great purity, and—on my part —a smile of surprise to see the strange product my blood had managed to evolve into.

Antonia reacted very decidedly against the free run young women were given after the war. Not only would she not dance, she would never leave the house unchaperoned. She always had to be accompanied by her mother or a maidservant, and at home, this created quite a problem, apportioning the watch-dog duties she insisted on. Sometimes, late at night, I myself had to go out to accompany her somewhere or to fetch her home. She was like a little bale of merchandise that could not move without a shipping agent.

And she was capable of defending her self-imposed bondage in the way Alfio defended his painting. When she talked about other girls she was as sharp-tongued as a disappointed old woman, and listening to her one tended to forget her fresh little face and her youthful bright eyes.

But this desire of hers, to feel locked and sealed up in a strong-box, was a sign that she regarded herself as something precious: a jewel. In fact, she devoted great care to the adornment of her person, and her clothes constituted a rather sizable expenditure in our family budget. I suspect, too, that Augusta managed to conceal part of this expense. It was not difficult because, except when I am in a black mood and want an outlet for bad temper, I do not worry about money matters.

And Augusta was like me; she trimmed her attitude to the prevailing wind. If she felt, for instance, that she needed my support to guide and educate Antonia, she could be first to complain of her daughter's extravagance. If, on the other hand, I brought it up first, I was told that Antonia was an extremely modest young lady who bought no more than other girls of her station. It made me cross with Antonia, and with Augusta too, as it seemed expressly designed to put me in the wrong. It is hard, anyway, now that I am old, to accept being in the wrong; but it infuriates me to find myself in the wrong through no fault of my own, simply because of other people's pernicious stratagems.

But all this has been forgotten long since and I recall it merely so as better to understand what is taking place now.

When she was fifteen, Antonia had only one friend: a rather plain, ill-shaped, dumpy-looking girl whose sole beauty lay in her black eyes—eyes with a curious lustre and that seemed to have been set in her head to admire and envy the beauty of others. The girl's name was Marta Crassi, and come what might she was destined to become Antonia's sister-in-law. I say "come what might" because Antonia had got herself into so strange a position in our community that there was no likelihood of her marrying anybody except one or the other of Marta's two brothers: she had fallen in love with an entire household—which, if truth be told, was nothing new in the family. Not much but certain faint traces of my physiognomy survive in my family.

I used to think that some more important traits had survived; and receiving word from Florence that whenever Eugenio, one of Marta's brothers, was on leave he went to see Antonia, and that he was showing signs of great affection for her, I thought to myself that the poor young man was in for a sorry adventure. But, as will presently be seen, I did not know the least thing about my own stock.

I had taken a fancy to poor Eugenio myself. Big-hearted, careless of his own interests, fired with ideas of humanity and Fatherland, when the war broke out he fled from Trieste and enlisted in the Italian Army. All the while he had been in Trieste he had not revealed his fondness for Antonia to anyone. The way I see it is that later, when he was able to free himself from trench life and to go running to visit his sister, with whom he would find Antonia, falling in love became a simple matter—for Antonia's sitting-room, naturally, was in every respect preferable to the trenches. I do not know whether the two ever discussed love. Augusta—and she knows her daughter—says no. It's her opinion that before speaking of love Antonia would have first wanted to speak of matrimony—and her opinion can be accepted as more or less certain.

But love, unquestionably, there certainly had been. I know, because when Eugenio died Antonia promptly agreed to get engaged to his brother Valentino, who was much less nice. This hasty decision was an open declaration of love for the late brother. Poor Antonia!—what a substitute she had to put up with!

With hardly a thought for his own welfare, Eugenio had rushed off to Italy to do his bit for the Fatherland. He had deposited his Austrian bonds, which he had inherited shortly before from his father, in a bank and had not given them a second thought; so that, when the enemy trenches receded, due in part to his own soldiering, he had unwittingly destroyed his own holdings. (A magnificent example of heroism and absent-mindedness.) Then, a few days before the armistice, he stumbled on a mine, which blew him to bloody fragments, and so he died.

Poor Valentino (very poor, because now he too is dead) also volunteered, but life in the trenches apparently did not appeal to him, and he found his way back to Milan, where he obtained a good job with an insurance company. God knows that I don't wish to speak ill of him, but he was certainly not the right husband for my poor little daughter. Fat, and faintly unhealthy-looking, he impressed me so unfavourably when I saw him after the war—that is, before the marriage—that I said to Augusta "Is *that* the husband for our beautiful Antonietta?"

Augusta gave a gesture of resignation, as if to say that she had not chosen him. But then, wanting to remain on friendly terms with everyone and to be left in peace, she added, "But he does promise to go on a reducing diet. Besides, he's not ugly, if you look closely at him."

I did my best to get used to him. But he was so pedantically sure of his own judgement. In his mouth the most fascinating bits of information became boring, I am not certain why—whether it was the nasal sound of his voice or the superior air he assumed in telling it. And how he knew what he did know! He knew it from every point of view, and down to its minutest details. It meant that every time he opened his mouth, he ended up giving a lesson. I later got in the habit of paying close attention to his voice, from which I first used to flee. To be spared having to put up with it for too long—one had to accept it cheerfully from the outset, studying it, noting its every nuance, since he wouldn't let one go until one had understood everything.

But I should not like to speak too harshly of him. In the first place, he is the father of little Umbertino; and secondly, he left Antonia a handsome fortune.

All I mean to say is that I did not quite understand how it was that Antonia fell in love with him. Nor did I understand why she remained so attached to him, that it never crossed her mind to betray him, even though his dieting was a failure. Well, the evolution of flesh is a great mystery. Whenever I hear that history repeats itself, I can readily believe it; it does, but there is no telling where it will. There lies the surprise. A second Napoleon could be born in my house today without its startling me in the least. And everyone would claim that history had repeated itself, whereas actually there has been nothing to prepare its way.

Suddenly, a year ago, Valentino's plump body began to shrivel, without getting any thinner; his face got more livid and he started breathing in a new way, always like a fish out of water, but noisily too, sometimes almost groaning. Dr Raulli saw the seriousness of the situation at once and sounded the alarm. Antonia crouched at the bedside of her husband and did not leave it again until he was dead.

My nephew Carlo explained the malady to us—it was premature senility: "Suddenly, in a matter of a few weeks, his organism became like yours is now, Uncle. But what you're capable of bearing at seventy or more, he couldn't bear at forty. You need less air, Uncle, less circulation. Everything in you is less alive. That's why you go on living . . . all the same."

None of this struck me as being very logical. But I didn't say anything. Instead, I withdrew into myself, into my aged organism, so as to protect it from such insults and go on living . . . all the same.

What do they know about human life? My mind, at this moment, is more active than poor Valentino's ever was. At least I don't get lost in matters of no importance, analysing them *ad nauseam* and dropping them only after everyone round me has been bored to death. That ought to be proof that my respiration must be better than his ever was. Nowadays they berate me because my mind wanders, because I can't remember names and faces. But I have always had these defects to a greater or lesser extent, and if they are the defects of an old man, then that is proof that I was able to withstand old age at birth, whereas it killed Valentino at the age of forty.

With Valentino dead, we were left to gasp at Antonia's demonstrations of mourning. At first, we all admired her. She moved us to tears; indeed, she carried on in such a way that I can say I have never wept over a death as much as I did over poor Valentino's. Even Carlo and Alfio, who had made much more light than I of the dead man's starch and circumstance, forgot their dislike of him and loved him in Antonia's grief. Who could be so petty to remember the man as he had really been? Fate had struck Antonia a fearful blow. Everyone was ready to assist and sympathise with her.

But a week later, Carlo took the lead and protested when he noticed that Antonietta's sorrow, rather than abating, was expressing itself more and more extravagantly in her speech and actions; it was draping everyone and everything in mourning, not only herself and Umbertino, who managed to make black the gayest of colours—but Augusta, Alfio, me, and my car as well; each day she found cause to weep even more copiously and to force us to torture ourselves to wring tears from our exhausted ducts. All during the first week Carlo had been very kind, so sweet indeed that afterwards Antonietta missed him, and, no longer seeing him about, bore him a grudge—which, at first, Alfio shared with her. But before long Alfio found so much sharing of grief beyond him, and he left Augusta, Antonietta, and me to weep over poor Valentino by ourselves. To make up for the two truants, Antonietta wept louder than ever. She coined new phrases to describe her incredible, her heart-rending tragedy, and with one of these she cut me to the quick. Every day when she saw me, she would exclaim: "Before killing him, Fate had to dishonour him by making him an old man!"

At this, I withdrew too, much offended. Old age a dishonour! It must be the world war that had taught people to say such things. Later, I had to explain the reason for my absence to Augusta, and she passed it on to Antonia, who, instead of waiting for me to go and weep with her, now had an excellent excuse for coming and smothering me with her mourning again. The performance served her as a very useful outlet but left me like a crumpled rag, not knowing whether I was on my head or my heels. In black from head to foot and shrouded in veils, she flung herself at my knees, crying and screaming that old age, in which I flourished, had buried Valentino in the tomb. And certainly, it occurs to me, this was another reason why my old age was not dishonourable, whereas Valentino's was a disgrace.

Once again, though, I was touched, as if Valentino had just died. I comforted her, and put my arm round her shoulders. I spent several whole days together with her. I was anxious to help her, the poor girl, so innocent and so unhappy. I experienced, as it were, a genuine reactivation of paternalism; and to purge myself of remorse at having hurt her, I anxiously explored my soul for sorrow and pity. Never had I loved poor, unfortunate Valentino as I did in these days—Valentino who, having lived half-dead, was now quite completely dead, but who, both before and after dying, had been able to kindle such an intense affection.

The scene I could never afterwards forget took place one evening after supper. It was in early September. It was still very hot, and Augusta, Antonia, and I were sitting under the pergola in front of our villa, where once we had been able to look out and see the city and the harbour, and now could only catch scattered glimmers of the distant sea from behind vast, sordid barracks. After expounding her (very original) theory about honourable and dishonourable old age again, Antonia continued to sob, her head lolling on my shoulder. Her tears were a far better weapon than her talk. Augusta was crying too, but I knew that her thoughts and ours were poles apart. She was not crying over Valentino, like us. Shortly before, I had explained to her, once again, how Antonia was mistreating us and disturbing the closing years of my life. She hadn't perceived that I had now come round to Antonia's side, and I could think of no way of letting her know. All she was weeping over was the division within herself—just as she had wept, not for the sake of Alfio's painting, but over the differences between him and me which she herself had caused. She hated quarrels, which, between human beings, and particularly between fathers and sons, were inevitable, though she had eliminated them from her vast menagerie of dogs, cats, and birds—animals to which she devoted the better part of her time.

A drunken man went by along the footpath that runs alongside the villa, leading to the mountain. I knew him very well. I had spied on him so many times. Wine sharpened the musical instinct in him, and he let himself go completely in his harmless, leisurely way. He only knew two old ballads— a very limited repertoire—which he sang with minor variations only, so you could hardly call his inspiration disorderly. Nor was his voice disorderly, merely gentle and weak and very tired. What a fine chap he was, happy with the wine he had already drunk! And modest!—singing so much without a public.

And as Antonietta wept, my thoughts turned to the drunk, who had so easily solved the problem of living. By day, work, and in the evening—not the night—music! The gentle strains grew fainter, then faded away.

"Poor man!" Antonietta sobbed.

"Who?" I asked, terrified she was still talking about Valentino.

"That poor man singing so sadly on the path," she murmured. "He must have lost someone and is consoling himself with wine."

It was too much for me to believe that everybody who got drunk did so because he had lost someone, though perhaps statistics might prove it so. But I was much obliged to her for having meant my poor lonely minstrel and not the late Valentino. I snuggled against her and, acting on an impulse of generosity, proposed that she should give up her broken home and come with Umbertino to live with us. At first she refused so vehemently that I dared not insist. But Augusta looked up, her face cleared of its despondency: she saw the dawning of agreement, and that for her was the prime aim in life. She was pained by the fact that everybody was deserting Antonia, just when her daughter wanted the world to sit at table with her and weep for ever. Some months later even Augusta rebelled, but not because she had run out of tears to share with her daughter, but because Antonia would have nothing to do with all the animals Augusta devoted her time to and wanted to get rid of them. She detested animals, because one of the things they lack completely is mourning. A dog sniffs its dead playmate's body with curiosity. For a moment it seems surprised, then it scampers off joyful that a similar fate has not befallen it.

That evening all we succeeded in doing was making Antonia weep and protest: Never would she abandon the house in which he had died! And besides, where was their room in our villa for all the furniture Valentino had so lovingly collected and which she would never part from?

But Augusta did not give up. First she convinced me that the ground floor, formerly used for receptions, no longer served any useful purpose, and that, having it done up a little, we could give it to Antonia. I had nothing against the idea, having already committed myself with the offer made under the influence of my beloved drunkard and his touching song. Augusta took measurements to see whether all of Valentino's massive, mastodontic furniture would fit into its new abode. It would, though there would be less elbow-room for the occupants.

But with spectacular obstinacy, Antonia turned a deaf ear to all proposals, and every offer became a fresh occasion for weeping and wailing, that filled the house with its sound.

Then, exactly on the nineteenth of the month, some three or four months after Valentino's death, she changed her mind. In the morning we had been told that she wanted to go to the cemetery. We went to pick her up in the car. She was surprised not to see Alfio with us. Alfio was not feeling well, I explained. Augusta added that besides not feeling well, he had had to stay at home to wait for a friend. A double reason for not coming along, which filled Antonia with such bitterness as to hamper her display of grief that day. She pottered about the new grave, strewing flowers. We were waiting for Carlo, who had promised to come if he could get away from the hospital, but we waited in vain. When all hope of seeing him had vanished, Antonia ceased to occupy herself with the flowers and, collapsing in our arms, devoted herself wholeheartedly to her sorrow.

The day was rather hazy. It was one of those misty autumn noons, perfectly clear, but as livid as chalk, the sun being hidden. I feel that on days like that things can be seen better— the cypresses, the tombs, their inscriptions and images, the encircling wall, the dark chapel. Being struck by this, I mentioned it to Alfio, who had been out painting, before writing it here.

"Pure indirect lighting," he said laconically. "Perfect!"

And I have not forgotten my little baby either, the way she threw herself about in my wife's arms merely because, after some moments, I had strolled off for a little respite. Under her veils, her lovely little face was still glowing with youth and vigour. She was doing a great deal of crying, and we had to lend her our support; all the same she was better off than we were.

Presently someone came towards us from the entrance gate. I thought it was Carlo; it was his very way of walking, holding himself erect, yet sauntering along in a nonchalant manner, his nose in the air and his spectacles gleaming.

"Carlo!" I called.

For an instant Antonia stopped crying and also looked.

"No, it's not Carlo," she said.

And in fact, staring at us somewhat curiously, the youth went on his way.

Antonia calmed down, and shortly afterwards we left the cemetery. She was silent for a long time in the car, her eyes red-rimmed, fixed on the road, which she was certainly unable to see. Then, suddenly, she turned to Augusta and asked where her servants' quarters would be, if she moved in with us. Augusta told her. Antonia turned her eyes, those beautiful eyes of hers, back to the fleeing road, and when next she looked at us she said softly, "I'd like to try it. If I'm not happy with you, or if I see I'm putting you out at all, I'll go back to my own house."

And so it was that she decided to come and live with us. And whenever I look back upon her in that chalky light, with that little face of hers that, with its dimple in the chin, still kept some traces of infancy, I think: "You dear, beautiful little sorceress, who want so much to cry but don't want to cry alone."

And so it was, too, that Umbertino came to be nearer me and assumed more and more importance in my life.

UMBERTINO

Translated by Ben Johnson

I · Umbertino

I AM A MAN WHOSE BIRTH WAS IN EVERY WAY ILL-TIMED.
When I was young, the only people held in high esteem were
the old; and I can testify that the old people of that period did
not even allow us young ones to talk about ourselves; they told
us to hold our tongues even upon matters within our com-
petence—like love, for instance. I remember being there one
day when my father and some of his contemporaries were discussing a rich Triestine who had fallen madly in love and was
being ruined in consequence. They were all men in their fifties
or older, and in deference to my father, they had let me remain
in the room with them, affectionately dubbing me "the colt".

Naturally, I respected the old as the times demanded and
eagerly looked forward to learning even about love from
them. But on one point I needed further clarification, and to
get it I intruded in the conversation: "In a situation like that,
I—"

My father promptly cut me short: "So now even the fleas
want to scratch themselves!"

Now that I am old myself I find that the only persons highly
regarded are the young. So I have gone through life without
ever once commanding respect. This must account for a certain
antipathy I feel both towards young people, who are the ones
who are respected now, and the old, who are the ones who used
to be. I am alone in the world, even my age having perpetually
been a handicap.

And in fact, I think I must be so fond of Umbertino because,
so far, he doesn't belong to any age. He is seven-and-a-half and,
as yet, has none of our vices. He neither loves nor hates. For

him, in fact, his father's death was more of an interesting experience than a distress. The evening that Valentino died, I heard him asking his nursemaid, in a tone of great wonderment and surprise: "Then you can even kick a dead man and he won't get angry?"

He had no intention, certainly, of kicking his father—of revenging himself for the long-winded lectures Valentino had given him: he was simply curious. For him, all life is nothing but a panorama from which he is so completely removed that neither good nor evil can reach him, provided he avoids colliding with it—merely snippets of information.

Certainly, I began to be fond of him while it was still only a matter of my seeing him from time to time. Once a day I used to call on my daughter and son-in-law, and there I saw my little hero growing up, blond and handsome, and with two negative recommendations: he had no desire to recite verses which he had learned by heart, and he did not want strangers to kiss him. I didn't kiss him, nor did I want to hear his poetry. Every day, however, I did take him a little box of sweets, always the same kind. I was still not so fond of him that I would try to surprise him with different presents; setting out daily to visit him, I simply stopped for a moment in the same sweetshop in our neighbourhood.

I noticed that he looked forward to my presents anxiously. And one day he surprised Antonia by showing her how he could put the little boxes together and make a house—a house for Grandpapa, who could live in it comfortably if you cut part of his body off, indeed all of it except his head. And the little man looked at my head and then back at the house, establishing the proportions between the two.

Antonia protested: "You don't want Grandpapa to die, do you? He couldn't breathe with only a head."

The child studied me.

"But don't you see he breathes *just* with his head?"

This wild fantasy of his upset me. I spent a restless night—so restless, in fact, that I translated his idea into a hair-raising dream. My entire body had been cut off and all that was left was my head, sitting on a table. I could still talk; and, apparently, I was eager to carry out Umbertino's every wish; but I was naturally short of breath and desperately panting for air, and I thought: "How long will I have to go on breathing like this before my body grows back?"

The nightmare disturbed me so much, that all the next day I couldn't shake it off. And I thought to myself: "One ought not to have to live a life in which such monstrous things can be imagined."

And to think it had been conceived in that little blond head of Umbertino's!

As to the sounds Umbertino makes, with all their grace and individuality, I should be at a loss to reproduce a single one of them; they are the sort of thing one understands but does not remember. One remembers only how one smiled at them. But there is one thing I know (this is a discovery of mine): Umbertino's face becomes peculiarly expressive when he's stuck for a word. His big, bright blue eyes open wide, so as to see better, shut to assist him to concentrate intensely; they look sideways (giving his rosy face a furtive look of criminality) as they search for words in the corner of the room, and up to heaven, trying to find them in the sky. Yes, that's it! It is the failure of words that gives rise to the expressive gestures.

I am greatly taken by everything I discover.

Little by little I found out Umbertino, whom not everyone knows how to observe, and that makes me love him. Everyone around me—I know, because I notice everything—complains that I see and hear less and less. It may be so; but what I do see and hear always leads me to interesting discoveries.

Since he moved in with us, I have sometimes found Umbertino a nuisance. Large as the house is, he found no place he liked as much as my study, and before long he was always under my feet. Eventually my books came in for use by him— to build pyramids. The mess was appalling. And then, he likes to see the gramophone in action; but unlike all other music-lovers, he finds the records too long. If he can reach it, he stops the turntable; and if he could break the records, he would do that too. The first time I stopped him, he said to me, quite simply, "Grandpapa, why don't you go away?" Any curtailing of his freedom he regards as so improper that he considers my presence near him as quite accidental and arbitrary. That child is a genuine protest against his father, though. I am convinced that heredity sometimes is nothing but a gesture of impatience, whereby an old stock is extirpated and a wholly new one evolved.

I do not like being left alone in the house with Umbertino. By himself, and if he has nothing to do, he becomes aggressive. I have no talent for telling him stories. Poor Valentino (with that imagination of his) could talk to him for hours. Sometimes I listened to the stories as well. The child would lie motionless in his father's arms, gazing up at that mouth from which, to his great delight, the fairy tales proceeded. Antonia, who also listened rapt and attentively, once told me: "He's heard the same story five times now."

But he liked it, the story about the fairy who visits all the little children to pick out the best one, only to find it's the one who always thought himself the worst. We grown-ups, on hearing a story told a second time, break in impatiently. My little grandson, however, insisted on events being repeated. As the fairy went through the woods, the trees bowed down in salutation. And the child, becoming a tree himself, saluted likewise. It might be night, or on the other hand a bright sunny day: if it was night, Umbertino would open his eyes wide to avoid obstacles, if it was day he would screw up his eyes to protect them from bright sunlight. Then he became the little boy whom everyone had thought bad and was really full of goodness, though no one ever noticed it, it took a fairy to detect it! But Valentino's drone was a prime requisite. Without it, Umbertino's nerves failed to respond. Valentino's big mouth opened and from it issued words of such consequence as instantly to materialise into things and beings.

By the time Umbertino arrived at our house, he had learnt to get along without his father. He told the stories himself. He only knew two of them, I think; I can't repeat them, having never listened when he told them. Whenever I had to endure one, watching the interesting gestures he made as he struggled with speech, he would look at me to see if I had enjoyed it and ask: "Did you like it? Want to hear it again?"

I would suggest that he should retell it while I read or wrote or played my violin. But no, I had to listen; otherwise he couldn't feel his story as real. I would then try listening to him, but would soon feel the old storm brewing within me. "How good I am! How good I am!" And to be able to get on with my own affairs, I would send the child back to Renata.

Renata is a sweet, little, dark-haired orphan girl from Friuli. She is now eighteen but has already been with us for four years. She is one of those girls who reached maturity during the war and so did not have to lengthen her short skirts, which previously only little girls wore. She was no scholar and did not make discoveries as I did; but, perhaps because she is closer to the child, she can stand his chatter better than I. And in my room, from which Umbertino never liked to be too far away, I used to hear his childish voice, as it told its stories, being interrupted from time to time by Renata's fresh, frank, irresistible outbursts of laughter.

Umbertino and I finally came to an agreement. Indoors we were to see each other only at lunch time; but every morning we were to go out together for an hour's stroll. This schedule, moreover, coincided with the prescription, to get an hour's daily exercise, which Dr Raulli had given me.

When he had to walk, Umbertino did not tell stories, he simply trotted along, with his tiny, soft hand in my own great gnarled one. I had to be careful to keep a firm grip on his hand as he was always stumbling, seeing so many things as he did—a crumbling wall some way away, or tramcars with their splendid numbers, which he knew how to read; or a train, near at hand or far away, with its puffing engine; but never any of the things that happened to be in his way or the puddles he would have gone plunging into if I didn't keep an eye on him.

What a lot of things he saw! Though always the same ones over and over again, since owing to my weak lungs, our strolls about the town (where as soon as you reach the outskirts you find yourself climbing a mountain) couldn't be very long ones.

Every night, when Umbertino goes to bed, sleep, I think, must so completely remake him that when morning comes everything is new for him—so much so that it is new for me as well. Railway tracks, for instance. Why did he spend so much time looking at railway tracks? And what enjoyment did he find in walking along them? But so long as this required no effort, just to please him I walked along the tracks too. When, however, it came to negotiating the gravel between the rails, and the sleepers were laid so far apart that it was impossible to jump from one to the next, I lost patience and dragged him away. He would go on studying them all the same, the road bed where enormous trains skidded along mysteriously. . . . But it was important to find out where the tracks began, for a beginning is always of extreme importance; and it was a great deprivation not to be able to see that other important part, the end of the tracks. I laughed, and suggested he looked at the nearest extremity of the tracks, not as the beginning, but as the end. It was an entirely new concept for the child to cope with and he faltered before it. . . . Then he saw! Yes, that *was* the end of the tracks!

One day we climbed to the top of a wall and found ourselves spectators at a little scene. Below us, angrily charging round a small courtyard, we saw a horse followed by a strapping young man trying to lead it back to the stable. The horse was rearing and kicking in the air. And from his safe look-out Umbertino squealed with delight, enjoying himself hugely. His shouts of joy delighted me, though they also struck me as symptoms of the hysteria which had been fatal to his fore-bears. On this occasion his joy could harm no one because the poor devil below, struggling with the horse, was not able to see or hear us.

The young man got an idea. Disappearing through one of the doors that opened on the courtyard, he returned carrying a bundle of hay in his hand. The horse picked up the scent, and as the man backed towards the door the animal followed after, docile and straining forward hungrily, finally vanishing after the man.

Umbertino screamed: "Don't follow him! You're stupid! You're going to get caught!" And afterwards, whenever we passed the place, he would cast a glance at it and say, "The courtyard of the stupid horse." However, we never saw the horse or man again. And Umbertino thought: "Maybe it happened again, and the horse didn't let himself get caught, and he managed to get in a few kicks, and now he is free in some faraway meadow."

I wonder why watching Umbertino and his child's play amuses me so. As I compose my life in these pages, Umbertino, whom I see in my mind's eye walking beside me with his short, uncertain steps, leads me to analyse why irrational joy is always so irrationally distributed among humankind.

It is granted abundantly to infants; and in this instance—the sole instance—it can be called rational, seeing that they understand nothing anyway. Later, during childhood, when we begin to examine the colossal machine that has been consigned us—life, railway tracks that end where they begin—we still find no relation between it and us, and we study life with objectivity and joy, interrupted by lightning flashes of terror. Adolescence is terrible, because it is then one gets the first inkling that the machine is designed to bite *us* and among all its cogs and teeth one hardly sees where to put one's feet.

Peace of mind may have been late in coming to me because, on account of my illness, my adolescence went on beyond the normal bounds, whilst all about me my contemporaries were living life without noticing it, like the miller sleeping soundly beside his mill as it grinds and roars. But peace of mind, a mixture of resignation and unquenchable curiosity, comes to all, and I walk side by side with Umbertino, very like him in many ways. We go very well together. His weak pace prevents him finding mine too slow, and I am reduced to his by my weak lungs. He is happy because the machine amuses him; and I am happy too, not because I think the machine called life can no longer harm me, death being so near at hand to rescue me—

for to tell the truth, death, for me, is still something external, only realisable by an act of reason—but because I am now so at home with the machine that it frightens me when I think people might after all be better than I have always thought them, or life a more serious affair than it has always seemed to me. (I feel faint, the blood rushes to my head at this thought!)

Poor Umbertino! Sudden moments of terror disturb his joy and curiosity. One instance of such terror, dating back some years now, is famous in the family. He was never able to go to sleep quickly in the dark, and one evening his mother tried to convince him that he had no cause to be frightened, because there are no lions in our latitude; moreover, the doors and windows in our house are all shut securely. Whereupon Umbertino declared that he was afraid of the little men who slip in through the chinks. It was a great discovery for him that the doors and windows are never so well closed as to keep out danger.

Sometimes he exaggerates existing evils too. Once they gave him a new pair of shoes, shiny little ones with buckles. To set his mind at rest, he insisted on wearing the shoes to bed. I shall never forget seeing the little fellow, sunk in slumber and warmth, with his shoes on his bare feet, stretched out across the cot. Not even sleep diminished his vigilance. Clearly, life is better than he thought it was then, seeing that most people cheerfully take off their shoes on going to bed.

So a three-year-old is a little mechanical toy everyone enjoys playing with. You press a button at one end and there is a reaction at the other. I am guilty myself of having once upset the toy's working.

Invited to Valentino's for supper, I happened to arrive in time to find Umbertino finishing his meal with an apple. I promptly took one from the fruit bowl, and, pretending to take it out of his neck, told him it was the one he had just eaten. Umbertino was surprised and alarmed; but then, since it was his, the little fellow began to eat it, and I let him, pretending I thought this only natural. Extracting a second one from his neck, I was prepared to let him eat that one too. But since his little stomach could not feel the relief which my conjuring ought to have afforded, he stopped.

It was late—Augusta and I were getting ready to leave before I was reminded of it. Antonia wanted us to see her son asleep. He was lying in a cot with a net arched over it. The light had been turned on, but there was no fear of awakening him because they knew once Umbertino decided to sleep, he slept. We saw him lying with his head off the pillow and pushed up against the netting. His cheeks were flushed and—so it seemed to me at least—he was breathing faster than usual. Antonia started to straighten him, and the child, scarcely stirring, murmured, "I eat it. . . . There! . . . And then it's whole again!"

Antonia laughed: "That's his grandfather's doing!"

My heart was a little heavy.

Yes, that's it! Umbertino is a worrier. In his brief existence he has already been threatened and even punished. But then, fear is an attribute of the flesh. It is a protective envelope already covering it when it first meets the light of day. It may lead it astray, but it is certainly a protection. Little Umbertino is afraid of lions, even though there are none there, and of carabinieri, who are not concerned with him, nor, we hope, will they ever be. When he sees them he walks along more silently. Their duty, he knows, is to keep watch, and a more rigid watch than the one he is under himself; the one on him, however relentless and tiresome, is accompanied by caresses and sweets. He is by no means sure that the day won't come when lions will appear in Trieste and the carabinieri notice this little boy who sometimes provokes his father and grandfather to anger and makes his mother cry.

His grandfather's moments of anger were always short-lived and were immediately followed by tender words of explanation, and rebukes, directed at him and myself equally—these, however, only in a soliloquy, in which I figured as concerned but not ashamed. We got on so well, walking the city street together, I being much less distracted than he, being constantly called back to reality by the threat of motor-cars or by admiration of him, with his head stuffed full of foolishness. For that one reason we had less in common (but for that alone) —the fact that I wasn't free, like him, but had to act as watch-dog. Otherwise, we would have marched together very much alike, and often in silence, for Umbertino is already in the habit of not telling everything. The last time we were out together he stood in the shadow of a tree so as to observe how he, mysteriously, stopped having a shadow. He hugged him-self close, drawing in one arm that protruded, so as to be completely in the shade. He succeeded, and afterwards walked on without a word. Perhaps he found his thoughts on the matter too childish to divulge.

II · Bigioni

WITH THE ARRIVAL OF ANTONIA AND UMBERTINO, WE OFTEN had another nuisance on our hands—a nuisance but a hope as well, I mean Signor Bigioni. Not Baglioni or Grigioni—the names of two other of our family friends years ago—but Bigioni. Every time I speak to him he has to tell me his name, because with those three names I'm never quite sure; this is an obstacle to our getting on better with each other. I don't find him particularly likeable, as he has some of Valentino's traits; whenever he has an opinion he is positive of it; he states it, he comments on it, he illustrates it with the most down-to-earth and sometimes offensive figures of speech. When he first confided in me, he found it necessary to apologise for the fact that, Valentino being dead, the best way of mourning him he could find was immediately to try to marry the widow. He recognised, he said, that it was an odd way of showing his friendship, but it was justified by Valentino's extraordinary generosity towards him—like that of a sailor who, adrift for weeks on a raft in the ocean with a friend, dies in time to furnish him with a meal. Having struck out this atrocious simile, he was quite ready to repeat it to Antonia, in just the same words. This figure of speech explained everything; and he maintained that in this world it was important to understand everything.

I was the first to realise what his hopes were. I hinted at it to Carlo, who is more in my confidence than anyone else. Assuming that confident manner of his, Carlo declared that miracles didn't repeat themselves.

"What miracles?" I asked in wonderment.

"Like Valentino's marrying Antonia."

I was offended. Did it need a miracle to marry one of the loveliest young women in Trieste? She had been the darling of the family, that beautiful child of ours, a jewel, the envy of all our friends; and even now, whenever she is mentioned, people call her "beautiful", "beautiful as Aunt Ada" (whilst Ada's daughter, who is in Buenos Aires, is as plain as my darling Augusta was). Every human being begins as a mixture of ugliness and beauty; they must be given time for full development.

And to pay him back for the offence he had given me, I told Carlo about Bigioni's intentions, though I had promised to speak of them only to Antonia. He was so surprised that he dropped his cigarette. He began to laugh. So miracles do repeat themselves! And from then on, we all, including Carlo, put up with Bigioni's company more cheerfully. We took him under our wing, we were tolerant of him, we loved him—all except Antonia and Umbertino.

Bigioni (what a capital idea for me to keep writing his name down!) behaved in a manner corresponding perfectly with the sort of person he is—one blind to everything except his own desires.

We were on our way home from the cemetery—Carlo, Alfio, Bigioni, and myself—after having buried poor Valentino. In the carriage Bigioni comported himself with great decorum. He dwelt on his long friendship with Valentino; he said he was deeply grieved by his untimely end. He even added the remark, "What shall I do now that he's gone?"

At this point, however, I am convinced he smiled. I'm positive of it. At the time, I put it down as a nervous twitch of the lips, this hardly being the moment for smiling; it was pouring with rain and we were all drenched, and Valentino had scarcely been buried. But I admit I had smiled a little myself at the thought of Valentino in the crypt, crowded round by the dead who had gone before him, saying, with that well-known gesture of his: "All right now, easy does it!" But as for me, of course, such ill-timed smiles have nothing to do with malice. Bigioni, on the other hand, after smiling, began

to stroke his long blond beard in a satisfied manner and to
run his palm over his bald head—gestures like those of beasts
of prey after a good meal; though I was unable to interpret
them until Bigioni singled me out to confide in. He wanted to
marry the widow of the deceased and so had begun by climbing
into the family carriage.

But from one point of view it was ridiculous, his insistence
on discretion when he confided in me, because before letting
me in on his intentions he had, without meaning to, told no
less a person than Umbertino. He had done it on the very first
day, while the child was still wet from the downpour at his
father's funeral.

The large house seemed extraordinarily empty. Before the
funeral it had been over-run by a horde of friends and relations, who had abandoned us at the graveyard and left us to
go home alone. Bigioni gazed about him serenely. Look at all
the space he would have! Perhaps even too much! He felt
so confident that he may even have been considering subletting
part of it as soon as it was his.

And catching sight of Umbertino, who was in tears—because Antonia, by forbidding him to play on the day of his
father's funeral, had finally succeeded in saddening him—
Bigioni pulled him over and kissed him, though the child did
all he could to avoid contact with that beard of his (though
to tell the truth, it was well combed and not at all bristly),
and he told him that he should be pleased it was raining; it
was a sign that heaven was opening to receive his father. (I
know another Triestine saying to the effect that clear weather
is a sign of the deceased's good reception in heaven. My town
is full of good-hearted people. Were it left to them, everybody
who dies would be well received in heaven.)

The child grew very serious. He discerned the vague out-
lines of a new machine to explore, that of heaven as presented
by Bigioni. And seeing the little fellow so serious, Bigioni, in
an effort to comfort him further, let the cat out of the bag:
"Well now, here you are without a father. How would you
like to have another one? Me, for instance?"

This was another remark that stuck in Umbertino's mind. Meanwhile he escaped from the bearded Bigioni. And in his mother's sight, though without her realising it, he managed to play a game on the very day of his father's funeral. He played with that conception of Heaven: the gates stood shut for days on end, with the dead loitering outside because it was not raining; and then, at the first drops, they opened, and all flocked in.

But he was not entirely convinced, and asked his mother: "What if it doesn't rain when somebody dies, does that mean he can never get in and has to wait for ever at the entrance?"

Shaking herself from the torpor her despair had plunged her into, Antonia told him to explain himself. He did, and so she learned who had been disturbing the poor child's ideas. She then kindly asked Bigioni not to tell the child any more such tales—very kindly, because Bigioni had not yet occurred to her as an aspirant to Valentino's inheritance, but rather as his closest friend, so that he was treated better than everybody else, better even than her father, her mother, brother, and cousin.

Umbertino expunged the story of Heaven and the rain. Little children have a great faculty for expunging things. Ah, so that's it! The gates of heaven don't have anything to do with rain. Signor Bigioni was mistaken, and there was no need to speak of it further.

But there remained another toy, the idea of having a second father. And while being put to bed, he consulted his nurse-maid: "How many fathers can a person have?"

The old nursemaid told him that, unless the person were born again, he could have only one. The idea of being born a second time was another interesting thought for him to play with. Umbertino slept on it but did not forget it. The morning after, Antonia had a great job driving such bright ideas out of his little head. And in doing so, she naturally found out about Bigioni's rash remark.

And she never forgave him. Bigioni was no longer regarded as a friend of Valentino's but as his enemy, which meant he was the enemy of Antonia, his widow, too. She told me about it next morning, interrupting a long fit of weeping in my arms to cry: "And this awful tragedy of mine—the greatest any woman has ever known—is magnified by every conceivable offence!" Whereupon she told me what Umbertino, with fair accuracy, had reported to her.

What she said was full of exaggerations. Every conceivable offence? Poor Bigioni had committed only one—that of proposing marriage so soon. And let us pass over her other exaggerations, for instance the one about her misfortune being the greatest any woman had ever known. One should allow all sorrowers the satisfaction—indeed the joy—of exalting their sorrow. The same sort of thing in Job, when I read it, sounded to me like a cry of triumph.

I now expected poor Bigioni to be sent flying from the house in a shower of kicks. But nothing of the sort happened. He was an enemy, but he had also been a friend of poor Valentino's, so respect was owed to him. Nothing in the house that had any association with her husband was meddled with; and that included Bigioni, who smoked with me and helped Alfio with his painting, Carlo with his medicine, and Augusta in attending to her menagerie. He was also permitted to speak to Antonia about Valentino, but about nothing else; neither was he allowed to spend too much time with Umbertino. For my part, it was only unwillingly that I put up with his company during our excursions. However much he tried, he fitted in badly with us two, the old dreamer and the young.

One day he was out with us when we arrived above a tunnel in the mountain, where Umbertino had once seen a train disappear. Not long before, we had passed very close to the opening and Umbertino had scarcely glanced at it. Now, however, being above it, he had clambered up on to a low wall and was staring fixedly at the gaping mouth, viewing it now for the first time from that vantage-point. Bigioni didn't know what was in his mind, and yawned. He had seen the tunnel himself a short while ago, from near at hand, and it hadn't interested him. What point was there in the boy's staying in so uncomfortable, and indeed dangerous, a position, where I had to watch him with such anxiety, merely to look at the same thing from a distance? But Umbertino was in luck. A locomotive with its tender came screaming out of the hole. Umbertino burst into squeals of delight; and Bigioni, alarmed, grabbed his jacket too.

"Now he's shying," he said. (Poor Bigioni! Before taking on Antonia, he had spent most of his time with horses.)

Anyway, he was not thrown out of the house. Antonia said, tearfully: "I can't maltreat a friend of Valentino, however much of a traitor he is." She put up with him. And the curious thing is how, as the day of poor Valentino's death gradually receded, her behaviour towards the friend became harder and harder. Before long she would scarcely reply when he said "Good morning." Sometimes she pretended not to be aware of his presence. It was as if she were experimenting how far she could go without actually throwing him out. I don't want to speak evil of my own daughter, but if these notes of mine are to have any value, I must be sincere, and in my opinion Antonietta found Bigioni's presence an excuse for prolonging and exaggerating her mourning over her husband's death. It tended to become more violent when he was there to upset her.

What's more, I must admit that all of us followed her example; I mean we all tried to find how far we could go without actually kicking him out. And first and foremost myself. It was a few days after Valentino's demise that he came to confide in me and ask my advice. I listened to him, curious and interested and not once letting him know that I had heard it all from Antonia, who had herself got it from Umbertino. Antonia had told me to comport myself in this manner because she felt that once he declared himself she would be compelled to show him the door.

I did not dislike listening to this story of a man who wanted to marry a particular woman, that one, and none other. Antonia had rid me of the notion that Bigioni might be after her money. No, he was rich—far richer than Valentino had been, and having had various business dealings with him he knew all about his circumstances. In an embarrassed way, Bigioni told me he had never been in love in his life. I at once pretended to believe him, as it was a thing I sometimes said about myself and I always regarded people who believed me as particularly courteous. But a little later, having got to know him better, I came actually to believe him. He was utterly unaware that there were other women in the world beside Antonia. It was enough simply to walk in the streets with him to realise this. He simply didn't see all the bare legs, sheathed in flattering silk stockings, that were on parade.

He told me that he and Valentino, who had been slightly younger than himself, had been close friends since boyhood. They had thrown in their lot together with the selfish aim of getting rich, with the effect, apparently, that such expensive and compromising things as women were strictly ruled out for them—not consciously ruled out, they had merely never given them a thought. They laughed at any man who embarked upon love, recklessly risking his own future. How could one do such a thing? The two of them lived like bears, refusing to have anything to do with society. Clearly, it needed his brother's premature death to make Valentino take a wife, and Valentino's own, for Bigioni to embark on the same adventure. And with great ingenuousness he explained to me the effect Valentino's marriage had had upon him. As things stood, the law—the code that had governed their lives —had been violated. He felt himself liberated, like a man who makes a pact with another not to smoke and the other breaks it. But how was he to make use of his liberty? Continuing to shuttle between his office, his home, and Valentino's house, Bigioni could not bring himself to search the great world for a wife, and, though determined to marry, he bided his time. Naturally, at Antonia's he did not find any women friends of hers. But in the course of biding his time, he fell in love with Antonia herself.

He swore it had never crossed his mind that Valentino might die, nor had he ever hoped he would. As far as Valentino's death was concerned, he was perfectly innocent; however, when Valentino had died, he found he was fonder of his friend now than when he was alive. Up to now he had always lived in the reflection of Valentino's happiness. And now, he said, he wanted to marry Antonia herself, since she had proved the ideal wife for a modest, hard-working, man. As for me, I could see that he was not only in love but worked up to a pitch of mad desire by the obstacles facing him. Something of the sort, I remember, had also happened to me. Of course, nowadays, after so much experience, I find such madness beyond comprehension. Better to have women of all sorts of different types—big and small, blonde and brunette. I am speaking, of course, for those whom this applies to—the young, the strong, the handsome, the ones who can hope to be loved.

But, owing to Bigioni, I gave a good deal of thought to that one woman who might satisfy the desires of a man; a woman of such-and-such measurements, equipped with a particular smile and sound of voice, and a distinctive way of dressing that hangs about her even when naked. And, plainly, if I could understand him, it must mean I'm not as old as all that.

So that first interview of mine with Bigioni was fairly pleasant. He studied me as though his very life depended on a single word from me. And I in turn studied him, understanding everything about him, detecting in his manner a shade of humiliation at having to rely so heavily on someone else's whims and wishes, a humiliation he submitted to with resignation and with no thoughts of rebellion, as though to some sorrowful fate. At the same time, and with some anxiety, I was studying myself. Was it really evidence of youth, my feeling I understood him, or of hideous old age—of deafness, blindness—not understanding a thing? I *thought* I understood everything. But of course it was rather more difficult for me because we were not able to think of the same woman; I could hardly put myself in his boots, considering that his chosen woman was my daughter; I had to find another model for my investigations. And I thought of one—a tall and comely woman (as Aretino puts it, and he should know)—whom I occasionally meet and on whose behalf I even put on my glasses to look at her after she has gone by: a woman all harmony, all vigour, full of richness of form without excess, her feet not small but elegantly shod and her ankles neat in proportion. In short, a woman fit to be the one and only for a long time.

I could understand everything, and so Bigioni's confidences gave me pleasure. But I had to blunt his impatience, explaining to him that in a family like ours we observed mourning for a long time. After that, it would be for Antonietta to decide. And as for me I shook his hand cheerfully and friendlily, promising to do all I could.

But when he began seeking me out every time he thought Antonietta had treated him coldly, I found his confidential chats growing much too frequent. I put up with them, however, for a time, believing he really meant to quit the household, and having my own good reasons for wanting to stop him. If I had just turned my gramophone on, I would stop it and make the best of it. To tell the truth, I would go on, following the musical idea I had had to interrupt, and just let him talk. I am quite capable of listening to a person without hearing a single word spoken. It worked extremely well. Moreover I knew what he was wanting to tell me. And by way of answer I gave him what he was expecting, a hearty handshake and a word of sympathy. But then his visits to my study became altogether too frequent. Every act of indifference on the part of Antonia threw him into my arms. In he would come, expecting me to turn off the gramophone or to stop reading.

One day he showed up just when I had succeeded, with great difficulty, in deterring Umbertino from finding out what made the gramophone make its noise and in getting him out of the room. My patience being worn, I suggested to Bigioni that he should go on talking without turning the music off. I was playing the Ninth Symphony, a piece I treat myself to once a week; and interrupting such music was not to be thought of. I asked him to speak softly and promised I would listen to everything he said. He sat without saying a word, waiting for the end of the record, and when I got up to put the next one on he began to talk. He couldn't stand it any longer. Antonia left the house now as soon as he arrived. Why? Seeing that all he asked for the moment was to shed tears with her over her dead husband?

In the short time it took me to change the record, I told him that, by taking Umbertino into his confidence, he had shown a grave lack of prudence; and when the music began again I fell silent. I intended to listen to him, but certainly not to talk, through the *Ninth*. And very soon he left. He was a worthy friend of Valentino's in so far as music was concerned. Except that Valentino was tone-deaf and could listen to music for hours without a sign of impatience: he puffed his cigar, keeping time to the music with puffs of smoke. Bigioni, on the other hand, was a dog with delicate ears: he soon got nervous and sheered off. I patted my gramophone gratefully.

Bigioni, however, did not leave for good, even though similar experiments were performed on him by everyone else. Augusta continued to treat him kindly, but she also took advantage of him. She sent him out walking with her little bitch Musetta, and once, when the pup had the mange, made him rub her down with ointment. This was a privilege in Augusta's eyes. And not even this privilege succeeded in driving Bigioni away. Musetta regarded him as one of the family, and he was good to her.

Alfio's nature being what it is, he did not indulge in such experiments; rather, he took to behaving in a manner that was enough to drive everything out of the house, wall hangings and all, but not the flesh and blood Bernardo Bigioni. One day, in a sudden fit of sorrow in her suitor's presence, Antonietta mentioned Alfio, the way he was making everyone so unhappy with his whims and incomprehensible paintings. At last, here was an opportunity to prove his usefulness to the family and Bigioni undertook Alfio's conversion with the determination he put into all enterprises designed to bring him closer to Antonietta. What he said to Alfio, I don't know; but shortly after their discussion I saw him standing in the passage outside Alfio's studio. He was mopping his brow. His head—bald on the dome but thick with hair at the base, right down to his neck—sweated easily.

Alfio had no intention of changing his painting-style, but Bigioni made haste to change his own taste. He decided he must at all costs buy one of Alfio's paintings. He became increasingly convinced of the beauty of Alfio's work. But Alfio obstinately refused. He wanted to be sure that whoever bought one of his pictures (which I called "mud-bath painting") was able to appreciate it. One day Bigioni came to me, no longer asking me to persuade Antonietta to love him but simply to get Alfio to like him, and to ask him to sell him one of his pictures. Bigioni could no longer be said to be harping eternally on the same string, and this time I was not bored listening to him. Quite the contrary. But his request sent the blood to my cheeks as I suddenly realised I wielded no influence over my household. I could not get Antonietta to love him—I could resign myself to this, as it was not within my province—but I could not even talk Alfio into being nicer to him. There was simply nothing I could do, and so, feeling myself under a certain responsibility, and wanting to appease poor Bigioni, I proposed something that, with incredible naïveté, I thought might compensate for Alfio's refusal: I offered to sell him one of Alfio's pictures myself—the one I had hidden in a drawer—at the same price as he had sold it to me. But Bigioni didn't even want to see the painting, and rushed out as though I had put on the Ninth Symphony, looking at me like a man ending a discussion for fear of being cheated. This time it was he who struck me as rude, and I stared after him with resentment. Then I reflected: "Bigioni wanted to buy Alfio, not his painting." If he had bought the painting from me he would have been risking Alfio's wrath all the more.

But Bigioni would have left our house permanently, I suspect, as it was becoming a perfect torture-house for him, if it hadn't been for the presence of Valentino's sister Marta. After her brother's death, she, who was a few years older than Antonia, came for two hours every afternoon to keep her company. When she first appeared I didn't know how I would ever learn to like her. To begin with, I was not at all attracted to her, fat and dumpy as she was, with heavy legs for which the decently long skirts of my own day would have been so admirably suited. She had vivid, beautiful eyes, sometimes mischievously veiled when she smiled, but they were not the sort of eyes that went with her body and so they only made it uglier by contrast. Later, getting to know how good and sweet she was, I came to like her myself. Augusta, too, had an affection for her by then, largely as a matter of gratitude. Her ever-weeping daughter was a nuisance, and when Marta appeared Augusta enjoyed liberty for a full two hours. I have no personal experience of it, but Augusta assures me that in Marta's company Antonia cried much less. I can understand why. They agreed to shed a certain quantity of tears, and they accomplished this more quickly together.

What I liked especially about Marta was her behaviour to Bigioni. I was expecting that, as Valentino's sister, she would help to throw him out of the house. Instead, she was firm to him, but courteous. She confided to Augusta that she frankly believed a young woman like Antonietta would eventually re-marry. And, furthermore, that it was better she should marry Bigioni, who was a proven friend of Valentino, than anyone else. But Bigioni was certainly wrong in so soon wanting something he could lay no claim to. Her task, and the task of everybody, was to hold him in and preserve him for more propitious times.

I was enchanted by her. How much more practical she was than poor Antonietta, who understood nothing of the ways of the world. This was just the method. She was naturally grieved by her brother's death, but with those beautiful, limpid, too clear-sighted eyes of hers she was also shrewd and discreet. Indeed one has to get used to such eyes, for eyes can never be too clear. Marta's saw clearly even through tears.

From then on she was our favourite companion. When Antonietta's tantrums occurred in the morning, before Marta arrived, we were less irritated, knowing that solace would soon be at the doorstep. And so it was unfailingly. Notified of her arrival, with a deep feeling of relief Augusta and I went to meet her, ceremoniously accompanying her to Antonia's bedroom. She led the way, listening to us and cutting short our complaints to remind us of the gravity of the loss Antonietta had suffered. She was very scrupulous in meting out to everyone his or her due. And every day we had to have recourse to her, to enlist her help in calming Antonietta, who was furious with us when, in the midst of mourning, we had had a dinnerparty for some old friends, or to submit to her reproofs, because we had wanted Antonia, little by little, to shed some of her many veils, which would be so stifling now summer was approaching. One day it would be we who were in the right, on another the balance would tip in Antonietta's favour. But we were all willingly bowed to her judgement.

I often used to think of that ugly girl, who proved to me that our instincts can never be suppressed; at most they are perverted to uses for which they were not intended. Fundamentally, although deeply attached to her brother's memory— an attachment she demonstrated with great assiduousness, weeping over his demise with Antonietta every day—she could not help outraging it by supporting Bigioni's love. This is elementary: when people are deprived of the chance of making love on their own behalf, they are compelled, by an imperious instinct, to make it on behalf of others.

Our differences with Antonietta rarely broke out again in the afternoon. It was as if Marta's beneficent influence lasted right through to the next morning. Except that it entailed being careful of what one said; which, in my old age, I find difficult. *Gaffes* positively hound me in my declining years.

We were sitting on the verandah at that moment after supper when I normally heard the strains of my drunkard's song. We had chatted a little and, compared with preceding evenings, I might even say cheerfully, even if my cheerfulness was largely expended in bitter complaints against my nephew Carlo who, that evening, struck me as full of shortcomings, cold-hearted and trivial-minded. Antonietta had sided with me and that had helped to make me more eloquent and expansive. It was a great joy, having my daughter on my side. I am always so alone! I felt as if I were leaning on her arm as we were walking, or supporting her slight body on mine.

My *faux pas* came of having strolled over to the edge of the garden and to the footpath to see whether—as an additional pleasure—my drunkard had appeared. But that evening he did not turn up. I laughed, thinking perhaps he had drunk more than his usual measure and was singing his melodious song asprawl on some park bench. Though no singer, he would certainly find it impossible to sleep without music.

It was late and I felt like turning in too. But first I wanted to thank Antonietta for having made the evening so pleasant. Kissing her on the forehead, I said softly: "Thank you, my daughter. We've spent a very lovely evening together."

Her face suddenly clouded. She was silent for a moment, and then, as though having first examined her heart, she slowly said: "Yes . . . it was just as if Valentino were not dead. . . ."

She faltered for a second, and then, bursting into sobs, fled towards her room. Augusta hurried after her. Catching sight of her mother, Antonietta entered and locked the door behind her. Augusta stood in the passage and in a low voice begged her to open the door. Antonietta refused to answer; whereupon, indignant, I turned round and set off for bed. Not only was I indignant, I was also highly offended. Confound it! At the age of seventy it's hard not to resent acts of disrespect.

And my annoyance lasted for quite a while. I went to bed, but sleep did not come. Late that night, however, something else did: the suspicion that I was the one at fault. Why had I had to point out to her she had been enjoying my comments on Carlo's character? She always felt remorse when she abandoned her grief or stopped thinking of her dead husband even for an hour, and I knew it, and yet I had felt I had to tell her,

at once, when she had been doing so. And I recognised the possibility that a descendant of mine might be prone to total vows
of self-dedication. I could see myself as Antonietta, more per-
verse and even less loveable. It was a minor nightmare. And
was I also to blame for Alfio's painting? Now that, with the
gramophone, I had so much improved my music I remembered
that when I played the violin it had all been wrong notes and
botched rhythms, not too much unlike Alfio's painting. I
rolled about in bed, sick with remorse.

When Augusta came to join me in bed, I tried to compose
myself, to rebel against this interpretation of my conduct, this
view of myself as—even if innocently—the source of all the
nonsense that was poisoning my home. I asked Augusta:
"What did she say?"—pretending just to have woken up, as
a proof of my total innocence, the kind that is so akin to
sleep.

But when she told me what Antonietta had said to her—
how, on hearing me acclaiming the pleasure of the evening,
she had felt as if she had received a rebuke from Valentino's
own lips—I fell back on the pillow defeated. I defended myself.
All I had wanted to say was that that hour or two had been so
pleasant I had suddenly felt myself better disposed to sleep.
It wasn't in the least a question of joy making a mockery of
mourning.

Augusta pulled the easy chair, where her little bitch lay
tucked up asleep, closer to the bedside. Then she sighed, saying as she got into bed: "Well, you know the way she is
now."

I felt she meant I was to blame for making her as she was.
I said nothing. That evening I could protest no more. And I
pictured how much of my life had been spent in remorse and
regret, when, to tell the truth, I could not see I had committed
any crimes. Perhaps I had, but I couldn't remember them, just
as Antonietta couldn't really remember any. She had had all
the worst side of heredity. So many children inherit from their
father his ugly, long nose, while his fine physique or expressive
eyes go to their brothers and sisters. Antonietta inherited my

remorses, which were all the more unbearable for her, being completely irrational.

Presently Augusta's breathing, which has become noisier with the passage of years, gave notice she was already asleep. There in the dark, like an ill-bred brat, I stuck out my tongue at her. At the moment such innocence as hers struck me as excessive. Absolutely alone, I lay wallowing in remorse. It was fair enough, my punishment for talking out of turn. But it was tragic, it was intolerable, seeing my worst shortcomings being reborn in my children.

III · Carlo

CARLO IS SUCH AN ENTERTAINING CHARACTER, IT'S A PLEASURE
merely to talk about him. On the surface he's another child
owing nothing to his father. Does he have his self-assurance,
perhaps, the self-assurance of Guido when he played the
violin? (I'm looking for the most far-fetched analogy.) But
Carlo doesn't play any instrument, and displays his self-
assurance in the art of living and enjoying himself—living
intelligently, not committing ruinous mistakes, and enjoying
life to the fullest. He sometimes looks run-down, but apart
from his health (which he neglects, being a medical student—
which leads one to wonder about the value of his studies), he
jeopardises nothing else. He receives a monthly allowance from
home, which, though not particularly large, is quite sufficient
for him. Since he receives the money in a foreign currency, he
is opposed to the revaluation of the lira, which would work
to his disadvantage; but apart from that, politics have no
interest for him. It could be that he is disaffected from our
country by possessing an adopted one, but in fact I don't think
he bothers much about that either.

Now that he speaks Italian perfectly, I get the feeling his
talk is more alive than the rest of his contemporaries'. On
most of our tongues speech has withered from long usage.
Which of us makes the effort to improvise? He, however,
blithely translates expressions out of his Argentine Spanish,
and on his tongue everything somehow becomes fresh again.
He studies everything necessary to him. There are even certain
passages from Greek and Latin he has learned by heart, and
which he recites with passionate hatred, remembering the

drudgery of being made to memorise them. I have his own word for it that he became so thin from squeezing his way up from class to class through the key-hole.

He is a determined and devoted lover of women. Indeed, though he enjoys any game whatever (especially cards), he asserts loudly that there is only one real pleasure on earth. In fact, he can never stop making continual allusions to that pleasure, allusions which would be offensive if they didn't happen to be witty. Occasionally he makes jokes to Augusta, who never even remotely understands his *double-entendres*. We two, the sly ones, laugh a lot on these occasions, but never so much as she when she eventually fathoms the joke. When she does finally see it she nearly falls off her chair with laughing. A cheerfulness spreads over every gathering when he is part of it—that is, if the obstacles are not too formidable, like, as is the case in our house, an Alfio in a huff over his painting or an Antonietta in deep mourning.

But worries are never allowed to disturb his cheerfulness. For instance, he told us he had been hounded for several days by bad luck at cards: "The bad luck is not serious," he said with the air of a man making an extraordinary discovery, "if your hands are bad. In poker the heavy losses come when your hands are good. This week, unfortunately, mine have been good."

But as he was a better player than his opponents, he rarely lost. And he could play anything. For a few years now, I have known there exists a very difficult game called bridge. I learned of its existence at the same time as I heard that the best player of this game, which has just arrived from England, was Carlo. "Son of a bitch," I thought, forgetting that he was Guido's son, "he can play any game. And he is better than me even at the only one I still play, a not too complicated brand of solitaire." I gave up all other games long ago. Whenever in recent years I have sat down at a card table I've felt doomed, a feeling so distressing that I had to leave the table. It's curious, I feel so young and yet am so different from myself as a young man. Can this be the true, the grand old age?

With a glance, Carlo would point out a mistake I had made. Then he would go back to his newspaper, intervening in my game again later with another timely suggestion, a most helpful one, such as I, who had been studying the cards with full attention, still found very necessary. However—though I did not tell him this—his interference annoyed and disturbed me: I like solitaire because it is solitary. Then I resigned myself: it is well known that the onlooker understands the game better than the player, who is distracted by the very effort he is making.

I was very grateful for his company. I was still under Dr Raulli's care, but at that period my daily purgative was prescribed by Carlo, as well, in due course, as the expectorant (which, to tell the truth, at first struck me as miraculous, though it does so less now). Finally, and also on his advice, I dieted more and more stringently. My weight went down, and I honestly feel better now than I did years ago. If I continue like this there's no telling what frisks I'll be capable of at eighty! One simply has to give a diet time to act, as it is slow to take effect.

But for these reasons I am very attached to him. Whenever I feel low, instead of soothing me with medical nothings, he feels my pulse and makes fun of me. Derisive laughter on his pale and handsome white face has the effect of affection. There is no reason to be angry, anyway, because his face always has a faint look of derision in the upper lip, which is carefully shaved and a little pendulous, a slight puffiness noticeable at once in his precise, clean-cut features.

There is another thing too that attracts me to Carlo. He is the first person in all my life—which is to say in an entire seventy years—with whom I have been able to be sincere. It is wonderfully relaxing, sincerity, after so much, so much struggling. God only knows what made me so sincere with him. Perhaps, partly, because one daren't deceive one's doctor. But sincere though I was with Carlo, I was not wholly sincere. Not that he was indiscreet; but a hint from me was enough for him to grasp everything. I never mentioned Carla to him, nor any of the other women, and indeed he never even suspected the existence of my back-street escapades. He always enjoyed himself with me enormously, as did I with him. He was intensely vain of his own conquests, and vanity of this kind is so engaging I could not help enjoying it myself. For which reason I was a little less than sincere, in that I exaggerated a bit. Not greatly, however, and not often. Only in the number of women. What I often did was to exaggerate their charms. But I never claimed that any of them were princesses of the blood royal. I called one of them a duchess, but only to avoid saying she was the wife of a *commendatore*. I might have called her the wife of a *cavaliere* without indiscretion; but after all, I liked to appear important before Carlo. Besides, it felt so pleasant being sincere that it struck me that by exaggerating I was being even more sincere. In this way, perhaps, I was finding out what I would have done if others had let me. My confessions became sincerer than ever. And Carlo continued to be most discreet.

He had dinner with us every Sunday. For me, it was the best dinner of the week. He was so impervious to the fatuity of others, that he didn't notice bad temper until it was positively shouted aloud, and so he was able to laugh a good deal even with Antonietta in mourning beside him. He didn't offend against her mourning, because he simply didn't notice it. And as far as I could, I followed his example. Of course, there was never a moment when I could forget Antonietta's mourning and Alfio's grumpiness as he could. It was easier when Cima was there. The three of us were better able to contend with the long faces of those two and the embarrassed unhappiness of poor Augusta, my wife, who was capable of grousing herself, later, in a tête-à-tête with me, but was totally incapable of standing up to her daughter.

One evening there was talk about the fidelity of husbands. Naturally Valentino's was the first to be mentioned; though I hardly know why, because by that time his fidelity was evidently permanent. Augusta then had the poor taste to bring up mine; and it was discussed at sufficient length for Antonietta to remember that her faithful spouse was dead and to bemoan the loss of such a fidelity, while Augusta was lucky enough to have her husband—such a docile, good, and true one—still alive.

Carlo suddenly burst into laughter, and I suffered a terrible moment. He could hardly speak for laughing; so my embarrassment went on long enough for me to begin preparing my defence. I would defend the happiness of my marriage tooth and nail, as I had done through the years. I saw a way. I would say that I had lied to Carlo for the sake of the laughs we might have together. It was he who had been deceived, deceived by me, and no one else. That would be enough for Augusta. But what about Alfio and Antonietta, who were younger and more evil-minded?

When he was able to speak, Carlo asked me: "How many years has it been since you were faithful?"

I stammered: "I don't understand."

I didn't insist on my innocence, as I realised Carlo couldn't be meaning to bring up my recent transgressions, which may not have existed, and which, in any case, he certainly knew nothing about. But if he had asked how many years I had remained faithful, then I had an answer ready: "I've always been! You're the only one I've ever laughed at and deceived, you scoundrel!"

"Because," Carlo explained, "Uncle Zeno's present state can no longer be termed fidelity. I was just wondering how long ago he had stopped being faithful."

He was touching on a rather delicate point, but a less delicate one than he had at first seemed to threaten. I buried my nose in my plate, hiding my face and the confusion it might have shown.

Then I laughed. "It will happen to you too, to become faithful through sheer necessity."

But Carlo—and here he showed his tact—replied: "In my case it will be called something else, because it won't have been preceded by self-imposed fidelity."

I breathed freely, but I had spent a *mauvais quart d'heure*, and I decided that, however much I might regret it, when Carlo went back to Buenos Aires I would give up sincerity for good. Why expose myself now, for the mere love of gossiping, when I was safe from all other dangers?

Rumours had already begun to get round about an affair Carlo was having with some married woman. She must have been what was keeping him in Trieste, because I'm sure that even Buenos Aires suffers no shortage of people needing medicine. His mother had written asking him to return, but he had turned a deaf ear to her. Still, he was considerate of his mother, who lived only for him, he being her sole remaining child after the death of Carlo's twin brother, and he sent her a short postcard every day. But he hated being with her. She tormented him, apparently, with an overdose of affection and always treated him like a child in need of kisses and advice. I chuckled at the thought of those cards of his which must have arrived in Buenos Aires in vast accumulations. Resignedly, Carlo explained to me that, well, that's the way she was. She arranged the cards chronologically and verified that there was one for each day and would even complain if the days didn't match the dates.

"I know very well," he added with a sigh, "that I'll have to go back sooner or later." And then, "Of course, there are women in Buenos Aires too."

Ada's tendencies towards exaggeration interested me; or to be more precise, they rather relieved me. Her tendencies, alas, had all too clearly nothing to do with me, so the Malfentis must be partly to blame for the exaggerations in my family.

And one fine day, I wanted to prove it to Augusta. I learned for the first time what she thought of me. Smiling softly and affectionately, she confessed. I reminded her of Alfio. Both physically and morally. Women are never good at putting things precisely. She could not offer any proof to support her feelings. But she saw him, heard him, and above all loved him, in the same terms as she did me. And not only that, but Antonietta also was like me—which she couldn't prove, either.

"But there's something similar about the two of you, something I don't like, and don't like for the same reasons. But in you it gives me a feeling of pity, of not liking it for *your* sake, do you understand? Whereas in her it makes me a little cross."

The car was approaching Miramare. The sun had set a few minutes ago and it was bliss to rest one's eyes on the vast expanse of water, with its soft shimmer of tranquil tints which seemed of no kin to the dazzling colours they had replaced. I gave in to all this reposefulness, trying to forget the gentle woman beside me who had read my character better than myself (and, I hope, better than she herself realised).

For a moment I had a vision of human characteristics being handed down from one to another, completely altered in content but still so patently alike in their form that even Augusta, in a flash of intuition based on no reasoning, was able to recognise them. But then I inwardly rebelled: what good was the law of heredity if anything could give rise to anything? Better not to know anything about it if one had to accept that Carlo could be descended from that ass Guido and those little pests Antonietta and Alfio from me.

But by that time Carlo already had a reputation in town as a promising young doctor. He knew how to deal with everybody, sparing the dignity of those who mattered to him, sparing it not at all if it didn't matter, but always sparing his own. Raulli thought highly of him too, but, I think, was a bit afraid of him. It seems that shortly after his admission to internship Carlo, in the presence of all the other doctors, hazarded a risky diagnosis. Raulli, in front of the other doctors, accused him of ignorance. And Carlo defended himself with a remark that first spread among the staff, and then, once it had leaked out, created as much fame for him as if he had saved a dying man. Even now, whenever Dr Speier's name is mentioned, people laugh. "Ah yes," they say, "the 'ignorance and error' man!"

That was Carlo. He had told Raulli that young doctors were certainly ignorant, but—as was proved by the history of medicine—old doctors were invariably in error. Raulli was floored, and muttered, knowing himself in the wrong: "That might have been true half a century ago, young fellow, but not today."

And now just let anybody find a resemblance to Guido in Carlo—Guido who threw his weight about when he could be the aggressor, but became speechless at the first touch of an opponent's fist.

Certainly, all the business-like instincts of this brilliant young doctor—and it was the quality which most attracted me—might well have descended from his grandfather, Giovanni Malfenti. Except that the business instinct, I know, developed late in my father-in-law, it kept pace with the growth of his paunch. And so, how could the subtle Carlo have inherited the qualities of that coarse, fat ignoramus—qualities I had come to think of as part and parcel of his obesity and his sedate, middle-aged complacency.

Carlo was lively, with a touch of nervousness, which added to his vivacity. You felt in him, if he was sitting beside you, a real, inexhaustible companion. He was never still, often beating a rapid tattoo on the floor with his heel: "The heel refrain,"[1] he would say, smiling as though nothing could be done about it.

He smokes a good deal, but with pleasure, and always very choice cigarettes. Alfio smokes too, but furiously, and stinking Tuscan cheroots. Not even in his smoking has he inherited anything from me.

---

[1] Literally, "trill of the heel".

IV · Renata and Fortunato

MY GREAT AFFECTION FOR CARLO IS PARTLY EXPLAINED BY the solitude my children had left me in. This is proved by the fact that Augusta, who is more in need of affection than I am, first sought a Carlo for herself among her animals, and finding them inadequate, joined company with Renata, who is now her inseparable companion.

Renata entered Antonietta's service four years ago, replacing Umbertino's old nursemaid, who went home to her village. She moved in with us at the same time as Antonietta, and passed into Augusta's service when Umbertino, having started school, no longer needed her. Renata, however, continued to keep him company in the evening, because he still couldn't go to sleep alone, the room being filled with hordes of wild animals; and after supper Antonietta would sit with us.

Renata thus had a very leisurely but rather complicated life. She doesn't have much to do (now she only has to clean the dining-room, drawing-room and my study) but it keeps her busy all day long. She prepares the daily breadcrumbs for the sparrows on the terrace, she looks after two cages of canaries, and is also at the beck and call of Musetta. She obviously enjoys all this enormously, because she is always in a good humour. What a pleasure it is to be waited upon by smiling people. One can enjoy all the conveniences of it, with no pangs of remorse. To reach my study, I have to pass the kitchen, and without fail I invariably hear the slightly throaty sound of Renata's rich, sincere laughter resounding there.

Just as I was able to share Augusta's love for animals, so I found it easy to share in her love for Renata. Naturally, being so old, I am moved by merely paternal love. But I love seeing her, so young and trim, her tiny body mounted on longish legs, moving about so lightly and nimbly. Her head, though not perfectly shaped, is delicious too, with its curly brown hair, shining eyes, and superb teeth.

Once a year she returns to spend a fortnight in Friuli with her mother. But she always comes back a little thinner. Augusta wanted to see how she was treated there, and so we drove over to her village, which is near Gorizia. She had been told we were coming, and she was waiting for us in the tidy and clean little high street. Blushing, she said she had come to meet us because her house was in a little lane inaccessible to cars.

Augusta pressed her: "But I'd like to meet your mother."

"There she is," Renata said, turning beet-red and with a slight shade over her usual smile.

At a sign from Renata, a little old lady, who was sitting by herself under a horse-chestnut tree, got up and came over. She was very old-fashioned, with her long skirts and a kerchief knotted elegantly over her head; she was obviously dressed in her Sunday best. But everything about her, including her grey-haired and toothless self, was dim and faded. She kissed Augusta's hand. She spoke almost pure Friulian, so neither Augusta nor I could make head or tail of the confusing sounds which issued first from the right and then from the left of her decrepit mouth.

The intervention of Fortunato, our chauffeur, made things a little easier. Coming from those parts himself, he was able to say things to the old lady, in Friulian, that split her sides with laughter. She doubled up with laughing. It was overdone, perhaps to conceal some still-lingering embarrassment. Once Augusta had given her the presents we had brought, Renata sent her back home, where her brother, who would soon be back from work, would be expecting his meal. The old woman protested: his meal had been ready since morning. But she had already begun to obey. "So I should think," laughed

Fortunato. "Polenta can always wait! It's the most patient food in the world."

At all events, as it was clear that Renata did not want us to visit her home, we had to resign ourselves, and leave without seeing it.

I asked Fortunato how he happened to know Renata's mother. The rascal told us that from villages in that part everybody knew everybody, just as if they all lived in the same town. In fact, though, the word soon got round that he and Renata were sleeping together.

We didn't like this at first, because we felt it meant a lowering of Renata's dignity. Fortunato had been my chauffeur for only a short while—only since the death of poor Hydran, a magnificent horse who went broken-winded two years after I bought him and whom, out of misplaced kindness, we had let go on working till his death. Then, being so much upset by his death, we had no more to do with horses—on account of our great fondness for one horse, we refused to have any more to do with that species which had had such patience with man, until man, in his hurry, ceased to have any with it.

So, after a lengthy period of instruction, which left me for some months with neither carriage nor motor-car, Fortunato graduated from coachman to the dignified rank of chauffeur. He was slow to learn, but once having learned he never forgot. At first we never managed to reach our destinations; now, however, he drives very fast—sometimes too fast, because after every trip of any length I have endless speeding-fines to pay. Fortunato claims that the police are never satisfied, as traffic fines make up half their income. This may well be so.

As to Fortunato's ability as chauffeur, there are some breakdowns that leave him bewildered and indignant, and which he cannot cope with. As an old coachman, he would like to try the whip. Once we had to leave him out in the country, luckily not far from town, and come home on foot. He arrived home late that night and, from all reports, swearing. He had forgotten to check the petrol, and only later, much later, noticed the tank was empty. And from then on, whenever the car stopped, his eye automatically raced to the dashboard. Everything he learned, he learned from breakdowns, and I got distinctly tired of it.

"But we old people," Augusta said resignedly, "we don't like seeing new faces."

And so Fortunato stayed. He also acts as gardener, without much talent for the work, though a certain fondness for it. Anyway, he doesn't have much to do, which is proved by his having found the time to seduce little Renata.

She already treated him as her husband; that is to say, not very affectionately. She liked to call him "the breakdown man", which made me laugh wickedly, after Carlo had taught me how. There was also some friction over their work. She wanted him to look after the drawing-room, since there were some plants there too, and when he protested, she laughed: "But isn't it true that all I have is yours?"

He was much slower than her; she was quick and understood things even before one finished speaking. True enough, Renata would then often forget, whereas Fortunato, having made one expend vast amounts of breath to get him to grasp something, never afterwards forgot it.

It was curious the way, before he could understand something, he had to examine details which didn't remotely concern him. For instance, he would have been told to give some message to Augusta when he went to pick her up at the home of one of her friends: "So," Fortunato would recapitulate, "I have to be at the Guggenheim's door at six, and when the mistress comes down. . . ."

He would make a detailed analysis of everyone's movements. And losing patience with him, I would shout: "Let the Signora come down from the second floor alone! Thank God she can still walk without help."

He would give a violent start, as if I were making him dizzy, and I realised that one simply had to let him talk, to say everything necessary to the process of organising his thoughts.

And in the evening, undressing for bed, I said to Augusta:

"How can that child live with a man who's so short of intelligence?"

And Augusta answered: "I don't think intelligence is needed to be happy."

Whereupon I wondered: "Then God alone knows what the point of intelligence is."

But poor Fortunato was running quite a risk. We had decided to keep the little housemaid as close to us as possible. It entailed enlarging the cottage already occupied by Fortunato. I proposed adding another room, which would come in handy in the event of children. But one evening Augusta told me that they had decided not to have any children. They accepted the extra room, however—for the gramophone—something that made a din only when expressly instructed to.

And a few evenings later she told me that that hussy of a Renata had declared that if she felt the need for children, she was going to have them by someone a bit smarter than Fortunato.

Augusta and I laughed a great deal over that; she because she considered the statement idle and made in jest; I because I really liked it, and didn't mind if it was said seriously or not. But was Renata also pondering the law of heredity?

Carlo, to whom as usual I told everything, so as to submit whatever I felt I didn't fully understand to the comments of the younger generation, said: "But you're wrong, Uncle. She's not thinking of heredity at all. She's thinking of the needs of the moment."

I didn't understand immediately, but I pretended to laugh. And when I finally did understand, I laughed much more. Afterwards I turned it over in my mind. Perhaps Carlo was right; but then again, perhaps I was too. What are the needs of the moment? Aren't they perhaps dictated by some imperious will preparing the way for the future?

A CONTRACT

Translated by Ben Johnson

A Contract

I HAVE NEVER FULLY UNDERSTOOD THE REASONS FOR MY present inertia—I who during the war had a reputation about town as a man of enterprise and energy. My doctor nephew Carlo, whom I consulted on this question, because it has a bearing on my health, told me I was right to take it easy: I could go back to work when the next world war broke out.

That rascal hits a lot of nails on the head in that Trieste-Agentine argot of his. It was true, my activity had been a wartime affair, and when peace came I seemed to have lost the secret of it. I was immobilised—like a windmill without wind.

I am trying to remember. . . . If I had only stopped earlier! But I hadn't realised the far-reaching changes that had taken place. Finding that my native city was at last emerging from a kind of middle-ages, I cheered the Italian troops down in the streets; but then I went off to my office and conducted business as usual, as though Austrian soldiers and short rations were still the rule. And, moreover, I remember, when communications with Italy had been re-established, I made use of them to write an impressive letter to old Olivi, who had spent the war in Pisa. It was a pathetically innocent letter, for one could read between the lines that I imagined things would go on exactly in the same way now that the war was over. I said that destiny had so willed it that the possibility my father had ruled out had actually been realised: I had become the master of my own business. I described the flourishing condition of the firm under my management and the various transactions I had conducted, and I gave him an account of the actual profits made. All this with great casualness and modesty. There was no need to rub it in; the facts themselves were enough to make him burst with spleen. And burst is what he did. When a few days later I heard he was dead, I thought my letter must have been too much for him. In fact, he had died of the *grippe*. In my letter I had suggested, coldly, that things should go on in the manner that fate had willed—drawing rather a veil over my father's last instructions, which by this time were ancient history. I invited him and his son to continue as my employees, and said that he should be free to re-establish his old business connections, such as they were, while I attended to larger-scale affairs—in which I would equally expect an entirely free hand. In addition, he should be responsible for the running of the office. I was rather tired of this side of things, for all that I had had so little in the way of staff during the war.

I am not sure, but I think it might have been better for me if I had heard of old Olivi's death at once, instead of eight days afterwards. Indeed, though I have kept no account of the dates, it might have been a good thing if he had died a day or two sooner.

At all events, the disastrous deal I plunged into was certainly caused by a lack of perceptiveness on my part; that is to say, although knowing peace had broken out, I acted as though the war was still on. That, coupled with the fact that I was in a hurry to be involved in important negotiations, so that when Olivi arrived he would have all the more reason to admire me. Had I known he was dead, I wouldn't have made such efforts.

Anyway, several truckfuls of soap had arrived in Trieste from Sicily. Throughout the war, soap had been in universal demand in Trieste, especially among those who wanted to make money out of it; so I seized on the soap avidly, and paid cash for it. As had been my custom during the war, I was in much less of a hurry to sell it. Then at last, when I began to think about this, I found no one wanted soap in Trieste any more. I suppose they must have got out of the habit of it. Worse was to follow. I received further offers of soap from Italy, and at lower prices than I had paid. I now became alarmed; I realised that the new fact, peace, had even entered the soap's existence. However, it seemed to me that there was one hope left for the soap. My soap was already in Trieste, whilst the rest was still a long way away. I sent it off to Vienna without delay, so that it should be the first to arrive, and began to try to sell it there. For some reason or other (I still don't precisely understand why) my soap was now sequestrated. There were two possible reasons, apparently, for this ban on its sale—the acute shortage existing in Vienna, and the fact that the soap didn't come up to certain standards laid down by Austrian law (even I knew vaguely about these). Various negotiations ensued, lasting several months, and at last the restrictions were lifted on my soap. But in the meantime everyone had had time to stock up with this substance (which nobody gets through very quickly) and I had to sell mine below cost price, and for Austrian *kronen*, which arrived only when it was too late to exchange them. They were worth practically nothing.

The soap affair wiped away virtually all the money which, thanks to luck and my own initiative, I had piled up during the war; and I found it hard to reconcile myself to it. The more so since Olivi's son, who had returned from the war in the meantime (still in his second lieutenant's uniform), couldn't keep a straight face when he looked at my old balance sheets, with their handsome profits all swallowed up by that last calamitous deal. Moreover, he displayed a great contempt for wartime transactions in general, and remarked one day that it was perfectly natural for someone who had got accustomed to wartime dealing to be promptly ruined when peace came. He went on, under his breath: "If I had been in command, I would have everyone shot who traded during the war." Then, reflecting a moment, he added, unsmiling: "Except you . . . of course."

This once-shy lad had grown remarkably bold during the war. At first it frightened me. How could a man with such pronounced Bolshevik leanings look after my business? At every moment he kept spouting opinions against the rich. He and his father had gone off to Italy with their shares and title-deeds under their arm. Without a further thought, he had then gone to fight in the trenches, and when he finally succeeded in destroying the enemy's trenches, he discovered that by the same act he had destroyed his own property. This rankled with him profoundly.

"What about your father?" I ventured. "He was a business-man, too, you know. Not like me, a war-profiteer, or you, a man-at-arms."

"It never crossed his mind," sighed Olivi *fils*. "All he did during the war was wait for news from me. Poor old chap!"

Triumphantly, I exclaimed, "I was waiting for news myself, from Florence, but I was still able to attend to business. True, that damned soap meant I didn't actually add to my capital; but at least I didn't let it be destroyed."

With real bitterness, Olivi said, "No one in your family was being shot at. I was in the trenches." He seemed disappointed that my daughter hadn't been there with him.

But despite his Bolshevism, when it came to business he was exactly as his father had been—shrewd, alert, and hard. The staff had been spoiled by me, who was not a Bolshevik. He straightened everything out again. He saw to it that they kept to a rigid schedule, and whenever he could he cut their pay.

Before long, I learned that I couldn't talk to him, but that I could trust him. He set an example by his indefatigable activity. So much so that I began to take things very easy myself. There was one day at the beginning—a day which I remember, though nothing happened on it except a certain stirring in my mind—when I thought; "It's still a rise in the world, even if I'm reigning without ruling." For some time Olivi had been submitting important letters to me for signa-ture. I would hesitate at first and then sign with a grimace that was meant to imply: "They'll do." If I had rewritten them, they would have been better, of course; but not to give myself all that extra labour, I would sign, with a sigh.

The only transaction which Olivi refused to give any attention to was the soap deal. The Austrian *kronen* never arrived, and one day I exclaimed: "But after all, couldn't those Viennese be *made* to meet their obligations? Didn't we win the war?" He laughed heartily, so heartily that I gathered that among those who won the war I was not included. I blushed. I am very sensitive to reproaches of that sort. I didn't say anything to him just then, because I needed time to calculate that I was fifty-seven when the war started. The next day, however, I asked him: "Do you think if I had volunteered they would have taken me on as a general? Because I don't think I would have been accepted as a foot soldier."

"Well, we certainly had all kinds of generals," he laughed.

He was less malicious this time—less malicious than myself, in fact, for I had prepared everything I was going to say to him the night before. And so, paying no attention to his friendliness, I added: "Even second lieutenant wouldn't have been good enough for me, for you need good legs for that too— for advancing, and also for running away."

He didn't notice this dig. He grew sad. He was remembering a retreat.

He was slow on the uptake, like me, for it was not until next day that he said to me: "It's people who know nothing about war who think the good officer is to be seen in the way he leads an attack. I believe I was of value to my country, valuable in the sense that I instilled my own confidence into hundreds of men during the retreat."

"It's a question of legs," I said, adamant.

Whereupon he got angry. But not with me. With others. Various commanders who had capitalised on his fine qualities. And then he became angry with persons even more remote— that is, with the war dead. They were the heroes and people proclaimed them so so readily because it didn't cost much— just a grave and a bit of an inscription. And the living who had done so much were neglected: if they wanted to live they had to hire themselves out to Signor Zeno Cosini.

His dig escaped me at first, and it wasn't till the next day that I said to him: "It would be a nice affair if poor Zeno

Cosini had to support all the heroes who managed to survive!"

He gave a contemptuous laugh.

And I raised my voice: "You weren't fighting the war just for me. There must be others in this neighbourhood who owe you as much as I do, if you want to look for them."

I was still really timid even when I raised my voice. And I didn't enjoy doing it. After all, it was true that he had been fighting while I had been buying and selling. But the worst was yet to come. By dint of reigning without ruling, it wasn't long before I knew nothing about my own business. Whenever I happened to offer advice I was promptly laughed at. My advice derived from past epochs. I would mention offices I thought ought to be consulted but which no longer existed, and Olivi would say to me: "Why, you must think you're still in the times of Albrecht the Bear."

Or I would suggest something that could have been done under the old régime, and he would proceed to tell me how, in 1914, the Serbs had killed an archduke and that so many troubles had happened as a result that my advice didn't apply any more.

I began to be distinctly bored by the office. Sometimes I would take vacations from it. Out of my love for orderliness. I would tell Olivi the day before that I was not coming in next day. And he would say: "Suit yourself, suit yourself." Then he would chuckle: he meant to convey how happy it would make him to see me less often.

By then it had already become an effort to me to go to the office. I invariably went hoping to catch Olivi out in some mistake. I hoped I would find letters he had overlooked or misinterpreted, and I was always ready to prove the necessity of my presence to him. He never granted me this pleasure. Indeed, once when I thought I had found him out in a mistake, he said to me: "But can't you even read a letter?" And he showed me where I had misread it. Actually, once, many months after some such exchange as this, I realised I had by chance been in the right, but intimidated by his cocksureness I had been incapable of sticking to my guns.

And so, between disputes in which I was wrong and others in which, against all justice, the blame was heaped upon me, I began to present the appearance not of one who reigned, but of an encumbrance no one paid attention to.

The staff, though they were perfectly respectful, never—not even when Olivi was out—came to me for instructions. I pretended not to realise they needed any because I knew that whatever I said it would only end in my being proved wrong. I kept as quiet as a mouse, relieved that nobody asked me anything.

And then, one fine day, I was wantonly attacked.

That idiot of a son-in-law of mine (poor fellow! I'm sorry to have to speak of him in this way: now that he's dead I don't like to be disagreeable about him) was deputed by Olivi to negotiate the drawing-up of a new contract with him. Business was poor and it had become necessary to reorganise the firm, to find new outlets. Olivi, therefore, was getting ready for study-projects, journeys and work of every kind—he meant to devote his life to the task. This meant he ought to be paid on an entirely different basis. He wanted a salary slightly higher than what he was already getting—plus fifty per cent of the profits.

My son-in-law looked at me with that fat, rather misshapen, doughy face of his—I have never understood what my daughter saw in him—and asked me to forgive him for having agreed to deliver such a message. He had done it with the best intentions. Better for him to do it than someone else.

I was indignant. The whole story of my relations with the Olivis, both the father and the son, stood there incarnate before me. For so many years we had adhered to the conditions laid down by my father. If those conditions were altered, I would then be free to pry Olivi out of the office and install myself as head of my firm. But now I found myself fighting shy. The day when, suddenly set free from all restraints by the war, I had hurled myself into business, had long since gone by. And with diabolical astuteness, Olivi had managed to convince everybody of my incompetence. He had even convinced me. I had visions of myself besieged by people wanting instructions and only being able to say to them: "Ask Olivi!"

All the same, it wasn't true that my son-in-law was acting for the best in accepting such a commission. For one reason, I know he had a very high opinion of Olivi and a very low one of me. As lawyer to a big insurance company, he had once tried to get me to sign a general policy covering all our transport. At a certain point he realised that with me hesitating so much (not having been properly briefed by Olivi) we would never succeed in clinching anything, and he went off to Olivi, with whom, in no time at all, the policy got signed and —to tell the truth—with better terms for us than I would have dreamed of obtaining. Afterwards, Valentino apologised. "But you didn't explain this to me, or that . . ." he said. In fact, he gave Olivi better terms than he had offered me, and ended—this was the worst of all—in conceiving a vast respect for Olivi.

Which is why he had no business accepting such a mission. For the moment, I turned down every proposal and instructed Valentino to tell Olivi that he could consider himself dismissed—that I was thinking of replacing him with someone else, if I didn't eventually take over his position myself.

Typically the business-man, Valentino believed there was nothing in the world that couldn't be discussed. But how was he to succeed, not realising that, for the moment, I was more concerned to salvage my dignity in his eyes than to pursue my best interests with Olivi? And so he began to speak of Olivi's long years of service, his great experience. He had an unpleasant voice, poor Valentino; the sound it made was partly due to his big nose. And it was by no means a strong voice (for that matter, what was there that was strong about Valentino?) so that the tedium of listening to it was made worse by having to strain one's ears. I strained mine with the requisite effort, and then closed them so as not to have to listen to these things that didn't concern me. Poor Valentino was talking about my own interests, when the question was now something quite different.

At last he finished! He got up to join the others, and before leaving asked to be excused for having bored me. Whereupon I became affectionate, reminding myself that if there were anyone to be angry with it was Olivi, not Valentino; and I smiled, I thanked him, and I accompanied him to the door. Thus he was not even remotely aware that I was saying to myself, reproachfully, as I often do: "How good I am! How good I am!" (In spite of all conviction to the contrary, I go on "being" good.) I hope poor dead Valentino will forgive me, but at that moment, instead of smiling at him as I did, I would have liked to accelerate his departure with a kick.

I went to see a lawyer—Bitonti, the son of my father's lawyer, who was an old man like myself, but thinner and more decrepit, with a small face framed by white whiskers, but still with a lively, bright eye. It's curious the way some people, when they study a case, see nothing but that. Their entire self, and that of their interlocutor, disappears and only the case remains. Bitonti was not acquainted with the situation, except for what I told him about it myself, and I was incapable of thinking simply about that. He might have been lost, therefore, just as I was. But he managed to focus on the case itself, badly presented and misunderstood by me as it was.

He said to me: "You say that during the war you were able to handle your affairs by yourself. Well, now you have to see if you can do it in peacetime too. You say that in the office you are at least as important as Olivi. Well, then; try and see whether you can remain as important without him. But I don't think you should replace him at once. You must first take charge of your firm yourself. Later on, you can look round for someone to help you or to take your place."

I went away hating him, but without letting him know it. Luckily, too! Because after a while spent with my gramophone, I saw, full of self-pity—the most active pity there is—that I, poor old man that I was, had only two routes left open to me: either to set to work myself, with the fear that I shouldn't be able to manage, or to give in to Olivi.

And it was at this point that I decided to ask Augusta for her advice. Not for a moment did I think she would be able to tell me what to do, but it would help me to clarify my ideas if I could talk about them. At first I found her even more inadequate than I had feared.

"But aren't you the master?" she wanted to know. "How could he dare to do this? How could he *dare*?"

It would have been a fine use for my time, trying to decide how he dared. I was a trifle impatient, and for a moment I returned to my gramophone.

I wouldn't have said anything more about it to her if she hadn't asked, the following day after lunch, when we were alone together: "Well then! What have you decided?"

Whereupon I explained that I found it more or less just that I should give Olivi fifty per cent of the profits. At that time fifty per cent didn't represent much, for our profits couldn't be compared either with our pre-war ones or the killings I had made in the war. The main thing was for Olivi and me to devote ourselves to rebuilding the firm on a new basis. But if I was going to collaborate in this, why shouldn't I get the same salary as Olivi?

It was easy for me to decide to tell everything to Augusta. That idiot Olivi—by going to Valentino, who told everything to his wife, who in turn kept no secrets from her mother—had already committed me to total sincerity.

Augusta suggested I should ask for a salary twice as large as the one Olivi was demanding. I gravely assented, though it immediately occurred to me I could never get so much out of Olivi.

And in a desperate attempt to exclude Valentino from the negotiations, I went and made a direct approach to Olivi.

He did not seem at all embarrassed. He treated the situation with the same easy-going manner with which he would have accepted or refused a shipment of merchandise. I, on the contrary, couldn't achieve such a nonchalance. I smiled, I discussed, I considered, but it was perfectly plain I was like a dog stiffening at the approach of an enemy, curling its tail between its legs. The importance of the moment took my breath away. And at that instant, noticing the sure and easy manner he displayed under stress, and feeling myself wretched and insecure, I recognised his superiority and made up my mind to keep him in the firm, come what might.

I proposed that I should be given a salary equal to his and that the profits should be divided, or else that we should not trouble to fix a salary for either of us and should merely divide the profits. I had imagined I was making one single proposal in this, but it didn't appear like that to Olivi. He began by telling me that he was about to get married, and that if he accepted my terms, the money, as one could see from our previous balance-sheet, would not be enough to allow him and his family to live in a decent fashion. He would need his full salary, and half the profits as well, with no deduction for a salary for me.

"But if I'm not going to be paid for working," I said, "then I won't work. I'll just call in from time to time, but I won't lift a pen."

Hypocritically, Olivi said: "I shall be sorry to have to do without your assistance, but it seems there is no alternative."

It was merely his words which were hypocritical, not his determined attitude, which clearly meant: "The assistance you're offering me isn't worth a damn."

There was still a little resistance on my part. I asked him gravely: "How long will you let me have to give you an answer?"

He explained that eight days had already elapsed since he sent his original proposal. He personally was willing to wait until the closing balance, which, under the old contract, would come at the end of the month; but this was impossible because another party he was negotiating with had demanded an immediate reply. So I would have to give him an answer next morning. He wanted to be frank with me. He had given my son-in-law Valentino a letter from some people who wanted to employ him under conditions similar to those he was asking from me; my son-in-law would let me see the letter that evening.

I gave a start—and for two reasons. I gathered that, if he couldn't reach agreement with me, Olivi was preparing to compete against me, and—what gave me much more chagrin—once again a member of my family had been admitted into discussions which, as all the evidence showed by now, were bound to end in my discomfiture.

"But why," I stammered, "why did you have to bring in outsiders as intermediaries?"

"Outsiders!" he laughed. "Isn't he your son-in-law?"

I thought a moment and mumbled, "That's right, he is."

This was another thing that couldn't be discussed. It was enough to drive one mad. I always got the worst of it with Olivi.

I didn't dare discuss the matter further, but once more, for the last time, I asserted myself in the way that Augusta—and only Augusta—had counselled me to, as the master. "Well then, let's leave it like that. I'll give you my answer in the morning."

And the odd thing is, I left the office immediately—for the first time, I left just when the post was being opened. At that time of day, and time of year, it would have been more comfortable in the warm office than outside under a sky heavy with snowclouds. But I was acting the master—master of myself, I mean, certainly not of the office, where I left the real master, Olivi, working in the warmth of the office, while I had to go searching for what refuge I could find.

I walked all the way home to the villa. It was no time to conceal my defeat from Augusta, when Valentino would soon know all about it. To free myself from the incubus, I dragged her away from her housekeeping and her bath. I told her it was true, I was no longer fit for work. Was it my age perhaps? I was only sixty-three at the time, but it might have been a case of premature senility. I note as a curious coincidence that that was the first time this malady was mentioned in the house. And when it struck down Valentino, I suffered a pang of remorse, as though I had given him it myself.

And, speaking of my irremediable old age, tears filled my eyes. Augusta began to try to console me, ready to weep as well. She is very concerned about money, consuming a great deal of it as she does—but wisely, in the sense that she never worries about the expense when it's a question of her own comfort. But I don't think she formed a clear idea of the financial blow the new contract meant to me. She imagined it to be only a small affair, and used this as an argument to comfort me.

And in fact it was a small affair. It might become a big one, though, if we made losses, because then, besides the losses, I would also have to bear the burden of Olivi's salary; for under the new contract Olivi was not to be affected by losses, since he considered that he, as the working partner, should never have to submit to a cut in salary. In short, it was what's known as a well-drawn contract—from Olivi's point of view. And indeed I may add at once that though the new contract strongly favoured Olivi, I can't complain, after seven years' experience of it, that I have been much damaged, except (as I will explain) as regards my health. There were years when the balance-sheets were splendid, and our greatest difficulties were in trying to deceive the tax authorities. Other years were less successful, but there was never an actual deficit. At bottom, Olivi handled my affairs much as his father had, except that he was better paid—a true sign of the times.

That first day, after experiencing the chill and discomfort of the morning outside, I stayed at home. I had still not decided to stay away from the office for good. As I saw it, I was at home considering what line to take with Valentino, so as best to safeguard my dignity when he called on me that evening (as he certainly would). In actual fact, I didn't give it a thought. I don't know how to direct my attention where I want it to go. It is completely independent of me. I recall that the entire day, during all those hours I spent by myself, I sat motionless in the same position trying to determine whether, when morning came, I might stave off having to accept Olivi's terms, or whether I would not have done better to have told him to go to the devil, that I was going to take over the business myself. To tell the truth, my thoughts are always happier when directed to the past, so that they can improve on it—or rather, if possible, to falsify it—instead of to the future, where they have no place to settle, the pattern not yet having been created.

And so when Valentino finally arrived, I could think of nothing but to get rid of him at once (whenever I look at a mountain I always expect it to turn into a volcano); I told him I had seen Olivi a little earlier and that we had come to terms. Valentino seemed doubtful, puzzled. His gaze rested on me fixedly; he scrutinised me with those eyes of his which—to his misfortune—he never knew when to believe. He finally put his doubts into words; he had seen Olivi that evening at six, and it was now only eight. So he could not see how I had had the time to meet and discuss a matter of such importance with Olivi.

I don't like lying, and being forced to lie was an additional reason for me for disliking poor Valentino. And having said the first lie, I could not escape it. But why did Valentino have to be so insistent? Later—when he died—I understood, and I forgave him. It was simply the way he was made; he could not drop a matter until he had thoroughly explored it, and this took time, as he thought slowly and with great meticulousness.

I explained I had run into Olivi by chance on the street and that we had reached agreement in no time at all. The matter was not really an important one. I was also kind enough to tell Valentino the tiny margin of profit we had made the year before. So, obviously, the matter was of no importance to me, nor indeed to Olivi, who was so much poorer than me.

Up to that point I had been able to repress that turbulent voice, wont to cry out from the depths of my soul: "How good you are! How good you are!" But apparently the echo of my reproach finally reached poor Valentino. Still, he had abused my goodness. He set out to prove to me that, on the contrary, the affair was extremely important, because a financial year might result in tremendous losses, and these would be aggravated by having to pay Olivi's salary.

But what did that have to do with it? Why, all of a sudden, now that he had been told the matter was settled—however much he may have doubted it—was he advancing the arguments against a settlement? To grasp the situation better perhaps? I have no idea how he detected the note of impatience and fury behind my voice, for I went on speaking in the most measured tones: I knew my firm and I knew my business, and with a man as prudent as Olivi in charge, we could exclude the possibility of making losses. But anger and impatience must have leaked out clearly, and offensively too, because poor Valentino's face, normally rigid and absorbed like a model clerk's, suddenly twitched and went pale, and he hurriedly started for the door. He was so offended apparently, that he meant to forgo good manners entirely and leave without another word.

He stopped at the door, and in a voice that was shaky despite its support from his nasal passages he said to me: "Very well! The matter is clearly no concern of mine. I was only talking because Olivi asked me to, and anyway, it was in your own interests."

Lounging all the while in my easy chair, I looked up at him in some astonishment, trying to think which of the words I had said might have wounded him. I failed, though; partly because he confused me by overdoing the good manners, saying he hoped to see me later, at dinner, when we would speak of other things and never again about this particular affair. Never again? Wasn't that really going too far? I had too many things to think about at the one moment, and I never managed to find which word of mine had given offence. I think he must have been hurt more by the sound than by the meaning of what I said.

Hours of a strange uneasiness then ensued. I had, first of all, to caution Augusta not to tell Valentino that I hadn't been out of the house for hours; otherwise he would realise that I couldn't have seen Olivi. But how was I to tell her? Augusta was no doubt in the sitting-room with Valentino and Antonia. Moreover, I had to find Olivi that very evening and quickly come to terms before he had time to see Valentino again. So, in a state of anguish, ready to go out, with my hat and winter overcoat on, in my room which, as usual, was overheated, as Augusta insists on having it, I was standing in the door of my study, undecided whether I should hurry into the sitting-room and summon Augusta or go down to the Tergesteo where I knew I could still find Olivi, who did not stop working—in this respect he was like his father—until nine in the evening.

Just then Renata, Umbertino's nurse, went by. She could help me! I called to her. She looked up with those brown eyes of hers, surprised and apprehensive, it being virtually the first time I had spoken to her when she was not with Umbertino, while I, agitated as I was, could not help staring at her long, still somewhat girlish, legs, concealed only in silk stockings.

It was a little difficult for me to explain myself. I wanted her to get Augusta for me without the others knowing I wanted her.

She understood instantly. She had a voice with a strained, shrill quality about it, intensified by the laugh that now took hold of her. It was a voice with many different notes in it.

She proposed: "Signora Augusta sent me out to get her glasses. Here they are, but I'll tell her I couldn't find them. You can be sure then that she'll come out to look for them herself."

I was not at all convinced that that was the way it would work, but in my irresolution I let her go. When Augusta came running out, I couldn't help being impressed by the little nursemaid's cunning.

Fortunately, Augusta had not said anything that might have compromised me with Valentino. What's more, she was not at all surprised by the lie I had told: she not only sympathised, she seemed even to approve of it. This fact, which now strikes me as rather curious, I can explain, I think, by the fact that she herself, just then, had something against poor Valentino, on account of a quarrel he had had with Alfio. Naturally, then, she also agreed that I should go out and find Olivi and tell him that the contract he had proposed had been accepted long before Valentino's intervention, and she would tell Valentino I had gone out on an errand on her behalf. That was the only possible way for me to use the car, because the sound of it leaving the garage could be heard all over the neighbourhood.

I found Olivi at the Tergesteo. I cut a rather odd figure, finding myself as I did in a state of complete inferiority to him, though he was my subordinate. I had to hurry, there was no time to think, and I hurled myself at my *idée fixe*, that of eliminating my son-in-law once and for all from the negotiations.

I told him I was prepared to accept all the conditions he had laid down, provided he granted me one—just one—in return.

Olivi looked at me, hesitant. Then he began to talk, slowly, the way he always did when it was a question of business, with that stupid respect he accorded to such matters, as though they had an importance beyond the money one intended to get out of them : as if business were science, art, invention.

And so, in the moment that I was behaving like a child in a tantrum, I felt I was vastly superior to Olivi, who, for all his measured tones and solemnity, was bent on telling me things that didn't interest me in the least and which I didn't even care to discuss.

He began by saying gravely that before submitting me his conditions, he had given them careful study, and so did not see how they could in any way be modified.

Impatiently, I shouted : "But what if I'm not thinking of modifications? . . . I'm talking about something else entirely !"

And I then explained what I wanted—that Valentino should not learn that our agreement had come about because of his intervention.

Olivi was unable to conceal his astonishment. He had known me for years, but it seemed to him he had never seen me making so little sense. He eyed me closely, to make sure I wasn't joking. But if he never solved this to his satisfaction, what difference did it make to him? So long as the affair was settled, even as a result of a fit of lunacy on my part, it was not for him to worry.

He murmured reflectively: "It was I who engaged Signor Valentino. He seemed the best person for the negotiations—he's an old friend of mine and your son-in-law." He went on, murmuring to himself: "It would be perfectly possible. I saw Valentino at six, and I could very well have seen you at seven." (This is the way slow-witted people collect their wits, by speaking their thoughts aloud.) And he went on to say something very odd: "Now that I hear Valentino is not a son of yours. . . ."

"But he is!" I protested—"I merely don't want to seem like a man who lets his sons run his affairs for him."

I had spoken up firmly, but Olivi's strange *lapsus* worried me all the same. Was I not, in fact, acting rather badly towards my son-in-law, who had always treated me with respect, and so, in a way, towards my daughter Antonia?

I was haunted by this doubt for a long time, and it increased the wretchedness of my situation, already miserable after signing that contract—a contract which took away my whole occupation, and what's more, a substantial sum of money. Now and again, trying to recover my peace of mind, I would put the blame on poor Valentino, whose interference had rushed me into accepting the terms.

At Valentino's deathbed, and only then, my remorse became acute and inescapable, so much so that it made me quite unhappy. Olivi, with his usual earnestness, had kept his word and Valentino never learned about the trick I played on him. Precisely for this reason—with the weakness typical of us unbelievers who, when someone dies, think he will know everything in the next world—I would have liked to confess to him, to beg his forgiveness for that as well as for one or two other tricks I had played on him, for instance when I had spoken badly of him to his wife Antonia (who, however—from all appearances—was not in the least influenced by my remarks). But they never left me alone with him. He was already having difficulty in hearing, and I was ready to confess to someone who was leaving me for good, but not in front of a horde of people who would still be there to make fun of me or rebuke me.

And I must say—I will confess it here—I never had much liking for poor Valentino. I doubt whether it could have been otherwise, for he was terribly ugly, with that fat chest of his and short legs, and I felt he was impairing my stock. But for this reason, apart from some very bearable feelings of remorse, I was more or less unmoved at his deathbed, and capable of observing everything with a clear eye. It struck me that everybody round him had more urge to confess than Valentino himself—poor Valentino, who was being urged to it by his very pious wife. I fear this is frequently the case at death-bed scenes. Augusta had been a party to that trick played on poor Valentino and never felt a moment's remorse.

That evening, in fact, when I returned, she managed to corner me for a moment, and like a regular accomplice, asked: "Were you able to see Olivi and come to an agreement?"

At my "Yes," she breathed a sigh of relief.

All that night I tossed and turned. I was not even sure which of my doubts—and I had quite a few—had turned into a nightmare; but something was weighing on me terribly. Was it the contract itself? Or being doomed to lasting inertia? But, I thought to myself: "If I really do know anything about business, I am bound, before long, to find something else that suits me." But even this didn't restore my peace of mind.

I spent a couple of restless hours and then, unable to bear it any longer, I woke up Augusta. She gave me a sedative, the first effect of which was to make me talk.

"It's that accursed contract that's keeping me from sleeping," I said. "Also, I'm afraid Olivi's going to tell Valentino that my coming to terms was due solely to his intervention."

I didn't really believe what I was saying, because I'm sure I knew even then that Olivi, that hollow man stuffed full of seriousness, would keep his word.

Augusta was not much help. She was so blind wherever I was concerned that she believed me still to be the master; she suggested that, when I was at the lawyer's the next day for the signing of the contract, I should simply refuse, since the idea no longer appealed to me. She didn't realise I was already acquainted with every clause in the contract, some of them distinctly humiliating for me, and had accepted them.

I said: "If Valentino hadn't butted in, the contract certainly wouldn't have been agreed to so soon, but as things stand now there's no hope of backing out."

And having said this, I found a little peace that night. I had found a way of laying blame at Valentino's door, to compensate for my own.

Signing the contract was a painful business. Though I knew all the clauses, when they were read aloud by the notary they seemed new to me. One of them stipulated that I could intervene in my firm's affairs to give advice but that Olivi was free to accept or ignore it.

I signed immediately. There might have been a clause in it sentencing me to death, for after the one prohibiting me from even thinking about my business I stopped listening to the reading altogether. Instead, I turned my thoughts to the odious action Olivi had committed against me—the way he had wounded a poor old man like myself so deeply. The struggle was over. Which explained why I felt so weak, so defenceless. Thinking about my weakness and the strength of my adversary, it struck me that right was on my side; at last I—the miserable victim—was on the side of the right. And that feeling of being a poor, innocent victim, which was to stay with me for so long and finally degenerate into illness, was born at that moment, at the instant of suffering the reading of the contract.

Now, I felt the impulse to leave, to run away. It was as

though I had to get away from Olivi so that, in solitude, I might fortify my thoughts and devote myself to revenge. It is strange, that rage to escape from one's adversary the better to devise his punishment.

But I was not ready to say the word I wanted to say to him, far from ready in fact. Once having signed the contract, and anxious to get away as fast as possible, I instinctively stretched out my hand to Olivi, the way a gentleman does when he feels he has been bested at a game. (One makes the same gesture when one suspects one has been cheated but cannot prove it.)

Olivi wrung my hand and said: "You'll see, Signor Zeno— you'll never have cause to regret having signed this contract. From now on, I hope to see to it that your firm attains—not its former glories, because business can never be like that again— but enough activity of a solid and well-managed kind, as will guarantee its future existence."

His pretty speech placated me not a bit. What difference did a little income more or less make to me? They were throwing me out of my office, where I had been so happy while Austria had released me from my two tyrants, and now they wanted to console me. It was too much.

In a choked voice, I said: "There are certain clauses that should never have been in that contract. Not by any means! You should have remembered you were dealing with an old man who, by the very laws of nature, would have given up working before long anyway. That clause there, the one that barely allows me to open my mouth when I'd like something to be done, and something else not done, that ought to have been struck out!"

The lawyer leaped to his feet in horror. To tell the truth, I can't even remember the lawyer, as I didn't really see him. All I know is that in the most important chair sat somebody very young, blond or red-haired, who had more life in him than one could expect in a notary. I was struck by the gold rims of his glasses and the gold chain hanging from them, which, en route to his waistcoat buttonhole, ran behind one ear. I noticed the chain, perhaps, because it was so pedantically arranged as to seem the only thing truly lawyer-like about the fellow.

He burst out: "But the contract is already signed and sealed. I don't understand how you can think of changing it now."

Olivi broke in, in a voice so very solemn and serene as to suggest the full dangerousness of a man both extremely strong and extremely sure of himself.

"Never mind the seals," he said. "I certainly gave you time enough to think it over—until eight yesterday morning. But it doesn't matter. I can always fall back on the parties I told you about; they will always be ready to sign the same contract with me. If you wish, Signor Zeno, we can tear the contract up. I don't mind at all. You can have your entire freedom back. On the other hand, though, I must be given my freedom, too— at once—today. From today on, I'll never set foot in your office."

My head swam. I had been struggling to resign myself to the loss of my office. Now, out of the clear blue, I was offered it all back—all the worries, all the responsibilities; the utter slavery of it.

And seeing that Olivi, his mind made up, was crossing towards the table where the contract lay, perhaps even to tear it up, I shouted: "The contract is already signed and sealed, and it's up to you, sir, as a notary, to defend it! I never said anything about annulling it!" And at this point I tried to laugh, to give me time to think of what else I wanted to say. And it came to me. I cried out in triumph: "I only wanted to let you see that you haven't behaved as you should have done towards an old man. You could have obtained the same result without some of those clauses. And now it would make no difference if they were struck out. Once I knew you had ever thought of them, the crime was committed—irremediably!"

Brusque and self-assured, Olivi said: "Believe me, it couldn't have been done any other way, Signor Zeno."

"Well, all right then," I said. "Let's not talk about it any more."

I started to walk out. But then, for a second time, I went back to shake hands with the notary and Olivi again. Damn it!—one either was a gentleman or one wasn't. Gripping Olivi's hand, I let go of it at once, as if it had burned me. We were to behave like gentlemen; which doesn't include making a show of friendship one doesn't feel.

I left in a hurry, because it looked as though Olivi wanted to come with me. I wanted to be alone. Frequently, in solitude, I had been able to pull myself together again, to console myself, to regain confidence in myself, after succumbing to another's might. Who could say but that, calmly re-examining my position, I might come to see it as less unpleasant.

The weather outside was foul. Every now and again it began to drizzle. It was dismal, the air thick and humid. What a bore! I yawned, walking along the grey street, with my umbrella still unopened. At that moment in the office the post would be arriving. I paused for a moment, debating whether I ought to go there before Olivi and act the master by opening the letters. The idea struck me as so original that I turned round to start back up the street. Then I began to think about it. Hadn't I declared that since I wasn't going to be paid I wasn't going to work? And I about-faced and hurried off in the opposite direction, for fear that, having come back near the notary's office, I might run into Olivi again. And as I quickened my pace, a strange thought came to me: "You see! I'm already *doing* something."

At that very moment, how I worshipped activity! And, for the time being, the activity I was used to performing at that time of day. How delightful it was, opening letters! One took the letter out of the envelope, and one couldn't guess what it would contain. The suspense was a delicious business, not infrequently followed by tiresomeness and annoyance. True, after about ten letters or so, I usually couldn't face any more and let Olivi cope with the rest. But that merely meant I had exhausted a pleasure.

Still walking towards the harbour, I decided to postpone telling Augusta I was never going to the office again. It would be tantamount to confessing that the contract meant I had been thrown out. For the first few days, I would find something to do away from the house. Later I would tell her that I couldn't stand the sight of Olivi any longer, and so I wasn't going back to the office any more.

In the meantime, however, I had to find shelter from the rain, and I set off towards the Tergesteo. Then I ran into Cantari, a representative of a German chemical firm. It was a pity, because Cantari sometimes saw Augusta and might tell her he had seen me on the street. Having greeted him, I wanted to move right on; but he detained me. He had been commissioned by Olivi to find out the prices of certain chemical products and wanted to know if, by telling me, he could spare himself the trouble of going all the way to see Olivi in such weather.

I told him I doubted if Olivi (who, under the changed conditions in Trieste was in fact having to try every possible new kind of goods) would be able to handle chemical products. And I made a gesture of contempt—which came all too easily whenever I thought of Olivi—as if to say : "So I don't want to hear about your chemicals."

And so the worthy Cantari, whom Olivi thought so highly of, because he never lost papers or forgot to visit his clients or to give them the information they needed—in a word, a man who was order personified, because that was all his job required—hoisted his umbrella and went resignedly on his way.

Meanwhile, however, I had changed my mind. What was the point of aggravating my defeat by all the confusion, the effort—the pain, in fact—of deceiving Augusta? Besides, what difference did it make if Augusta suspected they had managed to throw me out of my office? Part of it could be concealed from her. I could tell her, this being the first time she saw me arrive home so early, that I had a violent headache. I shouldn't have much difficulty in faking an illness on this day, of all days. It would result, of course, in Augusta's making me take a purgative. But perhaps that was what I needed, with so many indigestible things to stomach.

Once in my study, having told Augusta something by way of explanation (which resulted in having my head wrapped up), I asked myself: "What do I do now?" I could find something to do, perhaps I might read or play my gramophone. With so much time on my hands, I might even make the great decision and take up my violin again. But how could I do anything while I was still quarrelling with Olivi? There were a lot of insults I still hadn't said to him.

Many days after signing the contract it occurred to me that if old man Olivi had not died, I never would have had to submit to such an affront, because he would not have permitted it. This was a remark that was sure to cut Olivi the Younger to the quick, considering the great respect he bore his father's memory. I could also tell him that if my father had known just what sort of persons would issue from the Olivi stock, he never would have left me in their hands.

And it was only then that I got round to examining the contract, of which I had a copy. With what diabolical cleverness it had been drawn up! Every clause was a slap in the face. If, for instance, I wanted the firm to be dissolved, I would be required to surrender half of the capital to Olivi.

That clause stung me so much that I had to look for some way to blow off steam, and I found it, I thought, in reproaching Valentino for helping to arrange the contract. I felt I could admonish him with a clear conscience, as I knew he was the cause of my signing so hastily. But he took offence. Hadn't he come to me and offered to discuss the contract clause by clause? And when he did so, hadn't he discovered I had already accepted every last one of Olivi's terms as though they had been one and indivisible . . .? Just like that, he went on.

I tried not to remember, but it was difficult because there had been witnesses. I had to retreat, having got the worst of it once again.

For some days, there was another thing aggravating my situation. My son Alfio—the painter—was going through a moment of doubting the prospects of his own strange art, and was looking around for another occupation. Among other things, he was toying with the idea of business, and of becoming a partner of Olivi's. But there was a clause that forbade that.

"After all," groused Alfio, who is not noted for his tact, "the business was a legacy of Grandpapa's and no one should have been allowed to interfere with it."

Whereupon I spent several days studying what concessions I might make to Olivi to get permission for Alfio to work in his office. I considered buying the permission with a huge sum of money. But in the meantime Alfio gave up the idea and went back to dirtying countless sheets of paper with tempera. I still felt I owed him something, however; and that made me even more timid in my already difficult relations with him.

Then came the day when, to my great chagrin, I learned that despite the contract and all manner of prohibitive clauses, Valentino had been able to obtain an important concession from Olivi; he was allowed to spend an hour every evening in the office, going over the ledgers on my behalf, checking them against the original documents.

THIS INDOLENCE OF MINE

Translated by Ben Johnson

IT IS NO GOOD LOOKING FOR THE PRESENT IN CALENDARS OR clocks; one consults them merely to establish one's relationship with the past or to move with some semblance of consciousness into the future. It is I and the things and people round me that constitute the true present.

What is more, my present itself consists of various tenses. To begin with there is one major, and interminable present, my retirement from business. A pathetic spectacle of inertia! Then there are a few important events that break it up, like my daughter's marriage: an event long passed and one that is becoming a part of another protracted present, interrupted —or perhaps renewed or, better, rectified—by her husband's death. The birth of my little grandson is now distant too, because the real present as far as Umbertino is concerned is my affection for him and his winning of it. He is not aware of this since he believes it his birthright. (Or does that small soul believe anything in general?) His present, and mine in relation to him, are merely his confident little steps, interrupted by painful moments of fear which, however, are relieved by the company of dolls when he can't have that of his mother or me, his grandfather. My present is also Augusta (poor woman!) reduced now to her animals—dogs, cats, birds —and her eternal unwellness which she hasn't the energy to cure. She does the little prescribed by Dr Raulli, but refuses to listen to me—who by superhuman effort managed to overcome a similar tendency to heart trouble—nor to Carlo, who is just out of the university and so knows the most up-to-date medicines.

Unquestionably, a great part of my present is provided by medicine. I can't recall exactly when this present began, but it has been constantly punctuated by new medicines and theories. Where now is the time when I believed I was doing all my organism required by gulping down every evening a good dose of licorice compound, or a simple bromide (powdered or liquid). Now, with Carlo's help, I command very different weapons against disease. Carlo tells me all he knows, but I, on the other hand, don't reveal everything I am imagining, because I am afraid he may not agree with me and, with his objections, may demolish the castle which I put such effort into seeking and which gives me a measure of tranquillity and security which people at my age don't normally have. A real castle it is! Carlo believes I accept all his suggestions so readily out of faith in him. Not quite! I am aware that he knows a great deal, and try to pick it up and apply it, but always with reservations. My arteries are not what they ought to be; about that there is no doubt. Last summer I reached a blood pressure of 240. Whether because of that or something else, I was very depressed altogether just then. Then generous doses of iodide and another drug, the name of which I never remember, brought the pressure down to 160, where it has remained till now . . . (I have just now interrupted my writing to measure it at the machine I keep ready on my table. It is exactly 160!). Before that, I felt threatened all the time by an apoplectic stroke, which I could feel coming nearer and nearer. The presence of death did not make me a kinder and better man, as I disliked everyone who wasn't threatened by a stroke; they had the disgustingly comfortable manner of people who sympathise, commiserate, and enjoy life.

But guided by Carlo, I even treated some organs which were in no need of help. But no doubt all organs must feel exhausted after so many years of work and are benefited by assistance. I sent them it unasked for. So often when disease strikes, the doctor sighs: "I've been called in too late!" So it is better to look ahead.

I cannot initiate cures for the liver when it shows no sign

of malfunctioning, but, all the same, I must not risk an end like that of a son of a friend of mine who, one fine day, at the age of thirty-two and in full health, turned yellow as a melon with a violent attack of jaundice and expired within forty-eight hours.

"He had never been ill," his poor father told me: "He was a giant, yet he had to die."

Many giants come to a bad end. I've noticed this and am quite happy not to be one.

But prudence is a fine thing. So every Monday I donate a pill to my liver, and this protects it from violent and sudden maladies, at least until the following Monday. I watch over my kidneys with periodic analysis, and until now they have shown no sign of malfunctioning. But I know they can stand some help. My exclusively milk diet on Tuesdays affords me a certain security for the rest of the week. It would be a fine thing if others, who never give a thought to their kidneys, should be allowed to keep them running merrily, whilst I, who make a weekly sacrifice to them, should be rewarded by a surprise like the one that befell poor Copler!

About five years ago I was disturbed by chronic bronchitis. It interfered with my sleep and every now and then had me jumping out of bed at night to spend hours sitting in an armchair. The doctor did not see fit to tell me so, but no doubt some heart trouble was involved. Raulli prescribed that I should give up smoking, lose some weight, and eat very little meat. As giving up smoking was very difficult, I tried to fulfil the prescription by giving up meat altogether. But even losing weight was not easy. At the time, I had a net weight of ninety-four kilos. In three years I succeeded in losing two kilos, so at that rate, to reach the weight Raulli wanted, another eighteen years would have been needed. But it was difficult to eat moderately when one was abstaining from meat.

And here I must confess that I really owe my loss of weight to Carlo. It was one of his first medical successes. He proposed that I should give up one of my three daily meals; and I resolved to sacrifice supper, which we Triestines take at eight in the evening, as distinguished from other Italians, who have lunch at noon and dinner at seven. Every day I fast uninterruptedly for eighteen hours.

I soon found I slept better. I felt at once that my heart, no longer assisting in digestive work, could devote every beat to filling the veins, to carrying waste matter from the organism, and, above all, to nourishing the lungs. I who had once suffered from terrible periods of insomnia—that great agitation of longing for rest and, for that very reason, not being able to procure it—would lie there quite still, calmly awaiting the approach of warmth and sleep: a genuine parenthesis in an exhausting life. Sleep after a sumptuous dinner is something quite different: the heart concentrates on digestion and neglects all its other duties.

What all this proved, in the first place, was that I was better adapted to abstinence than to moderation. It was easier not to eat supper at all than to limit the amount one eats at lunchtime and breakfast. On these occasions there were no limitations. Twice a day I could gorge myself. And there was no harm in it, because eighteen hours of autophagy followed. In the beginning, the midday meal of *pasta asciutta* and vegetables was topped off with some eggs. Then I gave up even these, not because Raulli or Carlo asked me to, but in accordance with the judicious advice of a philosopher, Herbert Spencer, who discovered some law or other to the effect that organs which developed too fast—through overnourishment —are less strong than those taking a longer time to grow. The law, naturally, pertained to children, but I am convinced that returning to it is a step forward—that even a seventy-year-old child would do well to starve his organs rather than overnourish them. Carlo, moreover, agreed with my theory, and sometimes wanted people to believe that he had formulated it himself.

In this effort to renounce supper, I received great assistance from smoking, to which, for the first time in my life, I was reconciled even in theory. The smoker can fast better than others. A good smoke numbs whatever appetite there is. It is to smoking that I believe I owe reducing my weight to eighty kilos. It is a great relief to have hygienic reasons for smoking. One smokes rather more and with a perfectly clear conscience.

At bottom, health is a truly miraculous condition. Being the result of the interworking of various organs, whose functions we never completely know (as even Carlo, who understands the whole science, including the science of our ignorance, admitted), perfect health can probably never exist. Otherwise, its termination would be even more miraculous. Moving things ought to move for ever. Why not? Isn't this the law in the heavens, where surely the same laws apply as on earth? But I know that diseases are predestined and prepared from birth. From the very beginning, some organs start out weaker than others, over-exerting themselves and driving related organs to greater effort; and wherever there is effort, fatigue results, and from it, ultimately, death.

For that reason, and only for that reason, a malady followed by death does not reveal any basic disorder in our nature. I am too ignorant to know whether in the heavens, as down here on earth, there exists the possibility of death and reproduction. All I know is that some stars, and even some planets, have less complete movements than others. It must be that a planet which does not rotate on itself is either lame, blind or hunchbacked.

But among our organs there is one that is the centre, a kind of sun in a solar system. Up until a few years ago this organ was thought to be the heart. At the moment everybody knows that our entire life turns on the sexual organs. Carlo turns up his nose at rejuvenation operations, but still, he doffs his cap when sexual organs are mentioned. He says: If the sexual organs could be rejuvenated, they would naturally rejuvenate the whole organism. This was nothing new to me. I would have known that without his telling me. But it will never come to pass. It's impossible. God only knows what the effects of monkey glands are. Perhaps a rejuvenated man on seeing a beautiful woman will be driven to climb the nearest tree. (Even so, this is a pretty juvenile act.)

One must accept the fact, Mother Nature is a maniac. That is to say, she has the reproduction mania. She maintains life within an organism so long as there is hope of its reproducing itself. Then she kills it off, and does so in the most diverse ways because of her other mania, that for remaining mysterious. She doesn't want to give herself away by always resorting to the same malady to kill off old people—a malady that would make the reason for death clear, a little tumour always in the same place, say.

I have always been very enterprising. And without resorting to an operation I decided to hoodwink Mother Nature into believing I was still fit for reproduction. So I took a mistress. It was the least disturbing affair I have ever had in my life. To begin with, I considered it neither a lapse of character nor a betrayal of Augusta. What I did feel was rather odd; it was as if taking a mistress was a decision equivalent to going to the chemist's.

Then, of course, matters complicated themselves a little. One finds out in the end that a whole person cannot be used as a medicine : or rather, another person is a complex medicine, containing a substantial proportion of poison. The episode occurred three years ago, when I was sixty-seven. I was not yet a very old man. Consequently, my heart, which was an organ of secondary importance in the affair and should not have had to figure in it, ended by taking part. And it so happened that on some days even Augusta profited from my liaison and was caressed, fondled, and rewarded, as she had been when I had had Carla. The curious thing was that it did not surprise her and that she was not even aware of the novelty. She inhabits her great calm and finds it only natural that I should occupy myself with her less than in the past; still, our present inertia does not weaken the bond between us, which is knotted with caresses and affectionate words. These caresses and words do not have to be repeated in order to endure, to exist somewhere, to remain alive always and always just as intimate. When, one day, seeking to salve my conscience, I placed two fingers underneath her chin and gazed at length

into her faithful eyes, she abandoned herself to me, offering up
her lips: "You have always stayed affectionate," she said.

At the moment I was a little taken aback. Then, examining
the past, I realised I had never in fact been so wanting in
affection as to deny my old love for her. I had even hugged
her (a little absent-mindedly) every evening before closing my
eyes in sleep.

It was somewhat difficult to find the right woman. There
was no one in the house suited for such a role; nor was I
eager to sully my own home. Still I would have done so, given
the need to hoodwink Mother Nature, to stop her thinking the
moment had arrived for my final illness, and given the enormous task of finding someone outside who would do for me, an
old man occupied with political economy. But, really, there
was no chance. The best-looking woman in the house was
Augusta herself. There was also a little fourteen-year-old girl
whom Augusta made use of for various household chores. But
I knew that if I were to accost this child, Mother Nature, not
believing me, would have struck me down at once with one of
those thunderbolts she keeps at her disposal.

There is not much point in relating how I came to find
Felicita. Out of sheer devotion to hygiene, I used, every day,
to go some distance beyond the Piazza Unità to buy myself
cigarettes, which meant a walk of half an hour or so. The shop
assistant was an old woman, but the actual owner of the shop,
who spent several hours every day there supervising, was
Felicita, a girl about twenty-four years old. At first I had the
impression she had inherited the shop; much later I learned
that she had bought it with her own money. It was there that
I came to know her.

We soon came to an understanding. She attracted me. She
was a blonde who dressed in a variety of colours, in materials
which I guessed were not expensive but always new-looking
and showy. She took pride in her beauty: the small head puffed
out on the sides with close-cropped, very curly hair, and the
elegant body, very erect, as if carried on a pole, and with a
slight backwards tilt. I noticed at once her liking for bright

colours. In her house, this taste was revealed everywhere.
Sometimes the house was not very well heated, and on one of
these occasions I took special note of the colours she was wearing: a red kerchief knotted round her head in the style of a
peasant woman, a yellow brocaded shawl round her shoulders,
a quilted apron in red, yellow, and green over her blue skirt,
and a pair of multicoloured quilted slippers on her feet. She was
a real oriental figurine; but her pale face belonged unmistak-
ably to our regions, with its eyes that scrutinised things and
people, calculating what she could get out of them.

A monthly allowance was agreed upon from the outset; and,
quite frankly, it was so high that I could not help comparing
it with regret with the much lower ones of pre-war days. And
as early as the twentieth of the month, Felicita, the dear girl,
began to talk about the stipend that was falling due, thereby
casting a cloud over a good part of the month. She was sincere, indeed transparently so. I was less so, and she never
learned that I had come to her as a result of studying medical
textbooks.

I soon forgot it too. I must say I still look back nostalgically
at that house, so humble apart from the one room furnished
with good taste and luxury corresponding to what I was
paying—very soberly coloured and dimly lighted—in which
Felicita appeared like some variegated flower.

She had a brother living in the same house—an honest,
hard-working electrician whose daily wages were more than
enough for him. He was extremely lean, but that had nothing
to do with his not being married; on the contrary, as one could
easily see, it was due to his tightfistedness. I spoke to him when
Felicita called him in to examine the fuses in our room. I discovered that brother and sister, being set on making themselves
some money as soon as possible, had become business partners.
Felicita carried on a very serious life between the tobacconist's
shop and the house, and Gastone between his repair-shop and
the house. Felicita must have been making more than Gastone,
but that did not matter, since—as I was later to learn—she
needed her brother's help. It was he who had organised the

tobacco-stall business, which was proving such a sound investment. And he was so convinced that he was leading the life
of an upright man as to speak scornfully of workers who
frittered their earnings away with never a thought for the
morrow.

All in all, we got on rather well together. The room, so
soberly and meticulously kept, smacked of a doctor's consult-
ing room. Only Felicita was a slightly sharp medicine that had
to be gulped down without the palate's having leisure to
savour it.

At the very beginning—before drawing up the agreement,
indeed, and to encourage me to do so—she threw her arms
round me and said: "You know, I don't find you repulsive,
really I don't."

It was really quite nice, because said so nicely; but it
gave me a shock. I had never really thought of myself as
repulsive. On the contrary, I had believed I was returning to
love, from which I had so long abstained through a misinterpre-
tation of the laws of hygiene, in order to surrender, to offer
myself up, to whoever wanted me. This would have been the
true health-regimen I was after; any other form would have
been incomplete and ineffectual. But despite the money I was
paying for the cure, I did not dare explain to Felicita how I
wanted her to be. And she, very frequently, in giving herself
to me, would spoil the treatment with her naïveté: "Isn't it
queer! I don't find you repulsive at all."

One day, with the brutality I am capable of on certain
occasions, I murmured gently in her ear: "Isn't it queer! I
don't find you repulsive, either." This made her giggle so much
that the cure was interrupted.

And occasionally, in my mind, I even dare to boast—so as to
encourage myself, to feel more confident, worthier, loftier,
and so as to forget having dedicated part of my life to the
effort of not being repulsive—that Felicita, in one or two brief
moments during our long relationship, actually loved me. And
looking for a genuine expression of her affection, I find it
neither in the never-changing sweetness with which she

invariably greeted me, nor in the maternal care with which she protected me from draughts, nor in the solicitude with which she once wrapped me in one of her brother's overcoats and lent me an umbrella, because a storm had blown up while I was at her place. What I remember is her murmuring, sincerely for once: "Oh, how I loathe you! You're repulsive!"

One day when as usual I was talking with Carlo about medicine, he remarked: "What you need is a girl given to gerontophilia."

Who knows? I did not confess to Carlo, but perhaps once I found and then lost just such a girl. Except that I do not believe Felicita was a thoroughgoing gerontophile. She got too much money out of me for me to think she really loved me for what I am.

She was certainly the most expensive woman I have ever known in my life. She studied me quietly with those cool, serene eyes of hers, often narrowing them to decide how far I would let myself be exploited. In the beginning, and for a long time afterwards, she was quite content with her allowance, because I, not yet a slave to habit, intimated it was all she would get. On several occasions she made a reach for my money but withdrew her hand from my pocket for fear of exposing herself to the risk of losing me. Once, though, she did bring it off. She got money out of me to buy a rather expensive fur, which I never laid eyes on. Another time, she got me to pay for an entire Parisian ensemble and then let me see it: but for one even as blind as I was, her multicoloured clothes were unforgettable and I found I had seen her in that suit before. She was an economy-minded woman who pretended to caprice only because she thought a man understood caprice in a woman more easily than avarice.

And this is how, against my will, the affair came to an end.

I used to visit her at set hours twice a week. Then, one Tuesday after I had started for her house, it occurred to me half-way there that I would be better off on my own. I returned to my study and quietly devoted myself to Beethoven's *Ninth Symphony* on the gramophone.

On Wednesday I should still not have felt such a strong craving for Felicita; it was really my avarice that drove me to her. I was paying a substantial allowance, and somehow, by not taking advantage of what was due to me, I felt as if I were paying too much. One must remember that when I undergo treatment, I pursue it conscientiously with the most scientific exactitude. Only by dint of doing so, can one decide, at the end, if the cure was a good or a bad one.

As fast as my legs would carry me, I was in that room which I believed to be ours. For the moment it belonged to another. Fat old Misceli, a man about my age, was sitting in an easy chair in a corner while Felicita lounged comfortably on the couch, concentrating on the flavour of a long and very choice cigarette—a brand which was not to be had in her shop. Essentially, it was the very same position in which Felicita and I found ourselves when we were left together, the only difference being that, whereas Misceli was not smoking, I joined Felicita in doing so.

"What can I do for you?" Felicita asked icily, studying the fingernails of the hand that was holding the cigarette aloft.

Words failed me. Presently I found it easier to speak, because, to tell the truth, I did not feel the least resentment towards Misceli. This fat man, who was old as I, looked considerably older because of his tremendous weight. He eyed me warily over the top of the shiny spectacles he wore perched on the tip of his nose. I always feel other old men to be older than I am.

"Oh, Misceli," I said forthrightly, fully resolved not to make a scene, "It's a long time since we've seen each other."

And I offered him my hand. He laid his ham of a hand in mine without returning my clasp. Still he said nothing. He was indeed showing himself—older than me.

By now, with the objectivity of the experienced man, I understood very clearly that my position and Misceli's were identical. I felt that, this being the case, we were in no position to resent each other. After all, our meeting here amounted to no more than a collision on the pavement. However painful it may be, one goes on one's way mumbling "Sorry."

With this thought, the gentleman innate in me asserted itself. I even felt called upon to make Felicita's situation more tolerable. And I said to her, "Signorina, I must have a hundred packets of 'Sport' cigarettes, top quality, as I have to give someone a present. The very freshest ones, if possible. The shop's a little too far so I took the liberty of dropping in here for an instant.

Felicita stopped examining her nails and became very gracious. She even got up and walked with me to the door. In a low voice, with intense reproach, she managed to say: "Why didn't you come yesterday?" And then, quickly, "And what have you come today for?"

I was offended. It was intolerable to be limited to fixed days, particularly at the price I was paying. I relieved myself by giving vent to my annoyance: "I've only come here today to let you know that I never want to see you any more! We're not going to see each other again!"

She stared at me astonished, and to look at me better stepped away from me, leaning even further back than usual. To be frank it was an odd pose, but it lent her a certain grace, that of a self-assured person capable of maintaining the most difficult equilibrium.

"As you like," she said shrugging. Then, to be sure she had understood me perfectly, just as she opened the door, she asked me: "Then we're not going to see any more of each other?"

And she searched my face.

"Certainly not!" said I a little querulously.

I was just starting down the stairs when fat old Misceli came bumbling to the door, yelling, "Wait! wait! I'm coming with you too. I've already told the Signorina how many 'Sports' I need. A hundred. Just like you."

We descended the stairs together while Felicita closed the door after a long pause, a pause that gave me pleasure.

We went down the long slope that leads into the Piazza

Unità, slowly, careful where we placed our feet. Lumbering along on the slope, he certainly appeared older than I. Once he even stumbled and almost fell. I helped him promptly. He did not thank me. He was panting a little, and the effort to be made on the slope was still not over. Because of that, and only because of that, he did not speak. This is borne out by the fact that when we reached the level area behind the town hall, he relaxed and started talking.

"I never smoke 'Sports'," he said. "But working-class people always prefer them. I have to give a present to my carpenter. And I wanted to buy the good ones Signorina Felicita always stocks." Now that he was talking he could only take short steps. He stopped altogether to rummage about in a trouser pocket. He pulled out a gold cigarette case, pressed a little button and the case flew open: "Would you like one?" he asked. "They're denicotinised."

I accepted one and also stopped, in order to light it. He stood there stock-still, waiting to put the case back in his pocket. And I thought, "At least she could have given me a more virile rival." In fact, I handled myself better than he both on the slope and on the flat. Compared with him, I was really a youngster. He even smoked denicotinised cigarettes, which have no flavour. I was more a man because, though I had always tried not to smoke, I had never stooped to the poltoonery of denicotinised cigarettes.

As God would have it, we arrived at the gate of the Tergesteo[1] where we had to part. Misceli was now talking about other things: affairs on the Exchange, on which he was an expert. He seemed a bit excited to me, even a little distraught. In a word, it seemed as though he were talking without listening to himself. He was like me, who was not listening to *him* but studying him instead, trying to guess exactly what he was *not* saying.

I did not want to part from him without having tried to find out what was really in his mind. With this in view, I

[1] *The Tergesteo*, a building close to the Bourse, containing offices and public rooms, was the favourite rendezvous of Triestine businessmen.

began by giving myself away completely. I burst out: "Felicita is nothing but a whore!"

Misceli provided a fresh spectacle, that of his embarrassment. His fat lower jaw began to move like that of a ruminant. Was this what he did when he didn't know what to say? Presently he said: "She doesn't seem so to me. She has excellent 'Sports'."

He wanted to prolong this stupid comedy for ever.

I became angry: "Then, in other words, you intend to go on seeing Signorina Felicita?"

Another pause. His jaw jutted out, swung to the left, returned to the right before fixing itself. Then, for the first time betraying an impulse to laugh, he said: "I'll be going back as soon as I need some 'Sports' again."

I laughed, myself. But I wanted further explanations: "Well, why did you leave her today?"

He hesitated, and in his darkened eyes, focused on the far end of the road, I detected signs of great sadness.

"I'm a little superstitious," he said. "When I'm interrupted in something, I believe in immediately recognising the hand of Providence, and drop everything I'm doing. Once I had to go to Berlin on important business but I went no further than Sessana, after the train was held up there for several hours, I don't know exactly why. I don't believe one should force things—especially at our age."

This was still not enough for me, and I asked: "You didn't mind when you saw me going to Signorina Felicita for 'Sports' too, did you?"

He answered with such decisiveness that his jaw did not have time to swivel: "What difference could it make to me? Me jealous? Certainly not! We two are old. We're old. There's no harm in our making love occasionally; but we mustn't become jealous, that way one starts to look ridiculous. We ought never to get jealous. Listen to me, don't ever let people see you jealous; they would laugh at you."

His words sound friendly enough on paper, but in fact they were said in a tone full of anger and scorn. His fat face flaming, he approached me; being smaller than myself, he looked up at me as though trying to find the weakest point to strike. Why was he angry with me at the very moment of preaching against jealousy? What else had I done to him? Perhaps he was angry with me because I had held his train up at Sessana when he should have been arriving in Berlin.

But I was not jealous. I should, however, have liked to know how much he paid Felicita monthly. I felt if I could know—as seemed fitting to me—that he paid more than I did, I would have been satisfied.

But I didn't have time to investigate. All of a sudden Misceli became gentler and addressed himself to my discretion. His gentleness changed into a threat when he reminded me we were in each other's hands. I reassured him: I was married too and was aware of the danger of an imprudent word from either of us.

"Oh," he said, with an offhand gesture, "I don't ask for discretion because of my wife. There are certain things that haven't interested her for years. But I know you're under Dr Raulli's care too. He threatened to leave me if I didn't follow his prescriptions—if I drank just one glass of wine, if I smoked more than ten cigarettes a day, even denicotinised ones, if I didn't give up . . . well, all the rest. He says that at our age a man's body maintains its equilibrium only because it can't decide in which direction to collapse. So you shouldn't suggest to it which part to choose, because then the decision would be easy." He went on, self-pityingly: "After all, it's easy prescribing for someone else, saying don't do this or that or the other. One might reply that rather than live like that it would be better to face dying a few months sooner."

He stayed with me a few moments longer, questioning me about my health. I told him I had once reached a blood pressure of 240, which pleased him enormously, because he had reached only 220. With one foot on the step that leads into the Tergesteo, he gave me a friendly wave and added: "Now, please, don't breathe a word about it."

I was obsessed for some days by Raulli's rhetorical figure of an old man's body that stays on its feet because it does not know in which direction to collapse. Of course, when the old doctor spoke of a "part" he meant *organ*. And "equilibrium" also had its meaning for him. Raulli must have known what he was talking about. With us old men, health can only mean a gradual and simultaneous weakening of all organs. Woe to us if one of them should lag behind, that is to say, stay too young! I suspect that then their interdependence changes into a conflict, and that the weak organs get bullied, with magnificent results for the general economy, one can imagine. Misceli's intervention must, therefore, have been desired by Providence, who guards over my life and even sent word how I was to behave by way of that mouth with the wandering jaw.

And I returned, pensively, to my gramophone. In the *Ninth Symphony* I encountered my organs again, collaborating and quarrelling. Working in concert during the first movements— particularly in the *scherzo*, when even the tympani, with their two notes, are allowed to synthetise what all the instruments are murmuring round them. The joy of the last movement seemed rebellion to me; crude, with a strength which is violence, with only slight brief gestures of regret and hesitation. Not for nothing does the human voice, the least rational of all sounds in nature, enter into the last movement. I admit that on other occasions I had interpreted this symphony otherwise —as the most intense representation of harmony between the most divergent of forces, into which, finally, even the human voice is received and fused. But that day the symphony, played by the same records, appeared as I say.

"Farewell, Felicita," I whispered when the music faded away. There was no need to think of her any longer.

She was not worth risking a sudden collapse for. There were so many medical theories in the world that it was hard to be ruled by them. Those rascally doctors' only contribution to life was to make it more difficult. The simplest things are too complicated. To abstain from drinking alcohol is a prescription of self-evident logic. Yet all the same, it is known that alcohol can sometimes have curative properties. Must I wait for the doctor, then, to allow myself the comfort of this potent medicine? There is no doubt that death sometimes results from a brief and sudden caprice on an organ's part, or a casual and momentary coincidence of different weaknesses. I mean, it would be momentary if it were not followed by death. Things must be so managed as to make the coincidence remain momentary. So aid has to be at hand, to stave off the cramps produced by over-exertion or the collapse induced by inertia. So why wait for the doctor, who comes running merely to scribble out his bill? Only I am able to tell in time when I need something, by a feeling of discomfort. Doctors, unfortunately, have not studied what can help in a case like that. I take various things, therefore, for instance a purgative and a sip of wine; and then I study myself. I might need something else: a glass of milk—with a drop of digitalis. And all taken in the most minute quantities, as recommended by the great Hahnemann. The mere presence of these minute quantities is enough to produce the reactions necessary for the activation of life, just as though an organ wants, not so much to be stimulated, but to be reminded. Seeing a drop of calcium, it exclaims: "Oh, look! I'd forgotten. I'm supposed to be working."

That is what was fatal about Felicita. It was impossible to take her in doses.

That evening Felicita's brother came to call on me. On seeing him I was seized with panic, particularly as Augusta herself showed him to my study. Fearing what he had to say to me, I was very happy when Augusta promptly withdrew.

He unknotted a handkerchief from which he took a parcel: one hundred packets of "Sports" cigarettes. He broke them down into five stacks, each of twenty packets, and it was therefore easy to verify the quantity. Then he had me feel how soft each packet was. They had been selected one by one from a large stock. He was sure I would be pleased.

And I certainly was pleased, feeling quite reassured, after having been so frightened. I at once paid the 160 lire I owed him and cheerfully thanked him. Cheerfully, because in fact I felt like laughing. A queer woman, Felicita. She might be jilted, but she didn't neglect her tobacconist's shop.

But the pale, lean man, after stuffing the lire he had received into his pocket, still made no move to leave. He hardly seemed to be Felicita's brother. I had seen him before, on other occasions, but better dressed. Now he was without a collar, and his clothes, though neat enough, were utterly threadbare. Strange that he felt he even had to have a special hat for workdays; the one he had on was positively filthy and misshapen from long wear.

He looked at me intently, hesitating to speak. It seemed that his slightly sombre look, rather out of place in the brightly-lit room, was inviting me to guess what was on his mind. When he finally spoke, his look became even more imploring, so much so that it almost seemed like a threat. Intense supplications border on threats. I can very well understand that there are peasants who end up punishing the images they have prayed to by hurling them under their beds.

Finally, in a steady voice, he said to me: "Felicita says we have reached the tenth of the month."

I glanced at the calendar, from which I tore a sheet every day, and said: "She's quite right. We *have* reached the tenth. There's no doubt about it."

"But then," he said hesitantly, "you owe her for the whole month."

A second before he spoke I understood why he had got me to look at the calendar. I believe I blushed at the moment of discovering that between brother and sister everything was frank and honest where money was concerned. The only thing that really surprised me was the out-and-out request for the whole month's allowance. I was, in fact, not sure whether I might not be owed something. In my relations with Felicita, I had not kept very accurate accounts. But hadn't I always paid in advance? So shouldn't the last payment cover this fraction of the month? And I sat there, with my mouth somewhat agape, having to look into those strange eyes, trying to determine whether they were imploring or threatening. It is precisely the man of wide and long experience like myself who does not know how to behave: knowing as he does that a single word of his, a single deed, may lead to the most unforeseen consequences. One has only to read history to learn that causes and effects can stand in the most peculiar relations with each other. During my hesitation I took out my wallet and counted and sorted my money, so as not to mistake a 100-lira note for a 500 one. And when I had counted the notes, I gave them over. Thus the thing was done while I thought I was merely gaining time. And I said to myself: "I'll pay now and think later."

Felicita's brother himself had obviously stopped thinking about it, for his eye was no longer fixed on me and lost all its intentness. He put the money in a different pocket from the one in which he had deposited the 160 lire. He kept accounts and monies separate. He bowed to me, saying: "Good evening, Signor," and left. But in a moment or two he was back, because he had forgotten another parcel similar to the one he had given me. By way of excusing himself for returning, he said to me: "This is another hundred packets of 'Sports' I have to deliver to another gentleman."

They were, of course, for poor Misceli, who couldn't stand them either. I smoked all of mine, however, except for some packets I gave to my chauffeur Fortunato. When I have paid for something, sooner or later I finish up using it. It is a proof of my sense of thrift. And every time I had that taste of musty straw in my mouth I remembered Felicita and her brother vividly. By thinking about it, I finally remembered with absolute certainty that I had, in fact, not paid the allowance in advance. After thinking I had been cheated on a serious scale, I was relieved to find they had only been paid for twenty days extra.

I think I must have returned to see Felicita once again, before the twenty days I had paid for had elapsed, and purely because of my famous sense of economy—the habit of thrift which made me smoke up my "Sports". I said to myself: "Now that

I have paid, I'd like to risk just once more—for the last time—the danger of showing my organism which direction it ought to collapse in. Just once! It will never notice the chance it's getting."

The door to her flat opened just as I was about to ring. Startled, in the darkness, I saw her pale, lovely little face as though in a visor, clamped in a hat that covered her head down to her ears and the nape of the neck. A solitary blonde curl stole from the cloche down her forehead. I knew that at this time she usually went to the tobacconist's shop to supervise the more complicated part of its book-keeping. But I had hoped to persuade her to wait for the short time I needed with her.

In the dark, she did not immediately recognise me. In a questioning tone she uttered a name, neither mine nor Misceli's, which I couldn't make out. When she did recognise me, she extended her hand friendlily, without a trace of coldness and with a certain curiosity. I clasped her cold hand in both of mine and grew bold. She let her hand lie still, but drew her head back. Never had that pole within her arched back so far —so far that I felt like releasing her hand and seizing her by the waist, if only to steady her.

And that far-away face, adorned with the single curl, studied me. Or was it actually studying me? Wasn't it really studying a problem which she had brought on herself and which demanded an immediate solution, then and there, on the stairs?

"It's impossible just at the moment," she said, after a long pause.

She was still looking at me. Then every shadow of hesitancy vanished.

She stood there, that lovely body of hers stiff in its precarious position, immobile, her little face pale and serious below the yellow ringlet; but slowly, just as if she were acting upon a serious resolution, she withdrew her hand.

"Yes!—it's impossible," she said again.

It was repeated to convince me that she was still considering the matter to see if there might be some way to satisfy me, but apart from this repetition there was no other evidence that she was really thinking about it. She had already made her final decision.

And then she said to me, "You might return on the first of the month, if you can . . . I'll see . . . I'll think about it."

It is only recently, only since I have put this account of my liaison with Felicita down on paper, that I have become objective enough to judge both of us fairly. I had come there to assert my rights to the few days outstanding on my subscription. She, on the other hand, was letting me know that by my renunciation I had lost my rights. I think if she had proposed that I there and then paid a fresh subscription I would have been less upset. I am sure I would not have run away. At the moment I was bent on love, and at my age, one is rather like crocodile on dry land—it takes a long time to change direction. I would willingly have paid for the whole month, though I was only going to make love for one last time.

Instead, things being as they were, I fell into a fury. I could not find words; indeed, I could hardly breathe. I said : "Ouf !" with intense indignation. I had the impression that I had said something articulate, and I even waited there for a moment or two as if I thought that my "ouf"—a cry meant to wound and give an outlet to my profound chagrin—called for a reply. But neither she nor I had anything more to say. I started down the stairs. A few steps down, I turned to look at her again. Perhaps on that pale face there would now be some sign contradicting such hard-hearted selfishness, such cold calculation. I could not see her face. She was completely absorbed in locking the flat, which she had to leave unoccupied for some hours.

Once again I said : "Ouf !" but not so loudly as to be heard by her. I said it to all the world, to society, to our institutions, and to Mother Nature—to everything that had permitted me to find myself on that staircase in that situation.

It was my last love. Now that the whole affair has been fitted into the past, I no longer consider it so disgraceful; for Felicita

—with that blonde hair of hers, that pallid face, the slender nose and inscrutable eyes, and the paucity of her words, only seldom betraying the iciness of her heart—Felicita was worth regretting. But after her there was no room for another mistress. She had educated me. Until then, whenever I was with a woman for more than ten minutes, I used to feel hope and desire surging in my heart. Of course, I wanted to conceal them both, but I wanted still more to let them grow, so as to feel an intenser sense of life and of belonging to life. And the only way to make them grow was to express them in words. There's no telling how many times I must have been laughed at. It was Felicita who educated me in my present role of old man. And I can still scarcely bring myself to realise that now, in the sphere of love, I am worth only as much as I pay.

My ugliness is ever before my eyes. This morning, on waking up, I studied the position I found my mouth in the moment I opened my eyes. My lower jaw was sagging on the side I had been lying on, and I felt my tongue out of place too, and stiff and swollen.

I thought of Felicita, whom I very often think of, with desire and hatred. And at that moment I murmured: "She's right."

"Who's right?" asked Augusta who was dressing.

And I promptly replied: "A certain Misceli, whom I ran into yesterday; he told me that he doesn't understand why one is born, lives and grows old—and he's right."

Thus I had really told her everything, without compromising myself in the least.

And until now no one has ever taken Felicita's place. Nevertheless, I still seek to deceive Mother Nature, who is keeping an eye on me to liquidate me as soon as it's apparent that I can no longer reproduce. With wise dosages, in Hahnemann's prescribed quantities, I take a little of the medicine every day. I watch women passing by; I follow them with my eyes, trying to discover in their legs something more than a mere motor apparatus, so that I may again feel the craving to stop them and fondle them. Even here, the doses are becoming more sparing than Hahnemann or I would choose. That is, I have to control my eyes lest they betray what they are looking for, and so, as you will understand, the medicine only rarely works. One can do without actual caresses, and still experience the feeling; but one can't feign total indifference without risking chilling one's own emotions.

And having written this, I can better understand my adventure with Signorina Dondi.[1] I bowed to her so as to be able to make some kind of gesture to her, and feel her beauty more fully. It is the destiny of old men to make pretty bows.

One should not believe that such ephemeral relations, entered upon merely to rescue oneself from death, do not also leave their mark, or help to embellish or trouble one's life, just like my affairs with Carla and Felicita. Sometimes—very occasionally—they leave an indelible memory. I remember a girl sitting opposite me in a tram. She left me with a memory. We reached a certain intimacy, because I gave her a name: Amphora. She did not have a very striking face, but her eyes, luminous and rather round ones, stared at everything with great curiosity and something of a little girl's inquisitiveness. She might have been over twenty, but I would not have been surprised if, for fun, she had tugged the pigtails of the child sitting next to her. I can't say whether because she had an uncommon figure, or because her dress made her appear to have one, but from the waist up her slender body was like some graceful amphora on its base. I was greatly taken by that bosom of hers, and I said to myself, so as to deceive Nature, who had her eye on me: "It's clearly not time for me to die yet; for if this girl wanted me to, I would still be ready to procreate."

My face must have taken an odd look as I gazed at the amphora. But I won't admit that it was the look of a lecher, for I was thinking of death. Nevertheless, others interpreted it as ill-concealed lust. As I now noticed, the girl, who must have belonged to a well-to-do family, was accompanied by

[1] See p. 12 *et seq.* The text reads, literally "old Dandi."

an old maidservant, who got off the tram with her. And it was this old woman who, as she passed me, looked at me and whispered: "Old lecher."

She had called me old. She was summoning death!

I said to her: "Old fool!"

But she went her way without replying.

REGENERATION

A COMEDY IN THREE ACTS

Translated by P. N. Furbank

DRAMATIS PERSONAE

GIOVANNI CHIERICI, an old man in his seventies
ANNA, his wife
EMMA RICCA, their widowed daughter
UMBERTINO (10 years old), Emma's son
GUIDO CALACCI, Giovanni's nephew
ENRICO BIGGIONI
DOCTOR RAULLI
Signor BONCINI
RITA, the maid
FORTUNATO, the chauffeur

Act I

Dining-room in the home of GIOVANNI CHIERICI. High
summer. One door upstage centre; one to the left of
spectator. To the right, a window admitting blinding
sunshine. There is a dining-table towards the back of the
stage and a little work-table near the proscenium
arch.

EMMA, dressed entirely in black, is working at the
table on a piece of material, also black. ANNA, likewise
dressed in black, is looking out of the window.

ANNA (shouts): Rita! Rita! Come here at once. (She cranes
her head out of the window.) Quick! Quick! Oh the horrible brute! He's got them in his mouth. It's all over. (She
rushes to the upstage door and then stops.) It's no good. I'm
too late. (Goes back to window.) Poor little things! It's all
my fault, all my fault.

RITA enters

RITA: Did you call, madam?
ANNA: I've been shouting and calling for you for at least an
hour, and now you come, looking all innocence. . . . It's
all over, in the garden. They've all been eaten.
RITA: Eaten? Who?
ANNA (almost in tears): The little birds. The poor little sparrows. And it was as if I'd seen them growing in front of my
eyes. They had got so big, they filled the whole nest. It
almost looked as if the nest itself had sprouted wings. I used
to watch them through the shutters. I used to spy on them,

and they never realised. They were so trusting—with me only a few inches away. I felt as if I were in the nest too. Even the mother never noticed me. Except that when we raised our voices, they lowered theirs.

RITA : Who interfered with the shutters? You said no one was to touch them.

ANNA : I did myself. It was my own absent-mindedness. I can't blame anyone else. All the same, there must have been something wrong with the mother's instincts. What could have induced her to build her nest there, between the shutter and the wall? It's Giovanni who's really to blame. He doesn't like the shutters ever to be closed in this room. Not even at night; because this room gets the first sunlight in the morning, and he comes and sits here. He believes the sun brings health and strength. And so the sparrows thought the shutter was part of the wall. Everything conspired against that poor nest. The sun was too fierce for me, so I thought I'd take advantage of Giovanni's absence and enjoy a little shade. I ran to open the shutters, forgetting what I was doing. Idiot I was! Poor little things! The nest split in two, and there was the mother inside it. She made a noise then, when she was flying away, the stupid creature! She didn't make a sound before, when I leaned out of the window—just let me get on with it.

RITA : There goes the cat, licking his lips.

ANNA : Poor beast! It's the way he's made. (*Clasping her hands in prayer.*) Dear Lord! From Thy hands there spring little birds, who for many weeks cannot fly, and likewise cats, born to lie in ambush for them. Could the tragedy have been prevented? No, no, certainly not. Otherwise Thou, who canst do all things, wouldst have prevented it. (*Leaning out of the window.*) You're right, he certainly is pleased with himself.

RITA : Who?

ANNA : The cat. (*Sighing, and addressing both* RITA *and* EMMA.) How lucky you are not to like animals. It's a strange muddle of a world they live in.

EMMA : You dare say that to me? (*She begins to weep, silently.*)

ANNA (*embarrassed*): Excuse me, I wasn't thinking what I was saying. (*Goes over to* EMMA *and puts her arms round her.*) Forgive me.

EMMA (*between sobs*): Animals are always there. But when humans die, they are dead for ever.

ANNA : But the little birds are dead too.

EMMA : Yes, but the cat's alive, and that consoles you.

ANNA (*timidly*): If you look for consolations . . . you find them. You ought to find a consolation too . . . for our sake, and for the sake of your child.

EMMA (*still in tears*): I can't. He was so young, so strong. And along came fate . . . and struck him down without mercy . . . humiliating him before it did so, making him look like an old man.

ANNA : Poor wretch! We feel sorry for him too, when we think of him. Last night, for instance, as Giovanni was coming to bed, he said to me: "See, here we are in our warm bed, and he's out there, under the cold earth." Neither of us said any more. We were both thinking, so sadly, of the dear departed one.

EMMA : I don't have to wait till bed-time to think of him. I think of him all day long—when it's sunny, and when it's grey and cloudy too. Whatever the day's like, one has the air to enjoy, one can move and be active; and I think how unjust it is—I still have my freedom and he's been robbed of his.

ANNA : You must be fair, dearest. What point would there be in our sharing your grief all day long? Wouldn't it make it worse?

EMMA (*ironically*): So you try not to think of him, so as to spare *me*?

ANNA : Well, we certainly don't want to add to your unhappiness.

EMMA (*angrily*): You couldn't add to it. It's too terrible. No, the truth is, you're happy with your cat and your sparrows and your games of patience; and Papa has his endless cures

and his diet and his two sleeps a day. You've no time to spare
for me or for Valentino.

ANNA (*choking with impatience*): You must permit us to live
our own life! And as for Papa, at his age, no doubt he knows
how to look after himself best. Do you want him to die too?

EMMA (*still in tears*): I want no one to die. I realise things must
be as they are. It's quite right for Papa to worry about
himself. If only Valentino had done the same!

ANNA: It would have made no difference. Guido says . . .

EMMA: What does Guido know about it?

ANNA: He has studied medicine. And Dr Raulli himself
says . . .

EMMA: When someone dies, the doctors always say it was
bound to happen. In fact, according to them the real proof
that someone had to die is that he does so. But where was it
written that a young man like Valentino had to die? Oh
he died, he died all right! There's no disputing it. And it's
shameful, shameful!

RITA: Poor madam. It was a real tragedy. When I came to the
house he was quite a handsome young man, and a few
months later he was really ugly, so ugly you couldn't bear
to look at him.

EMMA (*furious*): Ugly? No! He was never ugly.

RITA: I don't mean ugly. I mean plain, poorly-looking, not so
handsome.

ANNA: Ugly, no . . . he was never really ugly.

EMMA: No indeed. Physical decay made him look like an angel,
a heart-stricken angel. That gentle expression of his—his
disease made it shine all the brighter.

RITA: Just what I meant to say, madam. I don't know how to
express things like you.

EMMA: Which means that you should watch your tongue.
(*She gets up, dropping the piece of material she has been
working on.* RITA *rushes to retrieve it*, EMMA *says drily*)
Thank you. (*To* ANNA) I shall give up this sewing. I thought
it would take my mind off things. But it makes me more
unhappy than ever, having to forget my unhappiness.

ANNA : Perhaps it's because the material is black.

EMMA : It's because it isn't black enough! No! Even work is to be denied me. I will give this material to my dressmaker. I'll go tomorrow before breakfast. Now I'm going up to dress.

Exit left.

ANNA : I don't want to speak ill of that daughter of mine, and it distresses me to see her so unhappy. But she's driving us mad. We're almost ashamed to live, for according to her we should all be in tears the whole day long. The most innocent pastimes should be forbidden us.

RITA : I'm sorry I said poor Signor Valentino was ugly. I wasn't thinking . . .

ANNA : He was as ugly as sin. With his mouth hanging perpetually half-open, like an imbecile's . . . (*She imitates him.*)

RITA : Just what I said; but I'm sorry I did. It's always safe to say a dead person was good-looking. Even Fortunato would let me say that.

ANNA : What we need is a little frankness. For her own good. So much mourning, so much tragedy . . . so much dressing-up. She even begrudges me my poor animals. She says animals are always there. How could anyone be so stupid— at the very moment when those poor little sparrows had tumbled out of their nests to a horrible death? She will grow old too, and her son will treat her as she's treating me, imposing his own sorrows on her, as if there weren't enough of them in the world, and imposing his own pleasures too, perhaps—in fact, making her live his life. When that happens, she'll turn to animals too.

RITA : I love them already. And little birds as well. All pretty and fluttering at home—the dear little things. And made into a nice pie, like we used to.

ANNA : For shame! Eating little birds!

RITA : Fortunato loves them too, fried in a little butter. I'm supposed to share my future husband's tastes.

ANNA : And meanwhile you quarrel like savages. I heard you

yesterday in the kitchen. I didn't interfere, as I thought you were so near marriage you could be regarded as man and wife, and you had no home to quarrel in comfort in. All the same, you should show a little respect, and keep your voices down. It's a good thing Giovanni's a bit deaf.

RITA: I wasn't the one who was doing the shouting. I was being shouted at. It was Fortunato, he's so madly jealous. There was I, standing there quiet and patient, waiting for the storm to pass.

ANNA: Who is he jealous of?

RITA: Signor Guido.

ANNA: Guido? He must be mad. Guido's only a boy. Isn't he younger than you?

RITA: Two months, yes.

ANNA: What can Fortunato be thinking of? Guido has other things to think about. He has to study.

RITA: And I've got so much to do too.

ANNA (suspiciously): Sly little creature! So Fortunato's right?

RITA: No, it's a lie, you mustn't listen to him. I'm fond of Fortunato, but his way of going on makes me so angry, I often feel like leaving him. I like a bit of fun, you know. But I'm a good girl at heart.

ANNA: May I enquire what sort of thing you regard as "fun"? There are some things no good girl should think of as fun.

RITA: My idea is, when people are good, there's no need for them to take anything seriously.

ANNA (vehemently): No, that's wrong! That's wrong!

RITA: I know, older people don't like you to laugh at anything. My mother talks just like you. Fortunato and I used to laugh together to begin with. Then he got serious—and I was delighted. For a moment, I agreed with Mother. Then he got too serious. And especially with me. He hasn't the courage to quarrel with Signor Guido, seeing that he's Master's nephew—he's too worried about that cottage you're going to give us. So he takes it out of me.

ANNA: But what do you get up to with Guido?

RITA: We just laugh and gossip and have a joke. Nothing

serious, nothing serious at all, I swear to you. I love Fortunato. But haven't I the right to listen to the nice things the grocer's boy has to say to me? And the serious things—which make me laugh—that Signor Guido has to say?

ANNA: Ah, so he says serious things to you, does he?

RITA: No, *scientific* things, I should have said. He improves my mind. Yesterday he said to me, wasn't it strange: the human face is such a beautiful thing, and the two halves of it, from right to left, are so alike, whereas from below, the two halves—the brain part and the one underneath, I forget what it's called—aren't in the least alike.

ANNA: So the rascal got the conversation round to your head?

RITA: No he didn't. That's to say, he talked about my head because it's a human head like anyone else's. It made me laugh a lot; and Fortunato heard, because he came into the kitchen unexpectedly. That was all there was to it. I swear that was all.

ANNA: What was Guido doing in the kitchen?

RITA: He wanted a light for his cigarette.

ANNA: Well, then, it's quite simple. You must make sure there's always a full match-box in this room, and that will be the end of it.

RITA: Wouldn't it be simpler to tell Fortunato that he mustn't shout at me in the kitchen, or anywhere in the house? Then we'd have peace and quiet all week, except on Sunday, when I walk out with him.

ANNA (*drawing* RITA *to herself and looking into her eyes*): Tell me, little girl—with your short skirts and your short hair—don't you realise you're endangering your marriage? Don't you realise it means you don't love Fortunato?

RITA: Don't say that, madam. I love him very much when he's at the steering-wheel. And I admire him then, too. He's master of the whole road. So sometimes he *can* be a master, like you and Signor Giovanni and Signor Guido. And he's a serious man, so he'll be good to grow old with. Mama always says I must think of the future. But you can do that and still have a laugh at things, can't you?

ANNA: There are many things one can laugh at. But you shouldn't do your laughing with Guido. Life isn't easy, you know—either for you or for us. If Fortunato gives you up, I don't know what we shall do. We've already had the cottage in the garden fitted up for you. My husband and I are fond of you—we love your dear cheerful little face. But we need a chauffeur too.

RITA: Don't be frightened, madam. I honestly think Fortunato can't do without me now. So you can rest in peace on that score.

ANNA: All the same, I don't find your way of talking very reassuring. In fact, if I had heard you talk like this sooner, I wouldn't have put the idea of the cottage in my husband's head. A house is a thing with solid foundations, meant for solid families. We never talked like that when we were young.

RITA: I know. And I expect I'll say the same thing myself when I'm old.

ANNA: You're an impatient hussy. (*There is the sound of a bell.*)

RITA: Forgive me, madam. I didn't mean any harm. I realise, when you're old, you want everyone to act like old people.

ANNA: What a lot there is in that little head of yours. Yes, it's quite true, we old people love peace and quiet, not vulgar din and disorder, nor . . . sorrows unduly prolonged. All the same, we do think about the young. We've had an extra room built in your house, in case there are babies.

RITA: There won't be any babies. At least not to begin with. That's one thing Fortunato and I are agreed upon. What we'll do with the nursery is to put a gramophone in it. A gramophone only cries when it's wound up.

ANNA (*indignantly*): I've never heard of such a thing! Is that how you talk when you're together? Coming to an agreement not to have babies. It's as bad as coming to an agreement to have them. It's quite indecent. And in my house, too!

RITA (*disconcerted*): We discussed it outside, not in the house, I swear.

Three long rings on the bell.

ANNA: Surely that's someone at the door. Isn't Fortunato there?

RITA (*runs over to the window*): Fortunato! Hoi! Wake up. Can't you hear someone's ringing?

FORTUNATO (*shouting from the garden*): If you can hear it, why can't you answer it?

RITA (*indignantly*): I haven't the slightest intention of doing your work for you.

FORTUNATO: Who says it *is* my work?

ANNA (*rushing over to the window*): Have I got to answer the door myself?

RITA (*still at the window*): Come on Fortunato, show a bit of speed. When you've done it, we can go into whose work it was.

ANNA: Will you be quiet? Aren't you ashamed of yourself? (*She tries to be angry but subsides into laughter.*) That's good. That's really very good. I must tell Giovanni.

RITA: Ever since he's got so jealous, he won't do anything for me any more. But he wants to marry me all the same. How shall we get on if he won't work? Perhaps he'll get used to jealousy in the end. The master says one gets used to anything, even old age. . . . It's Signor Biggioni, Madam, the friend of poor Signor Valentino.

ANNA: He will be wanting to see Emma. She is getting dressed to go out. Will you tell her?

Exit RITA left. Enter ENRICO BIGGIONI.

ENRICO: Good morning! I was just passing by, and as I had something to give Signora Emma, I thought I would step up for a moment. I've only got a quarter of an hour—in fact not even that, as I haven't brought the car and I'll have to go back into town on foot.

ANNA: Do sit down. I've told them to tell Emma. She will be down in a moment.

ENRICO (*cheerfully*): Marvellous day, isn't it? I hope Signora Emma will go out and enjoy herself a little.

ANNA: Enjoy herself! She is going out, but only to go and see her dressmaker, and then she'll come straight home.

ENRICO: She would be better for a little change of air. Why doesn't she go with her father and Umbertino on their daily walk? I saw them a few days ago. They were seeing how fast they could walk. I followed them for a bit, and I heard Umbertino say to his grandfather: "It does you good to walk, Grandpa, and today you're really going to have to." They were practically running. I said "hullo" to the child and he nodded back, but he didn't say a word.—As for the old gentleman, he gave me a vague sort of look and stood aside for me to pass. I don't think he recognised me. And yet he sees me every day.

ANNA: Giovanni sometimes is a little absent-minded. He has always been like it, having so much to think about with his business affairs. And now he hasn't got those to think about any more, all that's left is the absent-mindedness.

Enter RITA.

RITA: Signora Emma says she sends Signor Biggioni her kindest respects but begs him to excuse her if she doesn't see him. She has a letter to write, and then she has to go out.

ENRICO: She was writing a letter yesterday too. She seems to have one to write every day. I just wanted to say good-morning to her and give her some letters from her husband that she asked me for. I was delighted for her to have them. But if she doesn't want them after all, then that's that. Look—here they are—they're all the letters I ever received from Valentino.

ANNA (*extending her hand*): If you like I'll give them to her myself.

ENRICO (*he is on the point of giving her the letters and then thinks better of it*): It will be better if I give them to her.

There is something I want to explain. This one is the only letter I had from him after he got married. No, it's better if I give them to her personally. (*He sits down.*) It's terribly hot today.

ANNA: Please make yourself at home.

ENRICO (*speaking on impulse*): Has Signora Emma ever told you I want to marry her?

ANNA (*startled*): No, never! What a strange girl she is. She spends her time telling me disagreeable things, and yet she's never mentioned that. (*Cheerfully, and full of curiosity.*) What did she say when you proposed?

ENRICO: She didn't seem to hear. And now she has heard of my proposal through other people she doesn't seem to want to have anything to do with me. As far as she's concerned, I don't exist. (*Sadly.*) The only way I know she knows of my proposal is from her attitude. She has never referred to it.

ANNA: What a pity! Would you like me to speak to her? Or rather, would you like me to be ready to speak to her sometime in the future, when she has begun to get over her grief.

ENRICO (*gratefully*): Thank you. (*Breaking down.*) Only what I don't understand is—how am I supposed to go on living in suspense? It would be easier if she told me to follow Valentino to the grave. But to do nothing! To hope one day and despair the next. I realise I began a little too hastily. When Valentino died we were all so unhappy . . . me as well . . . losing a childhood friend, someone who was almost a brother to me. And to console Umbertino, who was crying bitterly, seeing everyone round him doing the same, I took him in my arms and said: "Cheer up. Don't cry. If you've lost one father, you've gained another."

ANNA: Just like that? With poor Valentino lying on his deathbed?

ENRICO (*hastily*): No, no! We were coming back from the funeral. It was all over.

ANNA: All the same, it seems very hasty to me.

ENRICO: I wish I had waited till now, and now had no longer to wait. Four months! It seems such a short time now.

Though indeed, I didn't mean Umbertino to pass my remark on; and in fact I hope he wouldn't understand. But he's such a lively boy. Someone ought to be thinking about his bringing-up. Every time he sees me he says: "Mama doesn't want anything to do with you, Enrico."

ANNA: So he calls you "Enrico"?

ENRICO: You mustn't blame him for that. It's the one piece of intimacy I've obtained from the whole family. And even then, he only takes advantage of it to cheek me.

ANNA: What a pity you didn't consult me in the first place. I could have helped you so much.

ENRICO: Oh, if only I had realised. (*He kisses her hand.*) I would have been so happy to take you into my confidence— Mother.

ANNA (*smiling*): Gently now, gently! (*Pause.*) Anyway, it may be too late now. I know Emma through and through. She is a good woman, a truly good one. But she's as obstinate as a rusty old iron door. There's no shifting her unless you know the trick.

ENRICO: You know the trick, though. There's still a chance for us all—all except poor Valentino, lying there cold and stiff in St Anna's. All I said to Umbertino was that I was ready to be a father to him. True, Emma may have guessed how I thought this might come about. Still, I could always say the poor child misunderstood me and that the idea of marrying her had only come into my head now, four months later. What do you think?

ANNA: Knowing the state she's in, you would have no better luck now.

ENRICO: But at least she wouldn't be able to say I was rushing her. And truly—I can say this to you—it's quite unfair to say I'm rushing things. It's ten years since Valentino introduced his fiancée to me. And when I first knew her, I had no designs on her, I swear to you. I thought to myself: "You see, someone else has the courage to get married." I was twenty-eight by then, but I had never had the courage. I worked hard at my job, I spent my days tied to my desk, and I lived for the pleasure of making money. There had been women in my life—but never anything lasting. I wouldn't allow it. I had a theory about it—it was the only way to deal with such creatures, whose sole function seemed to consist in spending money. And now Valentino had had the courage I lacked. I studied his love-affair from all sides; in fact I studied it too closely—I discovered that Emma had the spending-habit too . . . and I realised I didn't care.

ANNA: You shock me. So you fell in love with Emma immediately she got engaged to Valentino?

ENRICO: If you are going to help me, you'll have to know the whole story. No, not immediately, but before the marriage. To begin with, I thought it my duty to hinder Valentino's getting married. I used to say to him: "Don't you see how shallow and flighty she is? She will be your ruin." And when I realised he was definitely going to marry this woman, whom I wanted for myself—who, in a sense, indeed, was my wife—it seemed quite natural to stick to the same language. After all, it would have been better, wouldn't it, not to have to look forward to Valentino's death? "Don't you see how she dresses herself up," I would say. "All show, from her curly head to her feet—her pretty little feet. She's a vain, shallow creature, and she will ruin you." Then came the marriage, with me as best man. And certainly, by the time they set about conceiving that child of theirs, I was head over heels in love. Ten years ago!

ANNA: Well, now I understand Emma's attitude.

ENRICO: I don't. I'm sure she never guessed what my feelings were. I had to carry Umbertino at his christening. I didn't drop him. And she wasn't a flirt. Anyway, I wanted to marry her, not to seduce her. So far as that household was concerned, I was always just Valentino's friend—nothing more. But when Valentino decided to die, my penance should have been over.

ANNA: *Decided* to die? Poor Valentino!

ENRICO: Poor Valentino, yes. It makes me grieve too, of course. But he's dead, you know. There's no remedy for him.

(*Pause.*) I was fond of him, very fond of him. Of course, when he fell ill, and started to get that ghastly look, with those bleary, gummy eyes and his jaw hanging open like an idiot's, I couldn't help thinking: "How will Emma be able to bear it?" But she did bear it. And that increased my admiration for her, but also my rage and jealousy— and it didn't stop me from being revolted by him.

ANNA: Take care not to speak to Emma like that.

ENRICO: You don't have to tell me. Once, as a consolation, I told her it was better for him to be dead, so as to be free from that horrible dribbling and slavering. Apparently she had never noticed it. As far as she was concerned, it had never existed. I wanted to call witnesses, but she sobbed so bitterly that I gave in and told her my eyes must have deceived me. But the result is, she now thinks I'm no friend of Valentino's. And it's true, of course. A dead friend isn't a friend any longer. As far as I know, there's only been one exception to the rule in recorded history. You remember those two friends who were shipwrecked and spent weeks together on a raft, at the mercy of the Atlantic. By good luck one of them died, and the other one ate him and saved his own life. Now that *was* a friendship which survived the tomb—if "tomb" is the word.

ANNA (*with a shudder*): You mustn't say such things to me. I don't even like hearing of little birds being eaten.

ENRICO (*astonished*): But why ever not?

ANNA: Never mind. You wouldn't understand. Let's keep to the matter in hand. Only four months have passed since Valentino's death, and in all decent households mourning is supposed to go on for a year.

ENRICO: There's nothing to stop one getting married in mourning. I wouldn't mind wearing mourning myself, for the sake of making Emma my bride.

ANNA: Will you take my advice? You can trust me, because to tell the truth, we both want the same thing. Though we don't express it in the same way—no, we certainly don't do that—I was very fond of my poor son-in-law Valentino, and I always mean to respect his memory. But I don't approve of my daughter's behaviour; I think she should accept what's done and can't be undone. She does harm to her husband's memory by all this grief of hers. Look at me; I loved him so much, yet it's positively maddening to have to keep remembering him.

ENRICO: Just what I say. Precisely. People who are dead and stinking have no place in houses for the living.

ANNA: You shouldn't put it like that. One must never talk of the dear departed as stinking.

ENRICO: It's not their fault. It's fate. Yesterday it was them, tomorrow it may be me.

ANNA (*losing patience*): Tell me frankly, what do you really want? Do you want the pleasure of *saying* things, or of *having* them? Good heavens! You manage to upset *me*, and yet you're surprised at offending Emma. Will you listen to me or not? Will you follow my advice?

ENRICO: I ask nothing better.

ANNA: Then don't *say* things. There's no need . . . at present. Don't even mention Valentino's name. Act as though he had never existed.

ENRICO: That's easy. Because he doesn't exist any longer.

ANNA: Don't mention him, I say! You only have to open your mouth for people to see how you loathe him.

ENRICO: No, that's unjust. You misunderstand me, completely. I was a loyal friend to Valentino.

ANNA (*with a shudder*): No don't . . . not even when we're alone. I can't bear it. (ENRICO *looks at her uncomprehendingly*.) As I was saying, if you think you will get Emma to listen to you before the end of the year's mourning, you're mistaken. Put the idea out of your head.

ENRICO (*gloomily*): And that's the best I'm to expect from someone who says she's my friend, my ally! What's the use of your advice if all you do is tell me to accept my fate.

ANNA (*in amazement*): But all I'm saying is that you must wait eight months.

ENRICO: That wouldn't be much, if I weren't already ex-

hausted after waiting 128 months. Why do I still have to
wait another eight?

ANNA: Ask yourself, whose fault is it?

ENRICO (*shouting*): I say that it's . . .

ANNA (*furious*): Be quiet! Be quiet! If you dare to tell me
it's Valentino's fault, for not having the good taste to die
sooner, you can go elsewhere for advice, I'm not going to
talk to you.

ENRICO: That wasn't what I was going to say. I was merely
going to state the facts of the case, coolly, without prejudice.
Clearly it's no fault of Valentino's that he's dead, or that
he didn't die sooner.

ANNA: Don't *talk* like that.

ENRICO: Honestly, I meant no harm. All I mean is that I fell
in love at the age of twenty-eight, and now I'm thirty-eight
and some months, and if I wait as long as you tell me to
I shall be forty. Remember the saying—when you're forty
it's only another year before you're sixty. The consum-
mation of my desires may come too late. And what if my
love for Emma dies in the meantime, what should I do then?

ANNA: Accept your fate. After all, Valentino had to die.

ENRICO: You see, you can't talk about him either without
making fun of him.

ANNA (*indignantly*): Not at all! It's not true. I swear it. Me
make fun of my poor son-in-law? You're an impossible
man. All you want is to wound people. That's all you're
after. You want to hurt people. I don't deserve such treatment. At the very moment when I'm trying to help . . .

ENRICO (*alarmed*): Believe me, I never imagined you could
mean to make fun of poor Valentino. All I thought . . .
and I was quite wrong, I see . . . was that you might be
making fun of death in general. But I'm sure you would
never do that either. It was a mistake. Please forgive me.

ANNA: I wasn't making fun of death. Make fun of the most
terrible—the most sacred—thing in the world? All I meant
was that if your love should die, it will merely be one death
more—the same tragedy as happens to things more real

than your love, and is sent by heaven every day—many, many times a day.

ENRICO: I was wrong. Forgive me. I sometimes laugh at death myself—perhaps that's wrong too. It's because it seems to me there are worse disasters than death. If you have so much pity for the dead, you should have some for me—since I have to envy the dead their peace of mind. Forgive me!

ANNA: Very well. I forgive you. But now, listen to me. Whether you like it or not, there's only one course for you —complete discretion. Try to make her forget the words you said in a thoughtless moment.

ENRICO: Thoughtless? But it could have been the most important moment in my life. Think of it—if poor Valentino's child had accepted me as a father that day, and his wife had accepted me as a husband, it would have been the finest possible act of homage to the dear departed.

ANNA (*impatiently*): Leave the poor man in peace, and let me finish. By discretion, I don't mean renunciation. Come to the house every now and then, without mentioning your reason for coming. Come to pay your respects to your poor friend's family—without mentioning his name, as you're incapable of doing so decently. And try to make yourself the friend of the whole household. Make a little effort. It may not seem so, but Emma is devoted to me and to my husband. When we die, she will weep over us just as bitterly as she ever did over her husband. As far as I'm concerned, you have my friendship already, though you don't deserve it. And as for my husband, it's easy enough to win his friendship.

ENRICO: Easy? On the contrary, it's quite impossible. I should know, having done nothing but pay court to him ever since I came here. He has never noticed my existence. He can't even get my name right. I spend half my time reminding him of it.

ANNA: It's just something which happens to him with names and numbers—and occasionally places. He got your name wrong the first time, and called you "Baglioni". People put him right; so now whenever he has to say "Biggioni" it makes him hesitate. But what does it matter?

ENRICO: It matters to me. Because when the old gentleman hesitates, he blames me. Indeed he gets quite angry. Yesterday, for instance, when he wanted to refer to me, he called me "that chap there". Well, that's not very polite.

ANNA: But what does it matter? You don't want to marry my husband.

ENRICO: You said yourself I need his support, and I assure you I'm never going to get it. He's just like Umbertino, who won't even accept the toys I bring him. In short your family is composed of Emma, who won't have me; the head of the family, who doesn't notice me; and Umbertino, who not only notices me but sees right through me. It's a lovely situation! Now do you see why I envy Valentino? At least he's escaped all that.

ANNA: My husband isn't really senile, you know.

ENRICO (*surprised*): Senile? No. (*Pause.*) No, he's not senile in the least. How can you imagine I meant that? I merely mean it's hard for me to win his friendship. It's not as if I haven't tried. Till ten years ago he used to do business in textiles; so I thought it might be a good idea to invest in them myself—so as to be able to talk to him about them, I mean, and know what I was speaking about. I lost a lot of money.

ANNA (*sagely*): It's a difficult line of business. You have to understand it.

ENRICO: I understand it well enough to keep clear of it now. I ran along to see him, full of hope. If he'd liked, he could have said what you said to me. He could have called me a fool and boasted of his own cleverness—how he had managed to make a fortune out of textiles. It would have been a bond between us. Being able to call someone a fool endears him to us greatly. But no, nothing of the sort. He asked to be so kind as to remind him of my name, and tried to memorise it. Then he told me that everything he was wearing was made of wool, and that was why he had such good health. I dropped the subject of my own affairs, and thanked him for his advice. I said I'd follow it. He seemed quite annoyed! He seemed sorry to think any advice of his might lengthen my life.

ANNA: My husband is a kind man, really kind—at heart. You don't understand him. Of course seventy-four is quite an age. You can't expect him to be as lively as Umbertino.

ENRICO: It would do me no good if he were.

ANNA: Really, you talk as if my family were a set of goblins. Why don't you give up the idea of belonging to it?

ENRICO: Do you mean I'm losing the one friend I've managed to gain?

ANNA: Not if you keep a curb on your tongue—you do too much harm with it, it's dangerous. I have the strongest desire to help you and guide you. It's all I ask for. But there are some things I won't sit and listen to. Believe me, when you're seventy-four you'll be no more alert than my husband. Even now you see things distorted.

ENRICO: All I wanted to say was that those eight months . . .

ANNA: I know, I know; they're too long.

ENRICO: On the contrary, they're too short; too short to win your husband's friendship. They're a long time, but not long enough.

ANNA: Well then, give up.

ENRICO: I would, if I had the choice. You should have told me that ten years ago. By now I'm like the poor brute who's thrown himself out of the fourth floor window; as he passes the second floor he hears people shouting to him: "Stop, stop, you'll do yourself damage!"

ANNA: You'll see, eight months will soon pass, and all the same they'll do the trick. My husband's a man who loves everybody. He even loves his nephew Guido, who's certainly a remarkable young man but costs him a great deal of money. Which reminds me. I notice you are paying court even to Guido.

ENRICO: There's no problem there. He's already most sympathetic. I keep pretending to be ill and asking his advice.

ANNA: I shouldn't take it. He's only a student.

ENRICO: Don't worry. I won't. Was he allowed to prescribe for Valentino?

ANNA: No, no. He's only been at the University a few months —Well at least it's something that you possess my friendship and Guido's. Guido can be a great help to you. He's very sly, very resourceful— And above all, be patient. Don't be afraid of being too old for marriage. Look at me and my husband. These last years of ours would be the happiest of our lives if it weren't for the tragedy that's befallen our child—that's to say her husband. Giovanni has got his cures to think of, and I help him to pursue them. Which means he is very attached to me. True, he wishes I didn't spend so much time on my pets. It's a tiny cloud in our sky, but it doesn't really count; when it comes to it, he lets me do as I like. So we go along peacefully side by side, just as we've done these forty years.

ENRICO: But you've had all sorts of other experiences . . . you came together in the first place for quite a different purpose. Whereas if I'm married in eight months' time, it will mean starting right away—she nursing me, if she's willing, and I helping her look after her pets.

ANNA: Nonsense. It's only quite recently I've spent so much time on pets. Only since my daughter married.

ENRICO: You old ones are tougher than us young ones. You're like a different race. I expect old age to catch up with me any week. I'm forty . . .

ANNA: Ten minutes ago you were thirty-eight.

ENRICO: Well thirty-eight then. But in order to get married I have to pay court not merely to my wife, but to everyone round her, father, mother, son, cousin . . .

ANNA: You have already won the mother over.

ENRICO: Thank you! And I hope it's for ever. We two have so many points of contact. Even pets. I love them all, except cats, which I can't abide.

ANNA: Poor brutes! They're the most slandered creatures in the world. I'll try to convert you on that point too.

ENRICO: I shall be delighted. (*A pause.*) And when will your husband be back, so I can start paying court to him?

ANNA (*laughing*): He'll be here soon. But don't look as though you were going to attack him. You might frighten him. You have got to go gently with Giovanni. He is a little set in his ways.

ENRICO: I know, I know. But if I don't put a certain amount of energy into it, he'll never notice me. What I think I'll do is to hang a notice on that wall there, with my name in great big letters. When he stumbles over my name, I'll just point to it and carry on with what I'm saying.

ANNA: You must stop making fun of my husband. It's not a question of his not understanding you. It's you who don't understand him. He is a deeper person than you. You think you can make fun of him without his noticing it. But he's fully aware of your dislike of him and returns it cordially. I assure you, my husband has always been regarded—indeed feared—as a man of great shrewdness. If you had really learned the lesson of your wonderful investment in textiles, you would get on better with my husband. Knowing what he succeeded in doing in the same line should make you admire him; and he would feel it, and things would go differently between you.

ENRICO: I'm sure I've never showed him any disrespect. He couldn't have guessed my feelings.

ANNA: You don't know him. He doesn't say much, and he finds difficulty in expressing things; but he understands everything and guesses everything too. Oh goodness, how he does guess things!

ENRICO: Then he should have guessed that I wanted to like him and win his good will.

ANNA: That was what you wanted him to believe, but he sees right into things. I should know!

Enter DR RAULLI (*an old man, very lively and sure of himself, indeed too much so*) *and* GUIDO CALACCI.

GUIDO: Hullo, Aunt. When will Uncle be back?

ANNA (*getting up, with a great show of respect*): Dr Raulli!
What a shame you should have come on a fruitless errand.
Giovanni isn't at home.

RAULLI: And I can't wait for him, as I've got to rush away.
But perhaps I can talk to you instead. (*He looks irritably at* ENRICO.)

ANNA (*introducing them*): Signor Enrico Biggioni, a friend of
the family. (GUIDO *shakes his hand.*)

RAULLI (*shaking* ENRICO's *hand*): Delighted to meet you!
Well in that case I can say what I have to say in your
presence. It's not worth trying to make a secret of it. I have
merely come to tell Signor Chierici that I am absolutely
opposed to his having a rejuvenation operation. That's all
I came to say. You live rather far away for me to call again.
So if you could just give Signor Chierici this message.
(*Slowly and emphatically.*) I am absolutely opposed to the
operation. That Giannottini fellow has come here upsetting
all the old men of Trieste. And instead of providing *them*
with youth he provides himself with . . . a gilded youth.

ANNA: I've heard something about all this, but I didn't know
Giovanni himself was involved. (*To* GUIDO.) Has there really
been a plan to operate on Giovanni?

GUIDO: Yes, Aunt. In fact it was discussed in your presence.

RAULLI: This young man here is an excellent fellow. He has
one essential quality in a doctor, a spirit of enterprise. It's
a good beginning, in fact more than that; but it's not
enough. When he knows more about things, when he
knows the human body and its secrets, a spirit of enterprise
will stand him in good stead. But till then, it's a danger.
It's like . . . it's like a train without rails.

GUIDO: But they're not my own ideas I'm applying, my dear
sir; they're those of Dr Giannottini, who's quite a respectable age.

RAULLI: He's thirty-five. He should spare us his opinion on the
operation till he's in need of it himself. What's a thirty-five-
year-old doctor good for? He can cure the diseases that have
been studied and cured before he was born. But for heaven's

sake, don't let him start innovating and inventing. You should have white hairs before you're ready to pass judgement on new ideas. At thirty-five one is still living and writing under dictation. As for you, wait till you've got your degree before you start talking. One day you too will be in a position to do what you like with the bodies placed in your care. But till then, it would be a crime—a disaster for our poor city.

GUIDO: Come, dear sir, it will only be like yourself, after you'd set up your ambulance. The place will get used to such disasters.

RAULLI: Allow me to continue. When I was that age I didn't think about reforming things. I accepted things as I found them. And you will realise, when . . . when you've seen a greater number of naked human beings . . . that Dr Giannottini is a meddling young fool, in fact a criminal. He just (*with a gesture*) goes ahead and slashes with his knife . . . hoping and waiting and trusting. Where are the documented cures, I ask you? Show me your cases of rejuvenation.

GUIDO: They exist, my dear sir, they exist. In other cities. The results are in print.

RAULLI: If you ask me, they've only experimented on mice. I haven't followed all their nonsense. I base myself on one definite, indisputably reliable, report. An eighty-year-old president of the French Academy of Sciences declared himself convinced of the efficacy of rejuvenation operations. Yes, well . . . in its previous session the Academy had declared that henceforth their president could not be more than sixty years old. That's the only rejuvenation-process I believe in. Do you get it, young man? D'you follow?

GUIDO: If I may be allowed to, at my present age, yes . . .

RAULLI: Don't interrupt, please. What if the operation were a success? That's to say, what if it managed to speed up the life-process and to shorten it? What then? Signor Chierici would rather go on as he is: digesting, seeing, hearing, speaking—in short, living—a little less intensely than other people, but otherwise with nothing to complain of—merely having to look after himself and take a cure from time to time. Why should you want to murder him?

ANNA: Good heavens! Giovanni has never thought seriously of such an operation.

RAULLI: He has thought of it, he has thought of it! Or rather his nephew, the future Aesculapius, has thought of it. Beware of those who know a little medicine. They know less than those who know nothing.

GUIDO: But my dear sir. If all the doctors who were born before we knew the great things we know today had not been allowed to speak, what a silence there would have been all these years. A most distressing silence.

RAULLI: It's not the same thing. You don't understand my meaning, young man. Aesculapius knew all the medical science there was in his time. He knew everything you could know at that period. (*Emphatically.*) He *knew* it, sir. He would not have taken liberties with a human body just for the sake of experiment.

GUIDO: But rejuvenation experiments have already been made. And by now they've been made on human bodies too. If we were to proceed on your plan, my dear sir, we should never get anywhere.

RAULLI: We must wait till the time is ripe; we must watch and observe. Don't let us murder people unless there's absolutely no alternative.

GUIDO: There never is any alternative. For surely it's obvious: I, having only just started my studies, am steeped in ignorance. But you, my dear Professor, who know everything there is to know up to now, you too are steeped in error. You need only look at the nearest history-book to prove it. And so, if we aren't allowed to murder people till medical science is perfect, we shall never murder anyone. How would the world get on then?

ANNA: How well he talks!

RAULLI (*after a moment's hesitation*): Yes, excellently. (*Reasserting himself.*) But he's wrong. I know he's wrong. If he had talked like that thirty years ago, when medicine was

still in its infancy, I might have agreed with him. But now
. . . now he's wrong. I will tell you why. Not knowing
enough medicine, he doesn't love it enough. He's a young
man of wit and spirit, that nephew of yours. He only goes
wrong out of ignorance.

ANNA (*enthusiastically*): But he's a young man of spirit?

RAULLI: It's a pity that there's no place for spirit in medicine.
We only use it for pickling our specimens. Ha, ha, ha!

GUIDO (*forcing a laugh*): Very good.

RAULLI: I'm not in favour of too much spirit. I believe in pro-
hibition, like the Americans.

GUIDO: Ha. Ha. Very good, very good!

RAULLI: I fear, too, that a rejuvenation operation can only
be an "operation of the spirit."

GUIDO (*tries to laugh, but cannot manage it.*)

RAULLI: An operation of the spirit, subject to maximum ex-
cise-duty. (*He laughs loud and long.*)

GUIDO (*same reaction.*)

RAULLI: Only, those who should be the customs-men are doing
the smuggling. Ha, ha, ha. Do you follow me?

GUIDO (*same reaction*): Yes, yes.

RAULLI: And I might add that the duty isn't paid by those
who drink the spirit. Ha, ha. Far from it. It's as if one party
felt like drinking and the other had to do the getting drunk.

GUIDO: One would never think you were against wit and
spirit.

RAULLI: But I am, I abominate it. Please forget I ever practised
it. In return for that I will forget that you ever favoured
rejuvenation-operations; and ten years from now, when
I see you working by my side, I will tell everyone—"Dr
Calacci never let himself be taken in by such charlatanry."
(*To* ANNA.) Well then, I rely on you. Tell Signor Giovanni
everything I said.

ANNA (*alarmed*): Everything?

RAULLI: Well, that I don't want him to let himself be interfered with. And that if he has the operation, he can look
for another doctor. I only like treating human bodies that

I know, suffering from diseases that I know. If they are going to make themselves ill for the fun of it, they can go to Nuremberg and get cured by the toymakers. Good day, Signora—and by the way, how *is* your husband? Is he well? Has he finished that medicine I gave him yet? I hope he's got over that theft by now?

ANNA: Yes, completely. He eats and sleeps as well as possible.

RAULLI: You see? And yet you talk of operations? What's the point of operations? Just to satisfy a caprice? If one medicine doesn't work, I prescribe you another. But what if your operation doesn't work, what then? Another operation? One to cut his throat, this time? Wouldn't it be better to cut your own? (*Pause.*) Give him my very best regards. I will try to see him sometime next week. Good day, Signora. (*He shakes* ANNA's *hand, then* ENRICO's.) Delighted to have met you. (*Nods to* GUIDO *and exit.*)

GUIDO: What a tornado of a man! I see there's no hope. When Uncle hears what his doctor says he'll never dare go ahead.

ANNA: And he'll be right not to.

GUIDO: Dear Aunt, don't jump to conclusions. Dr Raulli said that he mustn't have the operation because it hasn't been proved reliable. But when will it have been proved reliable? Uncle is seventy-four. Can he afford to wait till it's been proved reliable?

ENRICO: Yes, he's right. When you're seventy-four, it's not so easy to wait. It's not so easy when you're only thirty-eight. Tell me. I've heard about this operation, but I've never given it much thought before. What if someone's a bit run-down, feeling his years I mean . . . would it do any good in a case like that?

GUIDO: Oh, with young men it positively can't fail.

ENRICO (*with a sigh of relief*): He would get a prolongation of youth? A second youth, that's to say? One to make money in, and another one to spend it in?

ANNA: But as Dr Raulli doesn't believe in it . . .

ENRICO: Thank heavens, he's not my doctor. If the operation really does work, who wouldn't have it? Time wouldn't be such a worry; one could afford to wait for things in comfort.

GUIDO: You're not thinking of it for yourself?

ENRICO: Not at this moment, certainly. But who knows whether I won't be needing it in . . . eight years' time shall we say?

GUIDO: Hardly then, I should think. Unless you are struck down by premature senility, which I hope won't be the case.

ENRICO (*alarmed*): Premature senility? Wasn't that what they called poor Valentino's illness? So that if you had known of this operation only a few months sooner he would have been all right?

GUIDO: It would have been better if I'd known of it quite a time sooner.

ANNA: But didn't you hear Dr Raulli say he didn't believe in it at all?

GUIDO: Naturally. He wouldn't have been an old doctor otherwise. One's heard of old ship's captains, hasn't one, who refused to believe in steam when it was invented, and wouldn't take down their sails? Unfortunately, as far as Giovanni's concerned, there's nothing to be done. A word from Dr Raulli is gospel to him.

ENRICO: Couldn't I try to convince him?

GUIDO: Do you think you've got so much influence over him?

ENRICO: Not yet, not yet; but in time, who knows?

ANNA: If I was convinced it was for his good, I would try too. When it's been a question of things that matter, I haven't paid much attention to the doctor either. Heaven knows how much Pagliano[1] got consumed without Dr Raulli knowing about it. And, yet, really, we're all very well in the household apart from poor Valentino, whom Pagliano did neither harm nor good to. But when it comes to an operation . . . oh dear!

GUIDO: Like cutting your nails. Nothing more.

ANNA (*pensively*): And it does so much good? What would happen if everyone underwent it?

[1] A patent medicine.

GUIDO: Everyone? Only the old would. I wouldn't undergo it myself, for instance. If I did, they'd have to send me back to school, just when, thank God, I've managed to reach the University. I'd be sent down for infantile behaviour.

ENRICO: For the moment, it would seem to me, the most important thing is not to tell Emma about the operation.

GUIDO: Why?

ENRICO: I'm afraid of the effect on her, if she discovers that if Valentino had waited a bit, he needn't have died.

GUIDO: There'll be no difficulty about that, at least until my uncle has the operation.

ENRICO: But afterwards, too. And anyway, isn't there someone else we shall have to conceal it from? We mustn't let Dr Raulli know. Even if Signor Giovanni gets ill, we must still conceal it. With poultices, or somehow.

ANNA: Why should Giovanni get ill? As a result of the operation?

GUIDO: Why do you start thinking about illness?

ENRICO (*in desperation*): I'm only trying to help—trying to foresee all the possibilities. I don't *want* the old gentleman to be ill. But everyone knows that young people—and after his operation he'll be a young man—are more liable to illnesses. Has he had scarlet fever?

GUIDO: One only gets twenty per cent rejuvenated at most. So if the operation were successful my uncle would be fifty-nine after it.

ENRICO (*reflectively*): And a man of forty would be thirty-two after it. It's not bad . . .

GUIDO: Look. (*He takes a piece of paper out of his pocket.*) I have here the proof that it's exactly the right moment for my uncle to have the operation. At my suggestion, and at his express request, I made him submit to an analysis. Look at it, Aunt. Everything normal.

ANNA (*putting on her spectacles*): I shan't understand a word of it.

GUIDO: Yes you will, Aunt. I asked them particularly to put it in plain God-fearing Italian. Do you see? "Normal. Normal. Normal." The analysis would have cost anyone else fifty lire, but they do it for me for twenty-five. That was why Uncle asked me to arrange it.

ANNA : So you feel the difference should go to you?

GUIDO : No, no, Auntie Anna. The result itself is enough reward for me. No, I'm quite satisfied with twenty-five lire.

ANNA (*takes a purse out of the drawer of the table and gives him the difference*): You're a good boy, Guido.

GUIDO : It was money wasted, worse luck. We did the analysis to see if the operation would be safe. And now we know it would be, he's not going to have it. It's a pity.

ANNA (*struck by the argument*): Yes, it really is a pity. Naturally I shall have to tell your uncle what the doctor said. After that, it's for him to decide.

ENRICO : Couldn't you get rid of Dr Raulli and take on Dr Giannottini as your family doctor?

ANNA (*vehemently*): That's out of the question! Dr Raulli was such a comfort to us all through Valentino's illness. He was here night and day.

ENRICO : But from what I hear, he didn't save his life, all the same.

GUIDO : That proves nothing, absolutely nothing. It would be a pretty state of affairs if doctors were called to account for every patient who dies on them. There would be no one blameless left—except me. I think if Uncle decides on the operation, he might have it without Raulli knowing. He would never discover it for himself.

ANNA : But wouldn't he notice your uncle getting so much younger?

GUIDO : He would put it down to his little green pills. It would buck him up no end. Aunt Anna, dear. Think. This is the last moment when Uncle could still get benefit out of it. After all—dash it—he's seventy-four. If he waits any longer, "physiological" death will have invaded too much of his poor old body.

ANNA : Death? (*She shudders.*) Why should he die, if the report says everything's normal.

GUIDO: I'm not talking of the same kind of death. In medicine we call paralysis death too. When you see an old man doddering along you must remember that he is a combination of death and life. What's still alive in him is taking the rest for an outing. That's what makes him totter, as if he were carrying weights. And there's no operation that can bring back to life a part that's dead, definitively dead.

ANNA: But Giovanni doesn't totter.

ENRICO (*dubiously*): Nooo . . .

GUIDO: No, certainly not. If he'd reached that stage, the operation might revive the parts still alive, but the rest wouldn't be any the better for it—I'm trying to explain things to you in the simplest language possible, as you don't understand medicine—"physiological death" supervenes where the normal work of limbs and organs is prevented by general enfeeblement. The eye is in no danger of death because it is made to go on working, assisted by spectacles. The ear isn't either, being made to work with the aid of an ear-trumpet . . . (*Begins to giggle.*) Where there's no room for mechanical aids, organs die of mere disuse.

ENRICO (*sadly*): It's very true. When work is interrupted there's always the danger of death.

Enter EMMA, *in heavy mourning and swathed in veils, ready to go out. She greets* GUIDO *and* ENRICO *distantly.*

EMMA: Are Papa and Umbertino not back yet?

ANNA: Not yet, no.

EMMA: I'm beginning to be a little worried. Papa has been so vague and absent-minded recently, I'm afraid something may happen to them—the roads are so terrible these days.

ANNA: Do you want to deprive your father of his daily outing, when he says it's so important to him, it makes him feel so much younger?

EMMA (*losing patience*): I didn't say that. Though if those walks of theirs really were a danger for the child, they would certainly have to stop. Perhaps I ought to go with them, to look after Umbertino. But I know I'm not a very cheerful companion, and I might spoil their fun. And moreover, it's a very inconvenient time for me . . .

ENRICO: Could I go with them instead? I often take a walk before lunch too, and nothing could give me more pleasure than to spend my mornings with the dear little child—and his grandpapa, whom I love and revere too.

EMMA: I wouldn't want to give you the trouble.

ENRICO: It would be no trouble at all. I would regard it as a privilege.

EMMA: It's not for me to say yes. You must speak to my father. I am sure he would be delighted to have your company.

ENRICO: Couldn't you tell him that at his age he shouldn't be out alone with a little child, with the streets being such a danger. And that you expect him to take me with him.

ANNA: That would be charming!

EMMA: You see?—It would mortally offend my poor papa. No, instead, every day, I'll have to pretend a sudden longing to go out, just at the same moment, and ask if I can have his company. Perhaps he won't mind so much like that, though he won't be very pleased, as he prides himself he's the only person the child will trust or talk to. When Umbertino's with other people—however fond he is of his grandpa —he naturally turns to those who can understand him better.

ENRICO: Couldn't I turn up just at the crucial moment and say, casually "Won't you let me come with you?" Umbertino doesn't actually dislike me, even if he's not all that fond of me.

EMMA (embarrassed and irritated): It's all rather difficult . . .

ENRICO (crestfallen): Well if I can't, I'll have to go on taking my walks alone, as has been my fate ever since I lost my poor dear friend, Valentino.

EMMA: I never remember my husband going for a walk with you.

ENRICO: Before he married, we went for one every day.

EMMA: So when Valentino got married, it meant you lost a friend.

ENRICO: On the contrary. When I saw him so happy at being by your side, and I was allowed to spend an evening sometimes in your household, I felt I had my old friend back again, and in a sense enlarged—for I was fond not just of him, but of his household ... yes ... his household. Believe me, his death was a great loss to me. Those evenings at your house counted for a great deal in my lonely existence.

EMMA: The household went when he went. There's nothing left of it.

ENRICO: I know, I know. And I won't complain on my own behalf. It would be wrong to do so in your presence, when you have lost so much more, when you have lost everything ... more or less. To lose such a good, kind, handsome man. It's a comfort to me just to remember him; that's why I come here so often—so as to help bring him back to my mind. I've been talking to Signora Chierici about him, and it was such a comfort.

ANNA: It's quite true. He's always talking about Valentino.

EMMA (coldly): Thank you. (Pause.) I think I'll go out now, Mama. I don't know why, but I feel rather uneasy. For some days now Father's been so very absent-minded. Last week he had his watch stolen, and never realised it till he got home.

GUIDO: That proves nothing. The thieves in Trieste are so advanced, evolutionarily speaking, they could rob a man of his head—no matter how alert he was—without him noticing. The only reason they don't, is they wouldn't know what to do with it. Everyone thinks his own head's sufficient.

EMMA: It was his behaviour after the theft that I didn't like. Mamma immediately bought him another watch, but he wasn't satisfied; he wanted the one he had lost, it was a memento of his father-in-law. He seemed quite angry with us because we couldn't produce it.

ANNA: I was touched to see him so distressed—it showed his respect for my poor father's memory.

EMMA (*impatiently*): It wasn't just distress; it was bad temper. He was resentful against us, though it wasn't our fault in the least. It was as if we had egged the thief on. It shows that his mind is failing.

GUIDO: Yes, well of course. The old are the old, and a great misfortune to any family. I've always said so.

EMMA: That's not what I'm saying—poor Papa, a great misfortune! I'm merely saying that we oughtn't to trust him with the child.

ANNA: I think he had a right to be angry—a faint right, but a real one. I bought him a handsome, expensive new watch, but with no resemblance to the one he had lost, the one that reminded him of my father. Then I was more sensible, and changed it for one that looked like the old one; and at once he became the gentle, kind Giovanni we all know; in fact he thinks he's got the old watch back.

EMMA: Which only goes to prove what I'm saying.

ANNA: I don't understand you.

EMMA (*losing her patience*): There's no point in discussing it. (*Pause.*) Mamma, I think I'll go out now. I will be back in half an hour. (*Nods distantly at the others and exit by centre upstage door.*)

ANNA: You must excuse her. She's been living with her own grief so long that she gets impatient as soon as anyone disagrees with her.

GUIDO: She'll soon see a difference. When Uncle has been rejuvenated, he won't be so concerned with watches. Young people have other things to interest them. Look at me, for instance. Do you remember that marvellous watch Uncle gave me for my first communion? First of all it got converted into an ordinary metal watch, and then that went too, to breathe the bracing mountain air . . . of the *mont de piété.*

ANNA: You young villain! And so you haven't got a watch at all?

GUIDO: When I want to know the time, I stop the first passer-by and ask him. Everyone has a watch these days.

ANNA: A doctor without a watch! And how do you take pulses?

GUIDO: I compare them with my own—it's as regular as a watch.

ANNA: And yet Uncle gives you a perfectly adequate allowance.

GUIDO: Ah, if it weren't for those wretched books! They're so expensive. Otherwise it would be quite enough. But to keep abreast of our profession you're always needing books, and periodicals, and papers. It was by reading them I got to know about rejuvenation operations, before Giannottini. It was I who put him up to this business.

ANNA: This *business*? Didn't you say it was an operation?

GUIDO: Yes, I mean, the operation. It was a slip of the tongue.

ANNA: How much do you need to redeem your watch? I mean, the cheap one?

GUIDO: I pawned it for twenty-five lire.

ANNA (*takes the money out of her purse and gives it to him*): Here it is. Don't tell Giovanni, or it might worry him.

GUIDO: Thank you, Auntie.

ANNA: I shall expect to see it tomorrow.

GUIDO: You shall see it, I promise you. The very same one I pawned.

ANNA: But I shan't be able to recognise it.

GUIDO: It's a perfectly respectable commonplace watch, with . . .

ANNA: Yes, yes, you needn't go on—I must go. I've got lunch to attend to. (To ENRICO.) So we're agreed, Signor Biggioni. You will try to be sensible and tactful and above all try not to worry.

ENRICO: I'll do my best. In fact, you've seen me doing my best. I've made quite an effort today, though it hasn't succeeded. I'll try again tomorrow—this afternoon I'm needed in the office.

ANNA: It's better if you can have other things to occupy you, some of the time. It will make the nine months pass quicker.

ENRICO: Nine? Eight, Signora Chierici, only eight, please.

ANNA (*laughing*): I beg your pardon. Eight, of course. Good-bye.

Exit left.

GUIDO: Nine, eight? I don't understand all this at all. I know something about nine months. But then come seven; never eight! Eight means disaster.

ENRICO: I'll explain it all another time. It isn't a question of fixed dates. I wish it were. If it were, I could take a calendar and strike a day off every twenty-four hours. But as things are, days go by, and there's still just as many left. (*Suddenly becoming cheerful and self-assertive.*) Listen. Will you accept a present from me? Will you have my watch? It's a real chronometer. But I don't need it in the least myself. (*Takes the watch out of his waistcoat pocket, removing the chain, which he puts back.*) It will be more use to you than to me; the way I manipulate clients doesn't involve their pulses.

GUIDO (*with ill-concealed delight*): But . . . why should I?

ENRICO: I want to reward—in the best way I can—the far-seeing scholar who has brought such benefits to our town. Please accept it. It's a slight return for all the insults you've had to put up with from Dr Raulli. He made me furious. My blood was boiling. I expect he's annoyed with you because he didn't manage to hear about that operation first. I wish you every success with it. In a little while, maybe we shall be the one city in the world with no old men. What a place that would be!

GUIDO (*with the watch in his hand still*): I can't possibly accept it. I admit I'm not above a little—what shall we say —contrivance, when I'm in difficulties near the end of the month—I mean, any time after the fifteenth. But nothing serious, you know; and anyway it's between me and my relations, since out of the goodness of their hearts they've agreed to support me. My little manoeuvres are merely to correct their estimate of my cost of living—that is to say of my value to the world. All quite insignificant. For in-

stance, I charge for that analysis, when it costs me nothing;
or I get someone to give me the money to redeem a watch
I never pawned—because I'm not quite such a child as to
put myself in the hands of our friends the moneylenders.
(*Still clutching the watch.*) But this is a serious financial
matter. And you're not a relation. (*With a sudden show of
decision.*) I tell you what we'll do. For the moment, you keep
the watch, but we'll agree that it's mine. As soon as you're
part of my family you can return it to me.

ENRICO: How splendidly you put it. (*Seizing his hand and
shaking it warmly.*) Well then, it's a bargain. The watch is
only to become yours when I'm a relation of yours. But
meanwhile, why don't you keep it? It's a guarantee, a token
that I will become a relation. Keep the chain too, on the
same conditions. Here! I beg you. Don't refuse me. Think
how much pleasure it will give me. I haven't had such a
pleasure since poor Valentino died. But just one thing—can
I ask you to be a friend to me? Not on account of the watch
and chain, which don't mean a thing. But as a return for the
sincere friendship I bear you, do help me, do give me your
support.

GUIDO (*equally cordially*): Of course, of course! With all my
heart. There's nothing I would like better than to help you.
And on Emma's account too, since she refuses to see she
has the chance to start life again, under the very best aus-
pices. I'll look after the watch religiously—I promise you—
and the chain too, till the very moment of the wedding—
the very moment they finally become mine.

ENRICO: Actually, I want your help at this very moment—
that's to say your advice. Ever since we started talking about
that extraordinary operation, it's been on my mind. Do you
think it would be better to tell Emma?

GUIDO: Tell her what?

ENRICO: About the operation. Suppose she married me without knowing anything about it, and then she found out.
Mightn't it plunge her back into the depths of grief. Let me
put it more clearly. Wouldn't it be better for her to . . .

swallow both her present grief for her husband's death, and the bitterness of knowing the new cure didn't arrive in time for him, rather than to learn of his second misfortune later on?

GUIDO: That's a very important question. I would like to think before replying. At first sight, I'd say there was a case for leaving her in peace for the moment. When she's finally forgotten her husband, I doubt if any new fact will revive his memory. Whereas if she learned about the operation now, it would certainly aggravate her unhappiness. Leave it till later, and what then? Why, she'd say to herself: "Good heavens, if the operation had come in time, I would have two husbands now. That *would* be awkward."

ENRICO (*laughing*): I wish she could say that. But who knows, she might say that if the first one had stayed at his post, she would never have known the second. That's the danger.

Enter ANNA.

ANNA: Here I am. (*Shouts.*) Rita! Rita! No, of course, she doesn't hear. And she's supposed to be laying the table. (*To* ENRICO, *laughing.*) What a pleasant surprise!

ENRICO: I know you think I'm incredibly tactless. But I had something to say to Guido.

Enter RITA, *panting and at the run.*

RITA: Oh how awful, what a terrible thing! (*She collapses on to a chair.*) Excuse me, madam. (*Collapsing back in her chair she covers her face with her apron and falls into violent sobbing.*) Oh madam, what shall we do, what will you do . . . ?

ANNA (*also collapsing into a chair*): What is it? Tell me, Tell me, you stupid girl. (RITA *is unable to speak, and shakes her head.*)

GUIDO: Rita, you're frightening my aunt terribly.

RITA (*sobbing*): It's the old gentleman. He's downstairs. He's too exhausted to climb the stairs . . .

ANNA (*getting up*): Why is he too exhausted? Is he ill?

RITA: He's alone.

ANNA (*falls back in her seat*): And what about Umbertino?

RITA: Umbertino isn't with him. Umbertino's dead, run down by a motor-car.

ENRICO: If you'll allow me, Signora Chierici, I'll go down and find your husband myself. (*Nobody listens, and he goes out.*)

RITA: To think of poor Miss Emma; she doesn't know yet.

ANNA: But how do you know all this. Are you absolutely sure? Have you seen him yourself?

RITA: He's dead, he's dead, the poor little boy. The master said so . . . he saw it with his own eyes. Crushed to pieces.

GUIDO (*going to the door upstage*): It can't be true.

Enter GIOVANNI, *confused and excited, with his clothes in disorder and his hat askew.*

GIOVANNI: You see what terror, grief and hurry have reduced me to! (*Pause.*) My poor little boy. (*He sobs.*) And poor me, too. Poor Chierici! I told him twice: "Keep hold of my hand." And he grabbed hold of it all too firmly. I shouted to him "Let go, let go!" He was on my wrong side. But he wouldn't let go . . . till the car caught him . . . and smashed him to pieces. (*He shudders.*) I only just escaped myself—he was dragging me towards the car. (ENRICO *takes his hat off for him and tries to tidy his coat.*) Leave me alone, can't you? Can't you see I've got other things to think of?

ANNA: It can't be true. Tell me; it's not so, is it?

GIOVANNI (*sobbing*): I wish it weren't. It's true all right. I saw him myself, lying under the wheels. (*He shudders.*) I was out of breath, but I managed to shout at the chauffeur: I shouted "Murderer". But he just went on his way, putting his tongue out at me. Yes, he actually put out his tongue.

GUIDO: Why didn't you have him arrested?

GIOVANNI: I couldn't shout loud enough; though I tried. And I think I saw a policeman nearby, but he wouldn't do anything. So I realised I had nothing but enemies round me, and I ran away. Anyway, I was frightened of seeing the poor child's head, all smashed and bleeding. (*He shudders.*)

ANNA: Guido, what ought we to do?

GUIDO (*sadly*): They are certain to have taken his body to hospital. I'll go there myself, at once.

ANNA: No, no, don't leave us. We need you. I'll come with you later. I want to see my little angel too.

GIOVANNI (*aghast*): You want to see him?

GUIDO: Don't be afraid, Uncle, I'll go first and decide if it's all right for Auntie to see him. For the moment, it's less important to see the poor dead child than to help the living— I mean the child's mother. (*Miserably.*) What a blow for her! How's she ever going to bear it?

GIOVANNI (*brokenly*): To think I'm still alive . . .

GUIDO: I know, I know. (*He is puzzled what to say next.*)

ENRICO: Would you like me to go and tell her?

GIOVANNI: Oh, we should be so very grateful, Signor . . .

ENRICO: Biggioni.

GIOVANNI: Signor Biggioni. It would mean we needn't be there when poor Emma hears the news. (*To* GUIDO.) What do you think?

GUIDO (*enthusiastically*): Yes, Signor Biggioni, it would be a great kindness. Do go to her.

ANNA: She's at her dressmaker's.

ENRICO: That's in the Corso. I know, I know. I know the shop very well, though I don't know the number.

ANNA: I can't tell you the number either. (*Pause.*) What a tragedy! If my poor old legs would bear me I would come with you. Poor little Emma. To lose your husband and your son in the same few months.

ENRICO (*eager to be gone*): I'll run there; and afterwards, if you like, I'll go to the hospital too. I'll take charge of everything, everything.

ANNA: But be careful how you speak to Emma. If you break the news too quickly you might kill her. (*To* GUIDO.) Don't you think so?

GUIDO (*self-importantly*): Listen. Tell her first that the child was badly injured. Then go on making the injury worse. Tell her that he has had his legs broken, and an injured chest. Once you've got as far as the danger of death it's only a step to death itself.

GIOVANNI (*mutters*): As a matter of fact I think the wheel went over his head. I managed to shut my eyes in time, so as not to have to see . . . (*Shudders.*)

ANNA (*screams*): Oh, his poor little head. (*Pause.*) You mustn't tell Emma that.

ENRICO: Try not to distress yourself, Signora Chierici. Try to resign yourself. We must all be ready—despite our own sorrow—to console Emma. Meanwhile, I promise you I will do everything I can. (*Kisses her hand and exit.*)

ANNA (*repeating his words, dubiously*): "Everything I can." What can that idiot do?

GUIDO: Poor chap, he means so well.

ANNA: I can't, I won't see Emma till she has got over the first shock. Rita, come to my room with me. I don't want to be alone.

GIOVANNI: Do you think Emma is going to eat you? When it's nobody's fault. . . . For it wasn't anybody's fault. I warned the child of the danger. I said to him: "Hold my hand tight . . ."

GUIDO (*regretfully*): And he held it too tight.

GIOVANNI: Yes. His poor delicate little hand. I can still feel it in mine.

ANNA (*to* GUIDO): You stay with your Uncle till Emma arrives. (*To* GIOVANNI) Poor Giovanni! You must have suffered terribly too. (*She kisses him on the cheek.*)

GIOVANNI (*with self-pity*): You can imagine what I felt. As I was running back home I kept thinking: "Oh why didn't the car kill me instead of the poor innocent child?" And if he'd not been on the wrong side of me, it would have killed me.

ANNA: Poor darling! I know you would rather have been lying under the motor-car than here in this room. And Emma will realise it too, I'm sure she will. Would you like a glass of wine?

GIOVANNI (*after a brief hesitation*): No, no. Dr Raulli was so firm that I ought not to take alcohol.

ANNA: Emma will want to come to the hospital with us.

GIOVANNI: Tell Fortunato to have the car ready.

ANNA: Very well. I'll put on mourning, as I did on the day of Valentino's death. (*Exit weeping.*) Poor little Umbertino. I'll never see him again.

RITA (*genuinely overcome with grief*): Yes, poor little master. So cheerful and brave and proud of himself.

GUIDO: How sorrow improves people's looks.

GIOVANNI: Are you talking about Anna? A fine sort of beauty treatment! I would rather stay ugly for ever (*Pause.*) Poor Emma! God knows what she will say about me. And then we shall have to have the grandparents on top of us— Valentino's father and mother, from Gorizia. They wanted to have the baby live with them. It's a most extraordinary business. I was still telling the child to hold my hand, and there he was, dead. In a fraction of a second. And now we've got to face: (*counting on his fingers*) Anna's grief, Emma's despair and the Gorizians's anger . . . we call them the "Gorizians" among ourselves, Valentino's parents, I mean. The list goes on for ever! It's all over with me. I would have done better to die. And my own conscience won't leave me in peace, either. I'm sure I wasn't to blame. But it is true that a few minutes before—not then, a few minutes before—I was a little absent-minded. It was the poor child's fault. We had trudged up the lane to the Maddalena; I wish we'd never left it. We ought to have kept going up and down that lane. Up and down! It would have been monotonous, but if we had, I shouldn't be here now in this situation. (*Dreamily.*) A dear little lane that no motor-cars ever go up. I only saw one, and it was going as slowly as a crocodile. (*Pause.*)

GUIDO: Why were you distracted, Uncle?

GIOVANNI: Distracted? Oh yes. Well, as we went up that lane, all alone, we ran into two *carabinieri* in full dress uniform.

The child was worried and asked: "Do the *carabinieri* know that we're not thieves?"

GUIDO: Poor little boy!

GIOVANNI: I know, I know. First I said that they certainly knew. But then I thought that there was something more I ought to tell the child. But it wasn't clear what. For obviously the *carabinieri* don't arrest all the thieves there are. They only arrest some of the ones that actually steal. The others—and there are thousands of them—that don't steal, because they're too lazy to, or because they have so much already they can't make the effort, go free though everyone knows they're really thieves. But I couldn't find exactly the right words . . . and now the child's gone it's not worth trying. (*Mournfully.*)

GUIDO: It wasn't your mistake, it was the others', letting some-one of your age go out alone with the child.

GIOVANNI (*furiously*): No, I won't have that! You're talking utter nonsense. What has age got to do with it? What if I hadn't told you I had been distracted? Would you start say-ing I'm getting feeble-minded? I know why you're talking like this, you want to persuade me to have that operation, and I won't hear of it. What's age got to do with it? (*Pause.*) Well perhaps . . . a little. Not because I don't hear as well, or see as well or think as well as other people. But because I belong to an era when there were no motor-cars. When I was young we used to get ourselves run over by bony old cab-horses. The stupidity of Man, that's to say of the driver, was limited by the weakness of animals, that's to say of the cab-horse. All the same, I assure you, people were crushed to pieces by cabs and carriages too. And if our modern motor-cars suddenly arrived on the scene today, amid people accustomed to cabhorses, they would all end up under their wheels. And I belong with them. Wait another ten years or so, and I'll be more used to these infernal con-trivances. (*Pause.*) Except that I'll never really be used to them. Neither now, nor later.

UMBERTINO (*heard offstage*): Grandpa, grandpa.

GIOVANNI: And I hear continually, in that tender conscience of mine, the child's voice echoing . . . "Grandpa, grandpa, help . . ."

GUIDO: It isn't the voice of your conscience, Uncle. It *is* Umbertino.

UMBERTINO (*rushing in*): Grandpa, why did you go off without me?

GIOVANNI (*stammering*): Me? . . . Go off without you? (*He rubs his face.*) Where have you been all this time?

GUIDO (*bending over the child and kissing him*): On earth. God be praised. (*Shouts.*) Auntie, Auntie!

GIOVANNI: Don't shout. Your voice goes right through me. Don't you see what a state I'm in? Come here, Umbertino. I don't understand anything any more. Did you get tired of running under motor-cars? Give me a kiss. Tell me—what happened? Why did you run away?

UMBERTINO: I didn't run away, it was the car that did. I ran after it because I thought you were under it. I ran so hard and I yelled so loud the driver stopped. I looked underneath. You weren't there. The chauffeur didn't half curse.

GIOVANNI: The lout! I hope he ends up in prison. It's too bad. It's disgusting! Running about town with his tongue out, crushing people to death.

UMBERTINO: I put my tongue out at him. Like this. (*Demonstrates.*)

GUIDO: We must go and tell Auntie. The news has nearly killed her.

GIOVANNI: Wait a moment. (*Pulls* UMBERTINO *to him.*) Tell me the truth. Were you frightened? And it's true, isn't it—you thought I was dead too? You looked under the car?

UMBERTINO: No, no, Grandpa. I only thought it for a moment. Then I realised it would have taken more than a single car. I came home quite calm. I'm hungry. Why haven't you started lunch?

GIOVANNI: You're pulling my leg, you must be. Tell me the truth, I beg you. Don't worry about lunch—you can have as many lunches as you like today. You *were* under the car, weren't you? Only you managed to keep out of the way of the wheels?

UMBERTINO (*laughing*): Why do you think I would get under the car? I jumped over to the other pavement. And if you had been where you should have been we could have finished our walk.

GIOVANNI: Finished our walk? After all that happened. (To GUIDO.) Well, it's clear enough. I thought he was dead, and he thought I was.

GUIDO: It doesn't matter now. Let's go and tell Auntie. Don't frighten her. She's next door, in her bedroom. (UMBERTINO *goes in that direction.*) Wait a moment. How can we avoid giving her too much of a shock. Listen, Umbertino. Can you limp a bit? Make her think you've hurt your leg. It will help her get used to the fact that you're all right, if we do it little by little.

UMBERTINO: Did Auntie think I was dead too? Shall I dress up in a sheet and pretend I'm a ghost?

GUIDO: Come on, come on. It's no time for jokes. (*He takes* UMBERTINO *by the hand and they go off right.*)

GIOVANNI (*Gets up to follow them but thinks better of it and goes back to his chair*): No . . .

Enter FORTUNATO, *the chauffeur-gardener.*

FORTUNATO: Am I to wait any longer, sir? I've got work to do in the garden. Now master Umbertino's come back maybe you won't need me any longer. I knew all along nothing could have happened to him.

GIOVANNI: Don't be a fool, how could you have known? How dare you pretend to have known, when I was there and didn't?

FORTUNATO: It didn't come to me at once, sir. But after half-an-hour or so, when nobody came or telephoned, I knew nothing could have happened. If Umbertino had been dead, half the city would have come down on us.

GIOVANNI (*persuaded*): Yes, that's true. I hadn't thought of that. (*With a sigh.*) I'll go to Anna's room and give the child another kiss.

FORTUNATO: And can I get on in the garden now?

GIOVANNI (*surprised*): Of course. We don't want the car now. (*Exit.*)

Enter RITA, *jumping for joy.*

RITA: After that, we ought to call it a day. We shouldn't have to do anything on a day like this, when everyone's so happy. There should be no more work today—and especially no more quarrels.

FORTUNATO (*sulkily*): I have to work.

RITA: Well, go and work then. And you like quarrelling as well, don't you?

FORTUNATO: I quarrel with people when I have to. You go on saying the same thing time and time again, till in the end you win the argument. Or at least, you pretend you think you have. I can't go on repeating myself like that—so I'm in the wrong, because of not wanting to say things a hundred times over.

RITA: Don't you realise Umbertino's back—safe and sound— curly head and all?

FORTUNATO: Yes, I'm glad. I've seen him. Only I never believed he'd let himself be smashed to pieces by a car. The old gentleman was annoyed when I said so. It would have been different if they'd told me *he'd* fallen under a motor-car. I'd have rushed straight to the garage and put our car in mourning.

RITA: You're right. I see it too now. Umbertino could never have ended up like that. But did you say it to the old gentleman before?

FORTUNATO: Before what?

RITA: Before Umbertino reappeared.

FORTUNATO: I didn't think to. I told him afterwards.

RITA: That's a pity. Because they'll never believe you foresaw it. It's a shame, because everyone here thinks you such a fool.

FORTUNATO: I'd rather be me than them. Taking all that medicine, like the old master does, instead of wine! Keeping all those pets, like the mistress! Or wearing all those veils, like the young mistress!

RITA: They say you scalped all the trees in the garden, like the demon barber.[1]

FORTUNATO: They knew I was a country boy when they took me on—I wasn't brought up on mulberry trees. And when they made me wait at table I kept scalping . . . I mean, knocking things over. But I ask you this, where will they find another chauffeur like me—not an accident in two years? Just the occasional breakdown.

RITA: About a million breakdowns!

FORTUNATO: I don't claim to be a mechanic. But I'm improving even at that. I know when to blow up the tyres, and screw things up and unscrew things. I said to Signor Guido the other day: "A motor-car isn't like the human body. With the human body, all you do is give it a little castor oil; then you ask it 'How are you feeling?' I give the car oil, in the same way. Then I get back into the driving seat and ask it: 'How are you feeling?' But there's no reply." All the same, they haven't given me the sack. I've never killed anyone. And everyone knows how dangerous cars are nowadays. . . . They have to pay the odd fine, every now and then, and they ought to be glad to. Anyway, that's not what we're arguing about.

RITA: Yes it is. Don't let's fight about anything else. In fact, don't let's fight about that. What do you say, shall I forgive you? I feel like being on good terms with everyone, even you. I love the whole world, now that Umbertino's all right.

FORTUNATO: The whole world? Guido included?

RITA: It would be pretty mean to leave him out. What's he ever done to you?

[1] Literally: "pruned all the trees in the garden à la Fieschi". Fieschi was a celebrated anarchist, of the 1900 period, who wore his scalp shaven except for a little tuft in the middle of his skull.

FORTUNATO: Nothing yet, I hope. I know what he'd like to do.

Enter GUIDO.

GUIDO: So that's over too. (*To* RITA.) Signora Chierici says I'm to stay for lunch. So lay a place for me, please.

FORTUNATO (*respectfully*): Did she give any orders for me?

GUIDO: Not as far as I know. You had better go in and ask.

FORTUNATO (*embarrassedly makes towards the door on the left, then changes his mind*): No, well, if they need me, they'll call for me. I've got work to do in the garden.

Exit FORTUNATO.

RITA (*laying the tablecloth*): I'm so happy, it's a shame I can't just enjoy my happiness and not have to spread this cloth.

GUIDO: Shall I help? With two of us to do it, it won't be such a burden. And think of the pleasure it will give me.

RITA: With two of us doing it, and one of them you, I'll never concentrate. (*Hesitantly.*) There, you see, my happiness has gone already. It's as if Umbertino had never been dead and resurrected. (GUIDO *meanwhile has been helping to spread the tablecloth.*) Thank you. (*Makes as if to leave the room.*)

GUIDO: Wait a moment, Rita. It's so rarely I have a chance to talk to you.

RITA (*laughing*): And it'll get rarer. When I'm married I shan't be allowed to talk or listen to you at all.

GUIDO: Good Lord! Do you really mean that? *After* you're married.

RITA (*laughing*): Such a *sincere* young man, aren't you?

GUIDO: I've never said a word out of place. If Fortunato takes it into his head to be jealous . . .

RITA: I like him when he's jealous. It gives him a bit of zip. That's the kind of husband for me. Look! Do you see?

FORTUNATO *is heard knocking on the window with a pair of shears. Then he appears, blinking in the sunlight.*

FORTUNATO: Rita! Are you there? I've got to clip the creeper round the window. Damn the sun! I can't see a thing.

GIOVANNI *enters, absent-mindedly.*

GIOVANNI: God knows what really happened. That boy can't remember a thing. (FORTUNATO *disappears.*) Well, one thing's certain—and it's a miracle—the child's perfectly unharmed. Perfectly! I've examined him. (*Sits down in his armchair.*)

During the rest of the scene, RITA *keeps coming in and out, laying the table.*

GIOVANNI (*after a pause*): And it's clear that he saw me under the car. So it's nothing extraordinary that I should have seen him there too . . .

GUIDO: Don't worry about it, Uncle. In the joy of seeing Umbertino safe and sound, nobody's going to worry how it happened in the first place.

GIOVANNI: Do you think so? (*Pause.*) Anyway the Gorizians will never have to know about it. Thank God for that! I shan't have to face them till Christmas. As for the rest . . . (*He suddenly gets angry.*) Good heavens! If it hadn't been for that damned idiot running off like that to tell Emma, she would never have known.

GUIDO: She would have heard when she got back.

GIOVANNI: Yes, that's true. With so many confounded chatterers about the place. (*Pause.*) All the same, that chap . . . what's his name?

GUIDO: Who?

GIOVANNI: The one who's always hanging about on our doorstep. Confound him!

GUIDO: Ah! Biggioni.

GIOVANNI: That's it. Biggioni. Couldn't we chuck him out once and for all, so he can't keep complicating every slightest thing that happens?

GUIDO: But Uncle, Signor Biggioni wants to marry Emma. It's common knowledge.

GIOVANNI: Oh that's marvellous! So I'll have him under my feet for ever and ever. It would be better if Valentino had never died.

GUIDO: Well, yes, I suppose so. But seeing that he's dead, it's better there should be someone to take his place.

GIOVANNI: And Emma's ready to have him? Then why does she keep stifling us with all that mourning? Anna's at her wit's end.

GUIDO: Emma *isn't* ready to have him. That's common knowledge too.

GIOVANNI (*irascibly*): I knew there was someone she wouldn't have. I merely didn't know it was him. You can't keep up with everything in this place.

GUIDO: I know, I know, Uncle.

GIOVANNI: As for the car . . .

GUIDO: What car, Uncle?

GIOVANNI: The one that ran over Umbertino. They'll say my mind's going, but I did my best to look. The only difference between me and the child is that I didn't actually look under the car. It gave me the horrors to think of seeing him all smashed to pieces. Of course the silly child wasn't afraid to look. He argued that if I were underneath it would interfere with the wheels—and with an idea like that in his head it wouldn't worry him what he saw. And after it happened, I looked round everywhere—I swear I did—I searched meticulously. The child had completely disappeared. There's no doubt about that. True, I didn't watch that murderous car driving off. I was so angry at the gesture the chauffeur made. I couldn't get my own back, even by shouting; so why should I look at someone who had insulted me? (*Pause.*) So all there was left to do was to run home for help. And actually, I ran back full of hope. But when I got home I found all that chaos—you saw it yourself. (*Getting angry.*) And then I found that chap—the one who wants to marry Emma—carrying me up the stairs as if I couldn't walk. He nearly had me breaking my neck. Damned idiot! Everything was in confusion, and I got confused too.

GUIDO: Uncle, allow me to speak as a doctor. Confusion is nothing in itself, but it's a sign of age. Ten or twenty years ago you wouldn't have been so confused.

GIOVANNI: I know what you're after, you scoundrel. You want to have me on the operating table. But I wasn't born yesterday. In fact I was born seventy-four years ago.

GUIDO: That's just it, I'm not talking to a child. A man of seventy-four is a man of experience *par excellence*. He's not the sort of man to refuse a chance of rejuvenation.

GIOVANNI: But he refuses the chance of being sliced up. (*He shudders.*)

GUIDO: Even when it's no more than having your fingernails cut? Uncle, I beg you. Let me go on talking to you as a doctor. We must try to be objective, we must look at things coolly and scientifically. The confusion wasn't only in the house, it was in your head, which is usually so clear and judicious. Otherwise how could you have seen the child's head crushed by those monstrous wheels.

GIOVANNI: Now no one's shouting and badgering me, I can see things clearly, even without an operation. I am certain— more or less certain—that I saw nothing at all.

GUIDO: Well then?

GIOVANNI (*heatedly*): What do you mean, "Well then?" (*Pause.*) The child was undoubtedly hit by the car. So, little by little, the memory is bound to come back to him. You'll see! You need patience with children. They can't tell you everything at once. Anyway—I don't like saying this—but Umbertino is conceited. He wants to show he's a big man, walking the streets as he likes, paying no attention to motor-cars. Operation or no operation, though old men may not see well, young ones aren't able to tell you what they've seen. And yet they always know better than their elders. Umbertino's like that already!

GUIDO: It will never happen to you, even after the operation. You wouldn't have to go back to adolescence, after all.

GIOVANNI: Even if I did, no one would be able to accuse me of that fault. No one, I tell you! If I'm nothing else, I'm

modest. (*Pause.*) The truth is, the confusion began before
I even started on the walk. Emma loaded me to the eyebrows
with advice. And that fool of a Rita, as she was putting the
child's hat on and kissing him, said these precise words—
I remember them as if it were now: "The little curly head
under a car-wheel." It's perfectly natural they should have
left a picture in my mind. And I remember, when the child
talked about the *carabinieri*, I stroked his head and thought:
"Rita can say what she likes; he's still safe and sound."
(*Pause.*) So you see, everything is perfectly clear, and there's
no reason to be thinking about operations yet.

> EMMA *rushes in, in a great state of distraction, from*
> *the centre upstage door.*

EMMA: Father! All I've got to say is, when you go out with
a child, you should come back with him, or not come back
at all.

GUIDO: But Emma, the boy's safe and sound! He's in there
with his grandmother.

EMMA (*screams*): Where? Where?

GUIDO: In Aunt Anna's bedroom.

EMMA: Umberto! Umberto! (*Rushes offstage.*)

GIOVANNI (*after a pause*): Did you hear that? Apparently,
having lost her child, the only thing that would console her
is to lose her father too. She seemed to feel more despair at
finding her father alive than her child dead.

GUIDO: You must make allowances, Uncle. She thought she
had lost her only son.

GIOVANNI: And saved her only father. (*Pause.*) Nobody could
be more tolerant and understanding than I am. But it's hard
to live so long only to hear your own daughter wishing you
dead. It's hard, very hard! After devoting your life to your
family. After toiling for them unceasingly. Till a few days
ago . . .

GUIDO: Ten years ago, Uncle.

GIOVANNI: Well, I worked till I dropped.

GUIDO: Everyone loves you, Uncle.

GIOVANNI: Do they? Ask her what she'd give to have her husband back.

GUIDO: She'd give a lot, I'm sure.

GIOVANNI: It's not that she'd give so much, but that she'd give it so cheerfully. She'd give up her father and mother. Not her son—I grant her that. The young are all she cares about.

GUIDO: Well, if they're counting on burying you soon, they're quite wrong.

GIOVANNI: What a pity you haven't finished your studies and I could believe you.

GUIDO: Oh, Uncle. You don't need much knowledge to interpret that report of yours. Look! (*Takes the report out of his pocket.*) Everything normal. There never was anything like it, in a man of your age.

GIOVANNI: "Normal" . . . "Normal" . . . "Normal" again. And you tell me that in spite of not feeling very well and my digestion not being so good and not sleeping as I used to, everything is in perfect working order?

GUIDO: "Normal", "Normal", "Normal". When you're old, a certain degree of aging is *de rigueur*, and it shows itself in the symptoms you mention. But the report proves that your youth is still there, ready to be tapped.

GIOVANNI: By an operation?

GUIDO: By an operation. One which you couldn't have in any other circumstances, and which this is the last chance for— I couldn't recommend it, if you weren't still in perfect health.

GIOVANNI: I hope you won't mention the report to Anna or my daughter. I have a feeling they treat me better when they think I'm ill.

GUIDO: I won't tell anyone about it. It's been paid for. So that's that.

GIOVANNI: How much did it cost?

GUIDO: Fifty lire.

GIOVANNI (*takes five ten-lira notes out of his wallet*): Make sure there aren't six there.

GUIDO : No. Five exactly. (*Pause.*) I'm only talking like this because I'm fond of you, you understand? Yours is the ideal case for this operation.

GIOVANNI : It would certainly be nice to be young again. In this world of today one isn't allowed to be old.

GUIDO : It was never a very pleasant thing to be, in any world.

GIOVANNI : Not at all. When I was young it was only the old who were respected. Oh, I remember it so well. They called me "the young shaver". When they had something grown-up to tell one another, they said "See, even fleas have the itch!" And now I'm old, only the young are respected. I've never been respected myself my whole life through.

GUIDO : It's because this is the age for youth. And anyone who has the chance to be young ought to take it.

GIOVANNI : I know what you're getting at. The operation.

GUIDO : Exactly! No more doddering, no more feeble appetite, no more children under car-wheels.

GIOVANNI : As for children under cars, I only ever saw one in my life, and I hope never to see another. If it were merely for that, I certainly wouldn't face the risk and expense of an operation. The expense is enormous. Look! (*He takes out a little notebook and searches through it.*) You say the operation lasts for ten years. Well then, if that's so, that's to say if its effects last for ten full years of 365 days of 24 hours each, youth is going to cost me 82½ cents an hour. Would you like to check the figures?

GUIDO : Uncle! I haven't the slightest doubt they are accurate.

GIOVANNI : Well then! Doesn't it strike you that this youth you are offering me comes rather dear? And it comes all the dearer when you ask yourself; "What use is it to me when I'm asleep?" I might as well be without it.

GUIDO : You will sleep longer, Uncle.

GIOVANNI : So much the worse. It will add to the cost of my waking hours, already enormously expensive. And then, and then . . . I have the greatest faith in you, but still, you haven't finished your studies. What if my youth only lasted five years instead of ten? I would be losing fifty per cent of my investment. And that's not all. When five years were up I should have to have another operation and spend the same again. (*Pause.*) And after all, my family look up to me as a model. If in the meantime you discover how to rejuvenate women too, Anna will want to follow my lead. It's going to ruin me.

GUIDO: Don't worry, Uncle. For technical reasons, the operation can't be performed on women. And anyway, as it's men who invented it, you can rest assured they haven't troubled about women. There are too many already.

GIOVANNI (*hesitantly*): You should go and have another word with Giannottini. His charges are excessive. All the more so if the operation is only like cutting your nails.

GUIDO: If I were in your shoes, I wouldn't worry about the expense. What do you want to leave so much money for? Who to?

GIOVANNI: *Leave* money? I want to enjoy it myself. Just as you suggested. Why else should I want the operation? But you mustn't rush me. Dr Raulli said the operation might shorten one's life. Have you come across that possibility in your text-books?

GUIDO: You'd have to be a . . . master-mind like Dr Raulli to believe a thing like that. I mean, to believe that an operation to restore youth could actually shorten life. He makes me angry! He can't find any good arguments, and so he takes the first to hand, the weirdest he could find. Remember that by a few days after the operation the patient's blood-pressure will have gone down noticeably! Which means that he's a hundred per cent safe against his great enemy, a sudden stroke.

GIOVANNI: It would be very nice to be safe against one disease. But there are so many diseases in the world—more's the pity. And that's the one disease I've never been frightened of. Look at my neck. No one could call it a thick neck. It's the classic text-book neck, a neck as normal as my report.

GUIDO: Still, high blood-pressure produces all sorts of other bad effects: congestion of the kidneys, and the lungs, and the liver.

GIOVANNI: Dr Raulli doesn't agree with you. He says my blood-pressure is just right for my age. It's normal, if you take my age into account.

GUIDO: Sly old devil! If he told *me* my blood-pressure was right for my age, I'd be delighted, as I'm only twenty. But if I were seventy-four and they told me my blood-pressure was only what I could expect at my age, I would be in despair —in despair about my blood-pressure and in despair about my age.

GIOVANNI: What's that? I don't follow.

GUIDO: I'll explain it again, Uncle, after the operation.

GIOVANNI: I don't know what you're getting at. (*Pause.*) Anyway, I'm right in believing you think the operation cannot shorten life?

GUIDO: Yes, certainly. And what I'm also sure about is that even if it didn't actually lengthen your life, your remaining years would be more intense, more worth living.

GIOVANNI: But what I'm most concerned about is living a long time. For Anna's sake, and that ungrateful girl Emma's. And for the sake of that child that I'm helping to bring up and take for walks every day. Not for my own sake; as far as I'm concerned, since I stopped work I haven't found life much fun.

GUIDO: When you've been rejuvenated, Uncle, you'll be able to go back to work again too.

GIOVANNI (*emphatically*): No, no! That's all been arranged; I couldn't possibly.

GUIDO: Well then, we'll forget work. I wish I had the same arrangement over *my* work. But if you want to have the operation, don't listen to Dr Raulli. That must be the first operation—severing communication with Raulli.

GIOVANNI: Luckily that's one operation that won't cost much. But you'll have to speak to that doctor . . . that miracle-worker . . . what's his name?

GUIDO: Giannottini.

GIOVANNI: To Dr Giannottini, and ask him to think seriously . . .

GUIDO (*firmly*): It's no good, Uncle. You mustn't expect a reduction in price. Dr Giannottini has very high overheads. Apart from anything else, there's the expense of advertising.

GIOVANNI: I don't see why I should pay for Dr Giannottini's advertising. What's it got to do with me? It doesn't apply in my case. You were my advertisement. Does Dr Giannottini pay you?

GUIDO: I give you my word, he pays me nothing.

GIOVANNI (*mollified*): I thought so. I believe you. Seeing how much I give you out of love for my dead brother, you couldn't stoop to profiting out of . . . out of my heart's blood. Because that's what it would mean.—And so he'll deduct the charge for advertising, since it doesn't apply in my case.

GUIDO (*dubiously*): I'll see what I can do, but I'm afraid . . .

GIOVANNI: And then, I'm not going to rush into the thing. Now I've given up business, I've sworn I'll make no more bad deals. I've got plenty of time on my hands, and I'm going to think this out carefully. You explained to me that my operation produces a twenty-per-cent rejuvenation. Well then, if I have it at the age of seventy-four—take or leave a few days—I shall gain fourteen and a half years precisely. Now look. (*He thumbs hurriedly through his notebook.*) Here it is! I've worked it out exactly. By every year I postpone the operation I gain 73 days, reaching an optimum benefit at the age of a hundred, when I gain twenty years precisely. Look at the table I've drawn up. It goes up to 120. I got bored then, and gave it up.

GUIDO (*laughing discreetly*): It's a beautiful table. I like it awfully.

GIOVANNI: You can check it yourself. It's absolutely accurate. I allowed for leap years. And so I'm going to wait. I'm in reasonably good health. My legs really carry me quite well. You should have seen me running home this morning. I got here in a flash. I couldn't believe I was there. And my stomach's in perfect working order to.

GUIDO: I thought you hadn't been eating dinner for some time now?

GIOVANNI: Yes, but that's so I shall sleep better.

GUIDO: And those eternal purges . . .

GIOVANNI: Purges are an excellent thing, excellent. See how clear my head is. You saw that table I drew up. Could anyone have done it better, more clearly, more scientifically? First my different ages; next the years I have to deduct, to two figures of decimals; then the remainder. I'm as good as I ever was.

GUIDO: Well then, that's that. I've done my duty as a doctor. Let's forget about it.

GIOVANNI: No, let's go on talking about it. It costs nothing to talk about it. I know all about the operation by now. I've discussed it with various people. Before having it, there's something else to consider. You scoundrel, you! You wanted me to rush into it!

GUIDO: Into what?

GIOVANNI: Into the operation. And you didn't tell me that when I'd had it, I might defile my white hairs, going to the well.

GUIDO: Going to the well??

GIOVANNI: Yes, in search of servant-girls.

GUIDO (catching on): Ah, I follow. (He laughs.) You needn't worry. They don't go to the well any longer.

GIOVANNI: What difference does that make? You meant to disgrace me. That's what you wanted. And I refuse. I don't deny I'd like to live a long time, and enjoy myself, but not at the expense of my good name.

GUIDO: You talk of your good name and what you mean is your old age. You're so old, Uncle, you've got to like old age. It's very natural. But is that old man's attitude towards women—if "attitude" is the word—something to admire? Speaking as a young man, I don't think so. That's the result of being young. I don't like old age, and when you're young again, you won't either—sluggish, feeble, squalid old age.

GIOVANNI (*indignantly*): Impudent puppy! "Sluggish?" And why is it sluggish? Because virtue is more peace-loving than vice. For no other reason. A murderer is always less sluggish than the person he murders. It's in the nature of things.

GUIDO: And the other one is dead, anyway.

GIOVANNI: But I'm talking of him when he's not dead.

GUIDO: I understand, Uncle. I was only joking.

GIOVANNI: And what were the other vile things you called old age? Oh yes, "squalid". I wash more often than any young man. I wash my hands four times a day. It's the only answer to all the germs. In fact, I believe I owe my good health to it. I always change the water twice when I'm washing.

GUIDO: I wasn't talking about you, Uncle. I was talking about animals, which only have instinct to guide them. It's well-known that mice, when they're old, give up washing, but after they've been operated on they start washing themselves again scrupulously.

GIOVANNI: The old age of mice is an entirely different matter. You'll find what I say is true. As you grow older, all your good qualities will go on increasing, whereas your bad ones will drop away; they may actually disappear. Who knows whether Dr Giannottini's operation may not give me tendencies which will dishonour my white hair. A pretty thing if I took to running after women like a chimpanzee.

GUIDO: But you have your wife, after all.

GIOVANNI: Anna, do you mean? (*He grows thoughtful.*) Wouldn't it be better, all the same, to tell Dr Giannottini I want to remain virtuous. As virtuous as an old man, though as young as a young one too.

GUIDO: All right, I'll tell him.

GIOVANNI: Of course I don't mean I want the operation to be any less efficacious. You'll have to put two things to Giannottini. He must guarantee that, whilst I enjoy all the benefits of his operation, there is no danger to my morals—that's to say, to my good name. And secondly . . . There's

something else that we were discussing, equally important.
. . . Ah yes! I don't want to pay so much. I don't want to
have to pay more than eighty cents an hour—a waking
hour, I should say.

GUIDO (*in a whisper so that* RITA, *who has come nearer, shan't
hear*): eighty cents an hour is meaningless. You must state
an overall figure.

GIOVANNI (*who hasn't heard*): What's that? Eighty cents an
hour, I say; not a cent more.

GUIDO (*trying to distract* RITA's *attention*): How is Signora
Emma?

RITA: Poor lady! She hasn't taken her hat off yet. She's been
kissing her child ever since. (*She goes out to fetch more
crockery.*)

GIOVANNI: Don't bother about Emma. Where were we? You
thought the operation was cheap at the price? Well, that's
only your opinion. You don't have to pay for it.

GUIDO: That wasn't what I said, Uncle. All I felt was that if
I were in your shoes I wouldn't think about the cost of the
operation till after I'd had it, and had been rejuvenated.

GIOVANNI: Brilliant! Clinch the deal first, and then see
whether it was a wise one. Phoo. Have they been operating
on you. Have they reduced you to the age of twelve? You're
talking like a child. What am I to do if I have the operation
and then find I get no benefit from it? Can I return the un-
wanted goods?

GUIDO: No, you certainly can't return them! (*Laughs.*)

GIOVANNI: You think it's funny, you young scoundrel. You
don't have to pay the bill, or be chopped up, or see yourself
morally corrupted.

GUIDO: I wouldn't mind the moral-corruption part. That
might be rather enjoyable. But tell me, Uncle, why do you
think that getting your youth back is going to make you
immoral? Were you immoral as a young man?

GIOVANNI: No, certainly not!

GUIDO: Well, you would become what you had been, again.
neither more nor less.

GIOVANNI : That's true. And so, if the operation has no effect upon character, then . . . then I would relive a blameless life, a life without stain. Rather a fine thing, really; an example to others. Of course it would be costing me . . . but it doesn't matter; a fine example. I only ever loved one woman, and I married her.

GUIDO : Uncle! Aren't you forgetting Margherita, the one you told me about a week or two ago, that Sunday we went for a walk together.

GIOVANNI (*remembering*): Ah! Margherita. I loved her with a pure Platonic love, though. (*Dubiously.*) Wasn't that what I told you?

GUIDO : Yes, that's what you told me, and I believed it.

GIOVANNI : I know to you, you young Belial, it might not seem credible. You belong to a different era. I treated Margherita like a saint. I didn't even touch . . . her clothes. I gazed at her, I fell in love, and I wrote her a certain amount of poetry. Wasn't that what I told you?

GUIDO : You said you used to sing duets together.

GIOVANNI : Yes, but that was all we ever did. (*Pause.*) I wasn't allowed to marry the poor girl. No one else in my family liked her; they said she walked coquettishly. Stupid nonsense! The coquettishness wasn't in her clothes and walk, it was in her legs themselves, her figure. Anyway, if I'd married her, I wouldn't have been able to marry Anna. But whichever happened, everything would have been pure and above-board. Whether I'd married the one or the other, I mean, my conduct would have been irreproachable. I am a man of virtue.

RITA *keeps coming in and out. Enter* EMMA.

EMMA : Father! Can you forgive me for speaking so unkindly to you?

GIOVANNI (*chillily*): Yes, I can forgive you, I do forgive you. It is my wish to forgive you. All the same, you did say you wished I were dead.

EMMA (*bursting into tears*): No, no, Father.

GIOVANNI: I have a perfectly good memory. You said: "When . . ." Well, in short you wanted me dead. It was hard for me to hear my own daughter wishing me dead. It was a hard thing and a dangerous one too. When a daughter prays for her own father's death, the prayer might be heard. I haven't got over it yet. And not because I'm afraid of dying. As far as I am concerned, death would be a blessed release, the reward for a life of incessant toil—all for your mother's sake, and yours, and the child's.

EMMA (*still in tears*): Forgive me, Father. I didn't know what I was saying. They had told me my child had been murdered.

GIOVANNI (*mollified*): And instead, he was perfectly safe and sound, and you were going to see him a moment or two afterwards.

EMMA: But I wasn't to know that then.

GIOVANNI (*nonplussed for a moment*): But if you'd remembered that I have been going out with the child every day for two years, and nothing has happened, you wouldn't have screamed at me as you did. You should have thought, and considered, before wounding me like that. (*Pause.*) At all events, that's the last time I take the child for a walk.

EMMA (*gently*): Yes, Papa. That will be best. Either you don't go at all, or I come too.

GIOVANNI (*speechless for a moment*): So you don't trust me any more?

EMMA (*tearfully*): What can I say, Papa? That child is all I have in the world.

GIOVANNI: At least tears lead to the truth. So your mother and father count for nothing with you.

EMMA (*collapsing into an armchair*): Oh how cruel, how cruel life is to me! My life was over when my husband died.

GIOVANNI: I lost a great deal too, when Valentino died. He gave me love and respect. But the dead are always kinder than the living. He—the poor dead soul—he was delighted for me to go out with his son every morning, whereas you want to forbid me it—the one amusement I have in my endless day. (*Working himself up into a passion.*) And in those days the child was much younger than he is now. He wouldn't have been able to go running after motor-cars and looking underneath them. So what might have happened today, and didn't, could have happened . . . I mean couldn't have happened. (*He gets confused.*)

Enter ANNA *from left and* ENRICO *from upstage.*

ENRICO: What wonderful news! And here was I, with a heavy heart. True, the hospital hadn't heard of any child being run over, but that proved nothing. My warmest congratulations. I couldn't have asked for a better reward for all my errand-going.

ANNA: Thank you, Signor Enrico. You will find us all so happy, so relieved.

ENRICO: But Signora Emma is crying? (*Looking at* EMMA.)

ANNA: It's the relief, isn't it? (*Going over to* EMMA.)

ENRICO: If they are tears of happiness, let them fall. Tears of that sort can wipe out a thousand troubles.

EMMA *shrugs, crossly.*

GIOVANNI (*still on his feet, absorbed in his quarrel with* EMMA *and oblivious of everyone else in the room*): And there's another thing. I've been going out daily with the child for two years. So it's a simple matter of arithmetic—I've been out with him 720 times.

ENRICO: 730.

GIOVANNI: It makes no difference, ten more or ten less. Something was bound to happen . . . I mean, could easily have happened. You can't expect to do the same thing every day and things to go right every time. And now you want us to make a threesome of it! All the more chance for something to happen. Anyway, I'm not coming with you. Everything has always been all right when I was there. And here's the child, safe and sound and full of mischief, and yet you want to punish me.

EMMA: I don't want to punish you, Father.

ENRICO: But think if you *had* been seeing properly.

GIOVANNI (*disconcerted*): Do you mean I didn't? (*Pause.*) I beg your pardon, but what is it to do with you?

ENRICO (*alarmed*): I only meant . . . As poor Valentino's friend I merely wouldn't like any further tragedies to fall on Signora Emma.

GIOVANNI: Do you mean to say that if Valentino were alive he would say I was in the wrong? No, no; he loved and respected me.

EMMA: And I don't, you mean?

ENRICO: As poor Valentino's friend I bear you the deepest respect.

RITA (*approaching from upstage*): Lunch is served.

GIOVANNI: I simply don't understand why you keep tormenting me with an incident . . . which never happened. Let's sit down to lunch. I'm just going to wash my hands. (*Goes towards the door, left. Aside, to* GUIDO.) Guido! I've more or less decided to have the operation. With people like this round me, one simply can't afford to be old. I want to sleep on it, but I've more or less made up my mind.

GUIDO: Well then, I'll come tomorrow morning for your decision. When you've slept on it.

GIOVANNI: No, no. I'll have decided by four o'clock this afternoon. So go and see Giannottini in the interval, and arrange those two things I mentioned. You remember?

GUIDO: Yes, Uncle. The price, and the moral question.

GIOVANNI: That's it. And the moral question. And be back here at four. We'll fix the thing then. Can it be done tomorrow?

GUIDO: As soon as you like.

GIOVANNI: Don't tell anyone but Anna. Let's give them a surprise; let them suddenly see me a young man again. Perhaps that will teach them to pay me more respect. (*Pause.*) "We'll all three of us go for walks." Did you hear her? Well, I'll show her.

Exit left.

ANNA: What did he say?

GUIDO: I can tell you, Aunt Anna. It's first-class news. Uncle has agreed to undergo the operation, as we wanted him to.

ANNA: Poor darling, isn't that splendid for him. But what will Dr Raulli say?

GUIDO: Don't worry, Aunt Anna. We won't consult him till it's done.

EMMA: What's going on, Mamma?

ANNA (to EMMA, but so that ENRICO can also hear): Papa has finally decided to undergo the operation. I'm sure his principal reason is so that he shan't lose his beloved outings with the little boy.

EMMA: An operation? What operation?

ENRICO: It's one which produces rejuvenation—certain and immediate rejuvenation. Signor Guido, who knows much more than I about it of course, will be able to explain it to you. (Hypocritically.) Think how unlucky we have been, Signora Emma! If poor Valentino hadn't died six months ago, this operation—quite a simple one—might have saved him.

GUIDO: I was one of the first to spread the news of the operation. If it hadn't been for me, very likely it might have been too late for Uncle too. And as always, I shall get nothing out of it myself. When Uncle has been rejuvenated, no one will remember me.

ANNA: Till you've qualified, you can't expect anything. When you are, you'll get paid, whatever kind of mess you make.

EMMA (bursting into tears): It seems such a terrible, such an unspeakable piece of injustice! Only six months later, and Valentino could have enjoyed the youth that was his by right.

ENRICO: That happens in medicine every day, doesn't it, Signor Guido? Two of my brothers died as children from diphtheria. Their fault for not waiting for the cure to be invented.

EMMA: So everything happened just as you could have wanted it.

ENRICO: I never wanted my brothers to die. I swear it.

EMMA: Mama, I'll have lunch later. I shouldn't be able to eat

anything now. All these disturbances, and Papa's reproaches
. . . I must go and lie down. Look after Umbertino for me.
I'll send him in. Goodbye. (*She gives a faint nod to the company and leaves the room.*)

ANNA: Poor thing! Signor Biggioni, you of all people ought
to feel for her.

ENRICO: Oh but I do, I do nothing else. For eight months I
have . . .

ANNA: Yes, for eight months.

GUIDO: But my poor dear friend, why did you talk to her
about the operation, and about how it might have saved
Valentino's life? It's just what you were so frightened of
doing; and yet you plunged straight over the precipice.

ENRICO: I don't know why I did it. The thing was stronger
than me. But perhaps it's better this way. No doubt she
would have been better pleased to have been told about the
operation when it could still have helped Valentino. But
that's not my fault. She could see I told her as soon as I
could.

GUIDO: Yes, that's true! And one could also guess what
thanks you would get.

ANNA: You made a great mistake, Signor Biggioni, you really
did. I would have said nothing, if I were you.

GIOVANNI: Let's sit down to lunch.

He sits down at the head of the table, and ANNA *helps
him to put on his napkin.* GUIDO *sits down likewise,
but* ENRICO *walks to and fro, deep in thought.*

Where's Emma! You know I like everyone to be punctual
at meals.

ANNA (*embarrassed*): She has had an attack of nerves.

GIOVANNI: Out of annoyance at my not being dead. It seems
to me thoroughly rude, her not being at table with us, and
I hope you'll tell her so. I don't want it to happen again.
(*To* GUIDO, *aside.*) After lunch, go along to Giannottini
right away and make arrangements, then come and collect
me. (*To* RITA, *who is bringing him a carafe of water.*) Rita.

Tell Fortunato to have the car ready for me at four o'clock. I'm going out. (*Pause.*) Now for some soup . . .

> *Suddenly he gets up, with his napkin still round his neck, and brings* ANNA *forward with him to the proscenium arch.*

I've made up my mind, Anna. This is no world for old men. I'll have the operation, even if it kills me.

ANNA (*alarmed*): Kill you? But Guido says it's nothing at all.

GIOVANNI: Doctors always talk like that. And then, when they've made a mistake, they bury it.

GUIDO (*coming to join them*): What's the matter, Uncle?

ANNA: Uncle says that the operation might be dangerous. (*Distressed.*) Why take such a risk? As if we weren't quite happy as we are. I don't want him running risks.

GUIDO: Tut, tut, Uncle's only joking.

GIOVANNI: He's a doctor already—at least he's talking just like one. I don't trust him. When doctors make a mistake, they hide it underground.

ENRICO: Everyone agrees the operation's nothing to worry about. All too much so. If it weren't so, Emma might be less upset.

GIOVANNI: What's that? I don't understand a word. What's Emma got to do with it? (*Turning to* EMMA, *ignoring* ENRICO.)

ANNA: Emma is crying because the operation wasn't tried on poor Valentino.

GIOVANNI: Valentino? But he was rotten to the marrow; he was quite repulsive. How could they try anything of the kind on him? In my case, being perfectly normal, it's a different matter.

ENRICO (*delightedly*): Oh if only you dared say that to Emma.

GIOVANNI: Say what?

ENRICO: That poor Valentino stank.

GIOVANNI: Why on earth should I? (*Working himself up into a passion.*) But there are plenty of things I do want to tell her, and I will, too. (*Pause.*) But one of the things I don't

understand . . . not in the least . . . is, how did you know
I was having an operation? Who told you?

ENRICO (*after a moment's hesitation*): You told me so yourself.
(GIOVANNI *gapes at him in amazement.*)

ANNA: Signor Biggioni, please . . . won't you sit down . . .
won't you have some lunch?

ENRICO: No, it's very kind of you, but I mustn't disturb you.
Though I would like to say a word to Signora Emma before
I go. She said goodbye to me in such a strange manner . . .

ANNA: Sit down, then. (ENRICO *sits at the empty table.*)

GIOVANNI: Did I tell this gentleman about my operation?

ANNA (*hesitantly*): I . . . think so . . . perhaps.

GIOVANNI: I wouldn't have invited him to lunch myself. I
don't take to the fellow a bit. Why's he so pleased I'm being
operated on?

ANNA: I'm sure he thinks it's for your good.

GIOVANNI: What's his name?

ANNA: Biggioni. Enrico Biggioni. I had to invite him, or we'd
never have started lunch.

GIOVANNI: I see. (*They sit down.* GIOVANNI *looks in the direction of the window.*) That girl Rita's forgotten to get my
chair ready.

ANNA (*she rings for* RITA, *then shouts*): Rita, Rita . . . Margherita.

GIOVANNI: Margherita? Is her name Margherita?

ANNA: That's right. Rita! Didn't you know?

GIOVANNI: I never gave it a thought. (*He begins eating.*)
Margherita! Very odd. A housemaid. (*Goes on eating.*) I
brought her and Fortunato together myself. (*He resumes
eating, somewhat uneasily.*)

ENRICO: Would you like me to move the armchair?

GUIDO: I can do it. (*He gets up.*)

ENRICO: Please, let me do it. (*He moves the armchair to the
window.*) Do you like the sun?

GIOVANNI (*dropping his spoon in the soup-plate in fury*): What
the devil do you think you're doing? Do you expect me
to go to sleep in the blazing sunlight?

ENRICO: Don't worry, don't worry. (*He moves the armchair.*)

GIOVANNI: Not there! In half an hour the sun will have come round to there.

ENRICO: Don't worry. There! (*He pushes the armchair towards the proscenium arch.*)

GIOVANNI: Not so far! Not so far! Do you want to send me to the North Pole? What I want is some of the warmth of the sun and none of its light. Do you understand, man? It's perfectly simple.

ENRICO: I've done it. Look. Just as you wanted it.

GIOVANNI (*surlily*): More or less.

ANNA: Where's Umbertino? We must call him. Rita . . . Rita . . . Margherita!

GIOVANNI (*mutters wonderingly to himself*): Margherita . . .

Curtain

DREAM SEQUENCE

The same room. The sun has disappeared. The characters are bathed in a pale bluish light.

The stage is occupied by Dr Raulli, four other doctors in long white coats, GIOVANNI, and in the background, stretched out on the table, and invisible to begin with, RITA. The real GIOVANNI is also visible, asleep in his armchair.

GIOVANNI: I have summoned you here . . .

RAULLI: Let me speak, please. We know everything you have to say, so there's no need to say it. Talking is tiring for the patient. And anyway he wouldn't know what to say. And if he did, it would still not be worth hearing.

GIOVANNI: But listen. I want to say, about this operation . . .

RAULLI: We know, we know. It's all arranged.

FIRST DOCTOR: Yes, I managed to persuade Dr Raulli . . .

RAULLI: Persuade me? Don't be absurd. A young fellow like you, knowing nothing about it.

SECOND DOCTOR: It was really I who first explained to him about it.

THIRD DOCTOR: We all knew about it years ago.

FOURTH DOCTOR: That's right. Everyone knew everything.

RAULLI: Then we're all agreed. Let me say that why I didn't want my patient to have the operation was that he was too young, too vigorous still. (*To* GIOVANNI, *in an imperious tone*.) Wasn't that what I said?

GIOVANNI: I don't remember very clearly.

RAULLI: Wasn't that what I said ten days or more ago, in the psychiatric report?

THE DOCTORS: He did, he did.

RAULLI: The patient was perfectly normal.

GIOVANNI: Yes, that's quite true. It cost me fifty lire.

RAULLI: It was accurate, whatever it cost. And then, I had another reason for hesitating. What use is the operation to someone who means to be virtuous?

GIOVANNI: I said that myself—when I was talking to young Guido, for example . . .

RAULLI: I hope you mean it, when you say "for example". The matter is not to be discussed with Guido. That's final.

THE DOCTORS: Not to be discussed with Guido. That's final.

GIOVANNI: What about the others? My wife, my daughter?

RAULLI (*impatiently*): What's all this nonsense about talking to people?

GIOVANNI (*in desperation*): But what am I to do? Women aren't like they were when I was young. They don't take their jugs to the well any more. There's running water.

RAULLI: Running water in the house represents progress in hygiene.

THE DOCTORS: Now he's developed a grudge against running water. It's quite essential for him to be rejuvenated—as quickly as possible. Let's tie him up and hand him over to Dr Giannottini.

GIOVANNI: But I *asked* you here to get your advice. You'll get paid. Don't worry.

RAULLI: And you mustn't worry about the expense. It's nothing at all.

GIOVANNI: I wouldn't have said that.

RAULLI: Where's your little book? You've done the sum wrong. Give me the book.

GIOVANNI (*searching anxiously in his pockets*): I haven't got it.

RAULLI: Well then! I will inform you that the operation costs merely ten lire a woman.

GIOVANNI: Ten lire for every woman? Good God!

RAULLI: That's to say each woman in her original location. Transport comes extra.

GIOVANNI (*reassured*): Well then, I won't transport them.

RAULLI: That's up to you. Even younger men differ about that; some employ transport, and some leave their women in their original location. Everyone to his own taste.

GIOVANNI: What frightens me is those women with short hair and short skirts.

RAULLI: Short skirts never hurt anyone, and their hair's not too short to pull.

THE DOCTORS: Assuming they're feeling like a romp.

RAULLI: In fact, I want to have the operation too. Now, at once. While everything's still normal. Otherwise you can get another doctor.

GIOVANNI: And you can't reduce the fee?

RAULLI: Think yourself lucky it's so moderate. When they pass the decree compelling all the old men in Trieste to have the operation, then you'll see.

GIOVANNI: If I didn't have it, I should be the only old man left in Trieste. It would be a magnificent position.

RAULLI: No, no. There would be all the old men for whom the operation had failed.

GIOVANNI: I couldn't spend my time with them, I agree.

RAULLI: Well, then? Have you made up your mind?

GIOVANNI: More or less. I'd like to think about it just a little more, in my armchair there, while I'm having a nap.

RAULLI: Take a look at the first woman we have in store for

you. This one is provided *gratis*; that's to say she's included in the price of the operation. (*He leads him towards the table on which* RITA *is lying asleep.*)

GIOVANNI: A most improper spectacle. Rita asleep on the table.

RAULLI: You mean Margherita!

GIOVANNI: Ah! Margherita. Ah yes, I see. That's a different matter.

RAULLI: Do you find her attractive?

GIOVANNI: I've known her all my life! She grew up in my household. When she first came, she was only *that* high. When I say I knew her, I don't mean anything else. I was a virtuous old man. Of course, now that I come to look at her . . . she does have remarkably tiny feet . . .

RAULLI: Ah! Ah! It's beginning to have results.

He gives GIOVANNI *a poke in the stomach, and the stage is plunged in darkness.*

Curtain

Act II

The same dining-room. Early afternoon.

Enter GIOVANNI, *cigar in mouth, much more smartly dressed than in Act I, and well-brushed and shaved. He also walks more energetically, but with conscious effort. He enters briskly from the left, knocks his knee against the table-leg, and goes off to the right, limping and senile.*

Enter RITA *and* FORTUNATO.

RITA: He's the master's nephew. I can't possibly be rude to him. You said so yourself. You said "Keep him at a distance, but in a friendly way". That's just what I'm doing.

FORTUNATO: Yes, but you're overdoing the friendliness. You're a friendly . . . hussy. That's what you are.

RITA (*in tears*): You seem to think I'm a child. You seem to think he could . . . (*sobs*) without my realising.

FORTUNATO: You don't listen to me any more. You don't listen to what I say. For the last week I've been saying "keep him at a distance". Just that. Nothing about doing it friendlily. Do you understand?

RITA (*hesitantly*): No.

FORTUNATO: You're like a car with bad ignition. The engine's all right, the petrol's all right, but it won't start. Will you or won't you listen to me? When he wants to get you in conversation, when he tries to come close to you, all you have to do is turn your back. Tell him to go to hell.

RITA: Oh!

FORTUNATO (*imitating her*): Oh!

RITA: And what about our new house? What about our situation here?

FORTUNATO: What's that got to do with it? We're employed by Signora Anna, and she's fond of you, and Signor Giovanni, and he's fond of you too.

RITA: The old pig.

FORTUNATO: Nice language! "Old pig!"

RITA: He used to be our dear, sweet old gentleman, who made us laugh with his funny ways—for all his stinginess. Now he's an old pig; he's not funny, he's disgusting.

FORTUNATO (*laughing*): Do you mean he interferes with you?

RITA: He's a hypocrite! Even when the mistress is in the room, he manages to get his hands on me. Yesterday evening he asked me when the wedding was, and as he was talking he took my hand. Then, ever so gently, he worked his way up to my shoulders. He was trying it on.

FORTUNATO: Trying it on?

RITA: I know he was, because a few days ago he found me on my own, and he told me he loved me like a daughter, he wanted to look after me and my family like a father . . .

FORTUNATO: Well what's wrong with that?

RITA: Then he said he wanted to be *sure* that was all he felt. He said it just like that. He tried to give me a kiss on the lips. (*She wipes her lips.*) Ugh, disgusting! On the lips! With that toothless old mouth!

FORTUNATO: As long as you find him disgusting, there's no harm done. (*Pause.*) And was the test successful?

RITA: How do I know? The mistress came along, and he started fiddling with his collar, to give himself something to do. He was all red and embarrassed. I noticed it all right, though the mistress didn't. I don't think she's looked in his face for years. And you can see why.

FORTUNATO: Don't worry yourself, my dear. I don't believe in the great Doctor Guido's operation. I notice the old gentleman's teeth haven't grown again; and you can't eat without teeth, you know. I'll keep an eye on him. If I see him really being rejuvenated—when I see that look in his eye—

I'll warn the mistress and ask her to keep him in order. In the meantime, I shouldn't worry. The old chap doesn't worry me. There used to be a learned man in our village and everyone went to him for advice. One day a young girl went to him and asked him what to do about her old master—he was seventy years old but he kept running after her, and she didn't want to offend him. Do you know what he said?

RITA: What did he say?

FORTUNATO: He told her to open her arms to him, and say "Here I am, take me". He knew a thing or two, that fellow. That's what I call clever.

RITA (*alarmed*): And that's what you want me to do?

FORTUNATO: No, I don't say that. All I mean is, the other old chap didn't find it a bit encouraging. He said: "Now? Just like that?"

RITA: But he hadn't had an operation.

FORTUNATO: Forget about the operation. If he isn't put off when you say it, and wants to take advantage of it, I can trust you to deal with him. . . . At least, as long as you find him disgusting. When I find you don't any longer, then will be the time to speak to the mistress. What I want now, is for the business with Master Guido to stop. We don't need Master Guido's friendship any more.

RITA: He doesn't care a pin about me.

FORTUNATO (*raising his voice*): Stop lying, or I'll start thinking the worst.

ANNA *enters*

ANNA: What's all this shouting about?

FORTUNATO (*after some hesitation*): She won't believe that you gave orders . . . for your bedroom to be spring-cleaned today.

ANNA: I told you so myself, Rita.

RITA: I'd forgotten.

ANNA (*reprovingly*): Your fiancé shouldn't have to shout to make you listen.

Exeunt FORTUNATO *and* RITA. *Enter* ENRICO *from upstage door.*

ENRICO: Here's the silk-pattern, Signora Chierici. I've gone all over town for it, and I think I've got just what you wanted. Look; a sort of silver-grey.

ANNA (*examining the pattern closely*): Yes, that's it, exactly. Thank you so much, Signor Enrico. How much did it cost you?

ENRICO (*embarrassed*): Heavens, I've forgotten. How much would it usually cost?

ANNA: Between 50 and 55 lire.

ENRICO (*seriously*): I rather think I got it for slightly less— between 45 and 50. I rather think I remember that.

ANNA: Signor Enrico! You must remember, I don't expect you to make me presents. I shall be angry unless you charge me the proper price. I'm very grateful to you for helping me with little purchases, like this; but I expect to pay the normal price. (*Angrily.*) You're not trying to give me money, I hope?

ENRICO (*apologetically*): Wait five minutes and I'll go and find out the right price.

ANNA (*maternally*): The point is, you mustn't overdo things. Emma was beginning to give you little commissions too, you remember, but then she got suspicious about that coffee you bought for her, that superfine coffee. She decided you'd charged her too little.

ENRICO: You should remember I'm a coffee-merchant my-self. Nobody else could get that coffee at that price.

ANNA: But we had Signor Alfi here the other day. He's a coffee-merchant too, and when Emma showed him it, he said he'd buy a boatload of it any day at that price.

ENRICO: What did Emma say?

ANNA: She was very angry. That's not the way to behave with her. I've told you before not to make declarations to her. Giving her coffee is a declaration if ever there was one. You simply mustn't do it. You're doing quite enough making yourself useful, and we're very grateful. Today you can go for a walk with Umbertino. His grandfather doesn't want to go.

ENRICO: What time then?

ANNA: Four o'clock.

ENRICO (*looking at his watch*): Very well. But meanwhile I want some advice from you. I've found a little book by a learned Protestant theologian arguing that mourning should be abolished. His arguments are really quite persuasive. What do you think? Could I offer it to Emma as a present? (*He shows her the book.*)

ANNA (*taking it and examining with interest*): I would say no. It would be unfair to your pretty little book. She'd tear it up on the spot. Is it translated from English?

ENRICO (*eagerly*): It's extraordinarily interesting. Imagine, the author has had the patience to work out what mourning costs the English nation annually. He calculates that for every person dying in England, three people go into mourning, which means they will be living on a reduced scale. A vast quantity of people all working less, and spending less on clothes—or on the other hand too much—and neither widows nor widowers begetting legitimate children. Think of the waste.

ANNA: I don't think that's the book for Emma just at present. It would infuriate her. Keep it for better times, please, I beg you.

ENRICO: She'd find it very consoling, though. The author—with typical English practicality—recommends that mourning should cease immediately the funeral's over, but that in return, once a year—on a particular Sunday, when it would cost nothing in working-hours—there should be a national hour of mourning, when everyone could think of their own dead. What a comfort it would be! Instead of stupid, solitary mourning, poor Valentino, once a year, could feel the thoughts of the whole nation on him.

Enter GUIDO, *followed by* EMMA.

GUIDO: Aunt Anna, Signor Boncini will be arriving very soon. Can I ask him into the dining-room?

ANNA: If Giovanni has no objection, I have none.

EMMA: Who is this Signor Boncini?

GUIDO: He's a prosperous client of Dr Giannottini's. He wants, first of all, to examine the results of the operation on Uncle.

EMMA: And Papa is ready to oblige him?

GUIDO: Why not? If for no other reason, he might do it out of gratitude to Dr Giannottini for saving him from such an abject state of senility.

EMMA: I can't see that he has got all that benefit from the operation. He dressed more neatly, he shaves every day and spruces and perfumes himself up, but otherwise I notice no difference.

GUIDO: What did you expect to see? Do you want to see him running after women?

EMMA: You'd be pleased if he did; that's what you wanted.

ANNA (horrified): Oh I hope not. No one ever suggested that.

GUIDO (hesitantly): No! No one ever suggested that. They wouldn't have dared. Aunt Anna, did Uncle run after women as a young man?

ANNA (hesitantly): No.

EMMA: But he got married, Mother. He ran after you.

ANNA: And I ran after him, I suppose.

EMMA: And if the operation works, as you all wanted it to, what will happen then?

ANNA: What are you saying? Giovanni is a good man. He was good as a young man and he's good as an old one; and if he becomes young again, he'll be the same as he ever was.

EMMA: Luckily for you, Mamma, I don't believe in this operation. I agree it might have helped Valentino; but for someone who's really old. . . . It could spoil him, it could upset him, but it won't bring back his youth.

ANNA: No, no, good Heavens, not real youth. He has too much experience of life to become a real young man again—one of the ones who do such wicked things and injure their own

family and other people's too. But he's better for it already;
he's less absent-minded, less distracted. Don't you see that
you could trust him with Umbertino again, now?

EMMA (*bitterly*): Oh yes, I could. Oh yes, of course! Except
that he can't be bothered with the child. He has his bath-
time and his massage-time, and then his time for gymnastics.
Yesterday I caught him in front of a mirror doing contor-
tions. He's not much of a gymnast, really; he fell over, and
I had to help him up.

ANNA: But he's a good man, deep down he's a good man. Do
you know what he did today, you ungrateful child? He
asked me to go and lay flowers on poor Valentino's grave.
He told me that the less near he was to death himself the
more respect he felt for the dead. It brought tears to my eyes
to listen to him, and I agreed to go and do it for him—saving
him that long dusty walk.

EMMA: So he's getting further away from the dead? That's
what he feels, is it? Well, he's deceiving himself; and it's
destroying all his pity and sorrow for the dead, and they are
the noblest thing in life. He thinks: "Valentino is dead!
Well, so much the worse for him!" (*Pause.*) And anyway,
why can't he go to the cemetery himself?

ANNA: But good Heavens! He's an old man; it's up to me to
relieve him of burdens like that.

EMMA (*laughing unpleasantly*): Ah! Ah! So he is an old
man?

GUIDO: Emma, think, you can't expect the operation to have
its full effect in three weeks. Who knows, in a fortnight's
time, he may be thinking how he can spare Aunt Anna
burdens?

EMMA (*reflectively*): That would be terrible. It would mean I
had lost a father.

ANNA: I don't understand you. You would have your father
back—younger, stronger, more able to protect and help you.

EMMA: Oh Mamma, how naïve you are!

GUIDO: I don't understand you either, and I'm not naïve.

ENRICO (*sentimentally*): I understand her. She means that

when a father is rejuvenated, he loses the unselfishness and love that an old man possesses just from feeling close to the dead.

EMMA (*sobbing*): Thank you, Signor Enrico, you have expressed my feelings exactly.

ANNA (*rather pleased*): Well that's nice, then!

EMMA (*violently*): What's nice? What are you so glad about?

ANNA: I didn't mean it. I wasn't thinking of what I was saying.

Enter RITA.

RITA: There's a Signor Boncini outside, wanting to see Signor Guido.

GUIDO (*going out*): Here I am, here I am! I'll be with him in a moment. Rita, will you tell your master too, please.

Exeunt RITA *left and* GUIDO *upstage.*

EMMA: I don't want to have anything to do with this man, he's another old man trying to ape youth again. Goodbye. (*She gives* ENRICO *a chilly nod and exit right.*)

ENRICO: Oh dear, Signora Anna, you've spoilt a great day for me. It's the first time Emma has ever agreed with me.

ANNA: Do forgive me, Signor Enrico. I know what I said was shockingly tactless. Well, I've done it now. You are the interested party, and you have made so many *faux pas* yourself. It's not surprising I should make one too, sometimes.

ENRICO: What a badly-behaved girl your daughter is, you know! She was scarlet in the face with rage—quite unjustly. It was adorable! (*Reflectively.*) I seem to be bound to her by her bad qualities just as much as her good. I suppose I should hate Valentino; but sometimes I almost envy him.

ANNA: My poor friend. But there'll be another chance soon. And I promise you I'll be careful next time. You must be patient. Now I must go; I wouldn't know what to do or say with that man there.

Enter GIOVANNI *dressed in an elegant pyjama-suit.*

GIOVANNI: Why are you going away? This is a real bore. I only agreed to it to please Guido, as I owe him so much. And I don't know if the old fellow who's coming has been operated on or not.

ENRICO: He hasn't been, yet. He's come to see what effect it's had on you.

GIOVANNI: But how can he tell that if he didn't know me before?

ENRICO: Guido has got hold of that photograph they took of you just before the operation.

GIOVANNI: Did they take a photograph of me? Oh yes, I remember; I saw it myself. It's horrible. I was terrified at what I'd let myself in for. You can see terror written all over my face.

ENRICO: So much the better. The difference will be all the more striking.

GIOVANNI: So much the better? I don't agree. I'd like to have the photo destroyed.

ANNA: I'm going to my room for a moment, and then I shall be going to the cemetery.

GIOVANNI: There's no hurry. The cemetery is there day and night for those who are disposed to go there.

ANNA: No. It's better for me to go now; I'll be back in half an hour.

GIOVANNI: Oh well, in that case, take your time. I'd like you to pay a visit to my parents' tomb as well. And go and see cousin Antonio's, who died when he was thirty-four. And wait a moment. There's that poor Ricciardi woman, the one who died a few years ago . . .

ANNA: You mean thirty years ago.

GIOVANNI (*in wonderment*): Thirty years ago! Still, as far as she's concerned it's neither a long nor a short time. So please, will you go and pay my respects to her too? She didn't leave anyone behind to pray for her.

ANNA: I will, I will, dear, good Giovanni.

Enter BONCINI *and* GUIDO.

BONCINI (*in conversation with* GUIDO): Yes, anyone in the returned package business is always as crafty as they make them. He has to go round finding out where there are used containers and then where there's a demand for them. And he has to discover if the demand is urgent or not, and fix his price accordingly. It has to be low if other sorts of container would be just as good, and high if not. And so on.

GUIDO: Still, we're not interested in barrels today.

BONCINI: We'll all interested in them, to some degree.

GIOVANNI: Excuse me, I can't agree.

BONCINI (*to* ENRICO, *looking at him in a pleased manner and comparing him with a photograph he is holding*): So you're seventy years old?

ENRICO: Me? God forbid. I'm only just thirty-eight.

BONCINI (*to* GUIDO): But what was the point of operating on him then?

GIOVANNI: I'm the one who was operated on.

BONCINI (*offering his hand*): Pleased to meet you.

GUIDO *introduces them*

BONCINI (*after long pause, while he compares him with the photograph*): Yes, there's a certain improvement. You were certainly in a terrible state before. You'd lost half your staves and hoops. You really were a rotten broken-down old cask.

GIOVANNI: What's that, what's that? I don't follow you. (*Losing his temper.*) You must need the operation badly. Listen to the way you talk. Go on, hurry, get yourself operated on.

BONCINI (*ingratiatingly*): I beg your pardon, I didn't mean to offend you. You misunderstood me—very natural. I was using the terms of my trade. You've been kind enough to let me come and see you, to help me over a most important step in an old man's life. I am extremely grateful to you.

GIOVANNI: I've agreed for the sake of my nephew here.

BONCINI: I realise you're not doing it for my sake; all the same, I think you owe me a little consideration. We are the same age. There's only one difference between us, you've been operated on and I haven't. People of the same age should be kind to one another. Where should we be if even old men, like you, started taking the young men's side? Young men would have everything then, even the support of the old.

GIOVANNI (*mollified*): I . . . I've nothing against you. In fact, as you see, I'm ready to help you. But I won't take sides with the old. I don't mean I take sides with the young either. If I'm a young man, I'm an old man too. In short . . . Why don't you go and have the operation? Then we would have something in common. We would belong to the same category.

GUIDO : Certainly; society nowadays is divided into young old men and old young ones.

GIOVANNI : Precisely. I'm a young old man. (*Laughs.*) There also exist old young men. (*To* GUIDO, *pointing at* ENRICO.) What's that fellow's name?

GUIDO : Biggioni.

GIOVANNI : He's an old man, no matter what his age is. That's what I don't like about him. You'd have to have the operation in reverse to be as old as that. He's always under our feet. He's in love.

BONCINI (*who has overheard*): An old man . . . in love? Then he can't be an old man.

GIOVANNI : You don't understand. Lovers can be old too. Really young men may be in love with women, that's true; but they only think of them at intervals. Not the whole time.

GUIDO : What you've said is scientifically accurate. The proof of genuine strength is that it should show itself at the right time and place.

BONCINI (*hesitantly*): Do you think so? (*Gaining courage.*) In that case I shan't have the operation. Good day to you, sir.

GIOVANNI : What's wrong with him?

GUIDO : If you must go, you must. But it doesn't seem very polite to my Uncle to break off the interview in this way.

BONCINI : Well then, allow me to ask your uncle a few questions. Without interference from you. Signor Chierici, do you or don't you regret having spent so much on this operation? That's the nub of the matter.

GIOVANNI: It doesn't matter a damn to me whether you're operated on or not. There's nothing in it for me. However, as you are kind enough to ask me, I will confess I still believe—seriously—that Dr Giannottini charges too much for his operation. I think he's a shark.

GUIDO: Uncle, what are you saying?

GIOVANNI: I'm saying the truth. However, seeing that Dr Giannottini is the only one who knows how to do the operation, it's natural he should want to make a profit out of it. I'd do the same myself. Indeed I've done the same myself. Once I was the only man on the Exchange who could supply a certain kind of merchandise . . .

ENRICO: Coffee.

GIOVANNI: No, something quite different . . . something that came in boxes. I've forgotten what it was . . .

BONCINI: It's a bad sign when you can't remember things.

GIOVANNI (to GUIDO): What's he say?

BONCINI: Your hearing doesn't seem too good either.

GUIDO (knowledgeably): Hearing and memory are always the last faculties to return.

GIOVANNI: It's the sense of life itself that's been rejuvenated in me. Everything about me feels younger. I agree the operation does cost a lot. But I'm saving up to have it again in ten years' time. I can't wait. And I'll have it again in twenty years' time, and thirty. Of course I shall continue to hope it will get cheaper. And in fact—as I told Dr Giannottini—if he doesn't reduce his prices, I shall set up in business against him.

GUIDO: There's a young man talking, if you like!

BONCINI: I don't think so. I haven't been operated on yet, but I've always managed to buy my packages where they're cheapest.

GIOVANNI: Are you sure? (To GUIDO, then to BONCINI.): I didn't realise what youth had been like. I had to rediscover it. It returned to me, in all its sweetness and warmth. I can remember it now, all right. How I remember it! (*In a reverie.*)

GUIDO: Bravo, Uncle!

BONCINI: Forgive me, but can we come to the principal point. How do you get on with women?

GIOVANNI: With *what*?

GUIDO: With women—you know.

GIOVANNI: Women? What are you talking to me about women for? What have they got to do with it? I may be a young man, but I'm a respectable one.

BONCINI (*impatiently*): Even after the operation?

GIOVANNI: More so than ever.

GUIDO (*taking* BONCINI *aside*): You see, my uncle is an old man . . . I mean a young man . . . well, whichever he is . . . who isn't always entirely frank. He'd never admit to feeling sexual desire. At least, he'll admit it when it suits him . . . that's to say to the woman he's after, but nobody else. (*Laughs.*)

GIOVANNI: What are you talking about? Why are you laughing?

GUIDO: Uncle, what you have here is one of the ordinary run of men—the only thing he wants from the operation is the one thing you don't want.

GIOVANNI: Then I despise him.

BONCINI (*taking* GUIDO *aside*): So you don't think there's any hope of getting it out of him?

GUIDO: It won't be easy.

BONCINI: No, I can't see that. I can't get any sense out of this old fellow. He may have been operated on, but he's still as obstinate and prejudiced as the truly old. Haven't you got another old man you can show me?

GUIDO: I haven't got one ready, not really ready.

BONCINI: Well, then?

GIOVANNI: Since you've got so much to say to each other, I'd better leave you to it. I believe in doing good to my neighbours. But you can't expect me to waste my whole youth waiting on your pleasure.

GUIDO (*whispering to* GIOVANNI): He doesn't want to pay as much as you, Uncle.

GIOVANNI: I hope I'm not going to be cheated. (*Pause.*) Must I tell him exactly how much I paid?

GUIDO: Better not tell him anything.

BONCINI (*to* GIOVANNI): As you've been so kind, perhaps you'll allow me to see you again? Not here, though. Couldn't we go for a walk together? You'll be surprised; people say I'm very good company. Naturally, just at the moment, I'm rather preoccupied, this being the most important affair I've ever been involved in. I can't pretend to be *dégagé*.

GIOVANNI: Come now, why don't you tell the truth? You don't deceive me; you want to see me in motion. You want to see me walk. That's a perfectly proper request—not like wanting to see me in women's arms. Today I can't manage it. I've got something urgent to do. Do you hear that? Something urgent. Before my operation I'd forgotten what that meant. But tomorrow I shall be going out, at five o'clock precisely, as I always do before dinner. If you like to be here then, we can walk together. I'm neither good company nor *dégagé*, but I have the deepest respect for age, and I will come with you with pleasure.

BONCINI: Thank you very much! (*Hesitantly.*) As the older man, perhaps I might even give you a little advice . . .

GIOVANNI: No! No, I hardly think there'll be occasion for that.

BONCINI: Well, at least we can talk things over together, and see how to make the best use of our youth . . . if we have it. I don't mean you will have to *listen* to my advice . . . nor I to yours. But we can exchange views.

GIOVANNI (*severely*): Remember, our talk must be decent and respectable. I must insist on that. I want my youth to be dedicated to virtue. We can talk—but let it be so that the chastest ear would not be offended.

BONCINI (*looking at him contemptuously, to* GUIDO): Fancy paying all that for an operation, and then making no more use of it!

GUIDO: It's all words—believe me—just words. I sometimes talk like that myself, though not very often.

BONCINI: Anyway, so far I'm not committing myself at all. It's a pity you haven't got another old man available. It's such a nightmare getting anything out of this one. However, tomorrow we'll go for a walk. The streets are full of bare legs these days. I'll see what effect they have on him.

ENRICO: You'll see, you'll see! I went out with him once, just once. I thought he enjoyed looking at women. In fact he does it quite lecherously.

BONCINI: When I saw you and thought you were seventy I was ready for anything. What a pity it's not you who had the operation. A great pity.

GIOVANNI: Please do go on talking, I'm delighted. If you'll excuse me. I'll be reading the *Piccolo*.

BONCINI: I beg your pardon, Signor Chierici. But you understand, this is an important matter.

GIOVANNI: If I'd been like you, I'd never have managed to have the operation. I simply thought about it, decided I wanted it, and had it. I'm not as easily frightened.

BONCINI (*pityingly*): I wonder if he's better or worse for the operation? (*With a sigh.*) At all events, nothing is decided yet. I wish it were. I'll come back tomorrow. (*To* GIOVANNI.) Tomorrow at five o'clock, then. And many thanks for all your patience and kindness. Goodbye till tomorrow. (*To* GUIDO, *who accompanies him to the door.*) Don't say anything to Dr Giannottini yet. He's always ready and waiting, and so far I'm not.

GIOVANNI (*he has put on his spectacles and is reading, a little nervously*): Another man murdering his wife. The trouble all arises from sex. How much better off we should be without sex. (*Goes on reading.*)

ENRICO (*to* GUIDO): You saw how I interrupted just in time?

GUIDO: Yes, I'm very grateful to you. But I'm afraid it may be no good all the same. These old men! The job it is to chivvy them out of their cosy ways. I wish it were young men we had to deal with. All the same, don't worry too much, I'm still optimistic. You can count on the interest on your 20,000 safely. We're negotiating a number of operations at the moment.

ENRICO: It isn't the money I'm worried about. Have you talked about me to Emma?

GUIDO: I've mentioned you several times, and I watched how she reacted. It didn't encourage me to go on.

ENRICO: How unfair she is!

GUIDO (*hesitantly*): I wouldn't marry her myself.

ENRICO: What do you mean?

GUIDO: I mean I wouldn't marry her if I were in your place. Good Lord, do you realise how many women there are in the world?

ENRICO (*smiling*): As if I didn't! (*Pause.*) Anyway, she has agreed that I can take Umbertino for a walk every day at four o'clock.

GUIDO: That's because his grandfather can't be bothered with him any more.

ENRICO: I've got the impression that he's beginning to like me at last.

GUIDO: Who could dislike you? (*To* GIOVANNI.) I want to say what pleasure you gave me speaking of the benefit you had got from the operation. The whole thing has been very much on my mind. It was I who persuaded you into it, and I feel responsible.

> GIOVANNI *leads* ENRICO *aside and gives him an*
> *article to read.*

GIOVANNI: It's been on my mind too. What would happen, in God's name, if it all disappeared again? How on earth could I go back to the old way of life? That's the danger. What do you say?

GUIDO (*hesitantly*): No! No! Once the operation has been successful, it must go on having its effect for a definite number of years.

GIOVANNI: Ten, I think you said?

GUIDO: Ten, or a little less or a little more.

GIOVANNI: Well then, I must try not to worry, and hope that every morning when I get up I shall find the same warmth, the same enjoyment of life, the same radiance. Yes, that's it! I call it radiance—something that dazzles you.

GUIDO (*impressed*): Really?

GIOVANNI: Do you mean to say you didn't know?

GUIDO: Oh yes, I knew all right. Only this rejuvenation takes everyone a different way. For some, like you Uncle, it appears as radiance, to others as warmth. Some lucky cases feel it as electricity.

GIOVANNI: You might call it electricity in my case too. A sort of pins and needles all over the body. I feel I've got a body. I feel I've got soles to my feet. I knew I had them before, in theory, because they carried me; but now I know it because I feel them—and they carry me all the better for it. That old man . . . what's his name?

GUIDO: Boncini.

GIOVANNI: Well that Boncini fellow wanted me to tell him how I got on with women. I told him I had nothing to do with women. I'm sorry to have to admit it, but it wasn't absolutely true. Women still exist for me. Indeed, I suppose they never stopped doing so, in the same sense that the soles of my feet existed. I looked at them and thought: "Heigh-ho. There they are still, but not for me!" Now I look at them and think—especially when I remember what people would say—"They're not for me, of course; but they look awfully like the ones that, in my time, if I'd wanted, could have been for me."

GUIDO: I'm not sure I quite understand. They are like those that, in your time, if you'd wanted, could have been for you . . . ?

GIOVANNI (*impatiently*): There are some things, of course, which a young man like you—without the experience of a long life—can't understand. Yet it would be so nice if I could explain to you. What I'll do is not explain, but tell you a story—Immediately after the operation, I began to dream. I began at once, the very instant.

GUIDO: Immediately after the operation?

GIOVANNI: Yes, immediately. Till then I had simply lived within the twenty-four hours of the day. Suddenly, I had jumped outside.

GUIDO: Jumped outside?

GIOVANNI: At present, I'm mostly not here, in today, at all. Just as I can feel the soles of my feet, so I can feel my past. It would be wrong to say I remember it; it wouldn't be saying enough. I live my past. I live out my youth. The other one, I mean, not the new one.

GUIDO (*hesitantly*): What other one?

GIOVANNI (*dreamily*): . . . And all of a sudden I was reliving my marriage. In every detail. And also what went before. The first moment when I thought of marrying my wife . . . of leaving Pauletta and marrying Anna.

GUIDO: In fact, the usual story, deserting one to take up with another.

GIOVANNI: No, not the usual story. Now I think about it again, it seems a strange, an incredible, story to me. I look back on it with amazement as if it hadn't happened to me, as if it were someone else, not me, who was responsible. There was nothing wrong about it, you understand. There was never anything really wrong in my whole life. Unless it's wrong that I ought to have married Pauletta and finished up marrying Anna instead. But swear you won't say a word to Anna. Swear it!

GUIDO: I swear it, Uncle.

GIOVANNI: Well, then I married Anna because I didn't want to marry Pauletta. Anna was a jewel of a girl. I won't have a word said against her. We have been married for so many years, yet if I took a candle and searched, I shouldn't be able to find one thing she had done wrong. Everyone used to think her beautiful too. She walked so gracefully, and yet so modestly. As for Pauletta, everyone was unkind about her. The poor girl walked in rather a seductive sort of way. She moved like this... (*demonstrates*) like this. Well, there are sayings which say you should distrust women

who walk like that. Popular sayings are . . . sacred; you
have to respect them. All the same, they're sometimes dictated by malice and bad feeling. Who looks after popular
sayings? Who takes care of *their* behaviour? They run wild
about the streets and the fields, like any orphan. One should
be careful how one listens to them. That old man . . .
what's his name? (GUIDO *doesn't understand him.*) That
old man who wants to go walking with me?

GUIDO: Oh, him! Boncini.

GIOVANNI: Boncini wouldn't have understood me if I'd said I
still think of women, but only the women who were young
when I was young. How shall I put it? My life is all topsy-
turvy. My memory takes me back to the beginning of life.
You understand the operation—don't you think this may be
the very way one returns to one's beginnings? First you
look and remember the past, then you jump bodily into it?

GUIDO (*touched*): Yes, Uncle, that may be how it works.
(*Pause.*) But I have never talked as intimately as this with
my patients. You'll realise why. They're mostly dignified old
gentlemen who don't confide in the first comer.

GIOVANNI: One should tell one's doctor everything. It's the
first time I have talked about it—it's such a pleasure to be
able to! I feel as if I had to clutch at the things that happen
to me, so that they don't escape. I was on the point—on the
very point—of telling Anna about it. I stopped myself just
in time. Though I thought afterwards that she's so old now
there are some things she no longer worries about. All the
same, how could I tell her that my memories had taken me
back to Pauletta? After all, it was natural to her, her way of
walking. How else could she have walked with that face of
hers, that seemed like . . . a flame, a blaze, dazzling you
and scorching you? That was the reason—the only reason
—why I wouldn't have her in the end. (*Pause.*) And that's
the reason—the sole reason—why I want her now.

GUIDO: So for the moment, all you want is one woman. You
can see the operation is taking effect, though. When you
start wanting one woman, you can end by wanting dozens.

GIOVANNI: A fine way to talk, you idle young villain. I didn't say I wanted *her*! I said I wanted to *see* her, to see her move in front of me, with that face of hers and her provocative way of walking. That's all I want! Remember that! I don't want people to think me an old lecher.

GUIDO (*suppressing a smile*): By now Pauletta will have lost her pretty face and exciting way of walking. So what are we going to do?

GIOVANNI: She's dead. She died soon after she married, I can't remember her husband's name or I would have sent some flowers for the tomb. Anna would have taken them; she's just gone to take flowers for Valentino and various others. I told Anna that the further away I got from the dead, the more I revered them. I said it because it's the proper thing to say about the dead. They have a right to it. But in fact dead people turn my stomach rather. Have you ever seen a corpse? Yes, of course; for a doctor like yourself they must be as common as daisies. But as for me! The stench! Ugh! Emma insisted on my kissing Valentino's corpse—as if he hadn't been repulsive enough in his lifetime. I'll never forget that kiss. So I think about Pauletta all the time, but I don't love her, because I can't love dead people. It's not their fault that they should have died before the great new invention. Still, it was a little stupid of them. They're out-of-date now! Like when people let themselves be killed by horse-drawn carriages, since the motor-car hasn't been invented. (*Pause.*) It's a shame! Pauletta was so pretty—I'd send flowers for her tomb now, if only I knew where to find it. (*Searching his memory.*) Puc . . . Pucci . . . Puccio . . . Puccio. I can't think of her husband's name. And the worst of it is, I can't even remember her maiden name. However, Anna will know . . . if I dare to ask her.

GUIDO: Everything will come in time, Uncle. Even names. The main thing is that you're well. I've brought you the report.

GIOVANNI: Shall I give you the fifty lire?

GUIDO: Oh, it's such a trifle. You can give me a hundred when you have the next report. Look at it! It's magnificent.

GIOVANNI (*puts on his spectacles and looks at it anxiously*): "Normal" . . . "Normal" . . . "Normal." (*Aggrieved.*) But this is the same report as before.

GUIDO: You can't improve on "Normal", Uncle.

GIOVANNI: Well then, the report isn't worth a damn. "Normal!" I was normal when I was old. Here I am, all changed and renewed, and the report says just the same. I shan't have any more truck with reports. It's time for something else now. Why should I have to have reports, as if I were an old man?

Enter ANNA, *in outdoor clothes.*

ANNA: I'm taking the car to the cemetery now. After that, I've got one or two things to buy, so I shan't be back for an hour or two. Do you mind being left alone, dear?

GIOVANNI: No! No! On the contrary. I mean, I want you to enjoy yourself as much as you can. Life is short, as the ancients said.

ANNA: Is there anything you want me to get you in town?

GIOVANNI: I want some newspapers. Especially the Sunday comic supplement. I enjoy laughing. I've got to learn how to do it again.

ANNA: And you want to stay here, in the dining-room?

GIOVANNI: Yes! This is the room I feel most comfortable in.

ANNA: And you don't mind if Rita comes in to clean the windows and polish the brasses?

GIOVANNI (*trying to conceal his delight*): No, no, let her come. Let her get on with her cleaning. I shall be reading and shan't notice her existence.

ANNA: Well then, goodbye. (*Gives* GIOVANNI *her cheek to kiss. Then, addressing* GUIDO.) Come with me if you feel like it. I should like your company. One can think one's thoughts better in a cemetery when there's someone to keep one company. You start feeling so lonely, if you're on your own.

GUIDO: I would love to come, Aunt Anna, but I can't. I have to be at the hospital in half an hour.

GIOVANNI: Good! I mean, I'm glad you've got plenty to occupy you. As for the cemetery, my opinion is it's a place where it's better to be alone. The dead expect it of you.

ANNA (to ENRICO, as she leaves): Goodbye, Signor Enrico, I'm delighted with the silk.

ENRICO: Always rely on me, Signora Anna.

GIOVANNI: Couldn't Signor Biggioni go with you?

ENRICO: I'm so sorry, but I don't think I can. I've got to stay here till four. I'm taking Umbertino for a walk. (Looks at his watch.) It's nearly three now. (To ANNA.) Goodbye.

Exit ANNA.

GIOVANNI: Excuse me. Of course, I'm only too delighted to have you here. I enjoy your company. But I'm rather puzzled. Aren't you a business-man? Can you afford to waste your time like this?

ENRICO: I haven't much to do today. And anyway, you'll understand—(in a tone of great dislike)—it's far from a waste of time for me to be with you.

GIOVANNI (alarmed): Thank you, thank you! You're always so kind, so remarkably kind. (Pause.) But, I say. Wouldn't it perhaps be a kind act to see Anna to the car?

ENRICO: Of course, that I can easily do.

Exit ENRICO.

GIOVANNI: Guido, listen! Couldn't you go and ask Emma to send Umbertino out at three?

GUIDO: Why?

GIOVANNI: It's such a lovely sunny day, I'm sure it would do him good.

GUIDO: But she wants him to avoid the mid-day sun.

GIOVANNI: But you're a doctor; couldn't you tell her she's wrong?

GUIDO (hesitantly): I don't really think I could . . .

GIOVANNI: Oh, come on now. You tell us castor oil is good for us, when it suits you; and bismuth, when *that* suits you. Couldn't you decide that the sun would do him good, today.

Anyway, it doesn't strike me as very hot today. Rather a misty day, I'd call it.

GUIDO: I'm sorry, I don't dare! Emma doesn't regard me as a doctor yet. If I open my mouth, she calls in Dr Raulli. It always ends by my putting custom in a rival's way. I don't like that.

GIOVANNI (*in despair*): But then, how the devil am I to get rid of that Biagini fellow?

GUIDO: You mean Biggioni.

GIOVANNI: Biggioni. He's like a broom someone's left behind a door. When you open the door, out he comes, straight in your eye. Only he's like about ten thousand brooms. For months now, wherever I go, bang, there he is, on top of me.

GUIDO: I can get him out of the way for an hour or so, before Umbertino's ready.

GIOVANNI: Splendid! I'd be very grateful. I can put up with Rita . . . (*Uneasily.*) Where is Rita? Why hasn't she come? Listen, I can be frank with you. I rather enjoy looking at Rita.

GUIDO: That doesn't surprise me at all.

GIOVANNI: It doesn't? Oh, I see what you mean. You find her attractive too. But she's not for you. It's a different affair for me. I don't like looking at her because she's pretty. I like it because she's got a look of Pauletta. Don't you think she has?

GUIDO: How should I know. I never knew Pauletta.

GIOVANNI: What's that got to do with it? Don't you see that she walks like Pauletta? Just like her.

GUIDO: There are other things about a girl apart from the way she walks.

GIOVANNI: Of course there are, you oaf. But whereas the other things are all material things, the way of walking is a spiritual one. In a sense, they're the only ones who know how to walk—the ones who know they are beautiful, really beautiful. They're the most dangerous type, the ones who don't get married and who you regret later you didn't marry.

GUIDO: As she walks beautifully, then according to you Rita is a truly beautiful girl.

GIOVANNI: I can't answer that. That's none of my business.

GUIDO: Oh, I beg your pardon.

Enter RITA, *left, with a pail, a sponge and a cloth, and* ENRICO *right.* RITA *busies herself polishing the door-handles.*

GUIDO: Signor Biggioni, would you care to come to the hospital with me? I hate walking on my own.

ENRICO: I would love to, but I can't, I really can't. I've got to be here at four, punctually. (*Whispers.*) Actually, I'm hoping to see Emma—she hasn't gone out yet. (*Anxiously.*) At least, I don't think she has.

GUIDO: No, she hasn't. She's in there. (*To* GIOVANNI.) And you wouldn't like to come, I suppose?

GIOVANNI (*growls*): Go to hell . . .

GUIDO: Well, ta ta then, Uncle. See you at dinner-time. (*Goes out, rubbing his hands,* ENRICO *goes back to his newspaper, with a sigh.* RITA *gets on with her work.* GIOVANNI *throws himself into an armchair and watches her agitatedly. A long pause.*)

GIOVANNI (*who has been looking at* ENRICO *from time to time indecisively, finally makes up his mind*): You know, I think you would find it easier to read your paper in the other room—the one at the end of the corridor. And Umbertino always comes by there when he is going out.

ENRICO (*with much dislike*): Forgive me; I didn't realise I was disturbing you. (*Becoming positively aggressive.*) I'm always *entirely* at your disposition.

GIOVANNI (*sweetening his tone, out of nervousness*): If that's really so, my dear Signor Biggioni, would you do me a great favour? Would you let me know if anyone is coming?

ENRICO (*in the same manner*): I should be delighted.

Exit ENRICO.

GIOVANNI (*sitting down again*): That's a timid man with a

bullying manner—he must have been born like it. When he says polite things it's quite frightening. I would never marry him.

RITA (*yelling the words, as she goes on with her polishing*): I'm afraid that's what Miss Emma thinks too.

GIOVANNI (*delighted*): How well I hear now. Every word, as clear as a bell. Even my ears are improving. (*Pause*) So you think it would be a good thing if Emma married him.

RITA (*still shouting*): Of course. A rich, distinguished gentleman like him, and fond of her too.

GIOVANNI: Distinguished? God knows what he can be like when he's angry, if he can look so furious when he's friendly.

RITA: But I think he *was* angry.

GIOVANNI: Why on earth should that be? Who with? And why didn't he say so?

RITA: Well, in the first place, he wants to make you like him, and he can never manage to.

GIOVANNI: Why doesn't he say so, then? If he said so, I'd be perfectly ready to tell him I like him.

RITA: Signor Guido likes him now, and so does the mistress. That only leaves you and Miss Emma.

GIOVANNI: That's the main part, I'm afraid. But if he would watch the way he talks—I mean, not frighten me—I'd be glad to see him—only not too often. (*Pause.* RITA *goes on working.*) What was your mother called? Paula? Pauletta?

RITA: No, Giovanna.

GIOVANNI (*startled*): Anna?

RITA: Giovanna.

GIOVANNI (*reassured*): Ah. Giovanna! Still, it's very near. It's almost like fate. I ask for Paula and they give me Anna. But your name is Rita, definitely Rita?

RITA: Yes, that's right.

GIOVANNI: Well then, why don't you give me a kiss? It wouldn't cost you anything.

RITA: It wouldn't be right, sir. I'm engaged to Fortunato.

GIOVANNI: What's that got to do with it? I don't want to marry you. All I want to do is to kiss you. I want to test what effect it has on me. Say I were on my deathbed, and the doctor came and said to you: "You must give him a kiss, to save his life." What would you do then? Assuming you feel some gratitude to me, and the mistress and my daughter, what would you do then?

RITA: But you're not on your deathbed, sir. And if you were, the doctors would prescribe quite different medicines—chemist's medicines—much more expensive.

GIOVANNI: I would pay much more for a kiss. I would have you another room built in your cottage, the one you need so much and that Fortunato is always talking about. Remember, I've already paid Dr Giannottini a fortune, for practically nothing. (*A pause, during which* RITA, *in embarrassment, applies herself to the doorhandle.*) I know I look like an old man, but I assure you, I was young and good-looking once, and if what I hope happens, I'll be—not a young man exactly—but a fine upstanding man in the prime of life. But for that to happen, you'll have to give me a kiss.

RITA: I must ask Fortunato's permission first.

GIOVANNI: Permission for a kiss? Good God! That wouldn't *be* a kiss. I've got to steal it from you, force it out of you—as if we were lovers. Look. I've been thinking about this kiss for a long time. I want to steal it, I say—steal it as a young man would do. Sit there in the armchair, make yourself comfortable and go to sleep, or pretend to go to sleep. I'll creep up on you and give you a kiss.

RITA: On the mouth?

GIOVANNI: That won't be necessary, not to start with. I'll kiss you on the cheek.

RITA: And I get the room, the new room in the cottage?

GIOVANNI: I'll give the order today; I'll tell them to have it ready by the autumn.

RITA: Signor Chierici! Couldn't you do it without the kiss? A kind gentleman like you?

GIOVANNI: Please, please, forget about the bargain, and the room, otherwise there'll be no kiss anyway. Concentrate on the kiss. You sit there, in the chair. Go on, please, I beg you.

RITA *goes over to the armchair reluctantly, holding her duster in her hand. She sits down and shuts her eyes, covering her mouth with the duster.*

GIOVANNI (*looking round*): Good; everything seems set. (*He moves unsteadily towards her chair and sees the duster.*) Take that thing away. That's only for doorhandles. (RITA *drops it, and puts her hands over her mouth instead.*) Make it a bit more lifelike, please. Stretch out—as if you were in bed. Like this! Excuse me if I wait a moment now, to think. How the devil does one steal a kiss if one has to organise the whole thing first? (*He sits down on a dining-chair, covers his eyes and thinks for a few moments, then approaches* RITA *and leans over and kisses her on the cheek.*) Oh, Pauletta!

RITA (*looking at him in amazement*): What did you say?

GIOVANNI (*brusquely*): Be quiet, you. (*He stands lost in reflection.*) I enjoyed that, I enjoyed it very much.

RITA (*timidly*): Can I get on with my work now?

GIOVANNI (*brusquely*): Didn't I say "Be quiet"? (*Another pause.*) Of course, if you had been in love with me, it would have all gone much better.

RITA: But I'm engaged to Fortunato.

GIOVANNI (*brusquely*): What's that got to do with it?

RITA: What's it got to do with it? (*She goes back to her polishing.*)

GIOVANNI: Forget about the work. I've given you a kiss. That's all I'm asking for the moment. Can't you just come and sit with me?

RITA: But what happens if the mistress comes back? What will she say?

GIOVANNI (*importantly*): You can trust me to have arranged

things, you know. Anna won't be back for two hours or so.

RITA: If you'd told me that before I wouldn't have worked so hard.

GIOVANNI (*sitting down at the table*): Come and sit down with me here.

RITA: Only if you promise to be good.

GIOVANNI: I've had no encouragement to be anything else. I'll be good . . . be good . . . till you tell me not to be.

RITA: What do you mean by that?

GIOVANNI: Let me say what I like, please. Don't keep interrupting me, and correcting me.

RITA: Very good, sir.

GIOVANNI: And don't call me "sir". I don't like hearing it. You can say it in Anna's presence, but not at other times. At present, I want you to call me "My . . ."—well, just call me Giovanni.

RITA: I couldn't do that, sir.

GIOVANNI: Well, at least don't call me "sir". It upsets me . . . like another operation . . . in reverse. It's like going back to old age and decrepitude. Do you follow me?

RITA: No I don't, s . . . I don't. It must be so nice to have people call you "sir".

GIOVANNI: Well, that's as may be. But they've done it for years and years, and I'm sick of it. (*Coaxingly.*) Just for to-day, I'd like to call you "madam". Can't I? Can't you be the Countess and I your humble page? It would be such fun.

RITA: How can you think of such a thing?

GIOVANNI: You'd be surprised; there's nothing one can't think of, if one tries. You only have to want to, and you can think the North Pole has changed places with the South. Nothing is actually changed by it, but you've had a vision; that's what makes a man strong and master of his fate. Do you understand?

RITA: No.

GIOVANNI: It doesn't matter. I don't care if you do or not. I'm creating my own world; that's the main thing. (*Pause.*)

There's a bottle of Marsala in the sideboard there, only just opened. Bring it over to me, and a glass too.

RITA (*obeying*): Here you are, sir.

GIOVANNI (*pouring out some Marsala*): Well, if you must call me "sir", you must, I suppose I half enjoy hearing a beautiful woman like you call me "sir". It's rather exciting, a woman being submissive to you. If I'm the master, it should in theory mean I can do anything I like with you.

RITA (*alarmed*): Oh, oh!

GIOVANNI (*irritably*): I said "in theory". Why must you keep interrupting? Let me go on as I want to. Have some Marsala.

RITA: Me?

GIOVANNI: To please me. Why not? Once upon a time we always began by giving women drink.

RITA: But just me? What about you?

GIOVANNI: The doctor has forbidden me to drink.

RITA: In that case . . . I couldn't, it wouldn't be right.

GIOVANNI: Well, then, get me a glass too. After all, I'm no longer Dr Raulli's patient, though he doesn't realise it.

RITA *gets him a glass, and* GIOVANNI *pours himself a drink.*

GIOVANNI: Let's drink together. One, two, three. Hup! (*They drain their glasses.*) I enjoyed that. I like drinking with you. It means we're really doing something together for once. And I like my dependents to have their recreation-times, you know, like everyone else.

RITA: Now there's something I really agree with. I do.

GIOVANNI: How well I feel. Obviously my operation has been a complete success. This is the final proof. That old lecher—the one who wanted to go for a walk with me . . . What's his name?

RITA: I don't know.

GIOVANNI: It doesn't matter. As I was saying, that old pig said that, after the operation, what was important was how one got on with women. Sometimes old pigs like him say the truth. I've often observed it, in that long life of mine. Chaste old men are older than old lechers ... I feel splendid beside you. (*Stretching out.*) The ancient Israelites gave King David a woman. But he wouldn't take her, and he perished miserably. I'm not such an ass. Come on, drink. (*He pours her out some Marsala.*)

RITA: If you'll drink with me.

GIOVANNI (*filling his own glass*): Why not? Dr Raulli can say nothing to me now. (*They drink.*) But I want to make you happy and contented with life. You were beginning to see my point of view, weren't you, and were going to let me kiss you, in exchange for more space in the cottage? If there is anything you want, you must tell me at once—I beg you. I would give my life to see happiness—which is the true symptom of youth—on that little face of yours. Youth itself isn't enough for me.

RITA: But as the mistress runs the house, there's no hope of that. She wants everything just so.

GIOVANNI (*looking round uneasily*): Why do you say that? Anna is as kind a woman as ever existed—kind to people and kind to animals.

RITA: Especially animals.

GIOVANNI (*laughing heartily*): I like that. "Especially to animals" ... to dumb animals. But she's kind to me too.

RITA: There's nothing extraordinary in that. A husband's a husband. She tells me she's fond of me too. A hundred times a day she says to me: "Rita dear, do this, do that". . . . By evening, after so many "dears", I can hardly stand.

GIOVANNI: Still, there has to be order and routine. How should I get on if I found things weren't ready for me when I go to bed, and when I get up?

RITA: That sort of thing—a glass of milk or two, or putting your clothes out—is no bother.

GIOVANNI: Anyway I shan't be drinking milk any more. I've just decided. This does me much more good. (*He takes a drink.*) To hell with Dr Raulli. Guido must be right; when you know too much about a thing you end by knowing nothing, not a damned thing. See what that mere student-nephew of mine has managed to achieve. And yet I don't think he really knows much.

RITA (*with feeling*): He's a nice man, young Signor Guido.

GIOVANNI: He is, he's a splendid young fellow. Tell me, if you're to be happy and yet we have to keep the house in order, how are we going to manage?

RITA: There's three of us working for you at present. So, as we want to work only half as much, you will have to take on another three. And then an extra one to look after *our* rooms for us; if we have to work for others we can't do our own work too. Our own rooms are filthy.

GIOVANNI (*takes another drink, to hide his embarrassment*): Would we have to feed all these maids too?

RITA: Oh yes. Well, perhaps there could be a little distinction made between their meals and ours.

GIOVANNI: Honestly, I don't think you can have quite all that. It would cost more than the operation did . . . by the hour, that's to say. I'll work it out. Wait a moment. (*He takes his notebook and pencil out and puts on his spectacles. Then he changes his mind.*) I won't bother now. There isn't the time. Anyway, what have the cook and the parlourmaid got to do with us just now? This is hardly the moment to announce a general strike, surely? Let's talk about you instead. Couldn't we arrange things—when I've really got younger and can hop about and do exhausting things—so that I help you with your housework myself? I mean, without Anna knowing? It would cost nothing, and it would be a great lark for me.

RITA (*laughing*): That would be the day!

GIOVANNI: You're laughing out of ignorance. Scientists know better than you. I'll see if I can get Dr Giannottini to talk to you one day. The operation is infallible. Only that old brute . . . what's his name? . . . says the proof lies in how one gets on with women. So women have to come into it! I want you to understand, though; it's not a question of immorality any longer, not anything sordid and abominable;

it's just a simple, legitimate . . . holy defence of one's own health and youth. I wouldn't think of indulging in it otherwise, for I've always been a most chaste, most virtuous man. As for you, if you'll co-operate . . . (*Fills both their glasses and drinks.*) What was I saying? Oh yes! If you'll co-operate in this noble, health-giving work you'll have your reward, I swear to you. First of all, you'll have it from me; and then in Heaven . . . I'm sure all religions tell us to honour, help and protect old men. And I'm still an old man, even though I've become a young one too . . . I mean, I still have the right to respect and protection . . . because the years of one's age are still a fact; they're part of history. There's no erasing them.

RITA: Help you? What's Fortunato going to say?

GIOVANNI (*nervously and crossly*): Fortunato? No, it wouldn't be easy explaining it all to him. And even if one could explain it . . . he wouldn't let himself be convinced. I know it all too well. Men are always thinking about their honour. They are egoists. Even in such an important case, even over such a simple demand, he wouldn't be ready to help me. (*Dictatorially.*) I suggest you say nothing at all to Fortunato. What's it got to do with him? Aren't I his master, and yours too for that matter?

RITA (*maliciously*): I think everyone ought to be told. The mistress as well.

GIOVANNI (*pensively*): Anna? Well perhaps. (*Pause.*) It seems to me that if she's a good wife she ought to be delighted. (*Pause.*) All the same, I think it would be best to say nothing to her. Wait while I think about it. (*He drinks.*) Marsala seems to clear my head for me. Wait a moment. (*Pause.*) Him, and then her too! Good God, how many complications over one simple cure. (*Pause.*) Look; let's forget about it. I'll say nothing to Anna and you say nothing to Fortunato. That'll make us quits.

RITA (*bursting into laughter and drinking some Marsala*): Good for you, old fellow! You certainly know how to fix things.

GIOVANNI (*crossly*): "Old fellow!" Well, I suppose "old fellow" sounds younger than "old man". But don't call me that. I don't like it; it confuses me and cramps my style. (*Pause.*) Of course, in a fortnight the operation may not yet have had its full effect. I just want to know how I'm getting on. Listen, Rita! Why don't you sit on my knee?

RITA (*irritably*): No, no!

GIOVANNI: I rather like your not agreeing right away. I beg you, come and sit on my knee. Look! I won't touch you, I won't try to kiss you. Just sit on my knee, that's all I ask. See, I'm begging you. Your master is begging a favour from you.

RITA: Oh, very well then! If it means so much to you. And seeing that the operation hasn't had much effect yet.

GIOVANNI: Don't say things like that, please. It puts me off. Sit down, sit down, make yourself comfortable—Now I should start seeing life as beautiful, as grand and radiant. (*After a moment's pause.*) Ow! Ow! You're hurting me. Get off, please. My leg's hurting.

RITA (*getting off, laughing*): Don't blame me. It was your idea. (GIOVANNI *rubs his leg.*) Is that better?

GIOVANNI: Yes! Much better. You must have sat on a vein. (*He gets up and limps about.*) Much better, much better. My leg had gone to sleep. It's prickling like a swarm of ants now. Odd feeling.

RITA (*fills their glasses, in high spirits*): Have a glass of wine, sir. It will do you good. Love and wine.

GIOVANNI (*drinking thoughtfully*): Here's the wine all right. But how about the love? Wait a moment. Let's sit down on the sofa. There! I'll put my arm around your waist. As if it were a serpent, a real serpent. Eve's serpent. I always liked that story about the serpent. There! Love's partly a matter of being comfortable. (*He gently leans his head on* RITA's *shoulder.*) Can you sing?

RITA: Why?

GIOVANNI: Because I want you to.

RITA: Here, in the mistress's dining-room?

GIOVANNI: I give you permission. Aren't I the master?

RITA: Well then, would you like me to sing "Valencia"? (*She sings "Valencia" softly.*)

GIOVANNI: Stop, stop. Don't you know anything tenderer, more sentimental? What do I care about that damned place Valencia?

RITA: What song would you like? I know them all. A Charleston?

GIOVANNI: Wait a moment, let me think. (*He drinks.*) Do you know that one (*he sings*)

> Always alone, Morettina.
> You've left me always alone.
> Left me without love.

I can't sing. I never could, though I'd have liked to so much. But I remember that I was once with Pauletta . . . a certain Pauletta . . . who had a way of walking rather like yours . . . but wasn't like you otherwise . . . she was more amenable . . . odd—when I was young the women were all more amenable . . . and prettier too . . . I should explain: that song was being sung everywhere. I couldn't sing, and neither could Pauletta. But when we were together, the song used to echo up from the street, and the room above, and the room below. Do you know it? It's a true love-song.

RITA: No, I've never heard it.

GIOVANNI (*fighting the desire to go to sleep*): You're different from Pauletta in that too. She couldn't sing the song but at least she knew it. Anna sometimes whistles, but not very prettily. So it's better not to know the song. Much better really.

RITA: And I don't, do I?

GIOVANNI: No. Good. Now if you're going to be able to sing the song, you must listen to it first. I'll explain it to you— If Morettina leaves me, I am alone, no matter if there are a million people round me. Do you understand the wealth of meaning in those few words?—And I'*m* alone, too, without love . . . until I find someone new. I do feel tired. I never felt so tired in my life. It must be thinking about love, and making love . . . It's a healthy tiredness. It's like tiredness after a battle, or before a battle . . . anyway not during it. Just sitting here with you beside me! Sleep . . . wonderful!

> RITA, *noticing he has fallen asleep, gently disengages herself from him and props his head against the back of the sofa.*

GIOVANNI (*murmurs*): Pauletta, come back. (*He begins snoring.*)

RITA (*stretching and yawning*): Ugh! The old horror! (*She sits down on the sofa again, whistling "Valencia". The song dies on her lips as she falls asleep likewise.*)

> Enter EMMA and ENRICO.

EMMA: What's this?

RITA (*waking up with a start*): I was polishing the doorhandles.

EMMA: Don't talk to me! Get on with your doorhandles. (*Goes up to her father.*) He's asleep! (*With a sob.*) He's asleep, as if he had nothing on his conscience.

RITA (*trying to compose herself*): Believe me, Madam, there's nothing for him to have on his conscience.

EMMA: Be quiet!

ENRICO: It seems to me . . .

EMMA: You'd do well to keep quiet too. You cut a very strange figure, sitting out there on sentry-duty. Anyone must be mad to do such a thing!

ENRICO: I was there because Signor Chierici wanted me to be.

RITA (*collapsing into a chair*): I was present. I can give evidence.

EMMA (*screaming*): She's drunk, she's drunk. (*Rushes out of the room.*)

ENRICO: But Signora Emma. How am I to blame, for her being drunk? (*He follows her. There is a long pause while* RITA *stretches and rubs her eyes, trying to pull herself together, whilst* GIOVANNI *snores. Enter* ANNA *and* GUIDO.)

GIOVANNI (*murmurs*): Yes, Pauletta. Anything you ask.

ANNA: What's he saying? Is he asleep? And what are that bottle and glasses doing there?

RITA: I was in here polishing the doorhandles . . . The master offered a glass of wine to Signor Guido. (*She grimaces entreatingly at* GUIDO.)

GUIDO (*hesitantly*): Yes, it was very kind of him.

ANNA: We mustn't disturb his sleep. I think we'll probably find his nightcap in his coat-pocket. (*She gently extracts it from* GIOVANNI's *pocket and puts it on his head.*) He needs a rug to keep him warm, too. Go and get one from the bedroom next door. (RITA *obeys.*) I really think the operation is working marvellously. He used to suffer so much from insomnia.

GUIDO (*disagreeably*): I'm beginning to think so too.

ANNA: You're only beginning to think so? When you were the one who advised it in the first place?

GUIDO: I was expecting something more gradual. Only a fortnight! It took even me by surprise.

> RITA *enters with a rug and* ANNA *spreads it gently over* GIOVANNI's *sleeping body.*

ANNA: And now close the shutters. We can do so safely now. (*The three go towards the left-hand door across the darkened room.*) Rita, you stay next door and listen in case he calls. I'll tell everyone not to make a noise. (*Exeunt.*)

GIOVANNI (*interrupts his snoring to murmur*): Together always, Pauletta.

> A *transparent curtain comes down and gradually blots out the scene.*

INTERMEZZO

> Only the front of the stage is visible. GIOVANNI's *snoring is heard from behind from time to time.*

GIOVANNI (*looking the same as in Act II, but moving like a young man*): Rita, Pauletta! Come here. Quick! Time's passing.

RITA (*comes in running, looking exactly as in Act II*): Here I am, master.

GIOVANNI: But if you call me "master" you can't be Pauletta; Pauletta nearly became my wife, she nearly became Anna.

RITA: You're everyone's master, now you're old *and* young.

GIOVANNI: At last! Life becoming beautiful and radiant. That was what I needed. Women calling me "master". I deserve it, you know, Pauletta, I deserve it, because I've never stopped thinking of you. People only had to say the word "moorish" in my presence and my heart started beating. You remember that song of ours, about the moorish girl, the one we never sang ourselves but we heard everywhere while we were talking love-talk.

RITA: I've forgotten it.

GIOVANNI (*severely*): That's not nice of you. You should have been more careful. And you're still young—let me look at you. Yes, of course. Death keeps things fresh. Even Valentino—you couldn't call him old now, even if you still called him repulsive. But what have you been doing all these years without me?

RITA: I was waiting for you!

GIOVANNI: Ah. Splendid! splendid! I like that. The woman obediently waiting for the man, awaiting the arrival of Siegfried. But why didn't you come before, if you knew I wanted you?

RITA: I was waiting for the operation.

GIOVANNI: And I had it just for you— Do you hear what good love-speeches I'm making? I've learned how to do it, again. I've got it word-perfect. Saying I had the operation solely for you was like buying you an expensive present. It shows the operation's worked, the very fact I said it. Let me go on talking like this for a moment, just holding your hand, and resisting the temptation, which I'm feeling already, to make free with your lips. I tell you, Pauletta, I would have married you then, if people hadn't made so much fuss. They said you walked like a loose woman, and that you were extravagant, and would have bled me dry.

RITA : Well, it's true, I did like expensive things.

GIOVANNI : And quite right too. So do I. And I understand about them too. Women look better naked when they have fine clothes to take off. Now you're back with me again, I must always have you either naked or well-dressed. Always. I spent a lot on the operation but this new expense is absolutely essential. Otherwise there's no point in being operated on. I'm not a mean man. I don't mind paying what's necessary. Not more, of course, but what's necessary. Why should they all have clamoured at me like that, saying you were going to ruin me, and stopping me from doing what I wanted to do—doing what was necessary for both our healths?

RITA : Beautiful women are loved by a few and hated by all the rest.

GIOVANNI : Yes, that must be the explanation. And to think I was fool enough to listen to them! But now everything is happening over again, I'll do what I like. I want you, no one else.

RITA : And will you give me all you have? Your money, your time, your health?

GIOVANNI : My health? What do you want with that? That belongs to me. That's precisely what I wanted out of the operation, and out of you.

RITA : Didn't you know, women both give health and take it away?

GIOVANNI : Why's that? Why do they take it away if they give it?

RITA : They can't help it, the poor things. And it makes them so unhappy afterwards. But that's how it is. They must have everything you've got, and much more besides.

GIOVANNI : So I was right not to have told Anna how much I have?

RITA : If she's satisfied, she can't be a real woman.

GIOVANNI (*convinced*): No, that's true, she can't be. So for me to get what I want, I have to give you my health too?

RITA (*smiling*): I'm not in such a hurry as all that.

GIOVANNI: I'll give you my health, for the sake of my health. So come here, come into my arms.

RITA: I will. But on one condition. You've got to kill Anna.

GIOVANNI: Nothing easier. I feel strong now, and she's as weak as water.

RITA: You promise?

GIOVANNI: Gladly. Give me your lips.

Curtain

Act III

Same scene. EMMA *is talking to* GUIDO.

EMMA: I wanted to talk to you before taking a decision. You think that once that horrible operation has been performed there's no hope?

GUIDO: No hope? There's all the hope in the world. In fact, too much hope, in a sense. The old fellow took me by surprise, like you. How young he is! What vigour and enterprise!

EMMA: Be honest with me. The effect of the operation is only going to last ten days, or fifteen, or twenty, isn't it? Don't worry, I won't be angry with you for making papa spend all that money. But you must tell me the truth. I've half a mind to consult Dr Raulli before I make my decision.

GUIDO: What could Dr Raulli tell you that I couldn't? Once the operation has achieved its initial effect, the long-term effect follows as a matter of course. It wouldn't even surprise me to see him grow hair on his head again. In fact, I almost think I've noticed a light down already.

EMMA: In that case, I've lost a father as well. I lost my husband because he grew old before his time. And now . . . (*She sobs.*)

GUIDO: But just because he's rejuvenated, it doesn't mean he'll be any the less affectionate and fatherly. Anyway, what good to you was that old man who let children fall under motor-cars?

EMMA: The child was perfectly safe with him, perfectly. Nothing ever happened to him. (*Pause.*) I shan't stay in this house another day. Living with an old man who seduces the housemaids! I shall leave the house to save Umbertino from the bad example, if for no other reason.

GUIDO: Who do you want him to make love to? There are no queens and duchesses in the house.

EMMA: Please don't joke about it. And Signor Biggioni, too! Standing guard for him!

GUIDO: That's not true. Signor Biggioni was waiting for Umbertino, so he could take him for a walk.

EMMA: Indeed? When I caught him at it red-handed? A pretty occupation. He didn't recognise me, the corridor was so dark. He leaped out of his room to stop me, saying Papa didn't want to be disturbed. Then he stopped in mid-sentence, and started making excuses. He's got some interest in that operation business. It's no good telling me he hasn't. He told me so himself. He tried to make me think he'd got involved in it out of kindness to you. But in fact he's in it to make money, like the crafty business-man he is—making money out of corrupting and ruining old men. And now he's watching the results; he's supervising them; he's enjoying them. He's like a white-slave trader.

GUIDO: Why would a rich man like him want to? He bought a few shares, certainly: 20,000 lire. A miserable 20,000 lire. I've got them in my pocket now. All the same, it's funny he said he did it for my sake. Can I take him up on it?

EMMA: Do just as you please. I knew it wasn't true. What affair is it of yours if he decides to make a business deal?

GUIDO: None at all. Still, I suppose he may have thought he was helping me, as a cousin of yours, just as he's always doing favours to Aunt Anna and takes such trouble over your child.

EMMA: He won't be allowed to see the child any more. I wouldn't trust him with a man like that. I've been noticing for some time that the child has been saying queer things after being with Signor Biggioni so much. For instance, the other day, our next-door neighbour's son told Umbertino he was his friend. "Friend?" he replied. "Then I'll eat you up." When the other child asked him what he meant, he said: "Friends always eat each other up. That's the sign of their being real friends." Who could he have heard a thing like that from, if not Signor Biggioni?

GUIDO: I can't believe it. A mild man like Signor Biggioni say a thing like that?

EMMA: He does, he does. Nothing's sacred to him. While Valentino was alive he never looked at me. And the moment he was in his coffin, he was all over me with vows and proposals.

GUIDO: And you'd do well to consider them. Especially now, when you want to leave your father. You'll be so much alone, all the more so with that child to keep men away.

EMMA: It's my duty. It's what Heaven wills.

Enter GIOVANNI.

GIOVANNI: I slept like an angel, an angel with a slight headache.

EMMA: I don't need to tell you what caused the headache. You had too much to drink. When I came home you were asleep, with a bottle beside you nearly empty.

GIOVANNI: Me, drink? I had one little glass, that's all. Two little glasses . . . well, three maybe.

EMMA: Much too much for you.

GUIDO: She's right, Uncle. It isn't good for you to drink. Can I take your pulse? (*Gets out his watch and does so.*) Excellent, excellent. A little too fast, perhaps.

GIOVANNI (*delighted*): A little too fast, eh? It hasn't been too fast for a long time!

GUIDO: But you shouldn't exploit your energy like that.

GIOVANNI: Not exploit it? But what would be the point of having it if I didn't? What am I to do with my energy if I don't exploit it?

GUIDO: Just enjoy it.

GIOVANNI: Enjoy it? (*Makes a gesture suggesting gymnastic exercises.*) Like this?

GUIDO: More or less.

EMMA: Father, I've got something to say to you.

GIOVANNI: Say it, dear, say it.

EMMA: I've been very happy with you and Mama, but now I want to live alone again, with Umbertino. I've found a place to live. I'll have the furniture that's in store taken there, and in a week or so I hope to be able to start a solitary existence.

GIOVANNI (*stammering*): You want . . . you want to leave us . . . me and Mama? What on earth for?

EMMA: I would rather not say.

GIOVANNI: Well, it's your right. You've been married. You're a widow. You're your own mistress. So you don't have to give us any explanations. You want to go and live on your own. Well, that's that. There's no one to stop you. You see how right I was not to want to be old. Everyone deserts old men.

EMMA: Father! I didn't want to say this, but you force me to. It's because you're not old any longer that I have to leave you.

GIOVANNI: But why? Good heavens, why? Aren't I better than I was before—more alive, more capable, more alert? After having upset me so much over that stupid motor-car affair, aren't you satisfied, now you know you could trust me completely with the child.

EMMA (*sobbing*): What my child needs to look up to is an old man, not a young one.

GIOVANNI: I don't understand! What can the child know about it? My hair hasn't grown again, nor my teeth.

EMMA: Oh, children find out everything, everything.

GIOVANNI (*dubiously*): Really? Do you think Umbertino realises something?

EMMA: Children don't know things, they feel them. They imitate them. If I stay here who will the child have to consort with? You and Rita. You must see, it just isn't possible.

GIOVANNI (*in amazement*): Me and Rita? Me and Rita? But when could the child ever have seen me with Rita?

EMMA : If I could see you with her, so might he.

GIOVANNI : Quite impossible! There was Signor Biggioni out there.

EMMA : There was, this time. But if I am to stay here I would have to insist that Signor Biggioni never sets foot in the house.

GIOVANNI : I don't like him any more than you do. I wouldn't object. I put up with him for your sake. I chucked him out yesterday simply because I didn't want him in the room with me, though he seemed to want to stay. I don't need Pauletta all the time, any more than any other young man would. There's no point in causing scandal.

EMMA (in dismay): Pauletta?

GIOVANNI (embarrassed): Pauletta? (Pause.) Yes, Pauletta, or Rita . . . I'm not quite sure . . .

EMMA (staring at him in alarm): And what is Mamma going to say?

GIOVANNI (disconcerted): Mamma? Anna? Oh yes. I must beg you not to say a word to her. You know young men never tell their wives anything.

EMMA : Father, I must stay with you after all; I must stay here beside you, to look after you, and protect Mamma.

GIOVANNI : Good girl, good girl. Stay with me, and I will always look after you and your child, so long as you make sure Mamma knows nothing. I understand what you're saying perfectly. You're frightened of my immorality. But it isn't as bad as all that. I love virtue, I've always loved it. It's just that now, after that operation, I can't go on being virtuous the whole twenty-four hours of the day.

EMMA : Why not?

GIOVANNI : I can be moral the greater part of the day . . . all too easily. So there's no problem there. What's more of a problem is something else. I would like Pauletta . . . that's to say Rita . . . to have a different position in the household. She's complained to me she's got too much work to do. Couldn't you take her on as a nurse for Umbertino? He's a big boy by now. He can look after himself and watch out for motor-cars. There wouldn't be very much to do for him. I would be so grateful to you if you could do me that favour.

EMMA : How could you expect such a thing? Mamma would notice . . .

GIOVANNI : Anna never notices anything. If you only knew how remote she is from all such things. Believe me, she hasn't thought about them for years. She promised me love, and we enjoyed love for such a brief time. All she wants now is to be left in peace and quiet and look after her animals. She is fond of me, of course. But as if I were her father, or a son or a brother. And I'm fond of her. Last night I had a strange dream. Someone in my dream told me to kill Anna. You can imagine how upset I was, and how I protested. As if someone had told me to kill my mother, or my sister, or my daughter. (*Warming to the theme.*) If you knew how I protested, how distressed I was to hear such a thing suggested. It was only a dream, of course, but it's significant. You follow me?

EMMA (*sadly*): Only too well, Papa.

GIOVANNI : We can get on together, I'm sure. Why should we have to part? I'm devoted to you, and to the child especially. Perhaps I shan't give him quite so much attention just at the moment. But if I live, I shall become an old man again, and then I'll need him. And we two have got so much in common. Even disliking that Signor . . . Biggioni. He's no husband for you. Poor devil, he's a mere child. You can do anything you want with him. If you only knew! I bet you if I told him to sweep out my room, he'd do it. Not very graciously, but he'd do it. He'd make ferocious threats, but he'd do it.

EMMA : Poor man!

GIOVANNI : Poor man, yes . . . but he's a bit abject too. He's not a real man at all. So that's settled, dear. You stay with us. You're still so young, you need someone to support you.

EMMA (*making up her mind*): Yes, very well, I'll stay. I do need support, and I'm grateful to you for offering it. (*Kisses him on the forehead.*)

FORTUNATO: Isn't the master here?

EMMA: Come in, Fortunato. He's gone to dress.

FORTUNATO (*embarrassed and hesitant*): I wanted to talk to him.

EMMA: He'll soon be back. I tell you; he's gone to dress.

FORTUNATO: I'll wait for him. (*Long pause.*)

EMMA: Is Rita still in bed?

FORTUNATO: Yes, she's still got a headache. She won't be able to get up today. The mistress has called in the doctor. (*Pause.*) Well, you must know what I've come to tell the master. I'm not going to stay in this house, and I'm not going to marry Rita. She's not the kind of girl for anyone to marry. How would I be able to drive the car? My horns would stick through the roof.

EMMA: I don't understand what you're talking about.

FORTUNATO: Oh yes you do. I can't believe Rita's always lying, especially as she spoke to me at once, while she was still drunk and half-asleep. She said "We were woken up by Signora Emma coming in." Where she started lying was when she said she was in here with the old master. As if an old gentleman like him would want to waste his time with maids. What would be the point? At his age, your mind is on other things. For a long time I've realised two facts. First of all, Rita is being pursued by young Master Guido, who's not like a proper member of your family. Excuse the liberty. I've got past politeness. The second thing is that Rita's been trying to keep my suspicions off Signor Guido by pretending the old master is after her. She keeps talking to me about operations, and I don't know what, and how they can make even old men a danger.

EMMA: Such operations do exist.

FORTUNATO: I don't want to hear about them. Nobody with any knowledge of life would believe such a thing. And yesterday that young rogue Signor Guido—excuse me, I'm past caring what I say—got Rita drunk. She was drunk as a tick. And I know what I'm talking about. Do you mean to tell me that isn't disgusting? The girl was practically raving. In a state like that, anyone could take advantage of her. I'm not going to marry her. I was so angry, I started talking about Signor Guido, and all she did was laugh; she laughed her head off. Then as she got sleepy she stopped laughing in that uncouth way and went to sleep on the kitchen chair, but you could still see the laugh on her face —you could see her smiling in her sleep. She's probably still smiling, seeing that she's still asleep. I'm not going to marry her, and I want to give in my notice.

EMMA: Shall I go and talk to my father? Would you like me to tell him all you've said? Wouldn't that be a good idea? Perhaps if he hears all this about Guido he'll forbid him the house.

FORTUNATO: It's too late now. It'd be shutting the stable door after the horse is gone.

EMMA: Anyway, let me talk to him. Go back into the garden, and wait till I call you.

Enter ENRICO.

ENRICO: Excuse me. I hope you don't mind. Before you tell me I'm never to see you again, I'd like to try and explain.

EMMA (*mildly*): Sit down, Signor Biggioni. Sit down! I'll be with you in a moment. (To FORTUNATO.) That's agreed, then? I'll speak to my father, and I'll call you in a moment. My father is going out, but I'll ask him to see you first.

FORTUNATO: Very well, Madam.

Exit FORTUNATO.

ENRICO: Signora Emma, I would like to give you an explanation. Yesterday, when you found me in that strange situation outside the door, you said things that hurt me deeply.

EMMA (*embarrassed*): I'm very sorry I said what I did. I found out later that you were waiting for Umbertino.

ENRICO (*staring at her in surprise*): Thank you. It does me
good to hear you speak to me more kindly, now that we
shall never see each other again. But if I must lose your
friendship, I want there to be no falsity or hypocrisy between us. That kind remark of yours—the first you've ever
made to me since Valentino's death—was one I had no right
to. It's true I was waiting for Umbertino, but it's also true
I had been commissioned to guard the door and see that no
one disturbed the old gentleman, while he tested the results
of his operation.

EMMA (*in horror*): Oh, oh!

ENRICO: Have you noticed how even the chauffeur won't
speak to me? He's quite right not to. Once, to please young
Guido, I called him away and questioned him about the
motor-car, so that Guido could have a free hand in the
kitchen.

EMMA: But that's downright immoral!

ENRICO: As to that, I can't say, as I couldn't inspect the car
and the kitchen at the same time. Anyway, as far as I was
concerned I was only interested in winning Guido's friendship. My questions about the car were supposed to last a
quarter-of-an-hour, and last a quarter-of-an-hour they did.
Imagine the tedium of having to listen to explanations of
things I understood better myself. When the quarter-of-an-
hour was up, Fortunato still wanted to go on, but I interrupted him brutally. Perhaps I was too brutal, and he
guessed something—in fact guessed everything. Ever since
then, I haven't dared go into his part of the garden, because
if I do I get bombarded—pie-dishes and casseroles, hot and
greasy out of the oven, come flying at me. Fortunato says
he's very sorry, and laughs his head off.

EMMA: And don't you do anything about it?

ENRICO: How can I? When my job is to be nice to everyone.
How could I still be nice to everyone if I took notice of such
behaviour. To calm myself, I think something.

EMMA: Think something?

ENRICO: I'll tell you what I think: I think: "Go on and

persecute me now. When I've married Signora Emma, I'll see you get your reward." As things are, you don't care what happens to me; so it's your fault that I'm treated like a slave, as if I were someone of no account. They are simply following your lead. But if I really managed to take poor Valentino's place, then you would have to treat me better too. Isn't that so?

EMMA: I don't know. Up to now it's never occurred to me to think of you as a husband.

ENRICO: I know.

EMMA: But I don't like seeing even the people I'm not going to marry being servile, ignoble, inferior. I like people with self-respect and a proper sense of their place in the world. Poor Valentino was nice to everyone; but he wasn't a man you could take liberties with.

ENRICO: I remember how he bellowed when he wanted the nurse.

EMMA: You, on the other hand, curry favour with everyone— except poor Valentino, who wanted nothing from you.

ENRICO: You're right. I've been a fool! I've acted like a fool ever since . . . you know when.

EMMA: Yes I do. And it's something I can't forgive you. You started acting like a fool the moment Valentino died. Even for you, it would have been better, don't you admit, if he were still alive?

ENRICO (*pausing a second*): Oh, of course, of course. And one thing I can say. I never thought about Valentino dying till he actually did so. I swear it! But then . . .

EMMA: Don't let's talk about what happened then. Just don't act the fool, any more. I will always remember you said you never thought of Valentino's death until it happened.

ENRICO: Yes, never. Afterwards, of course, I couldn't help it.

EMMA: I don't want to hear about that. And there's another thing. I expect my friends to behave in a dignified manner, and not do belittling things. I want more naturalness, more dignity. Anything else is a great mistake. If people told you it was the way to win favour with me, they were deceived or lying. Do you understand me?

ENRICO: I only understand one thing—for the first time you are ready to think about me. At least I'm learning from the right teacher now. (*He tries to take her hand.*) And you could make the lesson even more effective . . .

EMMA: Don't try to take what has not been offered to you.

ENRICO (*earnestly*): I understand, I understand! And I'll do as you say. Let me just memorise your instructions. First: I mustn't mention poor Valentino any more.

EMMA (*disdainfully*): Even that's mentioning him too much.

ENRICO: But it's the last time. Goodbye Valentino; for me you now cease to exist. Secondly: I mustn't be anyone's slave. (*He heaves a sigh of relief.*) And not before it was time. It was intolerable. Can I tell Guido that he is a young cad?

EMMA: That's going too far, I think.

ENRICO: Perhaps so. It seems to have been my fate to exaggerate since poor Valentino's death.

EMMA: But I told you . . .

ENRICO: Give me time to get back to normal again. I'll tell Guido that as his cousin-to-be I've got the right to give him advice; and I won't hesitate to give him it.

EMMA: For the moment, I forbid you to tell anyone that you may be joining the family.

ENRICO: I'm glad you warned me. With you, though, in private . . .

EMMA: No, not even then. (*She bursts into tears.*) You, with your stupid behaviour, you've made me abandon all my good resolutions.

ENRICO (*distressed*): Don't cry. I can't bear to see you cry. I promise you I'll wait till the anniversary of Val . . . Anyway, as far as your father goes, it will all be plain sailing. If anything he's too much on the side of youth; he'll understand right away. He'll have to learn to make love a bit less publicly. I'll tell him: "Carry on with the good work, Papa. But do it discreetly."

EMMA: They've certainly made a kind of monster out of him. And to think he was once the pride of our family.

ENRICO: You wait, you wait. I'll help re-educate him.

Enter GIOVANNI.

GIOVANNI: Here I am, ready for that tiresome fellow, what's his name? . . .

EMMA: Wait a moment, Papa. I've got something to say to you. It's about Fortunato. He was here a little while ago . . . Aren't you going to say good morning to Signor Biggioni?

GIOVANNI (*negligently*): Good-day.

ENRICO (*in a friendly but frank manner*): Good-morning. I hope you slept well after getting so drunk last night.

GIOVANNI (*in amazement, takes* EMMA *aside*): What did he say? Did he say "getting so drunk".

EMMA: Yes, Papa.

GIOVANNI: Extraordinary impertinence. And he says insulting things in such a sweet obliging manner. Shall we kick him out of the house?

EMMA: No, Papa.

GIOVANNI (*amazed*): No? (*To* ENRICO.) Getting drunk? Me? I've never been drunk in my life. Kindly remember that.

ENRICO: All the same, that's what we young fellows call it— the state you were in last night.

GIOVANNI (*staring at him and then bursting into laughter*): You young fellows? So it's something that often happens to young men?

ENRICO: Especially very young ones.

GIOVANNI (*hesitates, and then forgets the whole subject*): What did Fortunato want with me? Why doesn't he come and see me?

EMMA: Because I wouldn't let him. Imagine, he refuses to marry Rita and wants to leave this house right away.

GIOVANNI (*astonished*): But what on earth for?

ENRICO (*in surprise*): You mean you can't guess? Don't you remember what happened here yesterday evening, between you and Rita? Oh come now!

GIOVANNI: I'd forgotten. You can't forsee all the consequences of things. Especially things you haven't much experience of. But who was the sneak who told Fortunato? (*Threateningly.*) It wasn't you?

ENRICO: I assure you I told no one. But Rita was drunk, and you were asleep and snoring the house down.

GIOVANNI (*to* EMMA): Do I really snore so loud?

EMMA: Occasionally, when you are very . . . tired. (*Pause.*) But Signor Biggioni wasn't here when Fortunato was speaking to me. Fortunato knows that Rita was drunk, but he didn't hear you snoring.

GIOVANNI: You see, people don't hear me.

EMMA: Mama had sent Fortunato into town to buy something. And now nothing will get it out of his head that it was Guido who got Rita drunk.

GIOVANNI (*pensively*): And you think he'll make a scene with Guido?

EMMA: I thought there was a threatening note in his voice. I was on the point of telling him that Guido had nothing to do with it, and that it was you who . . . who got Rita drinking. But then I thought I would speak to you first.

GIOVANNI: You did quite right. I don't like affairs like this at all.

ENRICO: It seems to me Signora Emma was wrong not to tell him at once that it was you.

GIOVANNI: What the devil do you mean? And what's it got to do with you?

ENRICO: I'm not supposed to talk about this. But as you're her father, perhaps I can tell you. Everyone here knows that I'm in love with Signora Emma, and that I'm living in hopes of becoming—on a certain anniversary, which I won't mention, but which is bound to come—of becoming your son-in-law.

GIOVANNI: Couldn't we make Fortunato believe it was you who got Rita drunk?

ENRICO: I don't think we can. I had been turned out of the

house, and just as I was leaving Fortunato came out too, and so he saw me.

GIOVANNI: What a pity!

ENRICO: There's something else I must say, Signor Chierici. When a thing like this happens to us younger men, we accept our responsibility. I'm sure that when you think about it a little you will realise that the only thing is for you to admit the whole business to Fortunato. Frankly, I think it will come down to money.

GIOVANNI: Money? Do you mean money?

ENRICO: As far as Fortunato is concerned, that's all it will probably be—a matter of money. But for you, it's something different.

GIOVANNI: Exactly. I give the money and he puts it in his pocket.

ENRICO: That wasn't what I meant. Did you make love with her?

GIOVANNI (*vaguely*): Me?

ENRICO: You needn't answer my question. In fact, when young men have made love they never answer. It's their duty to deny the whole thing, or at least to keep their mouth shut.

GIOVANNI: I want to do my duty too.

ENRICO: On the other hand, anyone who makes love has to be responsible for the consequences. And now Fortunato's quarrelling with Guido. That's something you can't permit.

GIOVANNI (*dubiously*): No, of course not.

ENRICO: No doubt it would be better if the whole affair could be hushed up. But that's impossible. You committed a foolish action—(GIOVANNI *makes an indignant gesture*.)—I realise there was some excuse, as you are inexperienced, despite your age . . . rejuvenation and all. But by now everyone in the house, to some extent or other, knows about the story. So decency demands . . .

GIOVANNI: Decency. (*Asserting his dignity.*) Let me tell you, my good sir, you're too young to teach me decency. I am perfectly capable of deciding what is decent, and have always acted accordingly.

ENRICO: I wouldn't think of denying it.

GIOVANNI: I'm glad. So don't let's discuss it any more. I'm going out for a walk now with that ass of a fellow called ...

ENRICO: Boncini.

EMMA: Father, Fortunato would like to talk to you immediately.

GIOVANNI: I can't just now.

EMMA: Signor Boncini could wait a bit.

GIOVANNI: What if he doesn't want to?

ENRICO: What does it matter if he doesn't? Let him get on with it.

GIOVANNI: Yes, you're right, let him get on with it!

EMMA: I'll call Fortunato.

Enter RITA, *followed by* FORTUNATO.

RITA: That Signor Boncini is outside, wanting to see you.

ENRICO: Let him get on with it.

RITA: What d'you mean?

GIOVANNI: Oh, Rita. How are you? Anna tells me you've not been very well.

RITA: I'm fine, sir.

FORTUNATO: Excuse me, sir; it never seemed possible to get to see you.

GIOVANNI (*nervously*): Are you angry with me about something?

FORTUNATO: With you, sir? I'm angry with a member of your family and it means I've got to leave it. I'm very sorry, sir, but I can't stay in this house a moment longer.

GIOVANNI (*meditatively*): A member of my family? That means Guido, doesn't it? Well, I don't altogether approve of his conduct myself.

ENRICO: But that's not really what Signor Chierici wants to say to you.

GIOVANNI: Let me talk. What's it got to do with you? My sense of decency's my own affair. And not only my sense of decency. My happiness too. You must remember that there's such a person as Anna. I don't want her to hear a word about this. Do you all promise not to say a word?

EMMA : Certainly, Father.

ENRICO : Absolutely.

GIOVANNI : And you've said nothing, Rita?

RITA : I don't know what you're talking about.

GIOVANNI : I want you to promise to hold your tongue and not say a word to Anna about anything that is said here.

RITA : I can keep a secret. It's the thing I find easiest in the world. In fact, it's talking I find difficult.

EMMA : Then you shouldn't do it!

GIOVANNI : Well then, Signor Biggioni, you go and take up the same post as last night, and if you see Anna coming, come and warn us at once.

EMMA : There is no need, Papa. Mother won't be back for half an hour; I know that definitely.

GIOVANNI : In that case, we can start talking. Fortunato, you believe Rita spent the evening and got . . .

FORTUNATO : Drunk.

RITA : I wasn't drunk. It's a lie.

GIOVANNI : Forget all that. We're not here to decide just how drunk you were. We want to know who got you drunk.

FORTUNATO : That's right. (*Threateningly.*) She wants to have me believe she spent those two hours with you, sir. Which, of course, is absurd. To think of you spending your time with a chit like that, sir, a girl who's had no education.

GIOVANNI (*nervously*): What would you say if I told you it was true?

FORTUNATO (*threateningly*): I'd say that you had all got together to make a fool of me.

ENRICO : My dear friend. You can't believe that of me. Signor Chierici told me to keep guard over that door. I was there for two hours, and I can assure you Guido never came near all that time.

EMMA : What difference do you think it makes to me if it was Guido or Papa with Rita? All I can say is, when I arrived, Rita was asleep on that sofa, and Papa in the armchair.

FORTUNATO: Oh, if only I could believe it.

RITA: You wouldn't believe it when I said it. I told you the only person I was here with was the master.

FORTUNATO (*running over to* GIOVANNI, *who backs away in terror*): Forgive me, sir. I'll stay here, I'll never leave you, never. Forgive me for upsetting you.

GIOVANNI (*sitting down to get his breath back*): I forgive you, I excuse you. I forgive you gladly. (*Pause.*) Only I don't quite follow.

Enter ANNA.

ANNA: The dressmaker wasn't at home. What are you all doing here? Rita, have you given the birds their breadcrumbs?

RITA: Not yet, madam.

ANNA: It's ten already. Go and do it at once. I hope you've prepared it, at least.

RITA: Only a little as yet, madam. But it's not my fault. Fortunato's been bothering me with his jealousy again. He thought I was here with Signor Guido yesterday evening, whereas I spent the whole evening with the master.

ANNA: You mean you were in here polishing the doorhandles.

GIOVANNI (*apologetically*): Actually, I let her stop for a little and keep me company.

ANNA: Well, what's wrong in that?

FORTUNATO: When they told me she had been with Master, I wasn't worried either.

ANNA: Do you like having Rita keep you company?

GIOVANNI (*embarrassedly*): Sometimes ... just occasionally ... yes.

ANNA: Then whenever you want her, you've only got to tell me, and I'll see that she's free. Now go along Rita. I'll come and help you grate the bread.

They go off together, followed by FORTUNATO.

GIOVANNI : And now I've got to go for a walk with that Signor . . .

ENRICO : Boncini.

EMMA (*kissing* GIOVANNI): Goodbye, Papa. I feel so fond of you again, now. I'll never leave you.

GIOVANNI (*reflectively*): Oh, I'm not as stupid as you all think. But wait a bit. The last word hasn't been said yet. I want to think about things a little . . . to try to make sense of them. (*He makes as if to leave the room, then returns.*) I believe I know what you all think. Only . . . I'm not sure what I think. (*Makes as if to leave and then returns, once more.*) We must get things clear. Either the operation works or it doesn't. If it works, I must be different from what I was, and you would have no right to laugh at me any longer. And I thought I *was* different. In dreams, certainly; but also in reality, and when wide awake. So what right have you to make fun of me? Why do you want to ruin it all?

ENRICO :⎫ (*together*) ⎧ Who's making fun of you?
EMMA : ⎭   ⎩ Make fun of you?

GIOVANNI : Hold your tongue, both of you. Hold your tongue, I say! I haven't lived to my age for nothing; don't think you can deceive me. There are so many ways of making fun of someone. Say a man's wife is unfaithful to him; fine, you laugh at him. But say he thinks he's being unfaithful to her, and finds she doesn't care a damn; you find that just as funny. (*Pause.*) That's not what I mean quite, but listen, I must make you understand. I don't say Anna doesn't care a damn about me. *She* doesn't make fun of me. But you do, you enjoy making fun of me. And it hurts. What am I supposed to have done? Only what I was told to do. I did. . . . I did what the doctor prescribed. So you shouldn't laugh at me. I shall take that doctor's prescription as my law, I shall follow it till my dying breath. I swear it to you solemnly, here and now.

EMMA : Father! Don't be upset. When you're upset, it makes me want to cry too.

GIOVANNI (*hugging her*): Yes, dearest, you would cry with me,

I know. Thank you for it. (*Pause.*) All the same, your crying
would be another way of laughing at me. But I'm old only
because I didn't die young. It will happen to you one day.
(*To* ENRICO, *loudly and aggressively.*) And you too!

ENRICO: Let's hope so. And then I'll have an operation.

GIOVANNI: I'm pleased to hear you say that! Talking like that
is better than making fun of people—much better—and
better than crying too. It's the first time I ever heard you
say anything intelligent; but you've done so now, and
done it at the right time. Why, it's really splendid! What
you've just said puts everything in a different light. It
makes all the difference. I'm quite ready for you to marry
my daughter now. (*To* EMMA.) You ought to marry him, you
know. It's better to have a man who talks intelligently once
in a way, when it's needed, than one who deluges you with
intelligence, so that you don't know what to do with it. Go
on, you should marry him. He'd be a useful chap to have
about the house. When you really need it, out he'll come
and say the right thing. It's something I can't do. You ought
to marry him.

EMMA: This is no time for thinking of marriage.

GIOVANNI: I know, I know. We've got to wait till 22 March.

ENRICO (*anxiously*): 22 February. Valentino died on 22
February.

EMMA (*reprovingly*): Please, don't say such things.

GIOVANNI: I'm glad you reminded me. What you said just now
was very good, really good. But remember, before I took the
step I did, I consulted the whole college of doctors—there
they were, in their long frock coats and white ties—and they
all agreed. Even Dr Raulli.

EMMA: No, Papa. Dr Raulli never agreed.

GIOVANNI (*confused*): Didn't he? I thought . . . But now,
thank Heavens, I don't have to think about it any more,
because it's been done. And it's up to me to make the most
of it. And one of the things which you earn a right to,
when you're rejuvenated, is love . . . though nobody seems
to think so. But there are other things as well: generosity,

kindliness. Old men are petty-minded and mean. Look. (*He takes out a handful of small change.*) Every day I give ten lire to beggars. And today, I'm going to give even more than that, because I shall be with that Signor . . .

ENRICO: Boncini.

GIOVANNI: Boncini. I'll give more today, so that Boncini can see I'm a young man again and will follow suit and have the operation. When there are several of us we shall be able to discuss things with one another, and clear our minds, and help one another. When we can be really frank with each other it will be easier to know what's illusion and what's real. We'll stick together, we rejuvenated men; we'll be a real band of brothers. I'm off. Goodbye!

He slams on his hat and marches out boldly.

EMMA (*delightedly*): Oh how I love him like that, so weak and doddering; an old man, a real old man. Poor darling! I must try and comfort him.

ENRICO: I would like to, too. I understand him so well, don't you? Even for young men like me love isn't all that much fun. So what can it be like for someone who hasn't thought about it for years.

EMMA: I'm not sure it's love that's involved.

Enter ANNA.

ANNA: Oh dear, that girl Rita! If I'm not here she forgets everything. There are certain times of the day when I ought never to go out.

Enter BONCINI.

BONCINI (*agitatedly*): Dr Raulli told me to come and tell you that there's nothing to worry about. Signor Chierici will be here in a minute, more or less safe and sound.

ALL (*in alarm*): What's happened to him?

Enter GUIDO.

GUIDO: Nothing, absolutely nothing. I was going by and I saw a crowd outside the chemist's shop. It was Uncle. Nothing had happened to him, nothing at all. It's a good thing I arrived in time, or Signor Boncini might have frightened you.

BONCINI (*angrily*): Did I frighten you?

EMMA: Not at all. But we want to know what happened.

BONCINI: I'll tell you. Now you're all calm again, I can tell you what did happen. It's extraordinary, marvellous! Good Lord, that operation is an amazing business. I want to have one right away. We were going along together, and I was noticing—with great pleasure, I must say—the brisk, youthful way Signor Chierici was walking. I told him so, and he seemed very pleased. In fact he started walking faster, so that I couldn't keep up with him. It was magnificent. Then he stopped to give a beggar some money. There was a car coming along the road—fairly fast.

EMMA, ANNA and ENRICO: A car!

BONCINI: A child—about eight years old—ran into the street. Perhaps from where he was Signor Chierici wasn't able to measure distances. I could see that the child was in no danger, as the car was level with him already and hadn't touched him. But Signor Chierici started shouting: "I'll save him! I'll save him!" And he hurled himself off the pavement at the car. I think and hope he never reached it, but he fell down as if he had been hit by it—flat on his back, with his legs in the air.

ENRICO: Silly old idiot!

EMMA: Good Heavens!

ANNA: Where is he? Where is he?

BONCINI: People went to find a taxi. Dr Raulli was going to bring him home. But I haven't told you the whole story. As he was lying there on his back, another car came along and would have hit him if it hadn't stopped in time. I stopped it by shouting at the driver. I saved his life . . . by shouting. I couldn't actually run, like him, of course; I haven't had the operation yet.

GUIDO: Otherwise you would have thrown yourself at the car too.

BONCINI: What would have been the good? I could do more good by shouting. (*To* GUIDO.) So that's settled, then. I'll come along to see you this afternoon.

> BONCINI *bows to the company and leaves. Enter* GIOVANNI, *leaning on the arms of* DR RAULLI *and* FORTUNATO *and with his head bandaged.*

ANNA: Oh Giovanni, what have you been doing?

GIOVANNI: Have you brought along the child I saved, so I can show him to my wife?

ANNA: There's no need for that, Giovanni. You've been so brave, but so reckless.

GIOVANNI (*they lead him to the armchair and he falls back in it exhausted*): One has to do one's duty. Where's the little boy? (*He shuts his eyes.*)

RAULLI: Let him rest a bit. Then we'll put him on the sofa, so he can have a sleep. Loosen his collar so he can breathe. (ANNA *does so. He addresses* GUIDO.) So much for your operation.

GUIDO: But he's all right, isn't he?

RAULLI: Perfectly. All he's done is slightly graze his neck.

GUIDO: So you see, the operation isn't so dangerous after all.

RAULLI: Only because it isn't effective. If he had been able to run like he used to, he would have ended up under the car.

GUIDO: Perhaps he will do better next time.

GIOVANNI: I've got something to say to my wife. But I don't want anyone to hear. (*They go over to the other side of the room, and he talks to* ANNA, *who is leaning over him.*) If someone tells you I wanted to kill you, don't believe them.

ANNA (*to* DR RAULLI): Is he delirious?

RAULLI (*goes up to him, scrutinizes him and takes his pulse*): No! He's perfectly sensible. He's merely a bit upset. You must have a sleep, Signor Chierici. Lie down on that sofa.

GIOVANNI: In a moment. But first I want to say something to

my wife. (*Pause.*) If someone tells you I married you without love, don't believe them. I've always loved you.

ANNA (*looking towards* RAULLI): I've always believed so.

GIOVANNI: You were quite right to. That's what one must believe if one's going to live happily side by side with someone. And when I went out walking with that Signor . . .

ENRICO: Boncini.

GIOVANNI: Can't you get rid of that chap, what's he called. . . ?

ENRICO: Biggioni.

GIOVANNI: Thanks. When I went out walking with that fellow Biggioni . . .

ENRICO: Boncini.

GIOVANNI: I mean, Boncini; I kept thinking: "I'm a virtuous old man, who loves all those who deserve love—that's to say, people like you. A virtuous old man, even if a rejuvenated one." I felt how tenderly I loved you.

ANNA: Just as always.

GIOVANNI: Yes, just as always, and a little more than usual.

ANNA: Thank you. (*She wants to kiss him; he lowers his head and she kisses him on his bandage.*)

GIOVANNI: You've kissed me on my bandage, the most glorious portion of my body. And now I'd like to lie down more comfortably, in bed, so I can think better, and understand everything that's happened.

RAULLI: Let's take him to bed.

ENRICO, FORTUNATO, GUIDO *and* DR RAULLI *escort* GIOVANNI *offstage, followed by the women.*

DREAM-SEQUENCE

RITA: Here it is, sir. This is the bit of earth you've got to dig.

GIOVANNI (*bandaged, and carrying a hoe over his shoulder*): This one here? It looks very hard to me. Couldn't we wait till the rain comes and softens it?

RITA: You've been chosen especially for the job, being so young and vigorous now.

GIOVANNI: Then go away and leave me to my work. People are so evil-minded! If they saw us together they would think Heaven knows what. Take yourself over there, and sing to me while I work.

RITA (*singing as she goes*):

> They told me Beppe had gone for a soldier
> And that they'd seen you crying all alone...

ANNA: You see, I've left Rita free so that she can keep you company.

GIOVANNI: Send her away. I'm a respectable man and have work to do. I want women given no liberties. And go away yourself! (*He gets on with his digging.*) Even as a young man I could see that women were all a mistake, all a muddle.

ANNA: All a mistake and muddle?

GIOVANNI: I don't know how to explain it. Perhaps it was the men who were all a muddle. Anyway, one chose a woman, and then it turned out not to be the right one.

ANNA: Do you mean you didn't love me?

GIOVANNI: I'm not talking about you. Don't interrupt. You women are always interrupting, you're always asking "What about me?" It's got nothing to do with you and me. I just know that what mostly happens is that a man goes to bed with a woman and then wants . . . to be in a different bed. We've got to change all that.

ANNA: But *didn't* you love me?

GIOVANNI (*angrily*): How she goes on! How am I going to silence her, so I can think my own thoughts? (*He digs.*) I always loved you. I worked for you, and I'll go on working for you. All the same, one woman may not be enough for a man. (*He digs.*) Or perhaps too much. (*Digs.*) I said *every*thing was topsy-turvy. But in the end you get used to it and live as if things were as they should be. So Dr Raulli was right, he was right to be against the operation. Because when you have had it, you start to examine your life and then you find out—you find out the mess and confusion it's in, you find out it's *all* mess and confusion. In fact you see that what you thought was life was really a kind of death. (*In a loud* *voice*.) Now I *am* talking about us. Can you remember when we last really looked at each other, before I had the operation? Because as soon as I had had it, I tell you, I looked at you—you didn't look at me, you were too busy looking at your birds and dogs and cats, but I looked at you, and I didn't like what I saw.

ANNA (*humbly*): I am very old, I know.

GIOVANNI: I'm not talking about age! As I looked at you, I remembered how we got married years ago, and what an absurd business it was, me in a dress-suit and you all in white, both of us eating and drinking as if we meant to go on eating and drinking the same way all our lives. Whereas there came a point when that ass of a doctor told me to stop drinking and I didn't drink; till yesterday, when I drank to please Rita. (*Pauses and digs*.) It was a futile business, that wedding, I tell you—because we didn't stay together. So what was the point of the dress-suit and the bridal veil, and all that food and drink.

ANNA: But we had Emma.

GIOVANNI: Yes and soon after that we fell apart.

ANNA: I don't remember it as like that.

GIOVANNI: Very well, then. The thing may still have gone on for a year or two, but then we fell apart for ever. And then I had the operation, and I found a world in chaos, a world where kisses counted for nothing any more. I kissed Rita . . .

ANNA: Yes, as a father kisses a daughter.

GIOVANNI (*furiously*): As a father kisses someone else's daughter. There's a difference! . . . And then you told me I could have her whenever I liked.

ANNA: I was only trying to be nice.

GIOVANNI: Thank you, but you overdid it. You gave me more than I asked for. You got the proportions wrong.

ANNA: You shouldn't complain. I thought I was making life pleasanter for you.

GIOVANNI: Make it pleasanter? You've made it a hell for me, treating me in that way, treating my operation in that way.

ANNA: Your operation: What did you expect? A miracle, after three weeks? You must be thinking of Pagliano.[1]

GIOVANNI: You didn't have faith. And it means that now I haven't faith either—I want no more to do with women.

ANNA: Not even with me? Won't you give me a kiss?

GIOVANNI: A kiss? No, certainly not! I love you. I never wanted to kill you. I love you, I say. For your sake I will love all the animals too, the sparrows, the cats and the dogs. And I will work for you. In your name I will keep and feed mankind. That is the task of us old men, us young old men, us old young men.

Curtain

---

[1] See footnote to p. 193.